Tears for Cambodia

Ed Mooney

First published by Dog Ear Publishing
4010 W. 86th Street, Ste H
Indianapolis, IN 46268
www.dogearpublishing.net

ISBN: 978-1-4575-2400-4

This book is printed on acid-free paper.

This book is a work of fiction. Places, events, and situations in this book are purely fictional and any resemblance to actual persons, living or dead, is coincidental.

Printed in the United States of America

Dedication

For Peggy

ACKNOWLEDGEMENTS:

I would like to express my sincere and undying thanks to my muse and staunchest supporter in this project since its very conception. My wife Peggy has played many roles since that afternoon in Prague in December of 2012, where she insisted that we outline the book's plot, while we sat in the Bud War Brewery sampling the original *Budweiser.* She was indispensable in my maintaining continuity and faithfully adhering to the plot's lengthy timeline. Her inputs were always germane and valuable. I believe she has reread the text almost as many times as I have. Her comments were always perceptive, spot-on, and added to the readability of the final product. She also provided the photos that were used for background on the cover. In addition to being a first-rate editor, she is an award-winning photographer. She is now prodding me to sit and outline the story for the next novel. What a treasure!

I asked a group of people to read the initial draft of the book late last summer. Their comments and suggestions have been incalculably beneficial to the novel in its present form. LTC (r) Jim Poe kept me faithful to military doctrine jargon and tradition and helped keep me mindful of the Vietnam-era culture. My sister Theresa Blazek, a clinical psychologist, helped me flesh out some of the issues that typically afflict combat veterans. Making Max more human and assisting in the characterization of Max's relationships were among her major inputs. Tom Harding put the text under a microscope and provided essential improvements to the flow and continuity of the overall text. My daughter Amy, who was born the December before I left for Cambodia in 1972, peppered me with queries that helped me clarify culture in America at that time. Her perspectives were extremely relevant to me, as I set out to expose the tenor of that era to people of her age and younger. Vicki Breaugh made some excellent observations concerning relationships and dialogue.

My daughter Amy and grand daughter Madeline Lewis greatly assisted with numerous iterations leading to the cover's final design.

For all the pertinent suggestions, inputs, and recommended fixes, I owe these people a tremendous debt of gratitude. I will never forget their support and encouragement.

Finally, I would like to thank my superiors and colleagues assigned to MEDTC, for their dedicated efforts to make American support to Cambodia successful. I am proud to have served with you.

EDM

November 2013

Introduction

In my research for this book, I encountered a surprising dearth of definitive American academic material dealing with the US involvement in the last days of Cambodia. There is very little literature of any kind that chronicles the heroic and resourceful efforts that were exerted on Cambodia's behalf by the United States. In our efforts to support Cambodia, there were many tragic turns. Yet, in my own return visit recently to Cambodia, I found plenty of hope and resolve left among the surviving, battle-hardened Cambodian people.

Thus, a brief introduction to this book's approach:

Max Donatello's story is based on actual events and real experiences. It is set against the backdrop of US efforts to extricate itself from the grip of the war in Southeast Asia. Max is subsumed into what William Shawcross incisively calls the "*Sideshow*" in his seminal book about the futile efforts of a wrong-headed US administration to prop up the corrupt and dictatorial pro-west Lon Nol regime in Cambodia in the early 1970s, as we ploddingly searched for a way to wrench ourselves out of Southeast Asia.

Max's experiences assigned to the US Military Equipment Delivery Team, Cambodia (MEDTC), represent a compilation of events actually experienced by the author, and several officer colleagues assigned to the team in those challenging days. So, this collage of remembrances, juxtaposed with cogent memories of the author, provides the grist for an inside view of one dedicated officer's tour in Cambodia, occurring in that period.

These collected, composite recollections also provided the author an opportunity to shed a bit of un-shrouded, objective insight on the expressed American policy toward Cambodia in the waning days of the SE Asian conflict.

More importantly, they gave me the opening to delve into the psyche of one officer, examining his futile attempts at making sense of his horrific battle experiences. Max's nightmares provided a voice for some long-held personal views about the Army's "warrior ethos," and its effects on the lives of returning soldiers and their families. These views were born and nurtured over the course of my twenty-two-year Army career, personally observing and studying our Army's culture firsthand.

Taking up these issues and cramming them into a historical novel was, I felt, the most expedient way for me to tell this story, while integrating the confluence of historical fact, prevailing policy, military practice, and American culture at the time.

Another major goal was to look at the impact of Max's combat experience through a powerful zoom lens, to gain a longitudinal perspective of how these events impacted his later life, and the lives of his family.

My greatest challenge, as an author, was providing the reader with enough authentic historical information to give a clear context of MEDTC's unique mission, while providing an accurate sense of the embassy atmosphere in wartime, along with some insights as to the pressure from Washington for the in-country team to serve up miracles on a daily basis. Finally, painting an accurate picture of the beleaguered Khmer Army (FANK), with all its foibles, was a tricky proposition, considering the complexities of Cambodia's political milieu.

I can honestly testify that MEDTC accomplished many remarkable near-miracles in its short organizational life, and I am proud to have played a small role as a member of this elite, if short-lived, fraternity. Unfortunately, as I describe in the book, the deck was stacked heavily against MEDTC's success at <u>many</u> levels.

EDM
November 2013

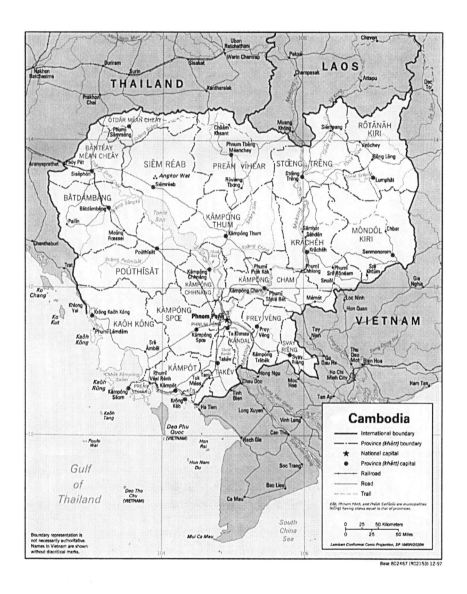

PROLOGUE

"Ironic how early fall seems to have the misplaced vitality and energy of early spring. When I look out the window onto the William and Mary campus, I see annual renewal and transforming taking place. Every year at this time, it's like nature in springtime. Instead of buds on new growth, a college town springs to life with its wide-eyed freshman class, returning upper classmen intent on inspecting the new flock, getting on with their own studies, their own lives." Max's brief soliloquy ended as he turned to Emily who seemed bemused by Max's impromptu reverie.

"You always had a vivid flare for words. Conceptualizing the reality of complex situations has always been your strength, my darling." Emily reached out her hand to Max who returned to her bedside.

"My biggest regret was not being able to come to terms and honestly verbalize the complexity of those awful dreams. I think life for you would have been a whole lot easier," Max said with demonstrative regret.

Emily squeezed his hand. "Not just for me, but for all of us, the kids, and especially you, Max." Emily cast her knowing gaze on Max, and inquired, "Have you had any of those nightmares lately?"

Max was silent for a while, as if not wanting to answer. Sitting at Peninsula Cancer Treatment Center with Emily, who was receiving yet another round of infusion therapy for her level-four ovarian cancer, Max realized that opportunities to discuss his war-induced nightmares with Emily were dwindling, as she grew progressively weaker. It wouldn't be long before her natural tendency to understand and express empathy would begin to wane.

"Truth be told, I had a doozy night before last," Max began. "I woke up on the floor soaked in sweat. Luckily it was around five AM, and I had to get up anyway to catch my flight from Denver to here. It caught me by surprise, because I haven't had one of these really vivid nightmares in a several months."

"Oh Max, not again," Emily sighed with genuine dismay. "You have suffered so long with this affliction. I have tried so hard to comprehend what you went through back then-seems like forever." Emily paused with exhaustion.

Emily continued before Max had a chance to speak, "Max, do you think you could you make an exception this once, and just tell me what you can remember about the dream?" Emily inquired with a kind of pleading tone, as if this may be her last attempt to broach the subject.

Max had been unremittingly reticent over the years about his experiences in Cambodia, and was especially tight-lipped about the chronic nightmares he still experienced. His unwillingness to seek treatment and obstinate, "I can handle it" attitude had been a major factor leading to their separation back in the early 90s. The subtle effects of his inability to relate to Emily and his family after his return had put unbearable stress on their twenty-plus year marriage.

Oddly, the separation had a calming effect on the relationship, one of bringing Max and Emily closer than even before his tour in Cambodia. They were still soul mates, still loved each other dearly. They now just lived in different parts of the country. Divorce was never discussed.

Max had recently come to the conclusion that if Emily ever asked again about the dreams, he would do his best to finally and honestly give her an account of his many grapples with the persistent gargoyles he brought home from war in his subconscious.

Max began slowly, "The bombing began without warning. We were in a noncombatant area inspecting a Khmer logistics rear echelon site, just outside of a town called Neak Leoung. No one expected to be a target that day, least of all the four Americans."

"As the explosions began ripping buildings apart, I somehow remember in the dream how harrowing it is to imagine that one of these monster munitions from the sky could be cosmically fated to find me. Who could know? In the process of its free fall, once released from the latches that held it in the racks above the B-52s bomb bay, I was as likely a target as anything around me at the time."

"By some means, I know that in spite any natural tendency to find refuge, take flight, or try to make it to our chopper on the other side of town, my destiny seems to have been determined. I am locked into the circumstances. I would have to stay and help. I had no alternative, no option. Stay, I must, even when escape was so compelling."

"In my dream I recognize myself as if I'm an observer, knowing the story well, having experienced it firsthand. As the observer, I strain to alter the course of that day, my own course, knowing the horror it would surely entail later in life."

"But, I seem to be trapped in Neak Leong. My observer-self had long since concluded that I would be stuck there, again and again. It was as if I was being sent back to find some lost, arcane clue that might release me from the torture of re-experiencing the scene in similar dreams."

"The scene in my dream clarifies: A wounded little girl, about eleven, comes up to me holding an inanimate infant, perhaps a doll. But, it's not a doll. It's a real infant, showing no signs of life. Amid the explosions, the older girl's crying, and the chaos, I observe myself cradling the baby in one arm, the skinny eleven-year-old in the other, scurrying across the town square in search of a safe refuge for these petrified kids. The jostling of my haste somehow enlivens the infant as we come to a halt near some large, burning trucks. Suddenly, the cradled infant comes to life, shrieks like a banshee, and proceeds to hurl the remnants of an earlier meal all over the front of me."

"The din from the repeated explosions merely adds to the frenzy. Townspeople scamper in every direction, as if to avoid the next explosion. The stench of burning flesh is horrific and unmistakable. I see body parts strewn all around the square, torsos without legs, legs without bodies, and feet with sandals but no legs."

"And, as is typical of so many of these dreams, the scenes relapse into a series of repetitive time capsules being recast as if to finally get it right. My observer-self realizes how horrific this scene is, but beyond the sweat and semi-consciousness of the dream, it seems normal, matter-of-fact. The scene rewinds again and again as if to remind me that I would surely live, but deep in my soul, I would just as certainly have accepted death than to see this dreadful scene even one more time, much less on a repeated basis."

"My dream observer watches as a four-man American team sets up a rudimentary triage center under a crude tarp canopy, just off the town's square. This dream observer is aware that the team is all these poor people have in the way of assistance or first-aid treatment. Their cries for loved ones seem to highlight the intense sense of guilt that befalls the Americans, who realize the travesty of this errant B-52 strike. The irony is fitting as the screams accentuate this sense of guilt, as they make their seemingly trivial efforts to help and comfort the survivors."

"The scene again focuses on collecting the wounded who just might live through this event. In the dream, I recall finding one woman who is sobbing quietly under a tin roof that has landed on her. Extricating her and carrying her over toward the triage canopy, I can feel the strength of her grasp. After a few steps, the grasp goes from solid to limp; she transforms from live to dead weight."

"I remember the eyes of the children, pleading and anxious, as if to say, 'you are all we have to keep us from being orphaned….please help my mother….'"

"My dream observer seems to know how desperately I need to self-implode, out of sheer physical and psychic overload. A meltdown might be what I needed at that moment. The thread of sanity that the Max of this dream held onto was the realization that there was a correspondingly dire need for him to remain calm, collected, and a beam of hope for both the dying and their surviving loved ones."

"And then, I'm awake in a pool of sweat, exhausted and certainly not interested in talking about either the dream, or the fact that it represented only one of several scenarios in which I found myself during my year in Cambodia, scenarios that are also settings for equally horrific nightmares. I can't think of anything that would top those scenarios as most-disdained discussion topics."

"The settings are really derived from my personal war experiences. They are painful reminders of regretful days I spent in the vain pursuit of personal honor and respect, as well as a naïve and misplaced sense of patriotism."

"Honestly Emily, my belief has always been that these burden were mine to bear, my pains to suffer, and my guilt to assuage. That's the reason I have been so reluctant, for so long, in sharing any aspect of the horrors I observed during those dreadful days."

As Max's voice trailed off, he noticed a grateful, peaceful smile on Emily's face, as he sensed her hand gently squeezing his.

CHAPTER ONE

THE PRESENT

*T*hunder clapped angrily as the sudden downpour began to drench everyone and everything surrounding the bleak Colonial Williamsburg cemetery. Max Donatello stood erect as he shivered in his fashionable, lined Burberry trench coat. He flipped its collar to the wind, trying to keep the chill out, but the chill was really in his heart. Max whispered to himself, "Damned chilly for November in Tidewater."

It also occurred to him that the universe could just be registering its own indignant objection to the loss of his precious wife Emily, whose burial was about to take place. He smiled wanly as if to encourage the plaintiff in its thunderous disdain.

His attention drifted from the sad proceedings, Max wondered, "How could another cherished life be snuffed out at only 63 years of age?" In Max's view, the universe had every right to complain vociferously. It was bordering on unjust when you think of all the lives Emily caringly touched and supported during her short sojourn in this life.

At 66, Max bore the countenance of a very senior corporate executive. Still a muscular 6'4" he could have easily passed for Tom Selleck's twin brother. He maintained the bearing of a retired military man. His height provided a lessening effect on the physical evidence of his less than Spartan days since retiring from the Army.

Max's mind wandered as the pastor read the final prayers over Emily's casket. Standing arm in arm with Chris and Melissa, one of his kids on either side, he felt unusual solidarity of family. Shared loss, shared grief, and the growing chasm between having Emily with them and the specter of her loss, made the scene more abject.

Max's penetrating blue eyes surveyed the crowd. He continued in deep thought, as the large crowd at the funeral seemed to thin out. The church had been packed with legions of Emily's admirers, friends, and business acquaintances. Max recognized members of Emily's extended family and her closest friends in the Tidewater area. It seemed a testament to Emily's unrelenting loyalty. With the inclement weather, he understood how the crowd at the cemetery might diminish. His mind swept back to the subject of these proceedings.

"My God, there are so many brilliant doctors and researchers out there spending billions of dollars a year in a delirious, uncoordinated, seemingly futile search for a way to eliminate cancer—especially the sinister forms of the disease that are the common among women," Max wondered about this, almost aloud.

Forms like the ovarian cancer, which had assaulted and summarily overwhelmed Emily. In spite of her noble fighting spirit and love for life, she was no match for the disease during her yearlong battle. All during her battle Max had been by her side and visited as often as he could. He was there just the week before her passing, but she seemed to have rallied, and he returned to Denver just to receive the call the following day.

Now, as the formalities came to an end, with Emily's significant life accomplishments, the family's numerous fond memories, and her life of service eulogized, the family shivered at the finality of the moment.

The casket lay atop the burial bier mounted just above a freshly dug grave in this godforsaken, mud-strewn burial ground, not far from Williamsburg, Virginia. The monsoon-like rains of the past few days had made the cemetery into a sea of shoe-sucking mud. But Emily Willis Donatello had expressed her wishes plainly. She wanted to be buried near the gravesite of her beloved mom and dad.

On his reflection of all this, Max finally shed furtive, heartfelt tears for the only woman he had ever loved, or ever would love.

---

CHAPTER TWO

*T*he day before the funeral, Max and his son Chris, and his wife Susie, decided to rent separate cars on their arrival from Denver at the Richmond airport. The idea was to give the extended family more flexibility getting around in the busy days ahead. Both drivers headed straight for the B&B that Emily had ably owned and managed since Max and Emily's official separation in 1991.

Emily's obvious success was due to her native warmth and cordial personality, a true caring about people, and an innate skill to listen to them. Her extensive travels allowed her to talk to her foreign clients about their country and life there. She was living her own dream.

Melissa, their youngest child, had accompanied her mother to Virginia from the first days after Max and Emily's separation. Melissa was then only 19 years old and was about to start her freshman year at The College of William & Mary. It was not long thereafter that Max and Emily jointly acquired the stately old manor, which was destined to be the culmination of Emily's life dream to own and operate a first-class bed and breakfast.

With daughter Melissa's amazing head for numbers, she would become an able assistant to Emily in accounting and financial matters.

Now years later, Melissa had finished her education, had her CPA, and was employed full-time at the B&B handling all administrative, financial, and related back-office affairs. She had many suitors but had always had a way of keeping her distance from men wanting to get too close to her.

Melissa, now in her late thirties, was a lot like her mother. She had summarily taken charge of all the details of planning her mother's funeral. Her efforts reflected her mother's own gracious, yet fastidious, way with things involving guests and family. Melissa seemed to know that her dad and brother would be of little real help to her. Her attitude was to assume that they would leave it all up to her anyway.

Melissa and her dad didn't have a particularly close or warm relationship. This distance could be attributed to the fact that he was gone much of the time she was growing up, often travelling or working long hours. She remembered her mother repeatedly making excuses when her father wasn't there at her first piano recital, her middle school graduation, or her senior prom. Then, she and her mother had moved to Virginia after her graduation from high school. Her mother always told her how much her father wanted to be there, but that she should realize that his important duties needed him more.

After graduation, Melissa found herself busy with her undergrad degree followed by marriage to her soul mate, whom she would lose tragically in an accident 18 months later. Then, Melissa buried herself in getting her Master's degree and helping her mom run the Inn.

Max had a way of keeping his distance, even when at home. Melissa had always known in her heart that her dad loved her and that he was proud of her, but there was still a perceptible gap, one that she could never quite traverse between them, almost a sense of distrust on Melissa's part.

It was her mother who had always been the heart and soul of the family. Melissa knew how much her mother loved her dad, but could never overcome the distance Max kept between himself and his family. What still seemed ironic to Melissa was, in spite of their 'separation,' how close and loving her mom and dad remained right up to her mother's passing. Melissa worried about how dad would live without her mom around to keep the family intact.

As for the funeral activities, part of the plan was that close, out-of-town friends and family would find refuge at the B&B after the post-funeral luncheon. This arrangement would hopefully allow the group to visit and get back in touch with one another. Mother Emily was always great at putting on an impromptu party and insuring everyone had a good time. Melissa calculated that this group of friends and family would be getting together just as Emily would have planned. Melissa knew that the one person who would surely have made it a resounding success would be the one missed the most.

*   *   *

Not finding Melissa when he arrived at the B&B the day before the funeral, Max breathed a small sigh of relief. Max was not looking forward to his initial encounter with Melissa under these difficult circumstances. He loved Melissa and was very proud of her, but he really didn't know his daughter. Max acknowledged that he had not been around much while she grew into an achievement-oriented young woman. On top of it all, there always seemed to be a kind of coolness between them.

Max took the opportunity to excuse himself from Chris and Susie, giving the excuse that he wanted to take a quick ride out to the old cemetery to check on grave preparation. On arrival, Max walked to the Willis family plot where there were three headstones: Emily's mother; COL Willis; and that of LT Pete Connors, Melissa's deceased young husband. The grave crew had already prepared the grave for Emily between her mother and that of Melissa's husband. An artificial grass cover was already placed on top of the fresh grave.

Emily's mom had predeceased her by ten years. Prescilla Willis had perished under the specter of the same brand of damnable cancer that would cause her daughter's interment here the next day. COL H.G. Willis had died suddenly on a golf outing, a little over a year before his wife's passing. Pete Connors had been killed in a tragic aircraft accident 18 months into his marriage to Melissa.

CHAPTER THREE

*A*fter Max walked around the muddy cemetery and inspected the Willis family plot, he climbed back into his cold rental car. He started the car to warm up, resting his head on the back of the seat. As he awaited the car's heater to warm up, Max was transposed back to his earliest days in the Army.

He would certainly never forget his first encounter with Emily's father, COL Herbert G. Willis, Director of Services, U. S. Army Transportation School at Ft. Eustis, VA. In December 1967, Max had just finished the Transportation Officer's Basic Course (TOBC) and had a couple of months before he would start his next course, the Aircraft Maintenance Officer's Course. (AMOC). Max, in those days, had the illusory goal of becoming an Army aviator. AMOC prior to flight school was one way the Army cued up young officers at Ft. Eustis to fit into the schedule glide path of the primary flight training classes at Ft. Rucker, AL, which was steadily churning out helicopter pilots for the ongoing Vietnam conflict.

In the Army's ineffable wisdom, they often kept officers awaiting their next course of instruction busy by assigning them to light duty in offices throughout the Army Transportation School. These officers were referred to as 'snowbirds,' because they were figuratively, 'here one day and gone tomorrow.'

After the holidays, Max was assigned as 'special assistant' to the Director of Services (DOS), Colonel Herbert Garrison Willis. With assignment in hand, and in a pique of interest from what the personnel folks described as something of Transportation Corps miracle man, Max drove with some immediacy to the Transportation School library to read the biography on COL Willis's distinguished Army career on file there.

Sure enough, his new boss was highly decorated for valor in Korea, with a distinguished record in the early years of Vietnam. Max could not imagine what possible need or useful purpose he could serve for this crusty, supposed legend, Colonel Willis.

As Max would find much later, the Office of the Director of Services was at the bottom of the pecking order for Transportation Corps full colonels. All the complaints, bellyaches, and prima donna demands came to the attention of the Director of Services. But, this assignment was COL Willis's final before retirement, and it proved the old adage that good deeds do not go unpunished.

Max's first day as a snowbird at DOS was marked with a certain degree of trepidation on his part, but, it turned out to be nothing but cordial introductions, brief banter, and high expectations expressed by COL Willis. The old full colonel seemed to take a shine to him. Then again, it was just the first day.

The more Max got to know COL Willis over the initial weeks, the more he admired him. Here was a straight-shooting leader who demonstrated enormous dedication to mission, results, and the welfare of his subordinates. His lanky, 6'5" stature towered over most of his subordinates, superiors, and colleagues. He used this height to his advantage, combining plain-spoken, wry observations with charming wit to win over any discussion.

In the course of the next few weeks, Max was given increasingly complex tasks. COL Willis liked Max's writing style, so had Max write responses for several worthy, but impossible suggestions submitted by overeager students and staff officers of every level. COL Willis was always astounded by the way Max could express the Army's appreciation, while tactfully telling the idealistic proponent of the suggestion that there was no way in hell the idea could be implemented in this lifetime.

After a week or two, COL Willis casually mentioned that Max should come over to the house for dinner some weekend soon. Invitations such as this were part of a long tradition in the Army allowing junior officers to get a glimpse of Army life outside the office, so to speak. COL Willis indicated that he hoped his daughter Emily would be available. Emily Willis had graduated early that past December from University of Virginia. Before long, COL Willis pinpointed the following Saturday for the dinner, but indicated to Max that he still wasn't sure Emily could attend.

"Wonder how she'll react to that?" Max immediately wondered silently. Max had been the brunt of way too many 'fix-ups' in his college years. Those were some of the longest evenings of his life. Max could just imagine himself arriving in the light of day, meeting this colonel's daughter, who may take a dim view of spending an afternoon with a 2nd LT, Max winced as he pondered what this girl might be like.

"Crap shoot is the likely odds," Max concluded. 'The colonel is a great guy, no doubt, but meeting his daughter could make this short-term snowbird assignment seem like an eternity."

What Max didn't know was that Emily had just graduated with honors from UVA with dual degrees in Marketing and Corporate Communications. She already had several job offers in the Tidewater area with major defense firms needing help with their corporate image.

Emily, it turns out, was a stunning, tall, statuesque brunette, brimming with the confidence and sophistication of a lady who had been carefully groomed and educated. Besides, she'd lived all over the world as an Army brat and had traveled extensively with her mom when dad was too busy doing his 'Army thing.' She could hold her own in most any situation—in hosting military social events or accompanying her dad at 'must attend' formal military functions, when mom was under the weather or otherwise indisposed. She could hold her sway in any debate with the most cerebral senior officers, and charm them to shame while doing so.

Emily was taking a month or so off after college to spread her wings and enjoy the liberation of being a college graduate. So, she was less than receptive when her daddy told her he was inviting "a lieutenant of good possibilities," assigned in his office to their home for dinner. Emily took this description as meaning he was OK looking, with a good personality.

As a rule, Emily didn't appreciate having her dad try to fix her up with young lieutenants. This occasion was no exception. Besides, it usually turned out that the guys were more interested in getting in good with her father than in her.

Not only that, but in those heady days Ft. Eustis was awash with stout-hearted young lieutenants and captains. The former were being trained to go to Vietnam, and the latter were here to show their stripes, providing training and guidance to these 'butter bars,' as 2nd LTs were referred to in those ominous times, where the life span of a new 2nd LT in Vietnam was measured in days, sometimes hours, depending on assignment.

So, some bright-eyed lieutenant was not about to turn her head, much less make much of an impression, not even if her daddy might think he was worthy. What's more, of late, she had been dating a dashing young Transportation Corps aviator, a captain no less, who was back to Eustis for a breather between tours in Vietnam. Word was, he was loaded in his own right; drove a flashy, new red Porsche 911 convertible; and was routinely invited to all the most lavish parties.

"Nothing serious, Daddy, mind you," but Emily declined the invitation to attend the dinner that Saturday at her parent's home.

CHAPTER FOUR

*M*ax had been sitting in the rental car and realized that he must have lost track of time, for when he checked his watch, more than ten minutes had passed. He was still not ready to head back to the B&B though. He needed this alone time to say his good-bye to the person who filled his life with love and happiness. He closed his eyes again and thought about Emily and their chance meeting.

"Heck, I might never have met Emily if I had to rely on my own connections, such as they were in those days," reflected Max with a wry smile.

Max thought back to that Wednesday evening in late January 1968, when Pete Carpenter, one of his officer roommates asked Max to join him for the Wednesday night festivities at the Ft. Eustis Officers Club dubbed, "The Pig Push," by all the young student officers. This moniker was applied because the club welcomed single ladies of legal age from the Tidewater community to come out and socialize with the burgeoning Ft. Eustis officer corps. There was always a live band, and it was usually quite a party.

Max figured, why not? So, after grabbing a sandwich in the Officer's Club casual bar, where they caught up with some of the guys, Max and Pete joined the festivities in the club's large ballroom. The evening dragged, however, and both looked at each other after about an hour or so. Max finally said, "One more beer, then we head back to the apartment. We both have to be up at the crack of 0545 hours. Six o'clock PT [Physical Training] comes mighty early."

They walked around the periphery of the dance floor like a couple of high school sophomores looking for a friendly female face. What appeared to be slim pickings prompted them closer to the exit of the enormous ballroom where these functions played out. Someone yelled at Pete Carpenter to "come sit down and meet his gang." Pete and Max shuffled reluctantly to a long table near the dance floor. Introductions were perfunctory yet cheerful, but soon the chatting resumed among members of the table.

Max had caught the beguiling smile of a tall brunette at the end of the table closest to the dance floor. He hesitantly returned the smile with a toothy grin, and went down the aisle and stopped at her place.

"Any chance you could show me how to dance this 'Funky Broadway stuff,'" he asked meekly, while holding his gaze and a goofy grin.

"It's a little late for dance lessons, I'm afraid," she declared with another nice smile. "Why don't you take a seat and wait for the next slow dance," inquired the rather self-assured young lady.

Max's native impulsiveness had gotten him into several ticklish situations in the past with the ladies. Now, here he was, stuck until the next slow song with nothing to say to this one. It was too loud for any kind of meaningful chatter, so he toasted his beer glass toward her, and she raised her glass to meet his.

Max must have pleased the gods that day, because just then, the band started playing a slow, romantic melody. The charmed lieutenant blurted, "Shall we dance?" She rose immediately and took his hand.

"I'm Emily, and you may tell me your life story." She looked straight into his eyes as if to say, "It had better be good, or I'll show you the exit personally." Max imagined her thinking. Little did he know that his life was about to change forever!

Max filled in Emily with his brief biography, outlining how he happened to be at Ft. Eustis at this particular moment in history. Then, he mentioned he was snow-birding for the Director of Services at the T-School.

Emily's eyes widened as the truth struck her, she exclaimed, "You're that lieutenant who works for my dad." Max was not sure if it was a declaration or an accusation.

"So, you're that Emily," retorted Max. They broke into embarrassed laughter, as they instantly caught the irony of having her dad and his boss trying to set them up.

As they finished the dance with periodic giggles and a few random squeezes, which drove Max through the ceiling, Emily finally said,

"I have a strict policy never to date my dad's choices for me. I'm going to make an exception with you. I need to know what my dad sees in you."

Emily's mind raced thinking silently, "*You're obviously a hunk, you have a cute dimple, you appear to be educated, my dad likes you, and you are probably trainable.*"

She continued, "Why don't you meet me at Nick's Seafood Pavilion near the Gloucester Bridge tomorrow evening at six forty-five sharp for dinner to allow me a chance to do a little one-on-one detective work to confirm suspicions?"

CHAPTER FIVE

*M*ax shivered when he thought of that moment way back then. It could have been last evening. There was a spark there from the very beginning. Was it those beguiling eyes? Was it her aggressive wit? Her self-assurance?

After a three-and-a-half hour dinner, as they strolled to her car in the restaurant parking lot, Max wondered if he had passed muster with this enchanting lady. The evening had been a friendly, free-flowing exchange of life histories, likes, dreams, and life expectations. In essence, they got along as if they had known each other since kindergarten. Max's mental scorecard went something like this: she was exciting, interesting, deep, devilishly intelligent, and a veritable dream to be with.

As they approached her car at nearly 10:15, she stopped and turned to face him. Out of nowhere, she stepped close to him, wrapped her arms around his shoulders, and gave him the warmest, sweetest, most luscious kiss that had ever been planted on his quivering lips. Max's head was spinning when Emily precipitously turned and somehow crawled ladylike into her MGB convertible. "Dad was right. Call me tomorrow, Max," she added as she zoomed off toward Denbigh.

Dazed, almost shivering, Max said aloud, "There has to be more of that."

CHAPTER SIX

The car was getting too warm; Max snapped out of his reverie. He knew he should be heading back to the B&B to see if Melissa or Chris needed anything from him. He had not slept more than a few winks since he received the call about Emily's passing.

He knew he would have to deal with the fact that Emily would no longer be there for him, even at a distance as it had been since 1991. No longer would she be there to buffer the rough edges of any residual resentment harbored by their daughter Melissa.

"Damned career always came first," Max reflected on his drive back to the B&B. It still was raining, and the windshield wipers were making Max drowsy. When he arrived, both kids were gone, but they had left a note for him urging him to join them at lunch at the Italian restaurant just down the block. Max realized he didn't need food. In truth, the soft, comfy bed upstairs was calling him.

*   *   *

The following day, after services at the family plot, Max was thinking about what a truly wonderful wife and mother Emily had been. "*How she tried so valiantly to be a good wife,*" thought Max as they finally got into the funeral limo to head back to the luncheon after the final prayers were intoned. Even after their separation in 1991, they were as close as ever, right up till the end. No twenty-four-hour period elapsed without them speaking at least once on the phone, and they still always ended their conversation with "I love you."

"*Perhaps she was right,*" Max thought to himself as he stood among family and friends this gloomy autumn afternoon. "*She only wanted for me to get over my nightmares, face my ghosts, heal my interior wounds, and put the past to rest. She only wanted to have a close and happy marriage like those years before my tour to Cambodia.*"

14

CHAPTER SEVEN

1968

*M*ax and Emily were married soon after his graduation from AMOC. Theirs was a whirlwind courtship, encouraged by Max's new best buddy, COL Willis, Emily's proud father. The dream-like love affair had caused Max to get into academic trouble in the AMOC course. At one point, he was placed on academic probation for scoring low on an important exam involving aviation propulsion. Truth was, he was spending too much time with Emily to spend any real time on his studies.

Max got the bad news a week later that he had not passed the physical for flight school due high blood pressure, which ran genetically in both sides of his family. So, with the help of his father-in-law, he traded eighteen months in Germany for a year in Vietnam later. This policy was new in the Army to entice young junior reserve officers, newly married, to stick around the Army longer, perhaps even opt for a full career.

Max was elated, and so was Emily. She had spent several years living in Europe with her mom and dad when she was a teenager. Max and Emily lucked out and got quarters immediately on base. Max was assigned to the Supply and Transport (S&T) Battalion of one of Europe's armored divisions stationed outside Nuremburg. At first, he was the appointed Maintenance Officer for the battalion; then, after six months, he was selected to command the battalion's enormous truck company, with over 190 soldiers and 85 trucks and trailers in his motor park. The division's basic load of fuel, in 5000-gallon tankers, resided in Max's motor park, since the semi-tractors for these tankers were the prime mover vehicles assigned to one of his platoons nearby.

Although they were poor as church mice, Max and Emily grew steadily as a couple, reveling in the German culture, eating in every Gasthaus they could find, and traveling around Europe whenever the opportunity arose.

Emily had changed their ordinary quarters into a charming home, and Max was always excited to get back there each night. They had been married only about six months when Emily told Max they would be expecting their first child in about seven months. Max was over the moon with joy, but they had decided to hold off on sharing their joyous news with family or friends.

Just a month later, Emily had a miscarriage, which broke both their hearts. Emily curled up in Max's arms at night and cried herself to sleep. The big lug didn't know how to take away her pain, so he just held her tight. Max grieved for the loss of their child, but he was more pained for Emily and how tough this all was on her. Gradually, over the next few months Emily was able to smile again and talk about their future. She threw her heart and soul into planning for their first anniversary trip.

On that trip, they drove to Paris, stayed in a little hotel on the left bank, toured the Louvre, the Eifel Tower, even the Opera. They drove to Versailles and walked the grounds in spite of a freezing wind that day. April in Paris—what a splendid delayed honeymoon.

They then drove on to Brussels, and finally to Amsterdam, taking a room on the fourth floor of a quaint hotel whose proprietors got them tipsy tasting the flavored Dutch gins. At the end of the night, it was a perilous climb up the steep staircases to the frigid fourth floor. To make matters worse, the privy was down the hall, a real challenge for a couple that had imbibed heartily earlier in the evening.

On a walk around Amsterdam, they came upon a flea market, Emily's eyes bright with joy. She just had to find something perfect for their home. She spend an hour looking over most of the stalls until she came upon the item she had been seeking: an old, three–gallon, light green glass wine bottle. So, Max carried it across town to their parked car, and stored it safely in the trunk for Emily. Max wryly thought, "I would have carried the whole flea market to the car, just to bring that joy and smile to Emily's face again."

The romantic trips seemed to just present themselves. A well-timed maintenance officer's course in Murnau, near Southern Bavaria's wood-carving capital, Oberammergau, provided an idyllic backdrop for a four-day get away. Then, another course several months later in

Garmisch-Partenkirchen allowed them to drive to Salzburg while they were so close to Austria. They took the tram overlooking the Salzburg valley, whose hills provided the opening scenes for the Rogers and Hammerstein spectacular musical, *The Sound of Music*. With each of these trips Emily got stronger and happier again, and her easy smile was back in evidence. These jaunts also allowed them both time to draw closer together working through their shared pain and healing.

Emily had made these little getaways possible through penny pinching, babysitting, and taking the neighbor's dogs for long walks. Each month, she would buy a few extra gas ration tickets, and she stashed them away until they had enough tickets to buy gas for another motor trip. She would pack small tins of tuna, deviled ham, and fruits to keep lunch and snack expenses to a minimum. Their trunk was always loaded with lots of canned soft drinks that Emily would buy in the commissary at rock bottom prices. She would bring enough salami and cheese to last a day or so. Max would stop in one of the quaint villages and pick up fresh *brötchen* (German crusty rolls) or a baguette. If they were staying the night in a village, they'd stop at a small market and buy a bottle of a good Riesling, or a couple of tall bottles of German beer for a late afternoon picnic.

These getaways, plus the unique lifestyle they enjoyed in Europe, made Max and Emily closer than ever. They were truly soul mates by the time Max had to return to the states came around. The future was truly bright for Max and Emily, because she had shared the news that she was expecting again, and was well past the dangerous first trimester. Their transfer came in mid-1970.

The Army scheduled Max for several courses before he would head out to Vietnam. One of these courses was at Ft. Lee, VA, the four-month Army Supply Officer's Course. They got to know several couples there well, and as Max's good luck would have it, one of his close friends from college was assigned to the Quartermaster School. So, their social life, as well as their golf games, got plenty of play.

Emily was glad to be around a couple of women who already had young children she approached her final months of pregnancy. She and Max enjoyed doing the mundane things like shopping for a baby crib, diapers, and enough newborn clothes outfit triplets. Emily was in the throws of nesting, and Max would only say yes to any of her requests.

Their son, Christopher Maxwell Donatello, was born in early September 1970, a healthy, eight-pound baby. Max and Emily felt that life couldn't get any better than this. Emily just enjoyed watching Max carry his son around marveling how much they looked alike. Emily thought Chris looked like a wrinkled old man, but she would never say that to Max.

CHAPTER EIGHT

1971

*M*ax was something of an odd character. He was by now an Army Reserve Captain in an era where few guys still responded cheerfully to what General Bruce Palmer called, 'The Summons of the Trumpet.' Still, Max believed that when your country asked for sacrifice, you did what you had to do to honor your family, and carry out your patriotic duty. His attitude now reflected his three years in the Army, and the subtle influence of his father-in-law. Max was beginning to assimilate the values of career officers, who believed what they were doing was a "calling," not simply a job. So, in spite of the fact that Max never entertained even a glimmer of an idea that he might make the Army a career when he was an ROTC cadet back in college, he had come to admire the character of men who served their country, regardless of the vagaries of politics or public opinion.

Max figured if you came back in less than one piece, either physically or mentally, that it was just the price you paid to acquit yourself honorably when the country taps you on the shoulder to serve. There would be no whining, no complaining, no *"Why Me?"* in any of his musings.

Max believed strongly that he had to serve, even in a war like Vietnam. Who else would stand up and defend the country, in the face of apathy and disillusionment that permeated the psyche of young people in the late sixties and early seventies?

Max understood that the war was essentially lost. He saw signs of it everywhere in the Army. Large units were being pulled out of SE Asia, entire divisions standing down, furling and retiring their colors. Truth was, in 1972, the war was indeed winding down. The citizens of America had rendered their verdict. It was "over, over there," as the lyrics of an old WWI ballad noted, in the eyes of most Americans. Certainly, public support for the war in Vietnam had eroded to its worst-ever ratings, according to all the polls.

One sickening indicator was the growing public hostility toward service personnel. American society had somehow come to hold soldiers, sailors, and airmen in contempt for involvement in SE Asia. Many ugly confrontations were experienced by returning GIs from SE Asia. Incidents such as people spitting on returning soldiers in airports prompted the Army to introduce a policy where soldiers were ordered to travel to and from assignments overseas in civilian clothes to avoid these humiliating spectacles.

It stung like a slap in the face to Max and his fellow comrades-in-arms. The sinews of Max's soul lamented sourly, *"What a crummy way to regard the supreme sacrifice of so many who would never make it back. Even more outrageous was the insult to the guys and gals who had done their duty and served in spite of personal reservations or disillusions."*

With his father-in-law's back-channel help with 'Mother Army,' Max had wrangled a 47-week course in Vietnamese Language at the Defense Language Institute East Coast (DLIEC) in Alexandria, VA. Here, he could finally demonstrate his language aptitude. Max figured that it would not only give him some concentrated family time at home (almost a full year), but it would also facilitate his eventual work when he finally got to Vietnam.

The language school assignment was really a godsend. Emily was thrilled. Not only was Max given a reprieve from combat duty for nearly a year, they were delighted that the school was situated in Crystal City, just down Route 1 from Arlington, Virginia. This assignment also meant that they would be only a couple of hours from Williamsburg, near her parents. They got to spend time with her parents, and Chris loved being with his doting grandparents. The language course wasn't easy, and Max had to spent hours listening to and repeating Vietnamese dialogue and words on his recorder.

A couple times each month, Max and Emily took Chris down to Williamsburg to see his grandparents. Whether it was a cookout, a lunch out somewhere, or an overnight stay, these occasions were always something that each member of the family looked forward to: Max and the colonel could talk shop; Emily and her mom could dote on Chris. Chris just reveled in the joy of the family's warmth and togetherness.

The language school was something of an oddity. Classes were held in the morning, usually concluded by 1:00 PM. This schedule gave students ample time to get home and work on their verbal and written lessons. It also gave Max plenty of time for exercise, and long, wholesome periods in his role as husband and dad.

Max had been assigned to a ten-man class where he was the only Army person among nine navy enlisted men. Not only did he stick out like a sore thumb in his classroom, the language school was inundated that year for some reason with Navy personnel. Max was one of two Army persons in a veritable fleet of two hundred Navy weenies!

Max got along well with the men, especially the three chiefs in his section. He learned more about the navy in those 47 weeks than he had ever hoped to know. The section's teacher was a drop-dead gorgeous French-Vietnamese lady name Ko Kim Chi. Classy and impeccably dressed each day, she easily kept the sailors in line. It was hard not to pay attention with her in front of the class.

*   *   *

Max had been informed by his assignment officer at the Transportation Corps's OPO (Officer Personnel Operations), that he would most likely be assigned as an advisor to a large Vietnamese logistics unit. This posting would be with one of the South Vietnamese organizations that were in the process of undergoing 'Vietnamization,' the hallmark slogan of the Nixon Administration's "Peace with Honor" campaign for re-election in 1972.

In June of 1971, Emily announced the wonderful news that she was expecting again. It wasn't something they had planned on, with Chris being so little and Max facing his tour in SE Asia just before this arrival of the newest Donatello. They regarded it as a blessing nonetheless.

Then, out of the blue in January 1972, just as he was about to graduate with honors from DLIEC, his usually chummy assignment officer telephoned Max with a great deal of excitement. It turned out that he had a new, special assignment for Max. However, it was not in Vietnam, but in a newly-formed, high-priority logistics team headquartered at the embassy in Phnom Penh, Cambodia!

Max's reaction was uncharacteristically harsh, "You mean to tell me that I just spent a year of my life mastering Vietnamese, only to be shuffled off to Cambodia, where French is the official diplomatic language; and Khmer, which is undecipherable even to the language geeks at DLI, is spoken by most of the Cambodian troops?"

The sardonic response of Max's assignment officer went something like, "In the Army, you need to be flexible, Captain."

"Calm down, Tiger," Max cautioned himself. *"Are you kidding me?"* wondered Max, as he sizzled over this patently ominous conversation. *"A new gift from the Army gods,"* thought Max ruefully.

In his estimation, this change was Army irony at its most wicked best, or worst, depending on your perspective. He was slated and ready to go to Vietnam to be an advisor to a large logistics unit, but, now his assignment officer was telling him that a new team had been established with the highest priority, and Max should feel honored to be hand-selected.

"Not sure if this hand-selection meant someone knew of him through COL Willis, or that this line was the same barf bag that assignment officers dealt out of on a daily basis," thought Max, without verbalizing his fury.

The way the assignment officer described the posting, things sounded too good to be true. Max's experience was that if something seemed that way, it was indeed too good to be true, and it should be avoided at all costs. Max let out the obvious question, inquiring what his options were.

At this point, the normally collegial Major on the other end of the phone got somewhat animated, and very strident, in his tone, "Captain, you are clearly confused about this process. You will report to the Military Equipment Delivery Team Cambodia's rear headquarters at Tan Son Nhut Air Base in Saigon, Republic of Vietnam, on the date we discussed. Written orders are being cut to that effect, as we speak. Options are not available at this point. Do I make myself perfectly clear?"

"Yes Sir, I'd love to go to Cambodia to serve my country," was all Max could muster as his desultory reply.

*   *   *

It was just before Christmas that Max settled Emily and Chris in Williamsburg in her parent's large home before his departure to Cambodia. It was a burden lifted from Max's mind that Emily would have her mother and father with her at the birth of their second child. Emily would need support with their two little ones and her husband overseas in a war zone.

CHAPTER NINE

*I*n the spring of 1973, when Max returned from Cambodia, he tried to fit in with his family, but Emily had been both mother and father to the children, and had run the household a year by herself. Their first assignment after his tour in Cambodia was to Ft. Lewis, Washington. It took months for Max to settle in and begin to feel comfortable again. He soon began to have some problems sleeping, and he always felt on edge. He knew his year in the Far East had changed him, but he resolved to work through this vale of tears on his own.

While he had desperately missed Emily, and could not wait to see her, he could not bring himself to share his wartime experiences, and he knew in time he would work through the remnants. They seemed so alien to this snug, home-front scene he encountered on his return.

Without knowing why, he had become emotionally distant, diligently suppressing a lot of the horror he had experienced during the tour in Phnom Penh, immersing himself in his military duties. The result was an often testy, impatient Max when dealing with his loved ones early after his return.

Emily began to witness disruptive outbursts late at night in Max's dreams as Max fought phantom hand-to-hand battles in his sleep. Sometimes, he would even wake up in a cold sweat, sometimes on the floor by the bed. When Emily asked what he was dreaming, he would only give some bland story that he had been tussling with a tenacious communist soldier on a hillside, which was why he had rolled out of bed in a heap onto the floor.

These occurrences embarrassed Max, and made him push the remembrances even deeper into his subconscious. Still, he sometimes lashed out in his sleep, punching walls, knocking over tables, and scaring the bejesus out of Emily, who absorbed several bruises from these nocturnal encounters with Max's demons in the months and early years after he returned from Cambodia.

Emily lovingly suggested that Max see a psychologist to identify ways to cope with terror and stress that had played such a big part in his experiences in Cambodia. Emily sensed from his letters home that he had omitted many details of his wartime experience, and his many distinguished decorations for valor attested to the violent and horrific scenes Max must had witnessed.

Max reminded Emily of the army ethic that officers worked through the rough spots, steeling themselves to their feelings and sensibilities long after experiencing combat in all its confusion and desperation.

CHAPTER TEN

1988

*M*ax had decided to opt out of his Army career at the twenty-year mark. So, in June of 1987, Max put his oar in the water. One of Max's retired Army buddies had spoken to the powers that be at Xerox, and Max was offered a good-paying job with a bright future in business development.

Back then Max had convinced himself that the right course for him was to throw himself at a promising second career at Xerox, and let time heal all his Army-induced psychic wounds. Emily welcomed Max getting out of the Army and fully supported him. She just prayed that it might provide him clearer opportunities to address his problems, and that it might also mean he could get help without putting a black mark on his career.

But the career change meant only that Max traveled more, which didn't help with the emotional distance between them. Despite her encouragement for Max to talk with other veterans about his experiences, Max was intransigent. Max had observed his own father's silence about all things military when he was growing up. While he was well aware of his dad's involvement in combat, he never heard a whisper of detail emanating from his father's lips.

Max's futile attempts at self-help did not provide any real closure for the many unresolved issues that continued to take a toll not only on Max's disposition, but also his benign treatment of his family. If anything, Max's testiness and frustration with Chris's lax pre-teen ways caused numerous instances where Emily had to intervene to protect the laid-back Chris. Max had even grabbed Chris one time and pushed him against a wall threatening bodily harm if he did not make amends. Emily's loving intervention saved both from an ugly scene.

So, by the time Max was making the transition to a second career, things had changed substantially between Max and Emily. What had all the promise early on of a marriage made in heaven before the Cambodian tour had morphed into a stalemate of distance and frustration on both Max's and Emily's part.

Max had often privately reflected on the miserable state of the mental health of the Army's officer corps. Alcohol abuse was a common, accepted form of self-medication. The glamorization of alcohol in the Army was a long, cherished tradition. It was also a major factor in the inevitable decline of many otherwise fine officers. Officer's calls, beer calls, military balls, formal calls on commanders were all part of the established milieu. The modern Officers' Open Mess was another illustration. These formal gathering places were nothing less than exclusive private clubs for officers to meet for a happy hour for a couple of discounted drinks before being joined by the ladies for fine dining and dancing to live bands, and, of course, the best-quality, subsidized alcoholic beverages served long into the night.

In Max's observation, there was almost a conspiracy of silence regarding increased instances of alcohol-degraded ability among mid-grade officers resulting from the residual shock received from the relentless horror experienced in an active war front where repeated one-year tours of duty every other year were expected and common.

One need only remember the WWII incident where General George S. Patton slapped a soldier in an evacuation hospital because he claimed that his nerves were shot from constant action and shelling. Patton slapped and rebuked the soldier as a "goddamned coward" in front of many injured soldiers. The primacy of bravery over the soldier's well-being was the operative axiom that was remembered throughout the Army, especially the officer corps.

Despite a formal reprimand by Eisenhower, making Patton apologize to his entire command, the subliminal message was clear. You must bury your psychic wounds, especially if you are an officer, especially if you have any hope of advancement up the chain.

By the time Max returned from Cambodia, not only was this unspoken ethic fully engrained in the Army's officer corps, there was a new and pernicious dynamic of careerism that manifested itself in the 'ticket punching' mentality that subsumed much of the professional dedication that had been the hallmark of career Army officers ever since Valley

Forge. Anything that obscured the path to advancement, such as a tendency toward mental illness, even if combat-induced, was anathema to an aspiring career officer.

What this set of traditions added up to was a sort of 'silent conspiracy' to bury war wounds, especially among Army leaders, ones that entailed flashbacks, mental illness, depression, even the long unreported, but inexorably growing problem of suicide in the Army as an institution, and even in the officer corps.

Max and Emily's friendship and dedication to one another was the countervailing principle during these years. Emily tried and failed to get the couple into joint counseling, on the hope that it would have a therapeutic effect on Max's buried wounds.

Max's staunch Catholic upbringing in a second-generation-Italian family did not admit discussion of divorce. It was not a valid topic in those middle years of their relationship. And, true to that philosophy of dedication and devotion, they hung together as long as they could, but, Max's near-complete absorption in his second career at Xerox made attempts by Emily at regaining past intimacy a tough bargain in anyone's book.

Max firmly believed that Emily deserved to be happy. He still loved her dearly, in his own intransigent way. So, the best thing he could muster was an amicable, uncontested separation. The settlement was reached, without the normal haranguing associated with marital rifts. Fact was, Max and Emily had always been a unique couple. In many ways, they were made for each other. Emily was well-educated and was about to be an empty nester. She needed to do something she had dreamed about. Max finally resigned himself to this arrangement.

The agreed separation took place after Melissa graduated from high school in early summer 1991. Melissa had already been selected to attend the College of William & Mary in Williamsburg, VA, and Chris had already started college in Denver. Emily's initial decision was to move with Melissa to Williamsburg to be closer to her parents. Perhaps there, she could follow her dreams and find a measure of peace and personal happiness.

To that end, within months of her arrival in Virginia, Max helped Emily find and arrange financing to purchase and restore a fine old colonial manor in Williamsburg, which they converted into a B&B, one of Emily's lifelong dreams. Within months, Emily was on top of the business, and having a grand time, even thriving. Over time, Max paid down the mortgage on the B&B with his annual bonus, and proudly presented the deed to Emily within five years.

CHAPTER ELEVEN

*M*ax's job demanded that he remain in Denver. College-age Chris decided that the Rocky Mountains suited him much better than Virginia. Besides, he was attending classes at the University of Denver. So, he ended back on Max's doorstep not long after the official separation.

Chris floundered around college, attending the University of Denver part-time, while working construction jobs in the summer, and teaching snow skiing at Vail on weekends in the winter. By the end of 1991, he still had two years left to earn a baccalaureate degree, but still had not declared at major. Chris lived rent-free in a small apartment above the garage at Max's spacious home outside Denver. The two had dinner out together often, and bumped into each other in dad's kitchen on most mornings. There were many long chats over coffee in those days between Max and Chris. Their years of struggling with each other had long passed.

Max loved Chris's adventuresome spirit. He was physically similar to his dad in almost every way. Tall, lanky but muscular, devilishly handsome, Chris was really a pretty good knock off of his old man in the looks department. Penetrating blue eyes and a boyish grin served him well in attracting the ladies. But unlike Max or Emily, he lacked organization, goals, personal discipline, and could hardly be accused of having any kind of personal world-view. Max, contrarily, saw clearly how the world operated, and hoped he could somehow bestow a bit of this earned wisdom onto his latter day hippy of a son.

Daughter Melissa thrived at College of William and Mary in Williamsburg. She was always a whiz kid with numbers, so she opted for a business degree with a concentration in accounting. Melissa was not as tall as her mom, but was still endowed with a striking figure and had classic good looks that attracted strong, athletic males with lots of brains.

As a very outgoing person who was very sure of herself, she had been student body president and homecoming queen in her senior year back in Denver. She was the only girl in her school to be elected to homecoming court as both a sophomore and junior. She had excelled in track, tennis, and debate. While she never had a steady boyfriend in high school, she had plenty of male suitors. Max always attributed this situation to her being very selective, even fussy with whomever she chose as friends, male or female. Her success in debate could also have contributed to her discriminating approach to guys. Not many ego-centered males could hope to keep up in discussions with her, much less disagreements.

Melissa kept up her tennis game at W&M, and still ran at least four times a week to stay in shape. She had stayed on campus only her first year, opting to have her own apartment after that. She loved her accounting classes, but took Romance Languages as a respite from all the numbers.

The success of the upscale B&B in a touristy town like Williamsburg thrilled both Max and Emily, although it was almost inevitable. The fierce determination that Emily brought to the fray, combined with Max's financial support and continuous encouragement, made success a relatively sure thing. Besides, there was a growing allure of visitors from around the world to the quaint authenticity of Colonial Williamsburg.

Emily's B&B was authentic specialty lodging, with a flair for comfort and congeniality, state-of-the-art bedding, bathrooms, and warm décor. She relished the appreciation that her guests exhibited with all the appropriate period appointments. Emily treasured the satisfied expressions as guests came down the circular stairway to enjoy the sublime breakfast, which would sustain even the heartiest appetite until long past mid-day. She basked in the friendly smiles of guests departing on their tours, only to return around 3:00 PM for their therapeutic, afternoon snooze. All these factors made Emily's dream come true in many ways.

The Williamsburg bed and breakfast, ironically, served to bond Max and Emily together again in spite of their physical separation. They talked on the phone incessantly, even several times some days. Emily was now content, and, since she was no longer present in Denver to observe Max's Type-A approach to work, and his inevitable suppression of his SE Asian demons, the physical distance between them seemed to quell Emily's chronic concern for Max's well-being. Emily was living her dream and she thrived....

Her typical frustration with Max's obsessive-compulsive nature appeared to have receded. It seemed like they were more like soul mates in their separate worlds than they were when they lived under one roof. Since cell phones do not reveal a person's location, Max's being on the road did not seem to irritate Emily so much anymore.

* * *

Neither Emily nor Melissa missed an opportunity to visit Emily's parents. One evening in the early summer of 1993, COL Willis was in the garden after dinner with his wife and Melissa, when an unexpected visitor came to call. It turns out that the young man, Pete Connors was cadet at West Point, and also the grandson of one of COL Willis's closest Army friends, the late COL Marvin Connors. This strapping young man related that his grandfather had instructed his survivors to deliver a picture of two young lieutenants, Willis and Connors, as they were preparing to lead an ammunition convoy to resupply the Marines at the Chosin Reservoir in December 1950. He had also been asked to bring along his grandpa's Distinguished Service Cross and Purple Heart for COL Willis to keep as souvenirs of those harried days together warding off the onslaught of invading Communist Chinese, who had chosen this precise time to join North Korea in its fight with UN Forces.

Willis was not often subdued, but this gesture from his dear friend came close to overwhelming COL Willis. While her grandpa gathered himself, Melissa invited Cadet Connors to stay for a cold drink. It was midnight when Melissa and Pete said good night in COL Willis's driveway.

COL Willis had taken a shine to Cadet Pete Connors, not unlike how he had with Max. As Pete got closer to graduation, COL Willis weighed in with some of his former subordinates still on active duty to make sure Pete got the schools and assignment he desired. In addition, in his own ineffable way, he made certain that Pete and Melissa had ample opportunities to spend time together. By the time he was about to graduate from the Academy, Pete had proposed to Melissa, and she had eagerly accepted.

Pete had his eye on flying Apache helicopters, so the wedding was planned for the first weekend after he graduated from flight school in June of 1996. He had done well enough to be selected for Aircraft Maintenance Officer's Course at Ft. Eustis, which gave the newlyweds some stable time together after the honeymoon, the same place where her parents had met.

Pete then got assigned as an Apache Instructor Pilot at Ft. Rucker, Alabama. The young couple loved their lives together, but after about 18 months, an odd twist of fate turned tragically their way. Pete was giving a green young Army pilot a test ride one stormy evening, when all hell broke loose. Investigators attributed the crash to wind shear as the aircraft was on short final approach to Rucker's aerodrome. The student pilot was at the controls, and the aircraft was too low to correct an unexpected and sudden tail drop. The aircraft's tailboom hit the ground and broke off the tail rotor, sending the fuselage into furious tumbles. Neither Pete nor the young pilot made it out alive.

Melissa surprised her family with her strength and stoic approach to the loss of her husband. She was devastated, but had the ability to buck herself up in face of this numbing tragedy. Melissa received permission to have Pete's remains interred back in Williamsburg, in a plot reserved for the Willis family.

Almost immediately after the funeral, Melissa announced that she would relocate to Williamsburg. Then, as soon as the next term began, she buried herself in Wiliam and Mary's graduate school to help cope with her loss.

She had graduated with honors from The College of William and Mary, had taken the CPA exam and passed it on the first try. All this success was before Pete could finish flight school. Now pursuing an MBA at W&M, she still helped Emily with the books at the B&B. Melissa was also still taking romance languages as her choice of relaxation from all the dreary business subjects.

CHAPTER TWELVE

*M*ax often rued his decision to let Emily go to Williamsburg on a permanent basis. She had been the love of his life, his only one. She was right about almost everything. He needed help, not only back then, but even now as the specter of her loss came home to roost. She had found happiness and peace running the B&B, only to be snuffed out by the same damnable cancer that claimed her mother ten years earlier.

"Is it too late for me?" Max asked himself. "Emily used to say that after the war, I should go back to Cambodia and reconcile myself with all the ghosts I'd brought home. Could I still do it?"

Max was now a fairly healthy sixty-six. He had been very successful in his career. Money was certainly not a problem. His kids had attended top-rated universities on his nickel, and he still had a substantial nest egg. He owned a large home in the foothills of the Rockies near Denver, and a retreat in the mountains of New Mexico for when things got too cold in Colorado.

"Why not retire, and finally take Emily's advice?" Max thought. He had always wondered what it would be like to go to the places he'd been assigned in the Army. Perhaps, he could refocus the scenes of those many repeat nightmares. Was it too late for redemption?

"Hmm, I could do it in Emily's honor, even though she'd never know," Max posited to himself. Doing it in Emily's memory had a surprisingly strong appeal to Max. Ironically, he had been intransigent all those years, discounting Emily's hopeless efforts to help him after his return in 1973.

"Good God, she had simply wanted to be close to me, and to share some of the burdens I had brought home with me," Max concluded. "If I had only listened back then," Max said, frowning, "I might have avoided all the suffering I've gone through over the years, and subsequently imposed on Emily and the kids. "Finally," Max thought,

"Emily would be vindicated in her sincere and loyal attempts to help me deal with the pain of Cambodia."

On the flight back from Richmond to Denver after the funeral, Max finally relaxed with a *Johnnie Walker Black* scotch in the first class cabin. He hadn't thought much about Cambodia in years, at least not consciously. Contrarily, forgetting Cambodia had been his original strategy for taming the ghosts he'd brought back. Now, he let his mind drift, and before long, he was pulling up memories and recollections of that tour. Before Max dozed off, he began to recall the frustration and indignation he felt when he finally read, *William Shawcross', 'Side Show, Nixon, Kissinger and the Destruction of Cambodia'* (1979). Max had read the book in 1981 when to his surprise, the Army selected him (more on this selection later) to attend the yearlong Command and General Staff College (CGSC) at Ft. Leavenworth, KS. Max had even quoted Shawcross in his Military History thesis presented before graduation from CGSC in 1982. In the thesis, Max had summarized the situation in Cambodia in 1970.

"In his thorough account of US policy formulation and execution, Shawcross uncovers the intricacies of the many political and military cloakroom activities that took place late in the nation's capital in 1970, including the establishment of the Military Equipment Delivery Team Cambodia, (MEDTC) to assist in the administration of what became a short-lived $300M/year Military Assistance Program (MAP), supporting the pro-American Lon Nol-led Khmer government. MEDTC's chief was an Army Brigadier General, who reported directly to the four-star Commander in Chief, Pacific (CINCPAC) in Hawaii. In this way, the team chief had autonomy from the influence of the nearby commanders in Saigon, who also reported to CINCPAC. And on the other side of the coin, CINCPAC could insure support to MEDTC, should the need arise.

MEDTC, at one point in time, consisted of 120 officers and NCOs from all branches of the service, about half of whom were eventually posted in a new building specially erected for the team on the grounds of the American Embassy in Phnom Penh. These officers had day-to-day interface with counterparts in the Forces Armies National Khmer (FANK), Army, Navy, and Air Force. They played a key role in requirements determination before material was ordered; and oversaw as to its use after its delivery. While a significant number of American officers assigned in Phnom Penh were skilled logisticians from each of the Service

Components, there was still a representative presence of combat arms officers who oversaw the requirements for force structure, and the scheduling and conduct of training for FANK (Forces Armee Nationale Khmer) soldiers, sailors, and airmen. MEDTC also had a rear detachment of up to sixty more officers hosted at the Military Assistance Command Vietnam (MACV) headquarters in Saigon. There, complex details of force planning, logistics, and distribution, as well as team administration, were conducted."

CHAPTER THIRTEEN

*W*hen Max returned to Denver, he went directly to the attic. He began moving boxes until he saw the one marked "CGSC" (Command and General Staff College). Max remembered his final Modern Military History thesis submitted before graduating. He gingerly rifled through the papers in the box. Finding the seventy-five page document, Max flipped it open and started scanning its contents.

"MEDTC was working around the clock to provide ammunition, arms, transport vehicles, and even armored personnel carriers to the FANK. Getting sufficient units trained was a constant struggle, because the so-called 'Nixon Doctrine' called for the Cambodian forces to bear the brunt of the load in the continuing conflict. Congress had weighed in with the Cooper-Church amendment, enacted in late 1970, and prohibited US military advisers in Cambodia. So the political work-around was the establishment of a Military Assistance Program (MAP), administered by MEDTC, with the stricture that the only function American personnel could perform was to determine requirements for the FANK, oversee the order, shipment, and delivery of war materiel, and perform 'End Item Utilization Inspections,' (EIUIs) to insure the activation, training, and payment of soldiers was not falsely exaggerated as had occurred in the past. Also, these EIUIs put the US officers on the ground with units throughout the Khmer Republic to insure the ammunition and materials delivered were actually being used, and not sold to the highest bidder, as had happened back in the 1960s, when the unsupervised American support to Prince Sihanouk went to all manner of fraudulent characters, making commanders wealthy and province chiefs increasingly more powerful.

Under Lon Nol, the corruption was equally egregious, if less obvious. Padded headcounts were still presented to their headquarters to support inflated payrolls (supported with US dollars), which, in turn, were almost certainly pocketed by the Khmer chain of command. In spite of evidence provided by the current EIUIs, protests by the Chief, MEDTC, and the American ambassador directly to Lon Nol were essentially ignored. The issue remained a source of consternation for diplomatic as well military officials throughout MEDTC's four-year existence.

The second most flagrant practice, which the EIUI was supposed to somehow thwart, was the sale of American-provided weapons to left-leaning paramilitary forces, and even communist forces in FANK's areas of operation. The idea was that the US government did not want the equipment intended for FANK forces to fall into the hands of the enemy, in spite of the well-honed propensity for self-aggrandizement among the FANK regional commanders.

This practice was exacerbated by the fact that much of the weaponry in Cambodia in 1971, and in the hands of Khmer units, was of Eastern European origin. Examples of these weapons were the antiquated SKS rifle, a smattering of AK-47s, left over from the Soviet era in Cambodia which ended just before Lon Nol took over in 1970. Trying to modernize the FANK's weaponry was a major challenge for early MEDTC planners, since at first there were so many types of small arms in outlying units. With so many types of small arms and mortars, ammunition re-supply was a monumental headache. The paucity of sources of supply for these munitions complicated MEDTC's ongoing ammunition supply nightmare. To simplify the situation, planners focused attention on standardizing weapons and ammunition. The doctrinal supposition here was that the soldiers should have and use the same weapons.

This situation was not resolved until the latter part of 1973, with the issue of the standard, American-made M-16 assault rifle to line FANK units. Mortars and artillery pieces were also finally standardized.

Max continued his reflection of his involvement with the team once he finally got to Phnom Penh. "And, what a crooked path he had taken getting there," Max grimly pondered.

Chapter Fourteen

EARLY 1972

*D*eparting from home and family had always been a scene Max dreaded. He hated tearful good-byes. He even went so far as to convince a very reluctant Emily that he needed to simply take a limo from her parents' home to Dulles for his flight to San Francisco and then on to Saigon to in- process with MEDTC's Rear Headquarters. No fanfare, no hullaballoo. He would simply fade away on the appointed morning in early February 1972. With COL Willis's sup- port on this issue, Max departed alone early on the day of his port call from his father-in-law's home.

In those days, the Army still required soldiers to wear Class A uniforms when traveling to new assignments. In this case, it was Army dress greens with buttoned coat, tie, and garrison cap. That worked fine as Max departed Northern Virginia, where the outside temperature was below freezing, and the tires crunched on the snow-covered pavement as he headed to Dulles.

As the plane settled on the tarmac the next evening at Tan Son Nhut, however, Max could immediately feel the blast of heat and humidity as the plane taxied to a halt, and the ground crew finally opened the cabin door to allow the weary passengers down the mobile stairway. Outside, at almost 11 PM local time, the temperature was still pegging in the high 90s. The air could hold no more moisture.

Max could not help but dwell on the irony of how things changed in a matter of hours. He left the states when it was as cold as a miner's behind in the dead of winter. He arrived in Saigon in a pool of his own perspiration. To add insult to his growing indignation, he was struck by how foolish it was for the Army to have all these poor bastards arriving, miserably hot and forlorn in their dress green uniforms, blouses but- toned and ties secure, when there was not a single GI in sight at Ton Son Nhut Airbase, who had been in Vietnam more than a day, who was wearing a Class A uniform! Max would rue this fact for the next 365 days, as he would not have occasion to take his Army Class A greens off their assigned clothes hanger once in that span of time.

Max spent a fitful, seemingly endless night, in a 'bathe-in-your-own-sweat,' bunk in the depressing ghetto of a transient Bachelor Officer Quarters. With precious little sleep, Max creaked out of the rack. He quickly cleaned up and reported, as ordered, to MEDTC's not-so-regal rear headquarters at Military Assistance Command Vietnam's (MACV) sprawling headquarters in his wrinkled, sweaty Class A green uniform.

Entering MACV headquarters, Max could not believe how cold it was in every corner of the maze of a complex. It was as if the Carrier Air Conditioning Company had donated their latest and largest industrial-strength cold air generators to the troops in the head shed in Saigon. "It's a wonder they don't issue arctic clothing to the staff components who are required to inhabit this iceberg of a headquarters," Max recalled saying to himself.

After overcoming the shock of the cold blast inside the MACV complex, Max took several mistaken routes in the massive, convoluted office building. He received erroneous directions from several different officers along the way.

Max finally arrived at the unremarkable offices of Military Equipment Delivery Team Cambodia (MEDTC) Rear. Here, he first encountered an Adjutant General Corps (AG) light colonel, one LTC Millard Shartzer, MEDTC Director of Personnel. LTC Shartzer sized up Captain Max Donatello as he strode through the door to a surprisingly open, bullpen of an office. LTC Schartzer occupied the corner cubical, with its one window overlooking the interior quad of the building complex.

This humorless, if aging officer, reminded Max of a rumpled, middle-aged university professor. His receding hairline; thick, wire-rimmed glasses; and premature wrinkling around his eyes made LTC Shartzer look older than he was.

His welcome was perfunctory and without expression. Then, without a word of small talk, he launched into his well-prepared orientation routine. Looking Max up and down, the stodgy personnel officer informed him that he would need smart civilian clothes (dress slacks, dress shirt, and tie) to wear at the embassy in Phnom Penh.

"*Whoa,*" Max thought. *'The only civvies I brought was a couple of tee shirts and gym shorts for daily physical training (PT), but, dressy civilian clothes?*"

"Surely, you jest, sir?" pleaded Captain Donatello. LTC Shartzer went on, ignoring the young captain's irrelevant retort.

"But, that might be a few weeks in the future. As you may know, the team now has a numerical ceiling of 60 MEDTC officers in country at any given moment. This ceiling was imposed by the Ambassador to keep Congress happy, and to impress on Congress that MEDTC is rigidly abiding by the strictest interpretation of the Cooper-Church Amendment, which limits our role in assisting the Khmer government."

LTC Shartzer went on to say that the ceiling was currently at its peak, and that Max would have to cool his heels for a bit until there was room for him in the headcount. Until then, Max would be attached for duty in the rear headquarters. Uniform was khakis.

"Khakis? You are certainly kidding me, sir. I was told I would be issued jungle fatigues the minute I stepped off the plane in Saigon." Max declared incredulously.

LTC Shartzer gave him a wry, knowing look. He said, "That is the current US Army Vietnam (USARV) policy for American units in the rest of the country, and it was the same here at the headquarters of Military Assistance Command Vietnam (MACV) until a month ago. But, I'm afraid General Abrams likes his khakis. So, jungle fatigues are history, except for operational areas outside Saigon."

"Oh, great," thought Max. "Not only am I short-handed in the number of khaki uniforms I brought, I am now going to have to get an immediate message to Emily to go out and buy, and priority ship, several pairs of slacks, dress shirts with modern ties, along with couple of pairs of up-to-date dress shoes, so I won't embarrass myself among the powers that be at the embassy in Phnom Penh, whenever I get the nod to go in-country, that is."

"Oh, and to make matters more interesting, " LTC Shartzer intoned, "you will still need to draw several sets of jungle fatigues from MACV Headquarters company supply to wear in-country, for when you go out on End Item Utilization Inspection (EIUI) visits to Cambodian units, once you are assigned in country on a permanent basis, that is."

Max murmured to himself, "And, are they going to issue me a British batman to lug all this crap from place to place?"

Max's next thought, which he immediately squelched, was, "*Perhaps, they'll simply issue me a Jeep with trailer and driver?*"

"*You wish, young warrior,*" was his subconscious self-response.

Max's orientation took a few days. He learned that MEDTC was a last-minute straphanger of a tenant command, on the already overcrowded bus that was MACV headquarters. Max surmised that MEDTC was sort of an "afterthought with high priority, if you can imagine that line of thinking."

To his relief, there was plenty for Max to do. While in Saigon, he would need to master the ins and outs setting up ammunition barge convoys, mustered and assembled in the Saigon River area, hooked up to tugs. They then would set off up the Mekong River toward Phnom Penh.

Max routinely visited Bien Hoa Airbase to coordinate Air Force ammunition transfers to the FANK at a rendezvous point near the Port of Saigon. Then, he was off to the staging areas near Cat Lai, where most of the rest of the ammunition categories were stored. He made numerous trips to Cat Lai and Long Binh to coordinate shipments, not only of ammunition, but also other material, such as tactical vehicles, trucks, and, of course, petroleum products.

Max became MEDTC's agent on the ground. His main job was to insure that what was ordered was what was delivered in the barge convoys. His job was to make contact with the mélange of contractors, US Army personnel, and Vietnamese soldiers that made up the cadre at each site: Long Binh, Cat Lai, Bien Hoa, Saigon Port. Max rather fancied his role as a kind of human lubricant that insured that items ordered for FANK use went to Cambodia, and then to the FANK via the river convoys.

CHAPTER FIFTEEN

THE PRESENT

*M*ax continued to page through his Leavenworth history the-sis as he began to take the proposition of returning to Cambodia seriously. His eye caught a passage that made him chuckle ruefully.

By far, the greatest tonnage of material transferred to the Khmer involved all types of ammunition. Military Assistance Program ammunition was trans-shipped by MEDTC from service depots around Saigon, such as Bien Hoa, for air force ammunition, and from Cat Lai, near Long Binh outside Saigon, for army ammunition. All these supplies were transported up the Mekong River on barges leased from the Alaska Barge Company, towed by powerful tugboats manned by intrepid, well-paid Philippine crewmen. River convoys constituted the principal Line of Communication (LOC) for ammunition and petroleum products. By far, the largest representative fraction of the ammunition pro-vided to the FANK from 1971-1975 arrived in Phnom Penh via barge con-voys. In emergencies, ammunition and supplies were parachuted to units caught in desperate combat situations. This practice took detailed coordination between MEDTC, FANK, MACV, and the C-130 fleet of the USAF sta-tioned in Utapao, Thailand. The airdrop of ammunition and rice to relieve the FANK forces surrounded by the Khmer Rouge at Takeo in the summer of 1972 was an illustration of this practice.

CHAPTER SIXTEEN

1972

*M*ax relished the fact that ammunition convoy management was time-consuming. It also carried with it the associated risks of an almost daily ninety-minute trek in each direction from MACV at Tan Son Nhut to Long Binh, Binh Hoa, or Cat Lai. Max's chariot was a vintage (early sixties), Navy grey Dodge 4X4, floor shift, tightly sprung pickup truck. He bounced his innards daily over pothole-scarred two-lane roads that sprouted out in all directions once Max reached the outskirts of Saigon.

It was bad enough weaving initially through mind-boggling city traffic, contending with grossly undisciplined Vietnamese drivers, but, there was also a very real threat. You never really knew whether the cyclo-taxi driver who would pull up next to you at a stoplight was Viet Cong (VC), and, it was hard to determine whether you had just become a juicy random target for his ready satchel of fragmentation grenades to be tossed in through the open cab window just as the light turned green. Max had witnessed several roadside attacks on South Vietnamese convoys in the first two weeks he was making this daily journey. The typical Viet Cong (VC) plan was simple: the lead vehicle in an Army of the Republic of Vietnam (ARVN) convoy would hit a VC-emplaced landmine on an unpaved detour. Then, all manner of hell would break loose. There would be a few Rifle Propelled Grenades (RPGs), some heavy machinegun chatter, and then there was nothing.

"Except a bunch of dead and wounded ARVN bodies littering the landscape and blocking the roadway," thought Max with little emotion.

"What ever happened to the proven Army tactical maxim, 'Scouts Out,' where the flanks front and rear are screened and secured by fast moving, gun shield-equipped M113 armored personnel carriers (APCs)?" puzzled Max.

His daily road excursion went on for a several weeks. Max began to think that his being assigned to the embassy in Phnom Penh was just a phantom notion, dreamt up by some delusional senior personnel weenie.

Max's letters to Emily tried to play down the frustration and unfulfilled expectations of his assignment thus far. He focused on the mechanics of daily life, explaining to Emily how things worked now that he was settled into a Bachelor Officers Quarters (BOQ) on the outskirts of Saigon. His BOQ was actually one of a handful of old French Indochinese four- and five-story hotels that the American contracting community had leased to house officers of every service who served at MACV headquarters. Initially, he was assigned alone to two-man quarters for junior officers. After a week or two, a young Navy ensign joined him to share the space.

Max told Emily that there was an officer's mess up on the fourth floor, where the residents took most morning and evening meals. There was also a small officer's club in the building where you could grab a warm beer before supper. Then, at precisely 7 PM, they would show a movie on the roof in the open air. Max refrained from voicing his concerns that the VC might choose that time to lob a few rockets onto the roof and take out about fifty officers. Luckily, that never happened while Max was in Saigon.

He told Emily that it was a hard transition from the frigid MACV headquarters to his sweltering trek to Long Binh. Then, he would return to MACV later in the day, dripping in sweat for the last couple of hours of the day to write up reports. Finally, he would hop back in his trusty non-air conditioned truck for the thrilling ride home through frenzied Saigon traffic. Upon arrival, he would make his way to his non-air conditioned quarters, with its three-bladed, one-speed ceiling fan to stir the air.

*   *   *

Then, one Saturday afternoon, Max was in his office at MACV, when a call came directly to him from a teammate in Phnom Penh requesting Max arrange an emergency airlift for one of the team's officers in-country.

It seems that some of the MEDTC team members had cooked up a hot game of softball. The third baseman on one of the teams, an Army major, had caught shrapnel in his posterior when a couple of teenage-looking kids drove by on a motorbike and lobbed a couple of well-placed fragmentation grenades near third base of the makeshift softball diamond!

Since Max had all the proper contacts as MEDTC's Movements Officer, he was quickly able to contact his new buddy, the Air Force liaison officer in Udorn, Thailand, and request an emergency Fragmentation Order be issued for a C-130 evacuation mission.

Max was in luck. The liaison was in radio contact with a C-130 crew homeward bound from upcountry Vietnam, who was just leaving Vietnamese airspace. The pilot had enough fuel to land at Pochentong, the Khmer Air Force base and adjoining civilian airport outside Phnom Penh. As always, there were conditions.

Max profusely thanked his Air Force buddy in Thailand. He promised him that an ample stack of Cambodian temple rubbings, from the famous lost temples of Angkor Wat, would be earmarked for the liaison office (no charge) on the next C-130 that landed at Pochentong.

Max notified his team counterpart in Phnom Penh that the team needed to rally and get the injured Army major out to the airfield at Pochentong post haste (ASAP), as the C-130 would land in less than 60 minutes and would not shut down. They would load the major and take off directly. The injured major would be attended to in US Air Force medical facilities at the aircraft's base in Udorn. Max reminded his counterpart in Phnom Penh that if there was no American Army major present at the end of the runway when the plane landed, the Air Force jocks would close up the Lockheed C-130 Hercules's cargo ramp and make her airborne without regret.

As expected, the diligent staff in Phnom Penh had the injured major stretched out in the back seat of the fastest, most comfortable riding sedan assigned to the team. They made it to the pickup point with time to spare.

Just as he had about wrapped up this little initiative, Max's newest 'buddy,' none other than AG LTC Shartzer, lunged through the door to the MEDTC (Rear)'s Logistics Office.

"Just the man I came to see," barked the aging AG light colonel.

"You will need to pack your bags and get yourself ready to be airlifted to Phnom Penh tomorrow morning. You have been designated to replace the injured major for whom you just arranged evacuation. He was, as you may know, a logistics officer just like you. "

"I have informed COL John Jacobson, your new superior in country, that you will be aboard the Air America shuttle that departs their operations facility tomorrow morning at nine o'clock sharp. In Phnom Penh there will be a team member assigned to meet you at Pochentong airport, and see to it that you get to the American Embassy for your in-country orientation."

"My guess is you'll take the wounded major's spot in whichever villa he was assigned. MEDTC has 15-20 separate enclosed villas strewn throughout Phnom Penh. They are separate to keep their target profile down. COL Jacobson will see to it that all the right skids are greased upon your arrival."

"Who will do the movements functions for the team?" blurted Max intently. "I have finally gotten a handle on these duties after these several weeks. I hate to have some sorry newbie like me have to go through and learn all the ropes like I just did."

"Don't worry, Max. I think you'll simply take the duties with you. We still have phones, you know," smirked the aging AG LTC. "They may even have a few other exciting projects for you once you get there and get settled in for a few days." Another wry smirk, then his eminence, LTC Shartzer, turned and departed as abruptly as he came.

Max's only reaction was to shake his head and say to himself, "*Irony of ironies, I simply cannot seem to shake the sense that this tour is absolutely fraught with the shit.*"

"*It all started with an ironic twist when I studied Vietnamese for a year, but near graduation, I was informed that I was being sent to Cambodia instead. Then, due to headcount ceiling limitations, I've been stuck in Saigon for weeks with all the wrong uniforms. Now, the logistics officer whose evacuation I just arranged will be making ceiling space for me in country by virtue of his medevac departure. Oh, and finally, I will be taking this poor, sorry bastard's villa place, and probably his functions, since he too was a Logistics Weenie."*

"Just my luck," posed Max rhetorically, *"It took a mighty big pain in that guy's ass to relieve the Saigon-based pain in mine. Irony!"* Max silently shrugged and left the office resignedly to go to his BOQ to get his things packed and check out.

"Lots of shit to ship," he concluded. *"Can't bring much more than a duffle bag and a suitcase, or, maybe, just one or the other. You never know how much room there'll be on that Air America bird."*

"Damn," Max thought, *"I don't even have a clue what kind of bird it will be. It could be anything from an old C-123, held together with chewing gum and bailing wire, or, if I luck out, it'll be one of those new Beech Craft King Airs. Or, it could be a Huey. Air America had lots of those."* Max had seen the Air America UH-1's poking holes in the airspace around Bien Hoa and Long Binh.

But, whatever Air America's base operations considered airworthy at any particular moment was what constituted the MEDTC shuttle between Saigon to Phnom Penh. Max resigned himself to the fact that he'd simply have to pack light, and pray that the rear detachment could forward the rest of his gear before his limited civilian clothes wardrobe got worn out or lost in the laundry.

CHAPTER SEVENTEEN

PRESENT DAY

*M*ax became obsessed with the notion of going back to Cambodia. His life of irony continued unabated. Within a month of Emily's funeral, he had informed the board of Xerox that he would be standing down, retiring. He was giving up the very career that he had placed between himself, his family, and the ghosts of Vietnam and Cambodia. The return to SE Asia that Emily had suggested so accurately so many years ago had now become his major focus.

Max remembered how he been sort of 'on the fence,' after Cambodia. Why would a Reserve Captain, with a marginal ROTC cadet performance record while in college, with almost no interest or aspirations for things military while in college, want to stay in the Army?

True, his record was pristine. He was one of the few logistics officers who came back from SE Asia with valorous awards, as well as laudatory commendations for meritorious service for actions performed while engaged against hostile forces. Hardly any company-grade logistics officers wore the Distinguished Service Cross (DSC), much less a Silver Star, a Soldier's Medal, a Purple Heart, and a Legion of Merit.

His efficiency reports were glowing, and Max knew that if he could stomach the bureaucracy long enough, he could possibly get his Regular Army commission and be able to compete with the best of the best. Truth be told, Max's war record looked more like a high-achieving Special Forces Airborne Ranger officer, wearing Infantry brass.

Max recalled the feeling. All he'd known since college graduation was being an Army Officer. Still, he could only now recognize how much of a role irony was playing out in his life. Here was at first an ROTC two-year man, who had encountered the Army at its best and worst, and was charmed by the experience. Taking his whirlwind relationship with Emily and her family into account, one could understand Max's fascination the life of a career Army officer.

Then, after a couple of successful assignments, Max was selected for Major, and, not long thereafter, to the Army's Command and General Staff College (CGSC) at Ft. Leavenworth, KS, the highly selective one year course for mid-career up-and-comers. Selection was considered an indication that the way was clear to make it as high into the Army's echelons as one could successfully achieve. What surprised Max was that he was selected, but he was still a Reserve Officer, a true rarity in those days.

While Max was moving to Kansas with his family, Congress passed the Defense Officer Personnel Management Act (DOPMA), which prescribed that any officer who had reached the ten-year milestone, and who still had a record competitive enough for CGSC selection, must be immediately given a Regular Army Commission. Soon thereafter, Max stood, with about sixty other Reserve Officers who were selected from across the Army for CGSC, in an auditorium at Ft. Leavenworth to take the oath as Regular Army Officers.

Max reflected that day that there were still sixty guys like him among the 800-plus officers selected to attend, who were competitive enough to be selected in spite of their Reserve status. Max simply took this rare situation as an oblique compliment, and the matter of staying in the Army never arose again until he got to the twenty-year mark.

CHAPTER SEVENTEEN

1972

*M*ax found himself that morning at the Air America heliport, thankful that his chariot for the hour-long trip from Tan Son Nhut Air Base in Saigon, Vietnam, to Pochentong Air Base in Phnom Penh was a relatively new UH-1H Huey, which didn't require a long runway. Once airborne, Max glanced out the aircraft's open door and could not help notice that the countryside was badly marred by bomb craters in decidedly clear patterns. In this manner the B-52s would drop their ordinance making a pathway along their approach to a target. As the shuttle neared Phnom Penh, he noticed an array of patchy areas along the runway that marked the near-constant Khmer Rouge mortar and rocket attacks from just beyond the outskirts of the airfield.

Max was surprised to see a civilian terminal without windows, and several WWII-era DC-3s owned by civil carriers like Air Cambodge, or Khmer AKAS, awaiting passengers to be marched to their flight. There was no difference here in the temperature or the humidity from Saigon. It was just that it was the onset of the monsoon season, and showers popped up all along the Air America route and were threatening the edges of the horizon with giant thunderheads rising like giant mushrooms as they converged on Phnom Penh.

Max wondered what type of conveyance would take him to the embassy and his new life in Cambodia. If it was an open jeep, they were destined for a drenching. So, not only at his Tan Son Nhut initial reporting to the team would he look like he slept in his uniform, now his newfangled civvies would get a chance to show their true colors after a steamy, wet trip from Pochentong Field into central Phnom Penh.

"Keep a sense of humor about this," Max said to himself, shrugging, realizing the threads of irony were still tugging at his sleeve, as he began the next chapter of his story's unraveling. At about this time, a tall, slender guy yelled out, "Max Donatello! Over here, I've got the

MEDTC embassy shuttle just outside," and grabbed Max's hand, pumping it relentlessly.

The guy introduced himself, "I'm Major Hank Bethke, ordinance specialist for MEDTC, glad to have you in country. We'll be working together on the logistics team under COL John Jacobson, who is a Quartermaster Officer, and an absolutely great guy." Bethke seemed like an affable character, certainly at ease in the sea of Cambodians pushing and shoving their way toward the ticket counters in the terminal. "Colonel Jacobson told me to inform you that you'd be taking Major Bill Hardt's space in our villa, and that we should stop and get you unloaded prior to proceeding to the embassy. I heard that you arranged Bill's evacuation yesterday—good show."

MAJ Hank Bethke carried his 6'3" frame without an ounce of portliness. He sported a David Niven mustache, and had a long thin stogie grasped in his teeth. It was as if he never let his lips actually touch the cigar, and it was the only affectation Max could detect from this otherwise engaging, friendly fellow. His receding hairline pleaded for a cap of some kind in this unrelenting sun. But, Hank Bethke didn't seem like a hat kind of a guy. Max had him cast as the 70s version of Boston Blackie...'here to solve mysteries.'

MAJ Bethke grabbed one of Max's bags and took off in the direction of what sufficed for a parking lot, not far from the terminal. He was headed directly for a late model Ford sedan, the sight of which Max prayed was their ride back to Phnom Penh. A uniformed Khmer driver opened the trunk of the Ford sedan and opened the back doors for them to enter. Thank God, the air conditioner was operating at full tilt.

MAJ Bethke filled Max in on how the team was housed. About four or five officers lived in villas enclosed in twelve-foot-high walls scattered around Phnom Penh for security reasons. Each villa was guarded by a squad of FANK soldiers, some of whom served as drivers, others simply sentries. A Khmer family maintained the villa, handling all cooking, cleaning, and laundry for the members. Each officer put in an equal share of the cost for food, beer, liquor, and other essentials. Since Max was replacing an officer, he would simply send the recently evacuated MAJ Hardt a check to "buy out his share." Each villa had a large freezer and several refrigerators, so stocking up was never a problem, in case for some reason, resupply from the commissary in Saigon got delayed.

The villas would share with each other if there were ever any spot shortages. Major Bethke mentioned that there was a high level of cooperation among the team, so sharing amongst households was never a problem. He went on to say that their villa normally had four officers assigned.

MAJ Bethke added, "The others in our villa are all logistics officers, the most senior of whom is a Transportation Corps LTC named Ed Czenko, who heads up planning for the Army Logistics Branch. Max, I'm afraid you are stuck with another ordinance officer in the last suite. That is Captain Larry Hemphill, who works on supply and ammunition requirements."

MAJ Bethke said that he was the team liaison with FANK HQ on weapons requirements, and that he constituted the fourth officer in the villa. MAJ Bethke was busy giving Max some great insider insights to the workings of the team when they pulled into the open gate at their villa about thirty minutes after they departed Pochentong. Max noticed that the driveway was wide enough for two vehicles abreast. They pulled in slowly, and the gates closed revealing a manned heavy machine gun pillbox that straddled the top of the wall that enclosed the villa. The grounds were covered with high palms that shrouded the direct rays of the sun.

As the driver opened their doors, the family came out of their quarters beside the villa to greet Max and MAJ Bethke. "This is Sakun, our chef, and his wife Tran, our diligent and most efficient house manager. These two munchkins are their children, Tak, and Els. Family, this is Captain Donatello. He will be staying with us for the foreseeable future. He will take Major Hardt's quarters upstairs, and he and I will share the bathroom adjoining the two suites.

"Very pleased to have you at this villa," said Sakun, as he grabbed both of Max's bags and headed to the rear entrance of the large, two-story house. "We will unpack your bags for you this afternoon while you are at the embassy. When you get home for dinner, your clothes will be all pressed, and you will be properly moved in to your quarters," added Sakun in near-perfect English.

"I just changed sheets and put a clean blanket on your bed," said Tran in broken English. MAJ Bethke mentioned to Max that Tran was from a Vietnamese family near the border of the two adjoining countries. Max could not let the opportunity pass to speak to Tran in pitch-perfect Vietnamese, causing Tran to glow with embarrassment as she broke into a delighted girlish giggle. "I must be careful not to tell household secrets in Vietnamese anymore," as she continued with genuine amusement.

MAJ Bethke showed Max around the villa. The kitchen was in the servant's adjoining quarters occupied by Sakun's family. Meals were brought in through the back entrance into a formal dining room. Next, there was a large sitting room with comfortable chairs, ottomans, and couches. The rooms were furnished with ample storage hutches, bookcases, and sideboards. Off the living room, there was another sitting room that housed a well-stocked bar, and all the matching glassware they would ever need. Near the bar, there was also a two-way base station and charging ports for four portable Motorola radios. MAJ Bethke pointed out that one of these radios would be assigned to Max today when they arrived at the embassy.

"These little babies can reach the embassy from as far as Pochentong. The base station is set up here to relay signals to the embassy network control center, which is manned 24/7 by the Marine Guards. So, you can always get help. You can even call the embassy on the radio, and they can patch you to an office phone either at the embassy or the land line at the villa." MAJ Bethke seemed proud of this setup, and added, "The embassy will also relay a message you have to another team member who is away from the embassy. So, you can pretty much chat with anyone who may be out and about in the Phnom Penh environs."
This communicationis system was a genuine relief to hear about , since Max never had the means to call back to Tan Son Nhut on his near daily excursions to Long Binh, Bien Hoa, or Cat Lai during his days back at MEDTC rear. There were a few times he would have appreciated the calming voice of someone American on the other end of a powerful radio network.

There was a one bedroom suite on the main floor. It was the quarters of CPT Larry Hemphill, who had the first-floor suite only because he had been resident in Cambodia the longest, abiding by the venerable, first-come-first-served rule. Senior officers who arrived in country later decided it was a good policy, and did not pull rank and cause the incumbent in the villa to move upstairs, in spite of the Army's long tradition of doing just the opposite.

MAJ Bethke patiently talked Max through the household routine. Then, he showed Max his suite upstairs, and suggested, "Why don't you take a few minutes to gather what you need to check in at the embassy, and freshen up, if you'd like? I'll wait downstairs. It is almost lunchtime, so we may as well stay and get a bite here. The others will be along directly."

Max entered his suite facing two large, wood-shuttered windows that faced the front of the villa. On the right, there were two more windows; the one nearest the suite entrance was equipped with an arctic-capable 8000 BTU Carrier air conditioner, humming quietly. As Max walked around the spacious interior, he found a well-lit, overstuffed chair and ottoman in the corner of the room.

He could not help noticing the two M-60 machine guns at each of the front windows, loaded and ready for action. At the first side window was an M79 grenade launcher with two crates of ammo. There was also a Thompson .45 caliber submachine gun resting on a stack of sand bags behind the overstuffed chair. Six double magazines strapped together sat next to this well-known people stopper. There was a case filled with 30-round .45 cal. magazines next to the M-79 ammo stock. Standing up next to the air conditioner was an M-16, fully loaded with multiple magazines stacked, loaded, and ready for duty. Max caught a glimpse of the boxes under his bed, and found six opened crates of fragmentation grenades, and two crates of WP (White Phosphorous) grenades. He unconsciously opened the walk-in closet doors to find a backup stash of ammunition for the weapons arrayed in his otherwise cozy chamber. There were flares, smoke grenades of all colors, and all manner of back-up weapons. On the top of the desk, Max noticed the .45 caliber M1911A1 semi-automatic pistol next to a 9mm Berretta semi-automatic. Looking into the desk drawers, he found an ample supply of loaded clips for each pistol.

"It looked like the recently departed MAJ Hardt was preparing for the next World War," mused Max after his initial survey of his new home away from home for the coming months. He did notice with amusement an impressive collection of 'Playmate of the Month' posters plastered neatly on the insides of the closet doors. "Aside from being paranoid that a battalion of the Khmer Rouge would target his particular room, the dude had good taste in pinups," Max concluded with a wizened grin. Max made a mental note not to describe the martial nature of his new environs to Emily in his nightly letter summarizing the day.

After a quick splash in the bathroom to wipe away the grime and pollution he'd accumulated between Saigon and there, Max joined MAJ Bethke in the sitting room downstairs. "Lunch will be served in fifteen minutes, according to Tran," reported the good Major. "We have a nice library that we share with the embassy staff. That way we get some of the newest releases. Our administrative officer works with the Embassy staff and the Marine Guards to insure we get a good circulation of recent topics, both fiction and non-fiction. He also coordinates films for circulation around the villas, so we get a fairly recent movie every other evening, on average."

Max asked about the bar. "How is that stocked and maintained, as I noticed it has a nice array of every kind of aperitif, after dinner drinks, not to mention the top-shelf brands of scotch, bourbon, gin, and vodka?"

"All part of your share, my good man. We all pitch in equally when the supply needs to be restocked. Booze is the cheapest of all the items of supply we maintain. Each villa has a liberal ration from the embassy, and, of course, they never run out. If we have a dinner party and need some extra bottles of wine, or anything else for that matter, the senior housemate is authorized to draw the needed augmentation, so to speak." MAJ Bethke went on to give Max a primer on the many embassy dinner parties the MEDTC team members were invited to in a given month. It was no wonder why the embassy had to keep a substantial stock of every kind of wine and liquor any normal person could imagine.

Just then outside, the gate opened and another Ford sedan lumbered through the gate carrying Captain Hemphill and LTC Czenko home for the two-hour lunch and siesta period observed daily by the embassy.

"*Some things never change*," thought Max, "*even during time of war and national emergency*." He had heard about the laid back lifestyle of the staffers at the embassy. He could not help seeing the obvious irony of all this high living amidst the war that clearly surrounded Phnom Phenh. It was as if all the weapons were there as a simple reminder that the Khmer Republic was grasping for life against tremendous odds. Nonetheless, the important business of keeping diplomatic appearances and social mandates were clearly evident in spite of the struggle that went on inexorably around them.

MAJ Bethke did a yeoman's job at the introductions, just as Tran came through the back door with a steaming tureen of hot soup. The conversation was animated over lunch, as Max marveled at the quality of the chicken and rice soup that was served and removed before the entrée was presented. The latter consisted of pork loin medallions sautéed in a savory sauce, arrayed with tiny potatoes and root vegetables roasted to perfection. Tran served a nice flan for dessert, topping off a meal that could have made mention in the Michelin Guide that year.

Max inquired, "Is the food always this good? No doubt I'll gain two pants sizes if I don't take smaller portions."

LTC Czenko's retort was not encouraging. "Sakun was an award-winning chef at the Hotel Phnom before the war. He was trained in Europe with an emphasis on French cuisine. Prince Sihanouk wanted him to stay on at the palace after a short tour as sous-chef there, along with the enticement of promotion to head chef, but, Sihanouk made the mistake of leaving the country on extended tour, allowing General Lon Nol to overthrow the government. That's indirectly why Sakun and his family here, and how he lost his job at the palace. He's a good guy, loyal to the core, and loves his family. This arrangement suits him and his family just fine."

"I'll simply have to take smaller portions and exercise more, I guess," was Max's less than enthusiastic response.

CHAPTER EIGHTEEN

*L*ater that day, the two sedans pulled out of the villa gate to begin the twenty-minute trek through Phnom Penh traffic to the embassy. Max marveled at all the old, beaten-up bicycles at a ratio of three to one over old French sedans spotted here and there along the route. Lane discipline was even worse here than in Saigon. It was like a mob at the starting line of a race at every stoplight. Everyone simply shoved his or her way forward to the front of the stopped traffic to find a spot, jammed next to car, motorbike, or cyclo-taxi. There never seemed to be a mere two vehicles abreast at a stoplight like in the states. While the crowd did not go until the light turned green, it was clear that no one appreciated having to stop for an electric traffic light. Their response was to crowd across the lane to get the best spot to launch onward to the next traffic stop.

MAJ Bethke remarked to Max, "We have the same security problem they have in traffic in Vietnam. You can never tell who is a simple peasant in town to sell his produce, or who may be a Khmer Rouge terrorist on an antiquated moped scouting for targets of opportunity. Blowing up an American sedan with two American officers, along with all the detritus, blood, and guts of everyone within a diameter of twenty meters, would make a Khmer Rouge operative a rising star. If you'll notice inside the briefcase I gave you before we left the house, there are two side arms locked and loaded should the need arise. You'll find more loaded clips for each in the side compartment. We also keep a bag of frag grenades under each side of the front seat, just in case we are accosted by any armed KR."

Max disengaged the briefcase strap and opened it slightly to see the two hefty semi-automatic pistols. Max couldn't help re-engaging the ominous foreboding he experienced when he walked into his room at the villa earlier in the day.

Max's sense of irony was instantly engaged with the thought, *"If we are assaulted, and the bad guys shoot first, we will likely be toast before we can unlatch these briefcases or snatch a grenade from under the seat."*

Max silently corrected himself, "*Too much to think about, big guy, just keep alert and try to identify threats.*"

"Certainly, there must be some intelligence that prompts these guys to make the villas as strong as Ft. Knox," Max surmised. "I must remember to ask LTC Czenko to go over the villa defense plan with me this evening." A twinge of trepidation crept into Max's gut as he considered how little he could remember of the principles of armed defense of a prepared position.

"*These guys take security seriously*," Max thought. Max inquired as to the use of alternate routes to keep the KR from sensing a pattern of travel.

"We have a plan to counter nearly every conceivable contingency. It's the unanticipated things that fall through the crack, like the fragging at our softball game the other day. But, as a rule, we have plans for the defense of the villas, routes that change twice a day to and from the embassy. We even switch around cars monthly between villas to keep things mixed up nicely. Our drivers never know which route we'll take until we exit the gate at the villa," MAJ Bethke posited. "The sedans rarely travel in tandem. Again, we try to keep the KR guessing, and not provide them too juicy a target."

Max was impressed again by the security measures taken before vehicles were allowed into the embassy compound. Two Khmer soldiers inspected each vehicle's under carriage with upward looking mirrors attached to what resembled a hockey stick. Trunks and hoods were opened, inspected, and occupant badges had to be shown upon entry, even if you had just left the embassy a couple of hours earlier.

CHAPTER NINETEEN

When the in-processing formalities, including embassy badging, and picture taking were accomplished, Max was escorted to a large Butler Building that stood behind the main embassy building. His escort dropped him outside the office of COL John Jacobson, Quartermaster Corps, Logistics Program Director, Military Equipment Delivery Team, Cambodia.

"Captain Max Donatello reporting for duty, sir," Max intoned as he knocked on the doorframe of what looked like a little broom closet of an office.

"Max, sit y'sef down and rest a spell," said COL Jacobson as he pumped Max's hand while chomping on the stub of chubby cigar that looked like the remains of yesterday's smoke.

"Ah heard a lot about you, doncha know? Ah done worked for yo' daddy-in-law on mah first tour to Vit-nam. Ah kep' in touch with the ole goat whilst I was headin' up the QM branch, up at OPO. I declare I do believe ole Colonel Herby Willis was the foh-ace be-hahnd mah makin' full bull. I surely do love that ole fella—how's he doin'? Awright, ah hope."

"Ahah! So, that's how I came to be chosen for MEDTC," Max quickly surmised. Here was evidence that it was not beyond the wiles of COL Herby Willis to pull strings until the last strand came through to make matters go in accordance with his liking. Perhaps his new boss with the Southern drawl could clue him in on the details of his father-in-law's skullduggery, if he could succeed in getting into COL Jacobson's good graces.

"COL Willis is healthy as a horse, and apparently still pulling strings in the logistics community," Max proposed delicately. "He insisted that my wife and son, and the new baby we have on the way, move back home with them while I'm away, so that he could have first dibs on making his 18-month-old grandson the next fan of Army logistics."

"Wust' thangs could happen, don'cha know?" came the grinning response.

COL Jacobson had a gleam in his eye when he looked at Max. A half grin and that smelly rope that he chomped incessantly made COL Jacobson have the air of a patronizing grandfather himself. Max suppressed his impulse to guess who the grandchild was in this arrangement.

Jacobson was a fireplug of a guy, maybe 5'10", with the shoulders and build of an ideal baseball catcher, that Yogi Berra sort of look. He had a graying flat top and knowing dark eyes. Max fashioned him as the picture of an Italian godfather. Perhaps he got his looks from his mother's side of the family, because Jacobson was certainly not an Italian name.

After another fifteen minutes of casual banter, COL Jacobson got down to business. He gave Max a run down on the hot topics of the day. He outlined the projects he wanted Max to concentrate on, and some others to put on the back burner, to get to as time would allow. LTC Shartzer's supposition that Max would hang on to ammo convoy duties was close to accurate. COL Jacobson said there was another TC officer in the pipeline who could take over the duties when he got on board in a few weeks. He did mention that MEDTC's team chief, BG Rex Clausen wanted him to get ready as soon as possible to go out on EIUIs to assess several outlying FANK logistics units, who were rumored to be funneling supplies to the bad guys.

"We bettah git on ovah to Gen'ril Clausen's office; we gotta three a'clock meetin' with him to innahduce yo' an git yo'ah mah-chin' oah-dah's dye-rect fum hee-um." COL Jacobson said, as he stood and grabbed his folder.

The short walk to the embassy gave us the opportunity to run into Air Force COL Throckmorton, MEDTC's deputy. After a quick introduction, they headed directly for the general's office as COL Throckmorton clued them in on the fact that the general was free at the moment, expecting them, and in seemingly good spirits. COL Throckmorton shook Max's hand again, giving him what Max thought to be another sincere welcome. He then disappeared into the embassy.

Chapter Twenty

*B*G Rex B. Clausen was a man of rather small stature, bespeckled and balding. He carried his left arm around the desk when Max and COL Jacobson entered the office. He had apparently lost control of his arm from a war wound. After the formalities of reporting, he directed his guests to have a seat. He seemed chipper, smiled readily, and asked us to sit on the couch across from his own overstuffed chair and ottoman. He turned to his aide and asked for fresh coffee to be brought in for three.

"Max, I'll get to the point," said BG Clausen, "I need someone to get smart quick, and get out there and perform End Item Utilization Inspections on the FANK logistics units. I have it on pretty reliable authority that not only are they padding their headcounts to inflate payrolls, but they are pocketing the excess salaries; stealing rations, weapons, and ammunition by the ton; and funneling whatever is left to the Khmer Rouge (KR), or to Vietnamese paramilitary units nearby, all for big payolas."

BG Clausen went on to enumerate his priorities for the team where logistics functions were concerned. Opening a deep water port was high on his list. The only real viable location for such an operation was Kompong Som, what was once known as Sihanoukville. Located on the Gulf of Thailand, the Russians had used it during the sixties to bring in equipment and weapons for the pro-Soviet Sihanouk regime of the time.

"I need you to get down to that port, as soon as you have your feet on the ground, and let me know what we'll need to do to get it up and operational," General Clausen urged. "Laying out a plan and getting the EIUIs started, along with the port evaluation, needs to happen in the next thirty days. COL Jacobson will guide you in arranging travel to all these locations." General Clausen finally paused momentarily, as if to gather his thoughts.

"We are glad to have you here finally, Max. I know you won't let us down," said BG Clausen as they rose to make his suggested exit. "One more thing, I have an inviolate rule, and that is that my officers never stop working on an action until it is dead and buried. None of this 'an action passed is an action completed,' BS you may hear in other head-quarters. When you take something on, it's yours until completed, period."

"Again, good to have you aboard, Captain Donatello," BG Clausen fin-ished and gave Max a big grin as they filed out. "Give my warm per-sonal regards to your father-in-law. He and I spent some quality time together in the hospital in Pusan early in the Korean War. That was right after I got my upper arm shot up, and he was tending to frostbit-ten feet and a couple of minor gunshot wounds. From what I've learned, he was quite a hero. It seems he was awarded the Distin-guished Service Cross for leading an ammunition convoy in relief of the Marines at Chosin Reservoir. My Marine colleagues told me Willis and his convoy had to fight their way through the North Koreans to get there, and then fight their way through Communist Chinese forces to evacuate wounded and get the convoy back to our lines. He got the Sil-ver Star for heading up that evacuation. Over 135 men were saved because of his leadership. I've gotta say, as I got to know him, I was impressed with his humble, down-to-earth ways. Great guy!"

As they were leaving BG Clausen's suite, Max and COL Jacobson could not help but notice a tall first lieutenant of Infantry about to enter the outer office of the Chief of MEDTC, with three steaming cups of the world's best instant coffee.

CHAPTER TWENTY-ONE

*T*he next seven days seemed to Max like he was drinking from a fire hose. *"So much to assimilate, in so little time,"* thought Max derisively. In a letter home to Emily at this time, Max related the stress of the surroundings.

His letter went on, "I'm already nearing the end of my second month on the team. Hard to believe, I know. But, I gleaned a great deal from the officers in MEDTC rear while I was there, and I'm becoming more attuned to the plight of the FANK forces. Our bosses have each of us read the message traffic daily between the Embassy and Washington, as well as all the traffic between MEDTC and the head shed in Hawaii. There are some real gems that pop out once in a while, especially when the intelligence community gets around to making appraisals. Some of it begs the question of how it could possibly be termed intelligence when it contains gross errors in fact, and in some cases ranked right up there in the stupid category."

"Enough shop talk! My darling Emily: I simply cannot wait for the next four months to pass when I will finally see you for R&R in Hawaii. Constant thoughts of you, and being here so far away from you, remind me that the two months have really gone agonizingly slow. I long to hear your voice and feel your soft skin next to me. I love and miss you more than words can express. Sweet hugs and lots of kisses,
Yours always.
Max"

*   *   *

Within a few days of sending that letter, Max was pleasantly surprised to receive a cryptic message from COL Willis informing Max that Emily had just presented him with a healthy new granddaughter. "Mother and daughter are both fine, and send their love, as do I, COL W." No mention of his paternal part, but this omission was his father-in-law's way of jibbing Max.

Max had been coaxing the Air Force C-130 pilots to bring him boxes of Philippine cigars in exchange for temple rubbings so he was well stocked with this commodity for this happy occasion. His toothy grin was prominent as he stalked the halls, knocking on doors in all MEDTC's offices, handing out premium Philippine cigars wrapped with pink ribbons to mark the birth of his new daughter, Melissa, in the traditional military manner.

*   *   *

By now, Max began to feel a bit more at ease in his new villa accommodations. However, all anyone talked about at the villa was their pet actions at the office, and how things were progressing. Every meal, every after-dinner drink, every waking moment was focused on what the team was doing to make the Khmer forces more effective.

Max was amazed that even at his first real embassy dinner, the evening was trodden with gossip about the Lon Nol government and how slow the FANK forces were adapting to the relief efforts the Americans were attempting. Even wives of higher-level embassy officials seemed to have a stake in the local gossip game. It wasn't long before Max was hearing stories suggesting Lon Nol had suffered a stroke and that he would be rendered a mere figurehead.

Max noticed that it took a day or two to vet this rumor, but in the end, the embassy and MEDTC gossip grapevine was validated when the FANK government, soon thereafter, made its announcement that Lon Nol had indeed suffered a mild stroke. The official release insisted that the general was hardly affected; the stroke only caused a slight slowdown in his rate of speech. While the American contingent in Phnom Penh understandably awaited developments with bated breath, Max filled his letters to Emily with wry commentary of the gossipy ways of the US Foreign Mission in Phnom Penh.

Chapter Twenty-Two

*M*ax was catching on fast. COL Jacobson was a great mentor, who took extra measures to insure Max understood the context of every action he was assigned. In the meantime, Max was planning his trip south for the following week to Kompong Som (KPS). Max thought he could size up the situation in less than a week.

It came as a relief to find out that MEDTC had a contractor already down at the port, working with the FANK personnel who were assigned to clear whatever shipping that was destined for FANK. There had been no deep-draft vessels. In fact, no watercraft that drew more than a foot of water had called at this port since the Russians quickly evacuated the scene back in the mid-sixties, as the political situation in Phnom Penh got more and more neutral in its orientation.

MEDTC's principal contractor, the Vinnell Corp., had hired a senior French-speaking port clearance expert to train the Khmer staff. They also brought along several Philippine port operations training specialists, as well as several South Korean port clearance personnel, who had a mix of stevedore, crane operation, MHE (Material Handling Equipment), and cargo off-loading expertise. These skills were intended to augment the FANK should the decision be made to schedule a bona fide deep-draft vessel for offload at Kompong Som.

Max was pleased to be accompanied the following week on his Khmer-AKAS flight to Kompong Som, by Navy Master Chief Petty Officer (E-9), Perry Carpenter. Carpenter was known for his skill in assessing port facilities from a technical perspective. He knew what to look for in pier pilings, load restrictions, proximate warehousing, and general readiness for a port to be opened to large ship traffic. He brought channel tables, charts of every description, as well as the latest known grids on the dredge paths approaching the port facilities and piers at Kompong Som.

The only lodging facilities for the two newcomers in the remote village of KPS was at a small beach resort, once abandoned, but now operated by an ex-pat French family. The facility was about five kilometers from KPS and the port. The Vinnell senior staff was also billeted here.

The bad news was that, in order to get to his quarters, Max had to traverse about three kilometers of winding roads from the town down to the beach. It seems that Kompong Som was built on a rise. The port was on one side of a small peninsula, while the beach resort was on the other. One had no choice but to traverse the moderate elevation change on switchback roads to get from the port to the resort. In relating this situation to Emily in a letter, Max said, "I've decided not to worry about the drive. There's no realistic way to defend myself if the KR decided to stop my chariot (an open Jeep) along the route at night. There were some reports of KR activity in the area a few months ago, but, the FANK recently moved several units nearby. I guess I will just have to remain stoic. I am armed, as usual, with my trusty .45, with one extra clip on my belt for good measure, but I am no match for an armed squad attempting to thwart my jeep's progress along a darkened, one-lane road to the beach."

"Some fight I'd put up," thought Max ruefully. *"More likely, I'd spend the next quarter century in the wilds of Cambodia, guest of the not-so-benevolent or protective brotherhood of Khmer Rouge."* Max, of course, omitted the latter thought from the letter.

"Perish that thought, old man, just take it one step at a time, one issue at a time, and don't let your mind play tricks on you," Max convinced himself.

*   *   *

On their arrival later that morning, Max decided to get started with an interview of the site Vinnell staff. The senior man, a French speaker, could provide a quick rundown on conditions at the port, its warehouses, and its fundamental ability to handle large vessels. The Frenchman had been on station for several months already evaluating FANK transportation units and warehousing procedures.

Max had noted on the twenty-five-minute drive from the escarpment overlooking KPS, where the airport was located, that there was not much in the way of port clearance infrastructure, except for this nice, wide, two-lane highway, with concrete drainage culverts on either side of the road to help with runoff when the monsoon rains started in earnest.

With the help of Monsieur Rene LeBeque, the Vinnell site manager, and Master Chief Perry Carpenter, the survey took only two days. En route back to Phnom Penh, Max finalized his recommendations. He had concluded that with some simple channel dredging, the port could easily handle a deep-draft vessel. Dredging of the channel was the fundamental first step.

Warehousing and port clearance were also matters of doubt and concern. Max's task would be to convince his bosses in Phnom Penh to twist some arms at FANK HQ, who, in turn, would have to order the local authorities at KPS to re-allocate space in the existing pier-side warehouses, and to transfer a substantial fleet of forklifts to the port to handle palletized cargo as it came off the ship.

BG Clausen was delighted with the news, and gave Max the full-speed ahead signal. Establishing a major seaborne, deep-draft vessel supply Line of Communication (LOC) had become essential to making the FANK forces viable against their formidable enemies.

Port dredging was the only sticky wicket. BG Clausen tasked COL Jacobson to have MEDTC's rear contingent modify Vinnell's existing contract to allow them to secure local coastal firms to perform the dredging.

With COL Jacobson's able mentoring, and through associations Max made in Saigon with Military Sealift officials, the Sea Train Maryland was earmarked to pick up FANK-destined cargo at Sattahip, Taiwan, and Vung Tau, with an estimated arrival at KPS within 45 days.

CHAPTER TWENTY-THREE

*W*hile all this deep water port business was taking place, Max was also busy planning his first EIUI. COL Jacobson had suggested a visit to two FANK support battalions working in the general vicinity of Neak Leoung. He had asked MAJ Hank Bethke to accompany Max, since he spoke French and had developed relationships with senior FANK logistics officers at their HQ in Phnom Penh. The Air America flight was scheduled for mid-morning the next day. The pilot would shut down near the EIUI site for two hours at each location, so they could look around.

Max and MAJ Bethke were at the Khmer Air Force hangar at the appointed time. They received a radio call that the UH-1D was inbound from a base in Vietnam, but it would be about twenty minutes late. Taking the opportunity to look around, the two curious officers headed out to an area nearby that was overgrown with shoulder-high elephant grass. Sitting in a row were five shiny, new MIG-21 Russian fighters that had been delivered just before Sihanouk pulled the plug on equipment deliveries from Moscow. These birds had been flown in, parked, and promptly abandoned. The tall grass was growing up into the wheel wells.

Back in the hangar, they chatted with a couple of KAF officers who told them that the Russians planned to train Khmer AF flyers to pilot these fighters, and to train indigenous crews to maintain them. This shipment was to be the first of four planned to fit out a full squadron of 20 MIG-21s. Apparently, it was envisaged that these relatively modern aerial weapon systems could be employed as interdiction against USAF fighter-bombers that were providing close air support along the Vietnam/Cambodian border. The plan also envisioned tactical fighter support for resupply columns utilizing the Ho Chi Minh trail.

Max marveled at the magnitude of this folly. Not only was the MIG-21 outclassed by both US Air Force and US Naval air-superiority aircraft, it was impossible to fathom the proposition that novice Cambodian pilots could gain the expertise needed in any reasonable length of time to hold their own against America's finest. Yet, here was the stark evidence. Here were five relatively modern fighters sitting on the runway gathering dust and deteriorating in the torrid tropical sun. "What a colossal waste," thought Max with a derisive smile. "Couldn't have happened to a nicer bunch of guys."

The Air America bird was on short final approach outside the KAF terminal. The two MEDTC officers hustled out when the Huey landed and hopped aboard. The pilot was a grizzled, portly, white-haired elf of a guy, wearing a light khaki flight suit with no insignia. He motioned to his passengers to put on headsets so all could chat privately, while the helicopter made its incessant, whining roar.

The pilot's name was Corky Finlen, and, he hardly stopped gabbing once on the 20-minute flight to Neak Leuong. It seems he had been an Army aviation CW4, recently retired, who couldn't resist the siren song of more flying, and the big bucks associated with flying in dangerous territory for the CIA's very own airline. He told the two spellbound passengers that he was a Master Aviator, and mentioned, quite boastfully, how many thousands of hours he had in rotary wing aircraft. Neither of the passengers had any idea if this sum was in any way significant, or whether he was merely engaging in SE Asia aviation BS (Belly Talk).

Corky added that the Army started getting strict on having its officers maintain weight standards toward the end of his thirty-year career. On his return from his fourth tour in Vietnam, the flight surgeon grounded him because his body weight exceeded guidelines by eight pounds. Corky submitted his retirement papers the following day, and was mustered out of the Army within weeks.

Within a month of his retirement, he was back to flying the ubiquitous Bell UH-1 and its variants for Air America in SE Asia.

Max couldn't help thinking that Corky would be the just the kind of guy to have along if things ever went to hell in a hand basket. Max consciously perished the latter thought.

As they approached Neak Leoung, Max noticed several jeeps heading for the Landing Zone (LZ). Hopefully, these vehicles would contain representatives from the First FANK Logistics Battalion, headquartered in a Log Base on the outskirts of the town.

Max had guessed right. The FANK greeting party meeting the helicopter was led by a diminutive FANK officer, named LTC Thak Chuong and his driver. LTC Chuong explained that he was the deputy commander of the Log Base. Speaking in very formal English, LTC Chuong did the traditional Khmer bow, with hands together at eye level as if in prayer, after returning the perfunctory hand salute from the American officers.

"Welcome, gentlemen, to our humble town. I will escort you to meet our commandant, COL Seng Leong, who patiently awaits your arrival. We have prepared a traditional Khmer meal for you. We will partake in what you call 'luncheon' prior to showing you around the Log Base, if that meets with your approval?" asked LTC Chuong with a humble smile and another bow.

MAJ Bethke assented for both of them, launching into a brief disquisition in French, wherein he apologized for our tardiness, offering the excuse that our flight was hopelessly delayed prior to arriving in Phnom Penh. MAJ Bethke indicated that they had initially planned to begin their tour of the Log Base on arrival, but that it made perfect sense to postpone it until after the meal, since, undoubtedly the Commandant had taken extraordinary measures to oversee its preparation. LTC Chuong responded in English that it was merely a simple meal, typical of was taken daily by Khmer personnel in units out in the provinces.

Max chuckled at the diplomatic repartee that was going on between the two allies. It was clear that MAJ Bethke knew his way around Khmer protocol and dining customs. Max made a mental note to sit opposite the good major to observe how he managed the various foods and toasts that would be inevitably be proffered.

LTC Chuong made it a point to invite their pilot and crew chief to join the entourage. Corky Finlen accepted without pause, and the group headed for the Log Base in the two open jeeps. The group traversed the small ferry town, and admired the view of the confluence of Tonle Sap and Mekong rivers, just off in the distance.

The meal was roasted chicken, with a rice-lentil concoction, accented with an aromatic sauce made of a mélange of local fruits mixed with a tasty fish sauce. The commandant, COL Leong, had his soldiers show the guests how the chicken was roasted. They somehow suspended a whole chicken in a covered, gallon-sized, used sesame oil tin. The secret was to cover the whole contraption with hot coals from a blazing fire, and roast the bird in this manner for at least an hour.

Max concluded that even for a tough, old bird, it was surprisingly moist, and had a hearty poultry taste. The challenge was in chewing the stringy, sinewy fibers of the meat. They also served a kind of unleavened flat bread. Max noticed the soldiers tearing off small bits, and using it as a scoop for the rice-lentil concoction.

COL Leong made several toasts with the aid of a good, yet tepid beer. It reminded Max of the good German beer that he and Emily had enjoyed so much in Nuremburg, Germany, while they were assigned there. Max was surprised to learn that this potion was brewed daily at a facility not far from the port of Kompong Som. Max made a mental note to visit the brewery on his next trip to KPS, after hearing that the place was run by ex-patriot Germans from southern Bavaria.

The traditional meal completed, COL Leong invited his guests to his small headquarters to brief them on particulars of the Log Base. No sooner had they boarded the jeeps than they heard a series of deafening explosions, one after another, continuing for what seemed like eternity, but really lasted only about ninety seconds. Max looked up to see several large bombs hit a school not far distant from the perimeter of the Log Base.

It appeared that a string of explosions was ripping through the center of Neak Leoung, continuing out from the periphery of the village, and approaching the Log Base itself. Max estimated thirty explosions before the last two bombs hit a motor park on the outskirts of the Log Base.

"It couldn't be artillery, because the Khmer Rouge only had 75mm pack howitzers, and the explosions were too large to account for artillery or mortars, or rockets, for that matter," Max related to MAJ Bethke, who was hunkered behind a water truck nearby.

"That, my friend, was an errant *Arc Light* (the code name for the Air Force's carpet bombing program in SE Asia) strike, and those were USAF two-thousand-pound concussion bombs raining down from a wayward B-52," yelled Major Bethke with some authority. Max had forgotten that his sidekick on this trip was a certified munitions expert, who had previously taught Army Ordinance Corps captains the fundamentals of explosives and munitions in their Officer Advanced Course at Aberdeen Proving Ground, MD, home of the Army's Ordinance School and Munitions Test Center.

"We need to collect Corky and his crew chief and head for the chopper. It has the only radio with enough range to contact the embassy to report this mess," MAJ Bethke barked.

Max had Corky in trail, along with the crewman. He commandeered the first jeep they came to and made a hasty exit. They headed for the route that would take them through town to get to the helipad on the other side of the village. As they hit the edge of the small town, they realized that they would be lucky if their helicopter was in one piece when they got their first full glimpse of the bombing's wholesale destruction.

The attack had essentially leveled most of the buildings. The hulks still standing were ablaze, and the road through the town was practically impassable, littered with tin roofs, ceiling beams, auto parts, and a ghastly array of limbs and torsos of the citizens caught in the firestorm. The remains smelled wretchedly like cordite and burned rubber. Max also thought he smelled what he recalled as singed hair. Clearly, this encounter was Max's first with wholesale carnage. He could not decide whether to get sick to his stomach or break down and cry.

Max yelled out, "Stop the jeep. These people need help. You can go ahead and make the report. I'll stay here to render what little assistance I can."

Just then, a little girl, no more than ten years old, emerged out of a pile of debris, holding a swaddled infant, bleeding from the nose, ears, and the sides of the mouth. The ten-year-old herself appeared to have burns on her legs, torso, and backs of her hands. Screaming, as if in horrible pain, she trudged down the street toward Max's commandeered Jeep.

"That baby appears to be still breathing. We've got to get it some medical attention," yelled Max as the jeep pulled away. When Max turned around, he encountered the lanky ordinance Major, who had hopped out of the jeep sending Corky to check on the chopper and make their report to the embassy.

"Two more hands might make a difference," was MAJ Bethke's only comment.

After surveying the immediate area, he continued, "Max, there's a market stall that's still mostly intact about 50 meters to our front. It looks as if it could provide some protection from the sun under that canopy for the wounded. Let's head in that direction, and make it an initial clearing station to sort through this mess."

Without so much as a moment's hesitation, Max swept up the ten-year-old girl and the infant and headed straight for the canopy. The baby that was being caressed by the girl, grunted just as Max had moved about ten yards. Not only was there an explosive upchuck, of surprising proportions, down the front of Max's fatigues, but the baby started to wail as if it hadn't eaten in days. "Well, all that emotion has to be a good sign," Max surmised.

As they progressed toward their destination canopy, they were exposed to an even more frightening nightmare. There were torsos still moving. Max and his human cargo encountered people without legs trying to sit up and move away from danger. Body parts, inadvertently strewn, were encountered at almost every footfall. Screams and moans echoed in a heartless harmony as fires were dying out. The victims seemingly moaned like an orchestra getting tuned, plaintively pleading their haunting, last soulful refrains.

Max tried to block out the unspeakable horror that presented itself starkly at every turn. He reminded himself that he needed to remain in command of his emotions, senses, and purpose. He could not subdue a compelling inclination to break down in a heap and sob his heart out. He knew he had to do something to help these poor, helpless victims. In the back of his mind, Max had a hateful thought, *"I want to testify at the court martial of those low–life jet-butt assholes who were responsible for this devastation."*

As his soul blistered with rage, Max made a pact with himself. *"I need to try and keep my cool in this unspeakable situation to provide assistance to these poor people. It is a sure bet that they'll never be able to speak a word in their own behalf.*" Committing to this pact, Max felt a resurgence of his psychic energy, and thoughts of breaking down receded quickly.

For the next several hours, Max and MAJ Bethke took turns going out on short patrols to find survivors to bring back to the 'canopy,' as they referred to their meager shelter. They found it overwhelming having to rummage through the remnants of buildings digging for signs of life or a plaintiff cry. Often, they had to move the charred remains of the dead who invariably lay in the path of the rescuer. Thus, they took turns tending to the canopy, rendering what assistance they could to the wounded who seemed likely to survive.

Max was overcome on one such probe, coming across a dead mother clinging to a dead infant, yet an arm's length from a crying five-year-old whose arms were stretched as if reaching for her mother. The five-year-old was covered with tangled roof support beams in the front of a bombed-out building. Max used every bit of his strength and bulk to move the fallen beams just enough to pull the girl to safety. As he lifted her up, the little girl threw her arms tightly around Max's neck and hugged Max as close as she could.

Max's eyes welled up as the little one continued to wail, and Max stumbled out of the wrecked building. With no way to stem the tears, Max trudged back to the canopy. There, they discovered that the roof beams had fallen across her calves, and both of her lower legs were broken. Gut-wrenching!

MAJ Bethke initially organized a group of unharmed older children to bring water from the river, both for drinking and to clean wounds. T-shirts came off and were torn into strips for tourniquets and bandages for those who appeared they might survive.

About an hour into this grisly collection process, they were relieved by the arrival of LTC Thak Chuong, who plowed through the aggregated mess with several truckloads of relief soldiers, laden with medical supplies.

"The town's medical station was destroyed in the attack, but we were able to collect what little we had in the depot to provide bandages and pain medication," reported LTC Chuong. "We will have to make do until we get relief, which we are told may take up to two days before we can expect further assistance. It seems that we are on our own here, for now."

About then, another wayward jeep made its way to their position. The driver looked angry, and remarkably like Corky Finlen.

"They did a job on our ride, I have to say," reported Corky. "There was not much left but a hulk of the airframe when we got back to it. She must've taken a near-direct hit. I would classify that aircraft as a total loss. I suppose you'd like to know if the radio equipment was still operational. Well, forget it," Corky declared emphatically.

Max looked knowingly to MAJ Bethke and interjected, "Guess that makes us stranded hereabouts for the foreseeable future. Why don't we make ourselves useful in the meantime?"

By morning, the civilian death toll was tallied to be in the low 100s. The number wounded was two- to three-times that figure. Max recalled the relatively few all-nighters he had pulled in college. This situation was a stark contrast to those last minute cramming forays at his alma mater. Thus, Max concluded that since he could tolerate the academic harassment that induced 'all-nighters,' the purposeful task at hand would not even be a stretch.

Max was getting used to making deals with himself. The more gnarly the situation, the more he was willing to give more of himself. This dreadful arrangement was no exception, and, the deals kept coming.

"Why do I have to make these mental deals with myself," inquired Max in the depths of his soul. *"I suppose it must be some sort of defensive coping mechanism gone awry. Besides, if I make it out of here with my sanity, I surely have a lot of years to thwart the offspring of these dastardly memories."*

Little did he know that the practice of suppressing horrific scenes such as these would cause a heavy toll on his long-term mental well-being.

Max had no idea of how foreboding this insight would be in his life after Cambodia. It was like practically predicting future nightmares and years of suppressing the manifest horror of his visit to Neak Leoung.

CHAPTER TWENTY-FOUR

*T*he hum of what would become prominent Huey blade-pops overtook the ambient noise of the still-burning fires that scorched the center of Neak Leoung. Bodies were still being stacked like cordwood. Horrified expressions hung on so many faces that Max personally strode along the piles of bodies, closing the non-seeing eyes of those who were still expressing terror, surprise, or abject panic.

Max was still railing inside that such a thing could have been perpetrated on so peaceful a village. Max concluded inwardly, *"It was such a travesty of justice, etched forever on the unknowing conscience of all American people. It is supremely ironic that almost no one knows of this needless, odious sacrifice."* Max promised himself that he would somehow, someway, testify to the truth of this senseless, American-sponsored slaughter.

An Air America helicopter, similar to the one that brought them here, circled the town center along with two KAF Hueys, apparently looking for a place to land. The Air America bird began its descent toward a clearing about 100 meters away from the canopy. The two KAF birds remained orbiting just overhead, as if covering the American chopper in case of any hostile KR activity. Two US soldiers hopped out as the high-pitched whine of the powerful gas turbine dropped away as the pilot seemed to snuff the engine to a low idle. They headed directly toward where Max and MAJ Bethke were standing. As they approached, Max noticed that one of them was BG Clausen, and the other was none other than their boss, COL Jacobson.

BG Clausen quickly surveyed the carnage and called Max and MAJ Bethke over to him. "You two need to get on that helicopter. Where are the crewmen who brought you here?" Just then Corky and his crew chief emerged from the other side of the canopy. BG Clausen motioned for them to head for the idling UH-1D.

"You can brief me on the way back to Pochentong,"

Donning a headset as the Air America bird cranked its gas turbine back up to a level where an almost direct ascent could be accomplished, Max was the first to speak, "We didn't expect any relief for another day or two. LTC Thak Chuong indicated it would be at least that long before FANK could get a column up in this direction. How did you get the word that we were stuck without a ride in Neak Leoung?"

BG Clausen chimed in almost instantly, "The air attaché at the embassy got a flash message from PACAF [Pacific Air Force] about the bombing error. CINCPAC [Commander in Chief Pacific] also called me directly. That was followed up by a call from MG Sosathene Fernandez [FANK Chief of Staff] at FANK HQ that COL Seng Leong had sent a flash message, in the clear, that the Log Base was catching Hades because of an errant American B-52 bombing run. His message stated that four Americans were headed back to their chopper. We surmised that since there was no contact from you via the Air America network, your chopper must have been destroyed. Then, yesterday, we got word from LTC Thak Chuong that you and your band of westerners were working around the clock to provide assistance to the wounded. It took us another 12 hours to set up this mission to extract you and insert trained medical staff from the FANK forces to provide assistance to the wounded. That's what the two FANK Hueys are carrying."

Max reported, "I counted over one hundred and forty-five dead, and they were still being dragged in. The number of injured was over two hundred at last count."

"Dear Christ," inserted Clausen. "May Your Perpetual Light shine upon on those poor, innocent souls." It was a rare scene for all aboard to see their sometimes standoffish, aloof leader shaking his head, and dabbing the corners of his eyes. "God damned Air Force hasn't made much progress in targeting since the Eighth Air Force leveled half of Europe in hopes of ending WWII. Didn't work then, and it still doesn't work. Some things never change."

BG Clausen was still shaking his head as Max and MAJ Bethke lapsed into silence. Corky Finlen was the quietest of all. This quietness seemed ironic to Max. Corky had been like Gabby Hayes on the way to Neak Leoung. Something had engaged his pause or mute button. The last thought to traverse Max's consciousness was how impressed he was with Corky and his crew chief. They had pitched in just as if it had been their own hometown hit by a tornado. Clearly, they both demonstrated true compassion to the wounded and great respect for the fallen citizens of Neak Leoung. In Max's mind, they both deserved Soldier's Medals. Max wondered as he finally dozed off, "*can civilians be awarded military decorations?*"

Max's esteem for MAJ Hank Bethke had reached the boundless range. He made a mental note to button-hole COL Jacobson and give the good colonel a full appreciation of his new best buddy's enormous humanity and cool demeanor under pressure.

CHAPTER TWENTY-FIVE

*M*ax and Emily had decided that in addition to exchanging letters, they would attempt a new technology in an attempt to stay close to each other. They bought miniature tape recorders for each other for the Christmas just before Max left for Cambodia. Max had made a vain effort to try to give Emily a sense of what took place at Neak Leoung. His description of the event was cryptic, incisive as to blame, and characteristically omitted details that would cause worry on Emily's part.

Emily's response, which arrived about two weeks after Max's evacuation, put Max well into his Kompong Som adventure. So, it was after his return to Phnom Penh that he was able to appreciate Emily's verbal perspective. (No mail was forwarded to KPS).

Emily's initial tape began with almost a litany of stateside activities that she and two kids had experienced since the last tape was received. She updated Max on what her mom and dad were doing these days, and, of course, she showered praise on her parents for being the 'backstop' for her, when his being away and Chris's demands as a toddler became onerous. She swore that the addition of a baby daughter made it seem as if she had three children instead of two, but, she reported, having her mom and dad to help with their extra sets of hands was a great blessing.

The latter part of the tape contained the thoughts and emotions of a lonesome Army wife, whose lover-for-life was off on some godforsaken military Odyssey. It was tough for Max to hear this tape because he knew he couldn't comfort her loneliness, or to be there for her to help raise their small children.

"Max, I know you will always take the upmost care of yourself, especially on these missions that have incredible, unscripted events that challenge life, and demand every ounce of your guile and essence to prevail. Never forget that your return is my most fervent prayer. Put yourself in my place. I am without power to influence your welfare. My only dream is to see you grace my doorstep. It would be a dream-come-true through heavenly intercession. You cannot imagine the torrent of hugs and kisses you'd receive. Just remember that, Max." Emily always put a tiny drop of her cologne, Max's favorite, next to her name on the wrapping paper. "With all my love, Emily."

Chapter Twenty-Six

*L*ife ratcheted back to near normal upon their return. There were two extraordinary events in the wake of Neak Leoung. BG Clausen, MAJ Bethke, and Max were invited to have lunch with Ambassador Ellsworth Hightower at his residence.

This lunch took place after an office visit, which was attended by Theodore Eckert, the Deputy Chief of Mission (DCM), the military attaché, COL James Ross, BG Clausen, and COL Jacobson. Max was not certain what to expect, but the Ambassador was extremely solicitous and seemed briefed on the B-52 tragedy. His interest was now focused on the welfare of MAJ Bethke and Max, although he expressed genuine remorse for the incredible loss on the part of the Khmer citizens. Mr. Hightower wondered aloud if the two American officers needed to take some time off to process the horrible spectacle, to somehow begin the healing necessary after a two-day living nightmare. BG Clausen injected that the two had been directed to take it easy and to plan an R&R as soon as they could get their wives to wherever they chose.

Mr. Hightower asked a few questions about the FANK response to this emergency. Max ventured an answer that led to the heroic depiction of LTC Thak Chuong's tireless efforts to alleviate suffering amongst his countrymen.

"That little guy was indefatigable from the moment he showed his face, a couple of hours after the attack. He seemed to be everywhere. Whenever we needed to calm a mother who was holding the remains of a dead child, he was there. Whenever we needed to communicate with a delirious patient, he was there. Cambodia should be proud of his dedication, patience, and sheer tenacity. If there was any heroics on the FANK side, all fingers should point to him," Max concluded.

Ambassador Hightower said, "We will insure the proper FANK authorities are informed of your strong testament."

Just then, Major Bethke chimed in, "Not only was LTC Thak Chuong commendable for his great humanity and resolve, he is blessed with the most remarkably gentle manner around casualties. You would have thought he was a seasoned emergency room physician,"

"Thank you for that, Major," added Mr. Hightower, "but, frankly, the purpose of this interview is to determine how we can provide adequate recognition for your heroic contributions, and those of Captain Donatello, to the welfare of those poor Khmer citizens. I am also concerned that, in spite of the Army's macho tradition, if you will pardon my use of the word, you may need more than a short vacation to somehow process the madness of those several days in Neak Leoung. No offense to either of you." Mr. Hightower swept his gaze to Max and Major Bethke.

BG Clausen inserted, "As far as recognition is concerned, we are preparing recommendations for appropriate military awards for their distinguished and heroic humanitarian actions. These decorations will be presented in short order. I will inform you as to the date, and perhaps you would do us the honor of making that presentation. As to your concern, Mr. Ambassador, for their emotional and mental well-being, we are in the process of scheduling both these fine officers for a trip to the Air Force's medical facility in Utapao, Thailand, the day after tomorrow, for a complete evaluation."

Hightower responded directly, "I want to be there to present these two superb officers the decorations they so richly deserve. Please ensure it is on my calendar the minute it is processed. Now, shall we adjourn to my quarters, as you call it, for a brief repast to honor these fine gentlemen?" Mr. Hightower stood, signaling the end of this brief encounter.

"I must beg your forgiveness, gentlemen," intoned DCM Theodore Eckert in an almost British, high English accent. "I will be unable to join you today. As you may be aware, we are about to host Vice-President Spiro Agnew in a few days. I must meet with the Secret Service advance team during lunch today to finalize the detailed itinerary for his visit. Please excuse me. I assure you I would prefer your company to these uncompromising blood hounds who are sent ahead of the vice president's oncoming entourage."

Eckert looked as if he had been churned out of the Ivy League, Max surmised. Not only was he exceptionally tall, his tailored, pin-striped suit accentuated his slender height. The long, blondish mane was swept almost straight back, giving an air of credence to his blue-blood pedigree. The oversized, tortoise-shell-rimmed glasses made his rather large head seem symmetrical with the other exaggerated features he possessed.

"We will miss you, Theodore," added the Ambassador.

Max was mystified by all this gooiness. Why all the hoopla? Why not simply send us on R&R, pin an Army Commendation Medal on our breast pocket, and be done with it? True, it was awful—a bona fide tragedy, if you took a survey of all those present. But, Max had a lingering suspicion that all the fanfare had to do with placating two scarred American officers who witnessed the horror that was perpetrated by an errant B-52 *Arc Light* Assault.

"*Keep it positive, fella,*" Max encouraged himself, but the rage was like a dose of yeast perking in a large batch of strong, autumn mead, not yet bottled. Max always had a natural tendency to catch himself when he felt negativity creeping into the scenery. "*Mustn't get cynical, old man,*" Max instructed himself.

The luncheon that ensued took on a character that omitted all discussion of the Neak Leoung tragedy. It seemed to Max like this was well-orchestrated sociable designed to make Max and Hank feel like the new rich folks on the block who need to be included in the social whirl. Max took rueful enjoyment in watching the proceedings. They could be attending any feting luncheon, anywhere in the Western world. The actors would, of course, change, but the inane, banal chatter would carry on without pause.

"*What sort of person aspires to this kind of superficial, shallow life, where protocol rules every action, and bland, mindless chatter permeates all meals,*" wondered Max to himself. "*I cannot decipher the motivation that drives these diplomatic types,*" Max admitted subconsciously. If it weren't for all the high–living, exotic locales to which they were assigned, Max could not imagine the brain-numbing boredom most diplomatic postings would entail.

* * *

The other manifest spillover of the Neak Leoung tragedy was a command visitation to the offices of Cambodia's President Lon Nol. This visit occurred the day after the Ambassador's interview and luncheon.

Ambassador Ellsworth Hightower and BG Rex B. Clausen were the only others invited. Stepping into the cavernous, messy executive suite, Max couldn't help but imagine what sheer wonders could be accomplished by a competent executive assistant. Clearly, His Excellency Lon Nol had no clue as to the state of personal disarray his office suggested.

The Americans were ushered in quickly and seated at a small conference table to the right of the enormous desk where Lon Nol conducted court. As they took their seats, his Excellency joined them from a small door off to the left of his desk.

"So, these are the heroes of Neak Leoung," Lon Nol began in broken English. "May I have the privilege of shaking the hands of the saviors of so many wounded Khmer citizens?" he inquired, as if someone might deign to disapprove.

"I have it on reliable authority that the fate of many of my countrymen rested in your hands for many hours while we struggled to marshal appropriate relief. I wish to offer my humble thanks to you for your undaunted valor during this terrible tragedy." Lon Nol grasped both Max's and Hank's hands, and brought them to his breast. "You will be remembered always in the annals of Khmer lore, as shining examples of humanity and compassion. My country's gratitude knows no bounds for your selfless contributions to the welfare of so many helpless victims in this, the darkest of moments in our modern history."

Max was impressed with how Lon Nol's diction clarified as he became more emotionally involved in his remarks. It was as if he had summoned a slumbering muse who finally caught the drift of his feelings, and it imparted a moment of clarity to his speech, inserting just the right strong, effective words to his manner of speech.

Max finished his initial evaluation of Lon Nol concluding, "*Here is a real patriot, trying desperately to save his country from destruction. He was clearly overwhelmed, exhausted, but hanging in there.*" Max observed no apparent symptoms of his recent mild stroke.

Lon Nol asked the senior American officials if he could be granted permission to bestow his country's highest honor on Max and Hank. "Of course, your excellency, you may proceed as you see fit," replied Ambassador Hightower.

Each of the two officers had a Khmer Order of the Angkor Medal pinned to the pocket of his jacket. Max took a moment to look at the red, blue, and white striped ribbon, from which hung a bronze medallion with a Cambodian phrase struck into the medal. Lon Nol proceeded to read the inscription first in a Cambodian dialect, and, as if he were eavesdropping on Max's thoughts, he said in English, "The words mean the following in your language. I had a scholar at the university translate it literally as, 'Conspicuous Valor and Brave Sacrifice,'" said President Lon Nol proudly. "On behalf of my grateful country, please accept my humble thanks for your service and bravery."

With a few remarks from Ambassador Hightower, and a quick aside with BG Clausen, the meeting was promptly adjourned. On the way back to the embassy, the Ambassador's limousine took on a somber tone as both senior officials lapsed into silence. Max and Major Bethke didn't make a peep.

On their return to embassy grounds walking back to the MEDTC offices, BG Clausen mentioned that he would ensure that the two decorated officers' military records reflected today's distinction. "The bad news is that you won't be able to wear the Khmer medal, or the ribbon, until after you retire, since the award has not been approved by Defense Department's Institute of Heraldry," remarked BG Clausen ruefully. "I have COL Throckmorton working an action to get several FANK awards OK'd by the Institute, but I fear that these matters sometime take years. They seem to move quicker through the process in direct proportion to the level of enthusiasm Congress provides for whatever action a particular award is fashioned to designate. I have to conclude that since Cambodia is not on many Congressmen's list of top priorities, we may be in for a long wait. You can be assured that I, for one, was bursting with pride during that presentation today. You two young warriors represent all that is good about America, and I thank you for everything you've done," concluded BG Clausen sincerely.

"Now, get your fannies over to Utapao for a checkup, and don't come back until the docs over there think you're ready. I don't want the

Ambassador pulling my chain about your welfare," he dismissed them with a rare big grin, as he returned the salutes of the two surprised young officers. "And give my regards to that old goat of a father-in-law of yours, Max."

*   *   *

Max's letter to Emily that evening contained a highly redacted outline of the day's events. "Today, Hank and I were escorted to a séance with Marshal Lon Nol, accompanied by BG Clausen and Ambassador Hightower. We were awarded the Order of Angkor, Cambodia's highest military honor in a brief ceremony in Lon Nol's office. I'm not sure what all this fanfare is about, but I'd like to get back to some semblance of normal."

"All the attention is nice, but it doesn't change the fact that our Air Force jet-butts from Thailand were way off course, and essentially vaporized a peaceful Cambodian village in their stupor. If my guess is right, that crew will never atone for the calamity they bestowed on the poor, unfortunate citizens of Neak Leoung. I am sick at heart with guilt for the holocaust at Neak Leoung.

Hank and I leave in the morning for a medical checkup in Thailand. I'll let you know if they come up with anything. About the only complaint I have is how cruddy I feel about all the carnage we witnessed. The hardest part for me was the injured and dead children. I could only think of my beautiful children home safe with you. I'm not sure how to deal with it since it keeps coming back every time I try to sleep, but, I am certain that lying around an Air Force clinic while they probe and prod is not what I need to turn the corner on this incident. What I do need is to get to work and sink my teeth into some useful project. Keeping busy is the key. You know how I hate just hanging around. I've got to be doing something, or accomplishing something."

"My biggest wish would be to have you with me in Thailand. You are my best therapy. You could help me while away the hours. With you, I am never bored or unhappy. I do so regret that we'll miss this opportunity for a few quiet days to focus on one another. You can't imagine how much I need you, miss you, and love you. Forever yours, Max. PS: I'm enclosing lots of kisses and squeezes for Chris and Melissa."

CHAPTER TWENTY-SIX

*B*y the time Max got back and settled into a routine in Phnom Penh, MEDTC got an unclassified Telecommunication Wireless Exchange (TWX) from the Military Sealift Command in Subic Bay, telling everyone who cared that the ship had stopped in Okinawa, "taking on bunkers." Max got a hand-scribbled note back appended to the TWX from COL Jacobson that read, "What the hell are bunkers?"

Max tried to add a little levity to his handwritten response. "'Bunkers' is a salty term for ship's fuel." The next day, Max received another note appended to the notes and the original TWX, with a scribbled reply from the southern Colonel addressed to, "Old Salty!"

Max had to get his planning hat on. This ship would be at KPS in four days. He would need to leave in the morning to coordinate with the Vinnell team to ensure everything was prepared for the first deep-draft vessel's arrival in KPS since the 1960s. Max arranged with the Embassy travel office to fly Khmer AKAS from Pochentong the next day at mid-morning, allowing one of the drivers to return to the villa to take him to the airport after they got the rest of the household safely to the embassy. The driver could then go directly back to assist in transporting Max's housemates home for the noon meal and break period.

*   *   *

Max marveled at the countryside from the air. He saw more pock marks in the landscape than he could count. These marks were always in a normal pattern as if four large cannons were aimed straight down at the earth from an aircraft of significant firepower. Max was familiar by now that these scars were the remains of *Rolling Thunder* and *Arc Light*, both bombing campaigns in eastern Cambodia designed to cut down infiltration and resupply along the Ho Chi Minh trail.

Then, Max rethought the scenario. He was headed south from Phnom Penh. Those innumerable pockmarks could not be part of the interdiction efforts in Eastern Cambodia. Rather, they were evidence of a much larger bombing campaign; one that had to be and was totally secret, especially from the American press (and the US Congress, as was later brought to light during the so-called Watergate revelations).

Max also noted large swaths of dead and dying vegetation, also in seemingly carefully-crafted patterns. By this point in the Vietnam conflict, it was well known that Agent Orange had been used on a wholesale basis to kill as much flora as possible to deny VC sanctuaries in areas where jungle and thick vegetation were effective cover for the always security-vigilant Viet Cong. Max wondered how many decades would have to pass before these areas could support life and oxygen-producing vegetation. "Not in my lifetime," Max concluded.

Max had asked Navy Master Chief Perry Carpenter, who had left Phnom Penh the day before to assist in the port preparations, to meet him at the airport at KPS, along with the senior Vinnell representative, Monsieur Rene Le Becque, the French speaker, so he could get updated on progress in the area since his initial visit a month and a half ago.

Upon Max's arrival at KPS, Carpenter launched almost immediately into an update. "We have acquired a small room near my quarters at the resort to install a powerful Harris single-side band radio (SSB), which will enable the KPS crew to maintain contact with the embassy on a regular basis. In reality, it is really our only means of communication to the outside world, unless we were try to rely on the primitive phone system. Mr. LeBecque has tried it to report to Vinnell, but the switching and toll system is a nightmare, and nearly impossible to understand," suggested the Master Chief ruefully.

"We got the big Harris installed yesterday just in time for the scheduled reporting time. The call is scheduled daily at 4:30 PM, even if we have no traffic to exchange. It's sort of a way to insure the link is still open," continued Carpenter.

"The bad news was that the radio is about 20 minutes from the port of KPS. Further, the embassy monitors the radio for only fifteen minutes before and after the assigned reporting time. This creates a situation that if there is ever an urgent need for assistance from Phnom Penh, one would have to wait until the next 4:30 PM reporting time. Thus, in an emergency, the time lapse that would occur would be from of the incident until that first scheduled reporting hour. Then, you'd need to add the time a response could be organized and dispatched to KPS from Phnom Penh," concluded Chief Carpenter woefully.

"Kinda dicey, if you ask me," proffered Captain Donatello upon hearing of the arrangement. We may need to increase the frequency of radio checks to insure our butts are somewhat covered in case all hell breaks loose," speaking with some authority concerning hell breaking loose.

"No argument from me. I had one helluva time convincing the communications weenies at the embassy that once a day was the minimum acceptable interval. They suggested once a week," remarked Master Chief Carpenter, shaking his head.

Max asked, "What about Vinnell, Monsieur LeBecque? Aren't they at all concerned about your ability to communicate with your headquarters?"

"I have been informed that we will be provided with another SSB, similar to yours, within the month," reported Mr. LeBecque.

"So quickly?" retorted Max sarcastically. "We will all be drawing old age benefits before they establish adequate radio coverage for this godforsaken paradise. We will be opening a major Line of Communications (LOC) for the FANK forces by virtue of the Sea Train Maryland's arrival. And, all we have is one radio to report it to the world. I'm beginning to know how Neil Armstrong felt a few years ago as he orbited around the moon. I wonder if he ever had doubts about the adequacy of his means of communication," Max paused thoughtfully, then continued, "I'll be totally frank with you both, I have serious doubts about this arrangement. I'll try to raise COL Jacobson this afternoon to see if he can weigh in to try and solve this issue before the ship arrives—before any wayward shit hits the proverbial fan."

Max was working off a checklist they had developed over the course of last thirty days. "Fill me in on Vinnell's progress in getting some dredging done on the channel into the port, Mr. LeBecque."

Monsieur LeBecque squirmed in his chair as he cleared his throat, "I must reluctantly report to you, *mon Capitaine*, that there has been no dredging accomplished. I am afraid the lead-time to procure the dredging equipment, and to have it transported here, was one week longer than we anticipated. Therefore, the dredging vessel is scheduled to arrive in about five days from now. That will make its arrival well after that of the SeaTrain Maryland."

Max strained to keep his cool, "You're telling me that one of the essential 'go/no go' requirements of this plan is one great-big bolo? How long has Vinnell known about this situation? Why have they not reported this condition to our headquarters in Phnom Penh? All we need is to create a worse fiasco by virtue of getting a major deep-draft vessel stuck in the channel muck, so the KR can use it for mortar and artillery target practice. The media would eat that up, and I am sure that Congress would shut this whole operation down if something like that occurred."

Monsieur LeBecque squirmed in his seat, "I share your outrage and concern. It is regretful that the Vinnell managers, who accepted this tasking, were overly optimistic in their assessment of the South East Asia merchant marine's ability to marshal and deploy specialized dredging resources. I am afraid the estimate they made of the time required to move this equipment was excessively sanguine. I, myself, was only notified by telegram of this condition late yesterday, too late to have the unfortunate information included in the daily report to MEDTC headquarters."

Max turned to the Master Chief, "What are the chances that this vessel will get stuck, Perry?"

Master Chief Carpenter immediately launched into a cryptic assessment of the team's chance for success. "Captain, the charts in our possession haven't been updated since 1967. Since we don't have any historical data about silt accumulation in this little corner of the world, it makes predicting whether this maritime monster will make it through the channel equivalent to shooting dice. I certainly would not even attempt to traverse it in anything but high tide. Then, your guess is as good as mine as to whether she gets stuck. There is a better chance she'll get stuck pier-side; as the tide ebbs, she'll surely settle into the muck. No telling whether the natural suction can be overcome after she's unloaded and makes an attempt at high tide to make a run for it out of the channel."

Max was completely incredulous, and waited a few seconds to compose his thoughts. "I will report this situation to headquarters this afternoon in case our friends from Vinnell Corporation high command have not deigned to submit an official report of this to our highers. Then, we'll just have to wait and see what our headquarters wants to do. I suppose we'll all wait to see what Military Sealift Command (MSC) wants to do since the SeaTrain Maryland is under charter to them. Who knows, they may leave it up to the vessel's master to decide whether to chance it."

After a few moments of buzz in the room, Max continued down the list of things about which he needed the latest information. "What is the situation regarding port clearance gear?" asked Max.

Chief Carpenter gave Max a run down on the FANK truck units that had moved into the vicinity in makeshift encampments. "They consist of a hodgepodge of American Army two-and-a-half–ton, multi-fuel vehicles, mixed up with some Australian Dodge and International Harvester flat beds," reported Perry, in a matter of fact tone.

"Forklifts are mainly old French-made, and LPG fueled. Most of them are being held together with chewing gum and bailing wire—if they work, at all. There are around ten of them, and they are strewn around the various warehouses adjacent to the piers. The warehouse managers treat them like they own the damned things, and the drivers treat them like bucking broncos, hot-rodding the bejesus out of them. 'Drive 'em till they drop in their tracks,' seems to be the FANK motto. Almost all of the operational ones need new tires. I guess they could muster six or seven of them on a wink and a prayer, if things got cooking real good," added Perry in his native Texas drawl.

"All very encouraging," Max snarled sardonically, "to go along with the great news about our stone-age communications gear and the glad tidings of our still un-dredged channel."

"Any other show-stoppers?" asked Max, as his tone changed back to his normal, direct approach.

Perry added quickly, "FANK hasn't really decided where they want to store all the gear headed this way. The warehouses by the pier are supposedly commercial, and the FANK have been ordered by the Port

Authority to have these stores, as they call them, cleared within a week of the cargo's arrival."

Perry continued, "I don't know who died and made the port authority King of the May, but FANK's only real warehouse is halfway to the KPS airport, about a twenty-minute, one-way truck ride from the port. If the port authority has its way, anything stored in the pier-side stores will have to be moved to the FANK store within a week's time. To net that out, it means not only will the cargo be handled as it comes off the vessel, the forklifts will handle it again to load it on the trucks, who will take it two tenths of a mile to be offloaded in temporary pier-side stores, for its third handling. Then, if the local authorities have their way, it will have to be reloaded onto the trucks for the trip up to the FANK warehouse. So, there will be five different handlings before it ever gets officially transferred to the FANK at their own warehouse. Then, the internal FANK distribution process begins. It's no wonder these poor bastards are losing the war," added Perry with a rueful twinkle in his eye.

Max interrupted, "We need a meeting with the local FANK area commander before dinner tonight to sort this mess out. His arm needs to be twisted to cut out at least three of those 'handlings,' as you affectionately refer to them. I know we are not here to advise the FANK, but we need to make certain we have all the coordination points covered. Perry, you and Monsieur LeBecque head to the local FANK HQ and arrange the meeting. I have to head back and try to raise COL Jacobson on the radio. I should be back here by say, 1715. With any luck we can be sucking down some of that Khmer/German brew by 1800," said Max with a twinge of hope in his voice.

*   *   *

When Max had contacted Phnom Penh, he asked the embassy communications office to patch him through to COL Jacobson's line. The marine duty officer informed Max that COL Jacobson was not available, but he could take a message and see to it that COL Jacobson received it ASAP. Max sighed to himself and said, "Please request that COL Jacobson be available for tomorrow's commo check at the normal hour. Tell him that the KPS site is in urgent need of radio equipment beyond what is currently available."

The radio crackled as the embassy responded, "Roger, received your last Lima Charlie (LC; loud and clear). Wilco. Anything further, over?"

Max squeezed the press to vox switch and began, "Urgent action required: Inform COL Jacobson ASAP that Vinnell has not, repeat not, accomplished dredging requirement making successful channel traverse highly questionable. Request guidance, over."

"Roger last," squawked the Marine Corps communications specialist, "will contact COL Jacobson immediately regarding Vinnell failure to accomplish channel dredging, over."

Max asked if there was any traffic for him, especially regarding the arrival at KPS of the SeaTrain Maryland.

After a SSB squelch break, the radio's speaker bellowed, "Have traffic indicating vessel arrival your location at 2230 local, this date. Also, have message for you from COL Jacobson that vessel has four, repeat four, Rough Terrain Fork Lifts (RTFL) lashed to main deck. Should assist in port clearance, over."

Max murmured to himself, "Ahh Shit! Those dipstick MSC weenies don't understand that this monster has to navigate an un-dredged channel, which has not been used for deep-draft passage for more than five years? Why not enter the channel at first high tide or first light? Or, better yet, both."

Max finally broke squelch and responded, "Roger last. Acknowledge vessel arrival 2230 KPS. Thank COL Jacobson for the info on the RTFLs. Negative further, out."

Max thought of the irony of COL Jacobson digging into the manifest to find the forklifts. As it turned out, it was one of the main discussion points Max wanted to bring up with his boss. Max wasn't sure what MEDTC could do about a shortage of forklifts in Cambodia on an immediate basis. But, he could sure as hell lay it at the good Colonel's feet. As Max walked out of the makeshift communication station, he noticed a sky full of hostile-looking clouds just along the horizon.

"Just what we need to kick things off right. Story Line: A frapping tropical storm lets loose to welcome the first deep-draft vessel port of call at KPS since the Soviet era! It does seem to be just the right touch to add a little drama to the proceedings," thought Max miserably to himself, as he slowly shook his head in acute frustration.

Back at the port, Max caught up with Chief Carpenter and Monsieur LeBecque just as they were boarding the nearly new, now defunct, Soviet-provided dredge vessel. The FANK had assigned the vessel to be used as a kind of headquarters for the Americans and Vinnell Corp. employees. The ship-to-ship radios still worked. Only the dredging gear was inoperative. Heck, the interior's main cabin was even air-conditioned. The auxiliary generator kept the lights and the a/c going.

The word Max got was that the dredge ship broke down on its maiden channel dredging mission a few years back. And, since there were neither parts nor technical repair expertise available locally, the nice-looking, sixty-five-foot vessel lay moored semi-permanently at the end of the main pier.

Master Chief Carpenter sounded off first. "Well Captain, the FANK area commander told us he would join us at 1730 sharp here at the ship."

"What a great break," replied Max. "Not only can I debrief you on the traffic from Phnom Penh, we can use the meeting to alert the FANK that our ship arrives at 2230 tonight." Max caught the shocked and incredulous expressions of his two colleagues.

"Holy she-it," was Carpenter's only comment.

CHAPTER TWENTY-SEVEN

*A*fter a fruitful meeting with the FANK area commander, LtCOL Sak Kheo, Max decided to adjourn back to the resort. Reflecting on the meeting, Max was pleased that LtCOL Kheo agreed that preparations needed to be made to transship as little cargo as possible to the pier-side stores. He agreed to prepare the FANK warehouse to receive cargo directly from trucks delivering cargo as soon as they were loaded directly off the ship. LtCOL Kheo also thought there should be no reason the offloading could not go on around the clock. He said he would need to chat with the FANK warehouse director, but he thought it would be possible.

Max could tell that port clearance was not LtCOL Kheo's strongest suit, but he reminded himself that, "The FANK needs to handle storage and distribution according to their own methods. We are not here to re-invent any of their processes."

Nevertheless, Max caught himself thinking, *"except to insure that they are not giving the cargo to the KR, or selling our precious military gifts on the burgeoning black market for personal gain."*

Max's final thought was *"On the most fundamental level, America had not signed up to replace the FANK logistics system with a modern US system. The FANK had to get it done using their own ways and means if they had any chance of survival."*

Besides, Max realized that time was running out for any further meaningful American presence in SE Asia. The public had made it plain that US involvement in Vietnam and Cambodia had to be curtailed, if not terminated, altogether. Max had long since concluded that the Nixon administration, with Kissinger bounding between Paris, Washington, and Beijing, had frozen their normal mental receptors of all things emanating from its citizens. Neither protest nor demonstration seemed to have any measurable effect on American policy or prosecuting the war. The 'powers that be' seemed to be relying on the ongoing drawdown to quell growing political unrest. The administration continued to repeat references to "Vietnamization," and "Peace with Honor."

These catch phrases were really nothing but sound bites, and they were correctly interpreted by average American citizens, even private soldiers, as nothing but, 'turning the damned war over to the Vietnamese.' The administration's spin about the drawdown was falling on deaf ears.

"What was going unnoticed by the policymakers was," Max thought, *"that there was a palpable downside effect on the morale of the remaining Americans in SE Asia, as well as the fighting spirit of our allies in the South Vietnamese Army (ARVN) and the FANK."*

"No one seemed to be taking note," reflected Max, *"and, who would care to listen to the musings of a low-ranking logistics officer stuck in Kompong Son, coordinating transfer of last-minute American military aid to the embattled Khmer Forces?"*

Max was beginning to answer himself in these cerebral discussions, *"No one of note, you can be assured, my fine young warrior,"* thought Max once again to himself.

Chapter Twenty-Eight

*L*tCOL Kheo turned as he was leaving and said, "*beaucoup le cargaison ici, mon Capitaine.*"

Max knew that the good Colonel was being wistful about the impending onslaught. "You are so right, sir. Lots of cargo here tonight, mon Colonel," responded Max. "*Ce soir, ici.*" "Here tonight," Max repeated in English as if to emphasize what he thought was the proper French phrase, but what he was really emphasizing that there would be more cargo than this or any other poor, feckless FANK officer had ever seen assembled in one location.

"*I hope you are ready for this,* mon Colonel," Max pleaded silently. "*I really hope to heaven that we are all ready for this,*" Max concluded in his sub-conscious contemplations.

Max turned to his colleagues and said, "Regretfully we will have to postpone trying that good KPS-German beer this evening. I recommend everyone get something to eat and a few winks of shut-eye before we have to deal with all this."

Max decided to go back to the resort, have a bite of dinner, and try to lie down and get a couple of hours of snooze time before all hell broke loose. It occurred to him that the surrounding clouds looked no friendlier than after his last visit to this shore-side paradise, as he surveyed the horizon as the last beams of light were sinking into the Gulf of Siam.

He decided to drop by the restaurant at the resort to see if he could find something light. What he really wanted was a glass of that heavenly French beaujolais he'd tried when he was here before, with petite medallions of beef adorned in a Bordelaise sauce, with mushrooms in a nice wine reduction. This entree was served with baby green beans mixed with julienned baby carrots, and bland radish hearts steamed to perfection.

Max decided he could do without the large meal. Perhaps the owner could stir up a nice French omelet to accompany that beaujolais?

Perhaps it could be accompanied with a hint of some of that divine double cream cheese he'd tried the last time during a pre-dinner cocktail.

All these thoughts of food made Max's mind seem to drift as he traversed the perilous S-curves of the dark passage that unfurled its hazardous coils down to the beachside resort.

CHAPTER TWENTY-NINE

*M*ax responded to the wake up call, which was nothing more than a clerk from the office down the path pounding on the outer door to his cabin. Noting on his luminous alarm that it was exactly 21:50 local, Max hopped off his bed and began lacing his jungle boots. After a splash on his face with a dose of the tepid local water, he grabbed his fatigue jacket and headed out to his open jeep, which was parked adjacent to his 'hootch.'

Max had remembered to strap on his shoulder holster under his fatigue jacket. He carried about twelve full clips of .45 caliber ammo in a cubby he had tailored between the seats of the jeep. He had a case of grenades tucked accessibly under the rear seat, in case things got really dicey. An M-16 was carefully set in place back there with 25 magazines stored like an old pro.

Master Chief Carpenter had intervened with the director of FANK stores (warehouses), to relinquish temporary control of three newly-refurbished jeeps. One was for a certain very senior Naval NonCom, of course. One was for Cap'n Max, as he was most often being called. The Master Chief was currently dangling the proposition that the last of these precious quarter-ton vehicles be assigned to Rene LeBecque, insuring his unswerving loyalty, and adding another set of independent wheels in motion to help control this complicated operation.

As Max mounted his steady quarter-ton steed, he thought, "The .45 cal M1911A1 would probably be a mere distraction if the KR decided to set up a road block on the route back to the port."

Max thought languidly, as he shifted through the gears of this gutless, god-knows-how-many-times rebuilt jeep he was driving. *"This mechanical marvel was a gift from the magnanimous graces of the United States of America,"* Max pondered. Little did Max realize that this little jeep was a part of an early Repair and Return Program (R&R, not to be confused with Rest and Recreation).

Max would not learn until much later the pedigree of this vehicle, which was that it was rebuilt in Okinawa after a horrific accident in Da Nang, Vietnam, in 1967 in its original life. It was then shipped to Taiwan in 1968, as part of an early American R&R program that recovered damaged chassis, hulks, and major assemblies of end items that had been provided to American allies for their use. In this manner, America was able to keep depot-repair organizations in operation in Okinawa and Taiwan as long as possible to support the war effort in SE Asia.

US policy masterminds decided which of our allies needed the rehabilitated vehicles most. Thus, Max was unknowingly tooling around KPS in a vehicle that had been in and out of SE Asia since the latter 1960s—a jeep with nine lives! But it was still a fine ride for an American officer in the outback of Cambodia. Max liked the old beast, at least until the skies let loose in one of the regular evening monsoon rainstorms. Luckily, Max arrived at the pier just in time to rush aboard the Russian dredge vessel to avoid total immersion in this storm's fury.

Monsieur LeBecque greeted Max, saying, "We have just heard from the pilot, who boarded the SeaTrainMaryland as it approached the channel. He says that the Master of the SeaTrainMaryland would like to be tied up at the pier tonight by 2330 to allow discharge operations to be initiated at the earliest hour tomorrow."

The storm outside took on a feverish intensity. Swirling winds, incredibly vivid bolts of lightning, and cavernous barks of thunder seemed to combine as if a dysfunctional family were simultaneously and synchronously raising their voices to plead their most strenuous, baleful arguments.

Max intoned, "I hope these merchant mariners know what they are getting themselves into. I did my best to spur our headquarters to warn MSC, and the owners of the vessel, that proper preparations had not been made to rid the channel of five years of sediment."

Not a soul had the psychic energy to respond. 'Nothing to do but wait,' seemed to be the accumulated attitude aboard the Russian vessel.

Max noticed that in spite of the storm, the Cambodian soldiers and dockworkers had dropped their fishing lines in the water along side the vessel. They used a technique roughly translated as 'flashlight fishing.'

The baited lines would be tossed over the side after dusk. When it was fully dark, the fishermen would train flashlight beams down their lines. Somehow, this light attracted the native squid to emerge to a shallow point that the fishermen could entrap the squid in nets trailing just below the keel of the Soviet vessel. In one swooping gesture, it would become dinnertime on the pier next to the immobilized Soviet vessel.

Before long, squid ink would be squirting in every direction. And, rudimentary tarp enclosures would pop up with hibachi-like fires dotting the entire length of the pier to cook the calamari.

"It was like a Cambodian fresh seafood culinary clinic, with rain thrown in as a challenge," thought Max. *"I guess one eats when the food presents itself,"* mused Max pensively, as he considered their few sources of protein other than seafood and chickens. While pork was also available, there was, for everyday Cambodians here in KPS, no refrigeration. Food had to be acquired fresh daily from the sea, market, or garden. Khmer food consisted of what remained after a day of fishing, or a day of trading in the marketplace for some other source of nutrition. About all that an average family stored in their stilted homes was harvested rice, fish sauce, and whatever root vegetables they raised in their large local gardens. Fruit, on the other hand, abounded. Bananas, local pineapple, papaya, as well as several citrus varieties were always available on shelves in the market.

Max had also noticed that there were very few butcher shops along the road from the resort to the port. It seemed that they were only opened when a large animal had been slaughtered and required butchering. Lack of refrigerated facilities dictate that every part of the slaughtered beast be used or sold. Another alternative was that select parts were kept by the family of the butcher for further processing into a kind of smoked sausage, or some other squeamish-inducing after-product.

*   *   *

The squelch on the ship-to-ship radio crackled with a call in Khmer to the Port Authority. An authority rep took the call and jabbered in the Khmer language that sounded like sing-song banter back and forth. One of the FANK officers came over to where Max was seated with Carpenter and LeBecque.

"The vessel master has ordered all stop and has lowered all anchors. The storm was pushing the boat off course and into dangerously shallow waters. He has ordered the crew to stand down until first high tide after daylight tomorrow to make another attempt. These orders will be effective depending on the storm, of course," added the diminutive FANK captain.

Max did some figuring out loud, "So, since first tide tomorrow after daylight is around 0930, it looks like late morning before offloading can begin, in even the best of cases. That assumes the weather cooperates."

Max told the FANK captain to get the word to the area commander over FANK channels, and to circulate this information to all concerned who were scheduled to take part in the initial offloading operations.

He then turned to his colleagues and said, "We'd best get back to the resort and get some rack time, while the gettin's good."

There was neither argument nor further comment, as all headed directly pier-side, where the vehicles were parked. "Let's assemble back at the dredge ship at 9:15 in the morning," was Max's last comment.

Carpenter gave his usual, "Aye, Aye, captain."

LeBecque gave his casual hand salute with a compliant head nod.

CHAPTER THIRTY

*W*hen the SeaTrain Maryland was finally and safely berthed at KPS, it was well after 1130. By the time the crew got a gangway in place, it was after noon. Max and Carpenter made their way up to the deck and requested permission to see the Master of the vessel. A crewman rang the bridge on a wall phone hanging nearby. An immediate welcome was offered, and the crewman escorted the visitors to the bridge.

The ship's captain was a mustachioed, prematurely grey, fireplug of an Aussie, named Fenwick. Fenwick reminded Max of the portly character actor William Conrad. His initial countenance seemed tense, but Max would find out later that the captain was indeed very laid back.

"Helluva channel passage, if ya ask me. That goddamned channel nearly beached us. Then, last night, the foockin' storm blew us off anchor. We had to crank her back up to get her back in position. Then, we were churning up sludge as thick as mud this morning at high tide," remarked the captain.

"Don't they ever dredge that piece of shit they call a channel?" inquired Fenwick, with a voice laden with sarcasm. "Furthermore, I wasn't sure there'd be enough water under us to get us to the pier, and since you may not be aware, I am pretty certain we are stuck on the bottom right now."

"It'll be a foockin' miracle if she ever floats again, even after we offload her. I'm concerned that the natural suction around the keel might make it impossible to get her off the bottom, even with no cargo aboard, and far less of a bunker load," concluded Fenwick's opening salvo.

After a spell of silence, they heartily introduced themselves, and Captain Fenwick seemed to ease up. "Well, we're here, is all I can safely report. So, why don't you fine fellas join me in the officer's mess for a bite of lunch. It's the least I can do to repay yuz, since I told yuz we'd be at the pier late last evening. Anyone beside me hungry around here?" inquired the Master of the vessel.

CHAPTER THIRTY-ONE

"*Master Chief Carpenter fit into this situation like a custom-made pair of fine gloves,*" Max concluded silently early into the lunchtime repartee. Fenwick and Carpenter were like Pete and Re-Pete, exchanging all manner of nautical belly talk during lunch, for all to behold, in what they surely expected to achieve utter amazement and adoring admiration from lovers of authentic sea tales.

Max was less than impressed. The food, however, was over-the-top good. Captain Fenwick said, "Is all yuz need to do, is ask the steward for whatever comes to mind. You want eggs and bacon? You got it. You want steak and lobster? How do you like yer steak? "

"You want meat loaf? Well, yuzza gotta come back for supper and give the goddamned cook time to brew it up for yuz. By the way, yuz and any of your Cambodian comrades or contractors are welcome at any meal. No need to call ahead for reservations. It'll be sorta, 'mi casa, su casa,' if you catch my drift. I mean that. I'll punish severely any discordance with this policy. Keelhauling will not be excluded from the options of the moment," Captain Fenwick added.

"I, therefore, hereby proclaim, as Master of this esteemed vessel, that while we are moored to the side of this godforsaken pier, you are ordered to feel as if this is your home away from home. Yuz' may take breakfast, lunch or dinner any time day or night in this mess, which I call my own."

"And, if you feel the need for a late afternoon retreat, I will provide three or four guest cabins for yer use to take a siesta. What I have in mind is, yuzs' may need a respite after yuz' join me in the afternoon for one or two cocktails in my cabin. The cabins are for your use while we are pier-side. You may choose to stay with us instead of going back to your beachside quarters, which I understand are a considerable distance from the port."

"Captain Donatello, you should pick one cabin and make it yours; the Master Chief another, the Vinnell guy another, and reserve one or two for the duty FANK officer during his watch. I will have the steward show you these accommodations upon conclusion of our meal."

Max thanked the Master sincerely, and told him that MEDTC and the US port clearance team were in his debt for all the truly gracious hospitality Captain Fenwick had shown, and was now extending. "I fear we will be more of a burden than you expect, if we accept this attractive offer."

"Nonsense," bellowed the Master. "We either feed our customers in port, or feed the fish when we are under way when the food goes bad. I prefer the former, in deference to future business, don't yuz' know?"

"Oh, and the guest cabins are vacant. Yuz won't be displacing anyone. The shipping line, in its inimitable wisdom, initially thought there might be a way to reinvigorate the old custom of taking vacationers or stranded travelers on our cargo vessels to and from exotic ports of call. So, they had all these ships built with guest cabins. Let's just say, the practice hasn't exactly caught on. So, I usually have about six cabins sitting empty on a normal cruise. Please let me know if there's a need to make a 'coupla more of 'em ready, in case of need," Fenwick's voiced trailed off.

Before anyone could comment, the Master inserted emphatically, "One more thing, I start to pour cocktails at precisely five PM local time. You are most welcome to join me. If yuz' don't show, it's your loss. The only thing I'm short of, is beer."

Chief Carpenter inserted, "That condition will be remedied before lunch tomorrow, to allow us to make a contribution of the local German-crafted lager to chill in your reefers all afternoon."

Thumbs up was the only signal from the vessel's Master.

The steward offered six different flavors of ice cream. He also recommended three types of pie and two kinds of cake as dessert.

Deliriously sated by all the fresh salad, the order-by-whim manner of serving main entrees, the steward had caught all of the displaced Americans pleasantly off guard. Not having dessert in weeks meant that the group ordered their favorite sweets proffered by the accommodating steward. A veritable buffet of sugary delights was arrayed before the men. When all were licking their forks and spoons, the steward took away six empty dishes without so much as a crumb to commemorate the bountiful repast.

This overindulgence resulted in what seemed like a gut-bomb ticking on a timer, pressing against their burgeoning waistlines. Then, the strongest coffee any of them had experienced in the South East Asia was served steaming hot to all takers. Suffice it to say, before long, sweat was pouring profusely off the visitors' foreheads. Whilst cautious sippers mopped foreheads, the assembled sat back and cherished the earthy, enlivening scent and taste of the ship's very best Sumatran Dark Roast.

Max reminded everyone, "When the ship departs, we're back to Nescafe and Sanka instant in our cups. So, enjoy it while it's available." Turning to the ship's Master, Max whispered, "You are spoiling us, mon Captain."

"My intense pleasure, mon Captain," was Fenwick's gracious reply.

CHAPTER THIRTY-TWO

*M*ax surveyed the initial offloading activities. It seemed remarkable that the FANK authorities had mustered six rather–battered, LPG-powered French forklifts and had a platoon of trucks queued and ready for loading just off the pier. The SeaTrain crew saw to it that the Rough Terrain Fork Lifts (RTFL) were the first items discharged off the main deck, even before the hatchways were opened for the stevedores to get at the break bulk cargo.

Max turned to Master Chief Carpenter and said, "Perry, could you oversee the de-processing of those RTFLs, so we can get some use out of them at the earliest opportunity? I've got my doubts that our FANK brethren will be familiar with all those levers and hoses."

Carpenter replied, "Vinnell has several Philippine dock workers who are supposed to be checked out in all the latest tactical Material Handling Equipment (MHE). I'll go round 'em up and see if we can't get a couple of those bruisers up and operational directly. By the way, I suspect the FANK warehouse will have an immediate need for one or two of the RTFLs given all the rain we've had over the last twelve hours. My money is that there's no paved outside storage. So, offloading and

stacking weatherable cargo in the muddy fields around the warehouse will be their biggest challenge."

Max shrugged, "I'll throw my money in with you. Murphy is out there waiting to bite us in the tail feathers. In fact, I admire O'Toole's corollary on Murphy's law, which suggests that Murphy was an optimist." Perry made an exaggerated snap to attention and a hand salute. Max returned Perry's salute, saying, "I'll catch up with you as soon as I get back from chatting with COL Jacobson on the radio."

*   *   *

Max made his way back to the resort to make contact with Phnom Penh via the daily SSB radio check. On the journey, he could not help but reflect on the many characters developing in this emerging plot:

Master Chief Carpenter, with his natural, perceptive way of assessing any given situation, then blending in with the scenery only to emerge when a guiding hand was needed.

Captain Fenwick, with his magnanimous offer to provide us food and quarters while the vessel was moored in KPS.

Most startling of all, Max was taken by the remarkable flexibility and unflappability of the FANK port officers even under stressful situations. Things got done quietly, without a lot of American-style hyper-stress or fanfare. Max made a mental note to check to see if there was any incidence at all of FANK officers suffering from hypertension.

Arriving at the resort just in time for the commo check, Max barely had time to make a deposit in Perry's commode before he heard the crackle of squelch preceding the call from Phnom Penh, "KPS, this is Phnom Penh, do you hear me, over?"

Max hurried from the bathroom and keyed the SSBs microphone and responded, "This is KPS, I hear you Lima Charlie."

"This is Log 6; that you Max? over" It seemed that COL Jacobson spoke without much of a drawl when using the radio.

"Roger, Log 6." Max intoned. "This is KPS 6, over"

"Self-appointed KPS 6," was Jacobson's dry, sardonic reply.

"No other choice of call signs available, so have assumed leadership call sign to identify transient role, over," was Max's somewhat pleading retort to the Colonel's jest.

"Does KPS 6 have traffic for Log 6, over?" responded Jacobson wryly.

Max grasped his zapping, static-electric-charged microphone and pressed the VOX button. "Just wanted you to know it looks like we landed a big one at our pier this morning. The storm caused about a twelve-hour delay, and the outgoing tide made passage through the channel impossible until first high tide after daylight. Final tie-up was around noon today, over."

"Sorry 'bout the Vinnell snafu on the dredging. By the time we found out about it and contacted Military Sealift Command, the ship was right around the corner from you," offered Log 6. "Our contract boys will get us a pound of flesh when those Vinnell muckety-mucks show up for their well-deserved comeuppance. But, I'm glad to hear you were able to land that big fella, over."

Max responded with, "Roger, over."

Max went on to brief COL Jacobson on the progress of initiating discharge. He included a list of concerns, including shortage of MHE, limited and primitive storage facilities, and, of course, sparse communications gear. Max emphasized his concern about lack of communications in the event of injury, attack, or other unanticipated calamity.

COL Jacobson acknowledged the concerns and assured Max that they would be top agenda items in discussions with FANK and with team planners. "Getting more MHE here may mean shifting shipment priorities, realigning the pipeline, maybe even using airlift," Jacobson ruminated out loud. "Not sure what the FANK can do for either, but we'll get the word to them that they need address the issue."

"Not sure what can be done about the commo stuff," Jacobson added. "We might have to just buy something commercial that patches into our existing network. I'll take it up with BG Clausen this evenin'. I'll get back to ya'll soonest on that one," promised Log 6. "As for the primitive FANK storage facilities, perhaps we can get FANK to go 'bout annexin' some a them pier-side stores for their use, 'specially while we got these dad-gummed deep drafters alongside. Ah'll have our log weenies take it up with them FANK staffers in the morning. What else yah got?"

"Negative further. Thanks for lending an ear, and for any future assistance you can give us on our issues. KPS 6, out," was Max's closing comment.

"Ya'll hang in there KPS 6, this is Log 6, out," as the squelch broke one last time.

CHAPTER THIRTY-THREE

*W*hen Max returned pierside, he took note that they were offloading what looked like fence posts. Pallet after pallet came over the side to waiting FANK trucks, which were heading off to the FANK warehouse. Not finding Chief Carpenter anywhere readily available, Max decided to drive to the FANK warehouse behind the next truckload of fence posts.

The Master Chief was right. The warehouse was situated on a bluff just off the highway, about halfway up a long, gradual sloping ascent to the top of an escarpment where KPS airport was located. Max could not recall seeing a warehouse on the day he arrived in KPS. When he arrived, he decided that the reason he'd missed the store was that it was an unremarkable, one-story building about five hundred feet long, and about half as wide. It had one main entrance/exit on either end. The folding doors could handle a fully-laden flat bed. Outside, there were open fields about twice the building's size on either side of the building, encircled by an almost six foot high chain link fence.

Max could readily see that outdoor storage was going to be a major issue. As Perry had surmised, there existed no paving close to the main building. Nor were there reinforced paths to the outside storage areas. Before long, even within a few hours, there would nothing but churned up mud, where the trucks had come and gone discharging cargo.

Max noticed a group of FANK soldiers trying desperately to extract one of the French LPS-powered forklifts from its muddy environs. "*What a nightmare*," thought Max, as he pessimistically envisaged the next several days.

Max then noticed a different group of soldiers who were unbundling fence posts. They were aligning them parallel, like so many match sticks, in a heroic attempt to build a makeshift pathway intended to be stable enough to support the French commercial forklifts and tactical cargo trucks, as they made their way around the fields adjoining the warehouse, without getting hopelessly stuck in the muck.

"These poor bastards are trying to achieve the effect you get with interlocking PSP sheets, as the GIs called them in Vietnam. They are essential to firm up the soil around motor parks, helipads, and warehouse areas." Max had seen the product put to good use all around Long Binh and Bien Hoa outside Saigon, especially in heavy traffic areas. They were 1/8" thick steel sheets, with flanged inch-and-a-half holes stamped out of them in rows up and down every 8'X3' sheet. Additionally, the slender sheets had notches on either side that allowed users to latch the sheets together to elongate or make a surface wider, and far, far sturdier.

Max contemplated this new issue, *"These poor devils don't have the benefit of the interlocking mechanism as with the PSP. Nor, has the ground they are laying them on been smoothed to preclude bending and sinking."*

Max had another ominous conclusion, *"This innovative FANK endeavor could even cause the offset posts to stick up in such a way that they could damage tires, or worse, the under carriages of trucks or forklifts,"* Max shuddered at the thought. Replacing vehicle oil pans and transfer cases was not high on his list of fervent wishes.

The fence posts were strongly made with hooks stamped out at various heights to allow wire to be attached. But, they were only 50" in length. The width was about 3". Max concluded, *"There had better be one helluva crop of these fence posts aboard the SeaTrain Maryland, if the FANK was going to successfully pave the fields around the KPS FANK warehouse with them anytime soon."*

"And, profuse apologies to the FANK units who were scheduled to receive fence posts in the near future," Max whispered to himself. *"And, I believe that all those damned RTFLs need to be on this end of the operation,"* concluded Max as he turned his jeep around to head back to the port.

Just then, he heard the high-pitched whine of an American diesel bouncing and chugging into the FANK warehouse receiving area. He looked up, and none other than Master Chief Carpenter and a Filipino driver presented themselves in the single seat driver's capsule of the Rough Terrain Fork Lift (RTFL). Chief Perry honked the obnoxious, screeching horn of the RTFL, as if to hail all observers. Max had to stop and get a report.

"Can I hitch a ride back to the port, Cap'n?" screamed Master Chief Carpenter the minute he hopped off what he called "this monster of modernistic technology."

"She's a 'beaut.'—Fully articulating at the hip to cut corners and fit into close spaces. That function alone will be worth its weight in precious metal when they start offloading the 50 metric tons of barrier material I just saw on the manifest. Believe it'll be that new concertina razor wire. It's strung in bundles that, when deployed, stretch 50 feet. Stowing that nasty-ass shit will have to be done by the RTFLs, no matter where in hell they decide to stash it," reported Perry Carpenter in his usual salesman's pitch.

"I'll take a dozen," Max replied in a smart-ass tone.

"Could you give me three minutes, sir," requested Carpenter. "I need to get things straight with that Filipino driver. I bet him ten bucks he couldn't figure out the controls on that hydraulic bitch before we left the port area. I lost."

"I also need to break the news to him that it might be morning before we can get another RTFL up here, along with someone to relieve him."

Perry finally emerged from the multi-lingual discussion of the FANK's forklift challenge. He hopped aboard Max's purloined quarter ton.

"But, then, it don't look like the FANK are hooked up for night operations—light sets and that shit—on this end. We may have to suspend offloading operations to deal with it. It's sure to piss off Captain Fenwick, who would undoubtedly love to be rid of our sorry asses," added the Master Chief in a way only he could put into words.

It wasn't long before Max was hearing of the manifest problems involved in de-processing an American Army RTFL. If it weren't for Perry's comical manner of expression, Max might have fallen asleep at the wheel.

The message Max did take away was that it would be at least several days before all the RTFLs were operational. Max ruminated, "*it may take as much time to offload this monster vessel as it did to load it and get it here.*"

114

"Keep Vinnell focused on getting the RTFLs operational, Perry," Max said with all deference to this highest-ranking of Navy enlisted man. Max made his point clear, "That goddamned FANK warehouse is going to be a sea of mud by tomorrow's morning light. We'll need every one of those hydraulic monsters, on station, 24/7 out there on the cliffs."

"Aye, aye, sir" was Master Chief Carpenter's sole retort.

When they arrived at the port, things appeared to be going along without problem. Max offered, "I think I'll go check in with the port folks on the Russian dredge. Why not meet me on the ship for a bite of dinner around 7 PM?"

"Great, that'll give me time to see how the de-processing is coming on the second RTFL. Any chance you can drop me at 'my' jeep outside the second pier-side store? That's where we set up shop to get these complex, technological 'angels of mercy' to descend to our most lowly plane of existence," jested the Master Chief.

"Amen, amen I say to you, that ye shall be anointed by the Most High, if ye deign to perform yet another miracle that resurrects even one of those ineffable marvels brought to our countenance by this merciful ship of deliverance, the SeaTrain Maryland," joked Max in his most preachy, comedic tone.

"Hey, I could get into this shit," he said as Max and Perry headed directly to the second pier-side store.

"Shit, in fact, I may be up all night rising to that occasion, mon Captain," was Perry's wise-ass reply. "I'm a God-fearing man, and don't you fergit it," was Perry's last comment as he climbed into his borrowed thrice-recycled M151A1 quarter-ton Jeep.

CHAPTER THIRTY-FOUR

*T*he next morning, Max found himself sprawled out on the bed at the resort. Still fully dressed, Max tried to figure how in hell he had made it back to this point as far from the port as could be? He remembered nothing from the time he begged off dinner aboard ship and left a note for Perry that he was headed back to the barn.

Yet, he had the god-awe-fullest aches running through his entire body. Max was actually concerned that he may have contracted malaria. The only mundane thing he could perform in his first hour of consciousness was to get his fatigue jacket off. In the next hour, Max struggled to get his jungle boots off. The most strenuous operation turned out to be getting his fatigue pants off.

"Woozy? Achy? Disoriented? All the above," was Max's next conscious thought. *"What the hell is going on? I have never felt so shitty since the glory days of enemas,"* Max mused in a vain attempt at self-cheering. He shuffled to the side of his bed just in time to allow him to get into a fetal position before he fell into the sack.

Max resolved to have Master Chief Carpenter check with the local medical authorities about regional diseases and their treatment the next time he saw him.

Chapter Thirty-Five

*T*he next moment of Max's consciousness was awakening to an annoying pounding sound on the outside of his wood-slatted-screen doorway.

"Cap'n Max, are you OK? Cap'n Max, you still with us? Cap'n Max, we need to come in and check you out," were Perry's pleading calls.

Max groaned, but thoughtfully cautioned, "I might be contagious. I've surely got some kind of creepin crud. Not sure what it is, but I can't keep anything down, and I need some drinking water—I'm dying of thirst. I must have sweated out twenty pounds since I talked to you last night at the pier."

"Not to point out your obvious loss of time and memory, but that meeting took place two nights ago, mon Captain," was Perry's gentle way of bringing the young Captain Donatello back to reality.

"You have been snoozing like there's no tomorrow, Mr. Van Winkle," prodded the Master Chief. "We still have an important mission to accomplish here, if you care to join us," jabbed the Master Chief with a bit of an edge to his sarcasm. "If you could find time in your busy schedule, that is." This little bit of palaver was over. Perry realized that humor needed to be put aside. Max sounded like someone poised on the dreaded edge of the abyss.

"I feel like a sorry sack of shit. But, I suppose I can be miserable just about anywhere. So, I'll meet you at the resort restaurant in about 20 minutes," said Max without much conviction.

CPT Max Donatello was now sufficiently, if woozily motivated, to get off his haunches and re-take the reins of the first-ever American deep-draft vessel delivery to the Khmer Republic. Illness or no illness, he was resolved to get cleaned up and back into the flow of life in sunny KPS.

Chapter Thirty-Six

*A*fter three glasses of orange juice, a large French omelet and two small baguettes, all washed down with what seemed like an ocean of coffee, Max felt a measure more human. He still felt achy and slightly feverish, but concluded that he could make it back to the port. After all, he could always use the cabin bequeathed to him by the honorable Captain Fenwick on the SeaTrain Maryland, in case he needed to lie down and rest. In fact, if something went awry, he would be better off there than way the hell out here at the resort. The only wrinkle was that someone needed to make the radio check late every afternoon. Perry could handle that if things got really dicey.

Max asked Perry to follow behind him in his jeep, in case he got woozy. Armed with three bottles of fizzy water stowed safely in his Jeep, they were off.

They arrived at the pier without incident, whereupon Perry suggested they use the Russian dredge vessel to get Max updated on the offload operations. Monsieur Lebecque was already on board, and, without fanfare, Perry and Rene began a detailed rundown of the past 36 hours.

"The principal obstacle is, of course, storage facilities, especially at the FANK store. The place is now awash with not only mud, but also fence posts, jutting out at every possible angle. This is a classic demonstration of the maxim that the solution to one day's emergency becomes the genesis of tomorrow's problem," remarked Master Chief Carpenter with rueful sagacity.

"Our FANK friends are decidedly game, but I am afraid that they are no match for the elements, nor the sheer enormous volume of cargo being bestowed upon them, all in a single deposit," concluded Mr. LeBecque. His non-verbal cues made him look as if he had been the last minute, gratuitously appointed defense counsel, at the court martial of a guilty-looking defendant.

Master Chief Carpenter added, "We are about two-thirds of the way completed with the offload, according to the vessel's second officer. He reports that it will be at least another 48 hours before the vessel can light her boilers."

"All the RTFLs have been de-processed and are busy off-loading trucks at the FANK warehouse. There are even a couple of promising young FANK soldiers who have caught the drift of the complicated array of levers on them. They are having the times of their lives atop these novel new monsters," Perry added with avuncular relish.

"You'd think these were his own children, the way he has adopted these FANK soldiers," said Monsieur LeBecque admiringly, in a manner that was meant to inform Max, obtusely, how impressed he had become with Perry's way with the troops.

Perry broke in as if shyly, snuffing any mention of his good deeds, while giving a smile and head nod to Monsieur LeBecque, "I am concerned that we are running way above the maintenance limits for these over-sized contraptions. They run at high RPM; two of them even have turbo-charged operations on board. We cannot simply run them into the ground. They are like aircraft, demanding periodic maintenance, based on hours of use. If we expect them to last through the offload, we need to take one or two offline at a time, changing the oil and doing some fundamental upkeep," pleaded the Master Chief.

"OK, what do we have in terms of facilities to accomplish these services?" inquired Max at his first opportunity to inject a comment.

"The FANK have a kind of an old-fashioned, in-ground service bay in one of the pier-side stores, where they do normal maintenance on fork lifts, trucks, diesels, you name it. We could run these babies over the oil change pit and get a few other things accomplished as well, not the least of which would be changing oil and cleaning filters, that sort of thing," added Perry as a sort of clincher argument.

Perry grinned a knowing grin as he heard Max's positive response. "OK, why not take the RTFL that was first de-processed offline in the morning for preventive maintenance. How are the FANK fixed for replacement oil, filters, hydraulic fluid, gaskets, etc.?" Max inquired dubiously.

"We offloaded multiple skids of engine oil and all manner of other Class III items (Petroleum, Oil, and Lubricants), and a basic load of RFTL filters in the last two days. I should think we could find what's needed in that booty to meet all requirements," declared Monsieur LeBecque.

"OK, let's arrange to get that first RTFL off the 'cliffs' [as the American contingent had started calling the FANK warehouse complex] at the first available opportunity tomorrow. Then, we can simply infiltrate these babies, one after another, as they have their periodic service performed," Max declared proudly as if it were his very own idea.

"Aye, Aye, Captain," was Master Chief Carpenter's gratified response.

Perry thought to himself, "this young Army officer has the makings of a real leader. He listens to his subordinates, does not criticize novel ideas, and, more than anything else, he supports the 'troops,' as it were, even when the stinky stuff gets hurled wily-nilly toward the fan by the powers that be."

Max soon realized that orange juice and eggs are a bad combination when administered to a tender tummy. Losing his breakfast, he spent the remainder of the day aboard the vessel in the cabin so graciously provided by Captain Fenwick. Max still felt damned woozy. The aches had returned. All he had for pain was the *Bufferin* that Emily sent him in the care packages that had arrived thus far. The latter potion was the pain reliever of choice in the Donatello family, as it had been for years in the Willis household, while Emily was growing up.

Much later, the ship's first mate, a slender, scruffy-looking Frenchman named Jake LeMonde, made a visit with the ship's onboard 'doc,' after Max failed to attend lunch or dinner, as invited.

The pharmacist mate, as they called him, took one look at Max, and said, "this man needs to be quarantined. He's running a temp of 103.5 and alternates between shivering, vomiting, and freezing. My guess is either dengue fever, or early-stage malaria. In either case, he must be isolated until the signs manifest a different determination."

The first mate said, "OK, let's get him down to sick bay and keep him isolated from all contact other than sick bay personnel." This order meant that the pharmacist mate and his orderly would be taking twelve-hour watches with Max to somehow keep the fever down. "So much for languishing on the exotic beaches of Cambodia," smirked the wise-ass first officer.

Captain Fenwick was not especially pleased to hear that he had on board an invited guest with a potentially virulent illness like typhus or typhoid. He could ill-afford to take chances, even if it was only dengue or malaria.

Fenwick turned to the first officer and said, "Jake, please pass a flash (Highest Priority) message to Military Sealift Command (MSC), informing them that we have an urgent medical situation here that could dictate our next port of call. Also, ask them to inform the American Embassy in Phnom Penh of our situation, since it involves an American officer assigned there. They may wish to execute a completely different evacuation strategy, especially if our boy Max takes a turn for the worse."

"Oh, and Jake, put it on scramble mode so we don't have every Khmer Rouge asshole within listening distance trying to make a name for himself by hijacking the SeaTrain Maryland on its first-ever port of call in Kompong Som."

The ship's secure teletype chattered relentlessly, as the word of the SeaTrain Maryland's unfortunate situation became news. AMEMB (American Embassy) Phnom Penh had sent an immediate reply informing Military Sealift Command (MSC) that Log 6 (whoever the hell that was,) was en route to KPS. Captain Fenwick asked to see the Master Chief, as soon as he could be scraped up, to apprise him of the situation.

Having no authority over a salty, old Navy E-9 was a bit frustrating for the commercial vessel's Master. A man in Fenwick's position is accustomed to being the 'Supreme Being' in the sanctuary of his vessel at sea. He was certainly not used to dealing with someone who, in the real Navy, might be an Admiral's chief enlisted man. Carpenter's lowliest possible assignment would be no lower than the 'chief of the boat', on some very large and significant vessel.

CHAPTER THIRTY-SEVEN

*C*OL Jacobson arrived at KPS at noon three days after Max had fallen ill. Monsieur LeBecque was the only one on hand to pick up Log 6, much to the good colonel's dismay.

"What in the world has happened to military protocol?" pleaded Log 6, not fully understanding all the implications of the realities on the ground at KPS. "Ah would've expected that dad-gummed Master Chief to git his dad-gummed tail feathers up here to welcome me to this 'god's little acre.'"

COL Jacobson went on in a mock tirade. "He mustah bin plumb ovah-taken by evints to uve missed his golden chance to impress me ev'un fu'thah than ah already ai-um," exclaimed the seemingly agitated Texas gentleman of an Army Colonel.

"No need for worry, *mon colonel, monsieur* the Master Chief is involved in the transfer of our MHE, as you call it. It seems we have been using it beyond its specifications. So, Chief Carpenter has instituted a program of *rotatiacione* [rotation] of the large rough terrain forklifts for what he calls '*maintenance necessicere' por le vie de les* RTFLs, as you call zem," proffered LeBecque, as if pleading for the Master Chief's absolution for failure to meet the American Colonel.

Mr. LeBecque went on to explain in his limited English lexicon that there were no facilities at the FANK stores to perform the many maintenance functions called for in the manuals to keep the RTFLs operational. It was already manifest that they were absolutely essential to the offload and storage operation.

Without them, the colonel was informed in no uncertain terms, that the SeaTrain Maryland would be looking at another couple of weeks of offloading time. By that time, it would surely be irretrievably ensconced in the pier-side muck, which leads to the as-yet-un-dredged channel.

Monsieur LeBecque described Captain Fenwick's concern about the force of suction on the bottom of a vessel stuck in the muck, with a keel footprint as large as that of the SeaTrain Maryland. *"Le Captiaine* Fenwick suggested that it may take zee *Star Ship Enterprise* herself, *avec les* grappling hooks, *avec* zee full warp-drive thrusters, to lift zees vessel off the bottom," declared Monsieur LeBecque, expressing serious concern about getting the SeaTrain Maryland out of this overwhelming pierside debacle.

"Capitaine Fenwick weeshes me to convey his compliments, and his sincere wish that you could join heem in zee wardroom *de les officiers* aboard the vessel today," added Monsieur LeBecque, struggling with proper English phraseology.

COL Jacobson threw his bag and briefcase into the open jeep and climbed in next to Monsieur LeBecque, who had positioned himself behind the wheel. As they began the slow descent off the escarpment toward the town and port of KPS, Log 6 asked about Max's condition.

Monsieur LeBecque updated Log 6 on the report he had heard that morning at breakfast on board from the first officer, Jake LeMonde. It appeared that Max was still struggling with fever and constant achiness. The fever had dropped to 100.8, but Max was still having trouble keeping food down.

Log 6 said, "Let's head to the port. I want to meet Captain Fenwick and get his perspective on the offloading situation, as well as to check on our boy Max," in almost dialect-free American English. It seemed that COL Jacobson had a way of turning his southern drawl on and off at will, depending on who was on the receiving end of his pretentious attempts at a southern gentleman's manner of speech.

CHAPTER THIRTY-EIGHT

*A*s they made their way down the long descent, they approached the FANK warehouse. LeBecque asked Log 6 if he would like to stop and see the ongoing off-load proceedings occurring there nearly around the clock. Rene added that they might encounter the Master Chief along the way, as he was scheduled to help with the RTFL equipment rotation.

"No, let's trudge ahead, Rene; I'm anxious to get to the port to assess Max's situation. I need to update BG Clausen this afternoon," was Jacobson's cryptic reply.

*   *   *

Less than a half mile beyond the FANK store, LeBecque and Jacobson came upon an ungodly sight. Just off the road in a concrete drainage culvert was an overturned RTFL, and, lying in a grotesque position about 50 feet away, was Master Chief Perry Carpenter, who obviously had been tossed off the overturning forklift.

"He must have lost hydraulic power," suggested Log 6. "It is essential to the braking function on these behemoths."

As the jeep ground to a halt, Jacobson was out of the vehicle in a flash, headed straight for the Master Chief. Carpenter looked as if he had landed on his right shoulder and, generally, the right side of his body. His torso had landed on the turf above the culvert, while his legs had slammed into the concrete as he came to rest in a curled-up, almost fetal position. It was as though he might have been conscious for a time after the mishap and had been reaching for his legs when he blacked out.

"His breathing is labored, he must be in a lotta pain, poor devil," was Log 6's initial assessment. "Rene, could you go back to the FANK store and commandeer one of those flat beds and about six strong guys to help get the Master Chief gingerly aboard, and then hold him down till we get him to the closest medical facility?" inquired Log 6 in a diplomatic, yet commanding tone.

Rene hustled faster than he had moved in more than thirty-five years, as he breathlessly mounted the jeep and hooked a U-turn on the sparsely-used roadway. "I shall return directly," was Rene's only comment.

It was about fifteen excruciating minutes before the FANK relief expedition started to arrive, with Rene nobly in the lead of what seemed like an oncoming column of vehicles.

"All we needed was a flat bed and a few soldiers," remarked COL Jacobson dryly.

"These are zee Master Chief's Khmer *amis*, buddies as you call zem, mon Colonel. Monsieur Perry is much loved by *tout les* FANK *ici*. They would carry him to safety on their backs, eef *ces't necessaire*," proclaimed Rene, trying graciously to give Log 6 a gauge of how high a regard the FANK had developed for Carpenter in these harried days.

"Well, let's get him aboard the truck, and do it damned carefully; he's a hurt'in, 'don't cha' know? *Tout suite*," commanded the newest senior officer in KPS, who possessed only the slightest command of French.

Rene related the order to the miniscule FANK lieutenant who had left his post to address this crisis. The lieutenant said something in French to Rene, and to the top FANK soldier of those there. In a very authoritative, efficient way, this FANK officer was setting in motion the steps that would keep Perry alive for the foreseeable future.

Within minutes the small convoy was headed to the only 'medical facility' in the area, a small clinic on the outskirts of the town of KPS. There were supposedly two trained orderlies present at all the times, and a Khmer doctor, who came to the clinic on an on-call basis. COL Jacobson was assured that Perry would be in good hands.

Upon arrival, COL Jacobson realized that the horror had only just begun. He had never before seen a Khmer medical facility, much less being in charge of delivering a seriously injured American senior NCO to a place that would match the obscene dread of a novel like *Murder at the Rue Morgue*, or some other spectacle of abject, intentional medical horror.

The place literally reeked of urine and some putrid antiseptic. No bed or cot was clean enough to be worthy of an injured American's future health to attempt the transfer of his broken body onto this odious cushion.

"Can this be the best we have?" inquired Log 6 with extreme exasperation. "If we don't get this man back to Phnom Penh by morning, there will be no more tomorrows for Master Chief Carpenter. Get some clean blankets, and completely cover one of those cots, so that no part of his body touches the surface of the cot," ordered Log 6 emphatically.

Monsieur LeBecque transmitted the Colonel's wishes to the FANK soldiers and the orderlies present. COL Jacobson worried, "It was still more than four hours before the regularly scheduled radio check with AMEMB Phnom Penh. How in hell can we alert MEDTC that we have not one, but two serious medical emergencies that require immediate attention? What about that damned vessel at the port; don't they have a secure teletype apparatus to get a message to MSC?" asked Log 6 recalling having received an earlier report of Max's sickly state. "I'm gonna saddle up and get over there to that ship to use their tele type. Rene, please stay here and make sure these folks handle Chief Carpenter in a most tender and careful manner," intoned the Colonel on his way out of the wretched medical clinic.

Jacobson said a prayer to himself, "Lord, ah implore You to keep a gentle and watchful eye on the Master Chief, whilst I go off to tend to his worldly disposition, and I offer my thanks in advance for Your Kind Intercession in this grave mattuh."

---

Chapter Thirty-Nine

*L*og 6 hustled up the SeaTrain Maryland's gangway and asked the first crewman who appeared to be a part of the ship's compliment where he could find Captain Fenwick. The seaman grabbed a deck phone and got the information for COL Jacobson.

"The ship's Master will meet you in the officers' wardroom, and hopes you will take the noon meal with him, sir. I will escort you to that area of the ship, if you will please follow me," suggested the seaman, who had very effectively come off like a fawning steward on a cruise ship.

On meeting Captain Fenwick, COL Jacobson shook his hand with vigor. "Mighty kind of you, Captain, to host me so soon after my arrival, and, thanks for the invite to lunch, but before the meal, could I impose on you to have a secure TWX sent via MSC to the Embassy in Phnom Penh. There's been a serious accident involving Master Chief Carpenter on one of the new forklifts." COL Jacobson filled Captain Fenwick in on the events of the past hour and expressed the need for immediate evacuation for Carpenter, and possibly Donatello.

Captain Fenwick immediately gave first officer Jake LeMonde instructions to send another secure, flash priority teletype describing the emergency medical condition of the two Americans, and the evacuation requirement for Carpenter, if not Max as well. LeMonde departed the wardroom, and headed immediately to the bridge, where the tele type apparatus was installed.

Captain Fenwick invited Log 6 to be seated as the steward began serving the lunch's first course. Fenwick and Jacobson took their time getting acquainted. Jacobson admitted this was his first experience aboard a first-line merchant vessel. Fenwick promised Jacobson a tour after their meal. The steward served an outstanding pottage of split pea and ham, followed by an entrée of medallions of beef tenderloin, adorned with a hearty Béarnaise sauce, tiny Yukon Gold potatoes, and an array of sautéed seasonal vegetables acquired on the last day at their last port of call.

COL Jacobson was duly impressed by the exquisite cuisine. "It's like experiencing fine dining in a godforsaken corner of the world where no one would expect it, like on an African safari, perhaps. My compliments to the chef and to you, Captain Fenwick, for clearly demonstrating your good taste in having him along," gushed Log 6, who had seemed to forget the purpose for his visit. "Unquestionably delectable; Five-Star; where on earth did you find him?" queried the American Colonel with an almost obsequious tone of admiration.

Before Captain Fenwick could respond, first officer LeMonde came through the passage waving a message. "I have already heard back from MSC. It seems BG Clausen had planned an unannounced visit to a large unit just north of KPS early tomorrow. MEDTC and AMEMB had scheduled two Air-American helicopters with the mission to ferry a large group of officers from Phnom Penh to the unit's location. It also states that BG Clausen has booted the officers off the second Huey. It will 'dead-head' to this location to pick up the two MEDEVAC candidates. They request landing coordinates."

COL Jacobson inserted, "Please tell them I will provide that information via Single Side Band radio this afternoon during the normally scheduled radio check. This interval will give me time to assess this situation further. Thank you, Monsieur LeMonde. I fear we have completely messed up your lunch today."

"A leetle excitement spices up zee uzzerwise routine day alongside zee pier, mon colonel. One can eat anytime. To be of serveece is mon pleazure, indeed," was the honorable reply of first officer LeMonde.

"Captain, I must decline the gracious offer of a tour of this wonderful vessel in deference to my duties. I thank you most earnestly for one of the finest meals I've had since arriving in Cambodia. Would you mind if I visited Captain Donatello instead?" asked Log 6 deferentially.

"He's been a pretty sick pup, but we seem to have the fever broken. That's a good sign. He has been hooked up to an IV for fluids for the last couple of days. Our ship has no means to test his blood to see what caused the illness. Neither malaria nor dengue fever is contagious, so we have been concerned that it might be something virulent. Since none of my medical staff have demonstrated any symptoms since Max came aboard, it gives me a pretty high degree of confidence that he is not infectious. Besides, he probably got dengue from a bug bite. Thankfully, the infection has only manifested itself in Max. So, I think it's OK to go down to sick bay. You understand that I am not allowed to accompany you down there. In accordance with the terms of my contract and license, it is very clear about how a vessel's master must act during an episode like this one. I hope you will forgive me," added Captain Fenwick with clear regret.

"No apologies necessary. Thank you again for the amazing hospitality you've demonstrated, not only to me, but also my contingent down here. I will insure that the authorities at MSC take note of the extent of your efforts to assist this operation," said COL Jacobson with genuine enthusiasm.

Captain Fenwick grabbed a wall phone and almost immediately an orderly appeared. "Please show my friend, COL Jacobson, to sick bay. I will notify the pharmacist mate that that the Colonel has my permission for a brief visit."

Fenwick turned to Jacobson and said, "Let us know where and when to deliver Cap'n Max in the morning, so he doesn't miss his evacuation chopper. Oh, by the way, if you wish to stay aboard tonight, I will have a guest cabin prepared," suggested Fenwick.

"I will let you know after I know where the LZ is established, and we have an approximate pick up time. Thanks again for your gracious hospitality, for everything," was Log 6's last remark before heading down to sick bay.

CHAPTER FORTY

$\mathcal{M}$ ax was still drowsy when the pharmacist mate attempted to bring him around. "Who is coming to visit? Was I expecting someone? Damned if I can remember last evening when you brought me down here," exclaimed Max, incredulously.

"Sorry again, Cap'n Max, but you have been keeping us entertained down here since night before last," responded the medic sardonically.

Max was struggling to remember this young man's name. He peered up to try to read his nametag, but, things were definitely still fuzzy in the sight department, and in the memory division, as well.

Just then, he heard the unmistakable drawl of his Army boss, COL John Jacobson, "The Mast-ah a this he-ah tub has accused yo' sorry aye-us ah malingerin', young warrior. What'cha got to say in yer defense? Do ah hay-uve to come day-un he-ah to give you an ol'fashioned suth'in whuppin' to get you off'n 'yo tail feathuhs an' git this ol' scow unloaded, and the Hades outta this he-ah poe-ut," inquired Log 6 in his thickest tongue-in-cheek drawl.

"Guilty as charged, mon colonel," responded Max, "Where do I report for this whuppin?" asked Max Donatello in the tone of a supplicant.

"Well, ah've not decided wuther ah should conduct this here whuppin' in pra-vit, or to do it in a public squay-ah, to warn uhth-ah slack-uhs that such trech'ry will not be tolerated."

Abruptly breaking up the repartee, Log 6 said, "How the hell are you, Max? You had us worried there up in MEDTC-World HQ."

"Don't know what hit me, sir. One minute I was planning to meet the Master Chief onboard for dinner, and the next I was in la-la land, sicker than a dog, and achier than a flu-ridden leper. I got here feeling woozy, drowsy, nauseated, and feverish. I honestly don't know what in hell is happening. I do know that I need to get the hell outta this dungeon and get to work, but I'm physically worthless," Max said, with considerable guilt in his voice.

Log 6 immediately broke in, "You don't fret yo-sehf. Y'all a 'bin thew a real bout of the ter'ble-awfuls. We gonna see 'bout gittin' you the heck outta he-ah in the morning. Yo-ah papa-daddy, Genril Clausen is sending us a MEDEVAC chopp-ah down he-ah to take ya'll to Phnom Penh for some real medical attention."

Max grew suspicious and asked, "Was that ya'll singular or plural, mon Colonel?"

CPT Donatello was not yet aware that it was Log 6 and Monsieur LeBecque who had policed up the injured Master Chief on the hillside site of the RTFL accident. COL Jacobson carefully gave Max the highly redacted version of the wreck that they had happened upon as they made their way from KPS airport to the port of KPS. Log 6 finally answered Max's questions about Perry's whereabouts and condition. "We gonna git the two a yuz the hell back to civilization a-fore you make a wust spectacle o' yo-selves," kidded Jacobson, back in his turbo-drawl.

"What about getting the vessel unloaded and outta here," queried Max.

"All in due time, young Cap'n. Don't you fret none. In the end, it is the FANK's problem. I'll stick around he-ah 'til the offloadin' is completely accomplished. Aftah thay-it, we gon' go back to deliverin' military equipment, just like our name says," concluded Log 6 in his inimitable way of simplifying things.

Max closed his eyes and thought about how easy it was to get your role confused in an operation like this. COL Jacobson was right. The role of MEDTC was that of handing over title to military gear that the US was providing to the Khmer Republic. Then, our role officially switched to overseeing its proper use.

What was specifically **not** the role of MEDTC, was advising, or carrying out functions, which should be led, managed, and executed by the FANK Armed Forces.

Max knew, in his heart of hearts, that the roles that he and the Master Chief had played were unquestionably advisory. In fact, there were times that they performed the essential leadership functions that would ensure a successful offload. Reflecting on whether he would change any of his, or Perry's, actions, *"If we were allowed to relive, by some God-given universal dispensation, these past several long days, we'd have done it all over again,"* Max concluded with unspoken conviction.

 Max's thoughts magnified this conclusion. *"There would never have been an offload without our guidance and personal intervention, on occasion. On the other hand, Perry would not be lying in a dump of a dispensary if we had followed the rules to a T,"* pondered Max, with wistful self-judgment. So, the question became one of choices: accomplish the mission the Army way, or abide by the rules of engagement? It was the MEDTC conundrum, in all its radiant glory.

COL Jacobson asked again about how Max felt.

"Thirsty and desperately hungry, but not bad beside that. Those awful aches seem to have subsided somewhat. They were the worst I've ever experienced. They turned my gut into knots. I couldn't keep anything down. Then, I'd feel alternately like I was in an oven, until I was sweating my guts out. Then, I'd be clamoring for blankets to ward off the chills. I'd call this condition the winter-summer flop-side flu, if I had to lay a name to it.

Max continued, "In my stupor, I saw complete replays of the wayward B-52 bombing of Neak Leoung, over and over again. Sometimes, I'd get to a wounded civilian, only to see someone worse off. I wasn't sure if it was the dengue, or my subconscious re-processing that 48 hours of abject horror," confessed Max. "It sure seemed real in those fever-dreams of the last day or so."

"You need to let go a that dream, Max, my friend," offered Log 6. "It was an unspeakable nightmare with roots in real life. You need to tell yourself that you acquitted yourself honorably there, far beyond what anyone could possibly expect. You need to take a lesson from your conscious reaction to that event, and to this, as well. You do a superb job dealing with the nasty realities that you encounter, but, I'm concerned about how you deal with them on a more fundamental, personal level."

"Ah ain't no psychologist, mind yah, but I do believe you have hay-ud yo-ah shay-ah a ugliness fo-ah the tahm bein'," COL Jacobson lapsed back into his so'thun way a speakin', as anyone else might turn a hose on to water the garden.

CHAPTER FORTY-ONE

At the crack of dawn, Max had been resurrected from sick bay and carried to the deck by four strapping young FANK soldiers. Four more replaced the first group for the treacherous traverse down the gangway. Always tuned to irony Max thought it a bit absurd to drag him up three or four decks to the main deck, only so they could tug and pull the stretcher precariously down the bloody gangway.

As it turned out, this normally ubiquitous device, the gangway, was particularly ill-suited for safely carrying a litter-borne patient of Max's hulking size. There were several steps on the downward trek where Max fully expected to be dumped into the narrow space between the pier and the SeaTrain Maryland.

Max had experienced a bad dream in one of his recent fever-driven fantasies. It seemed that he had actually stooped too far over the pier and fallen ignominiously into the pier-side abyss. His dream envisioned ink-swaddled squid and a man-eating monster squid surrounding him, just like in Disney's classic, *20,000 Leagues Under the Sea*. As Captain Ahab reported, "this is one of the most tenacious of all sea beasts," in George Mason's most convincing, pseudo-British noble dialect. Max's dream trailed off with Kirk Douglas strumming, "I've got a whale of a tale to tell you lads—a whale of a tale or two." For Max, it was then, of course, darkness….

Max shivered at the thought. Then, he caught a glimpse of the entourage carrying Perry to the LZ. It appeared that the Master Chief was caked in his own blood and wasn't making any movements except a sort of heaving motion of his chest to indicate he was thankfully still struggling to breathe. Their two litters came together, and Max reached to touch the Master Chief.

Perry actually turned to him and rasped, "Fucking RTFLs."

"Hang in there, Master Chief. The evacuation chopper is just over the horizon. You'll hear the blade pop shortly," encouraged Max. Just then, the wop-wop of rotor blades made the peaceful morning come to attention, as the Air America-Bell UH-1H made its presence known for all to see in the KPS environs. All, including Log 6, were surprised to see not one, but two of these silver birds whirling their way earthward in a steep descent, where several FANK soldiers had outlined an LZ (Landing Zone), with colored flags at each corner. An enthusiastic FANK LZ-coordinator flapped yet another pennant, as if to magically guide the helicopter so it responded to his every waving, opaque directive.

The first one to hit the ground looked pretty much loaded, but, in the prime passenger seat with headset at the ready, sat BG Rex B. Clausen, who promptly pulled off the headgear and jumped off the chopper in full stride, heading to the two casualties. He took one look at Max and flashed a "we've got to quit meeting this way," sort of grin. He scurried directly to the Master Chief, whispered something close to his ear, then turned and pointed to the approaching UH-1H, then to Max, and then to Perry, as if to say, "there's your ride back to civilization. You've earned it."

Later in the AMEMB dispensary when Max was back in Phnom Penh, recovering from his dengue fever ordeal, he awoke startled to this remarkable revelation of an idea. "Who in God's dominion is ever going to refuse an American Brigadier General, who is offering you a lift out of a hellacious situation to a cozy safe one, in this case, behind the walls of the US Embassy? Not any stranded and injured, still-sane American soul anywhere on this earthly trek," was Max's conclusion. And then, he was back to slumber.

Chapter Forty-Two

$\mathcal{T}$ he word around MEDTC was that the opening of the port at KPS was a remarkable achievement. A new LOC was now opened to bring wholesale levels of supplies to the embattled FANK. The trick would be how to distribute this cornucopia of military aid in accordance with the needs of the force structure that had been drawn up for Khmer forces by their earnest endowers from the West. It was not without concern that a relatively significant representative fraction of this largesse would inevitably find its way into the hands of the Khmer Rouge.

The truth was that valuable, scarce commodities like POL (Petroleum, Oils, and Lubricants) and barrier material were immediately earmarked for distribution. Weapons and vehicles migrated to top of the list whenever they arrived in large quantities.

Since ammunition was arriving routinely from Vietnam to Phnom Penh via Mekong barge convoys, that LOC became the principal source of ammo supply, distributed to units from supply stores in the capital area.

Max's arrival back in Phnom Penh allowed him a couple of days to sort mail, open care packages, and listen to Emily's latest tapes to him. She was, of course, not aware of his illness, and wouldn't be for at least two weeks. It took that long to get Max's tape from the Cambodian Embassy pouch to the Army Post Office in Saigon. Then, it would take the remaining time to get the tape describing his illness and the travails of KPS from Cambodia to Virginia.

Still shaky after the bout with dengue fever, Max took special care to sound relaxed and upbeat on this important tape. The tape was long on describing symptoms and side effects, and short on how badly it had wiped him out. Max also omitted the required evacuation from KPS, and he left out the whole episode of his friend Perry's accident.

Emily, in her latest recording, had taped a whole dinner party with her parents, allowing everyone, including their toddler, Chris, and infant

Melissa to babble their best wishes to their daddy far away. Emily saved
the last part of the tape for after the party when children had been put
snuggly into their cribs. Max savored these moments, and this particular tape made him both happy and proud, but also mildly aroused by
Emily's suggestive manner of speech.

Emily was a master at making Max feel like the most virile, wanted, and
loved person on the planet.

CHAPTER FORTY-THREE

*M*aster Chief Petty Officer Perry Carpenter was air-evac'd to Subic Bay in the Philippines after his wounds and infections were stabilized in the Embassy infirmary. Max saw him to wish him God speed on the morning of his evacuation. In truth, in spite of his native good spirits and positive outlook, Max thought he looked like shit, but he prayed that the Naval medical establishment would nurse him back to health.

Max wasn't sure what his next priority would be, now that the deep-draft LOC was established. Another logistics Captain had arrived to backfill Major Hardt, whom Max had evacuated and supplanted. It was almost immediately announced that the new logistics Captain would assume oversight of offload operations at KPS and Phnom Penh port as his principal duties. Max's focus would be on getting caught up on EIUIs.

BG Clausen was still hounding the senior Log folks to redouble their efforts in the direction of End Item Utilization Inspections (EIUIs). Max was beginning to feel the natural ebb and flow of American political pressure. Pundits offered commentary from about every stateside news source demanding that the Nixon administration perform some kind of hat trick to quell the growing dissonance that underscored the continuing US presence in SE Asia.

The bombing of Cambodia was another issue that made the administration look like it was speaking out of both sides of its mouth. Nixon had halted the bombing of North Vietnam in an effort to entice the North to crank up the stalled Paris Peace Talks. However, throughout 1972, the bombing in Cambodia only intensified, especially near the Cambodia/Vietnam border. Even Kissinger's "Peace is at Hand" speech on the eve of the presidential election was played down in the media, as the bombing in Cambodia went on relentlessly.

The pace of EIUIs also intensified. Max was scheduled for one every ten days in the fall of 1972. This pace was furious, when you consider there were now about 90 officers assigned to MEDTC forward at the

American Embassy in Phnom Penh, and, the frustrated MEDTC front office was clamoring for real, hard evidence showing that the FANK forces were properly using the Military Assistance Program hardware and weapons systems in keeping with the terms set out in Congress's 1971 Cooper-Church Amendment. Hopefully, this evidence would keep Congress from pulling the plug on support to the Khmer Republic.

Max had been on only one EIUI thus far in his tour in Cambodia. His detachment to get the deep-draft port open in KPS had taken him out of the normal rotation for EIUIs. Max's only one was so far was where an incredibly off-target B-52 had made Neak Leoung look like the surface of the moon, not to mention the body parts strewn in every direction.

CHAPTER FORTY-FOUR

On the way to the embassy on the morning before his next adventure, Max and MAJ Bethke were on a routine trip from the villa to the Embassy. They coincidentally pulled in behind the Ambassador's entourage as they turned onto a long Boulevard about two miles from the Embassy.

This entourage had two armed motorcycle guards out front. Then, there was a lead car with an American Marine driver and three heavily-armed American Marines, all of whose lives were sworn to protect Ellsworth Hightower, US Ambassador to the Khmer Republic. They were simply leading the way to the Embassy. Next, in the procession was the Ambassador's car, with a Marine riding shotgun, and two more armed FANK motorcycles trailing the entourage. They were all in touch with the others via closed-channel radios.

Max wasn't paying attention when the explosion occurred. MAJ Bethke noticed what appeared to be a cyclo-taxi filled with charcoal had been left by the side of the road. In truth, it was a command-detonated, improvised explosive device (IED). In practical terms, it was a roadside bomb, timed perfectly to take out the first two motorcycles and the lead car. The trailing motorcycles were knocked off their mounts, but seemed to recover quite quickly.

Two Marines struggled out of the rear of the lead car with weapons at the ready. The other two appeared either dead or severely incapacitated. The Ambassador's car pulled forward, and its doors opened for the two surviving Marines. Before the doors closed, the big Lincoln limousine burst away from the scene like a bolt, the trailing FANK motorcycles making a valiant attempt to keep up.

Max and Major Bethke knew that they could be entering an ambush KZ (kill zone) if this was, indeed, an all out attack, intended to complete the mission of taking out the American Ambassador. MAJ Hank Bethke seemed to sense that this target was simply one of opportunity. If there had been a full-fledged ambush, there would have been fire from all directions after the explosion, eliminating the Marines from the lead vehicle, and finishing off the trail party. That not being the case, he ordered the driver of their vehicle to stop to render assistance to those fallen.

It was an ugly scene. The two lead motorcycle-borne guards had taken the initial brunt of the blast. The scene reminded Max of the stench he'd experienced right after the wayward B-52 had rendered human life a matter of random selection in Neak Leoung. There wasn't much left of either the motorcycles or the two men who proudly led the entourage through the edgy morning traffic in Phnom Penh on this unfortunate morning. Assessing the situation, Max and the good Major focused on the two remaining Marines in the lead vehicle.

The blast had emanated from the right side of the entourage. The car behind the lead motorcycles was severely demolished on its right front side. The entire right front wheel assembly was missing when Max arrived at what had once been a sedan's passenger front door. The Marine guard was hanging from his three-point seat belt, badly wounded, emitting a gurgling sound endemic to upper chest injuries, involving perhaps a collapsed lung. Otherwise, he seemed in one piece. He did have a nasty-looking head injury.

Max yelled, "We need to get this one to the embassy clinic pronto. He's having trouble breathing, and I think he may have a punctured lung. I'm going to try to load him in our sedan, as soon as I can get him unlatched from this goddamned sling of a seat belt assembly." Max finally took out a bolo knife from his briefcase and made quick work of the seat belt.

Once Max had the Marine on the ground, he noticed that the gasping, gurgling noise had subsided. Under the sheen on the blood from his head wound, the Marine was turning scarlet. Max started CPR and got the gurgling to re-start. The Marine was like a limp rag. Max yelled for assistance from his sedan's FANK driver.

MAJ Bethke yelled out that the driver was simply out of it, knocked cold from hitting his head on the windshield as the car came to an abrupt stop. "I'm going to try to extricate him, but he's one burly dude"

"Let's do one at a time," suggested Max, "and let's do it together. My ass is still dragging from the KPS expedition," referring to his dengue-fever experience in Kompong Som a week or so before today.

"You got it," MAJ Bethke quickly agreed. Bethke was 6'3", and weighed all of 180 pounds soaking wet. If anyone was going to struggle with an injured client of any heft, it was MAJ Bethke, especially when the patient weighed about fifty pounds more than he did.

Max, Bethke, and their driver got the Marine who rode shotgun into their sedan. They then hustled over to the driver's side to witness the enormity of their joint task. Bethke suggested, "Let's ease him out onto the pavement, then we can figure out how to get him aboard our sedan.

This process took a full ten minutes. As the giant Marine was laid out on the roadway, Max caught a glimpse of movement in the Marine's arms and legs. Then, like a drugged wildcat coming off the high of a tranquilizing dart that downed a dangerous wild animal, the huge Marine bolted up as if to say, "No one is relocating me this morning."

This kind of hostile response, of course, meant that lifting or dragging the woozy Marine would be rejected as a course of action. It appeared that the Marine had a huge dent in his forehead, and his right arm was hanging limp. Nor could the oversized Marine remember where he was, or how he got here. It took MAJ Behtke's best command voice to convince the flustered Marine to join them in his sedan on the short trek remaining to the safety of the Embassy compound. The stocky Marine finally came to his senses, when he observed his buddy struggling for air in the back seat of the MEDTC sedan. Just then, another blast shook the landscape adjacent to the scene of the IED. A two-story, concrete-faced building just to the right where the cyclo-bomb was parked erupted in an outward explosion strewing all manner of debris onto the roadway in front of the sedan that was now laden with two seriously injured Marines and two very shaken up Army officers, who were expecting a leisurely morning drive to the American Embassy.

The driver had to back up two car lengths to get his sedan sufficiently clear of the rubble from the building's streetward expulsion of building debris. MAJ Bethke ordered their driver to haul ass, with no stops before they arrived at the US Embassy. Max had never seen this particular FANK soldier drive so aggressively. With clenched teeth, which ultimately caused Max a throbbing headache afterward, they arrived at the AMEMB without further incident.

CHAPTER FORTY-FIVE

*L*ater in the day, COL Jacobson came into the small office space shared by Max, Hank Bethke, and two other MEDTC logistics officers. He intoned, "Seems the American Ambassador to the Khmer Republic would like you, MAJ Bethke, and yo-se'f, Cap'n Max, to join him in his office, forthwith. In addition, BG Clausen requests that you stop by his office to allow him to escort the two a you sterlin' lads to 'God's Little Acre,' way up thay-ah. The Gen'ril would like me tuh make shoo-ah that you two young heroes don' git lost on yo-uh way to MEDTC HQ, which is down-stay-uz of way-ah the Am-bass-a-door has his office."

So without comment, the three marched out of the leaky MEDTC Butler Building to the main embassy office building fifty yards away. They virtuously stopped to pick up the general. Then, they were hastened to climb three flights of stairs at a double-time cadence, behind the undoubtedly oldest officer of them all, BG Rex Clausen. Without so much as heavy breathing, Clausen identified himself to the Marine guard outside the executive level of the embassy, without a trace of condescension. They were directed immediately into Ambassador Hightower's office.

Mr. Hightower was the first to speak, "Gentlemen, please come in and sit down. I have asked you here to offer my sincere thanks for the selfless measures you took this morning to rescue members of my personal security team, after the IED attack on our little entourage. Your decisive action, as it turns out, saved the life of one of the most dedicated and long-serving members of my team. You may not know that both of those Marines came with me from Africa, where we were all last stationed. They are like real members of my family. I have been with them daily for the last three and a half years. I trust them with my life. The burly one is in intensive care, as it appears his head injury is far more severe than first assessed, and his whole right rib cage was smashed, as was his collar bone and right shoulder."

Max could see that this expression was of genuine appreciation. He could not help but say, "The Marine Corps is famous for never leaving anyone behind. That anthem was going through my mind today after the IED was detonated. I know MAJ Bethke felt the same way. We simply had to get these brave Americans to a safe harbor, if you will pardon an Army officer's use of a nautical expression."

By this time BG Clausen burst forth. "Mr. Ambassador, you may recall that it was Captain Donatello who most recently oversaw the opening of the deep-draft LOC at KPS?"

Mr. Hightower seemed to perk up. "Let me get this straight. You two officers were the heroes of Neak Leoung, then, Captain Donatello and the intrepid Master Chief Carpenter, isn't it, made history in opening the port of Kompong Som to provide a much-needed deep-draft port for the FANK? And how are you feeling after your bout with dengue fever, Captain Donatello?"

"Getting along much better, these days, Mr. Ambassador," was Max's perfunctory reply.

"And now, the intrepid team of Donatello and Bethke were reunited again in yet another selfless act of valor, making the best of a truly ugly situation on our route to work this morning. Our country already owes you a very large debt of gratitude. General Clausen, would you please allow me to endorse a very robust recommendation for some very distinguished decoration for these two brave men?" proposed the American Ambassador.

BG Clausen responded by saying, " Mr. Ambassador, I have just received the Army's Soldier's Medals for both Bethke and Donatello, for their selfless and heroic actions on behalf of Khmer soldiers and citizens at Neak Leoung. Now, it appears that the two will be recommended for the Silver Star Medal for their actions, pardon the expression, 'cleaning up the battlefield,' this morning, exposing themselves, saving those two wounded Marines, and evacuating them to safety."

Truth be told, BG Clausen was at that very minute, seriously considering a recommendation for the Legion of Merit (LOM) for Max's extraordinary performance under exceptional adversity in KPS. The LOM was traditionally reserved for senior officers (COL and BG), as recognition for years of continuous achievements from assignments of increasing responsibility. General Clausen mused, "This young Captain is going to go home with a stack of ribbons, like no other logistics officer this general officer has ever seen, except one perhaps, his esteemed father-in-law, Colonel Herb Willis."

Ambassador Hightower quickly inserted, "You really must fill me in on the lineage and honor that accrue to the distinguished family, even the in-laws, of this remarkable young officer," giving BG Clausen an opening.

But, he went on regaining his momentum on the previous train of thought, the Ambassador exclaimed, "By Jove, we need to insure those decorations get approved very quickly. I wish to attend the award ceremony, and it should occur quickly. In fact, I will be speaking to Admiral McCain later this morning, and I will ask his permission to make the award as a Vocal Order of the Commanding General (VOCG), under his four-star authority, pending the necessary follow-up documentation, which we can provide later for the record. That way, we can award both medals at the ceremony. Perhaps, we could even make the award this Friday when Vice President Agnew is here for his visit with President Lon Nol.

I will get back to you, General Clausen, about these matters after luncheon today," added the normally dignified Ambassador in a gleeful expression, obviously pleased with his own inspiration, and this rare opportunity to plow through the military bureaucracy, cut red tape, and get exactly what he wanted.

A man of his word, Ambassador Ellsworth Hightower arranged not only the approval of the Silver Star Medal for both Major Henry Bethke and Captain Max Donatello, but he had inserted the award ceremony into Vice President Spiro Agnew's tight itinerary in Phnom Penh that coming Friday.

CHAPTER FORTY-SIX

*A*t precisely 11:30 AM on Friday, CPT Max Donatello and MAJ Hank Bethke stood stiffly at attention, next to BG Clausen in the foyer of the American Embassy building, as Mr. Hightower briskly escorted the Vice President of the United States to a place where they stood opposite the three officers who were dressed in black slacks; white, short-sleeved dress shirts; and dark, conservative ties. The Ambassador and Vice- President were attired in tropical-weight summer suits, with jacket and tie, of course.

The foyer was crowded and noisy, with a din of gossipy dissonance, with members of MEDTC, the Marine Guard detachment, and a smattering of Embassy officials. COL Throckmorton, BG Clausen's deputy, quieted the assembly when he loudly intoned, "Attention to orders."

He then read the CINCPAC General Orders awarding each of the two officers the Soldier's Medal for ineffably gallant, valorous actions at Neak Leoung, which saved countless lives of FANK soldiers, their families, and local civilians. He then read aloud the citation that chronicled the officers' heroic actions of those harrowing days and nights after the errant B-52 strike. Upon completion of the citation, he handed the medals to Ambassador Hightower, who in turn offered them, one at a time, to the Vice President for him to make the presentation.

"On behalf of President Nixon, and the people of your country, I wish to express America's sincere appreciation to you both for your conspicuous valor at the scene of the unfortunate, mistaken bombing of Neak Leoung." He then pinned the Soldier's Medal on each of the pockets of their dress shirts.

COL Throckmorton then announced the next orders, and read the citations for award of the Silver Star for each of the two young officers. The dignitaries repeated the previous award process, which allowed Mr. Agnew to present the actual awards.

"Gentlemen, your actions earlier this week have been related to me fully by Ambassador Hightower, who thank God, was not himself injured in the attack on his entourage. Your gallant actions, without regard to your own safety, in an unsecure kill zone, are most admirable. I am so very proud to have had the opportunity to make this presentation to recognize those intrepid actions," added the Vice-President, as he pinned a Silver Star Medal just to the left of their newly awarded Soldier Medals. He had been well rehearsed.

The highest award is always closest to the heart. So, even though these two medals were on an equivalent plane, the Silver Star, ranking third in the order of valorous decorations, took precedence over the Soldier's Medal. What is not normally well-known outside the ranks is that award of any medal on that level is reserved for exceptional valor and exceptional circumstances. Both elements were present that eventful morning several days ago.

Before he stepped away from Max, he said, "I understand you are the officer who has just overseen the recent opening of the Port of Kompong Som, allowing it to now receive large draft vessels?" Seeing an emerging grin on Max's face, the VP continued, "Yes, and I also understand that it was the SeaTrain Maryland, the first vessel to call at the port. I just want to thank you for your actions there."

"You may not be aware that I have particular affection for things named after the state that I recently governed, until Mr. Nixon and I were elected to Presidential office. Maryland was, and always will continue to be, my home. You make me proud that its name is part of the history of our honorable support here in Cambodia," said Mr. Agnew, with obvious pride.

Max could only muster, "Thank you very much, Mr. Vice President, for taking time out of your very busy schedule to make this presentation," as the two men shook hands. Mr. Agnew sputtered, then turned to BG Clausen, seemingly played out of small talk, and said perfunctorily, "You must be very proud of these fine, young men." Clausen readily agreed, and the two men had a brief chat before concluding the ceremony.

Ambassador Hightower then led the assembled audience past the two officers, offering his personal congratulations, and allowing the rest an opportunity to shake hands with the honorees. A brief reception took place immediately afterward at one end of the foyer.

It was only then that Max and MAJ Bethke finally had a chance to mingle. Max expected friendly kidding from his colleagues, to the effect that they had been lucky to happen on the scene. Any of the achievement-minded officers of MEDTC might have taken that particular route on that particular day.

There was a lot of friendly banter that clearly demonstrated that there were indeed officers on the MEDTC staff who coveted not only the opportunities to demonstrate valor, but a wish to take away these distinguished awards for themselves. In fact, a common thought was that these prestigious awards had been given to these two stinking log pukes, who by unadulterated sheer luck, happened upon two of the most propitious occasions in recent memory to demonstrate the mettle of American officers. Max's rueful contemplation was almost automatic, *"One never knows what evil lurks in the minds of men, capital sin or not."*

Max noticed that BG Clausen left after about another five minutes with the Ambassador and the Vice-President's entourage, obviously headed for their scheduled luncheon meeting with President Lon Nol and his staff at the Royal Palace.

Max knew all these details because he had worked a good part of the last week as an attached member of the MEDTC/Embassy liaison team, together with the Secret Service advance team, as they planned all the complex security arrangements that go without saying when the US Vice President or President makes a state visit.

*   *   *

Max's letter home that evening barely mentioned the awards ceremony. Max decided to downplay the significance of these awards and the fanfare associated with having the Vice President make the presentation. He did mention that he had received an award for helping some Marines who had been injured in an explosion that took place on their way to the Embassy a few days before. Max told Emily that he and Hank had happened along right after the incident, and were able to get the two Marines extricated from the wreckage and on to the Embassy, as they needed medical attention. Typically, he omitted reference to the Ambassador being the focus of the blast, or that Mr. Hightower was in any way involved in the episode.

Max did report that he was improving daily, making gradual progress on his way back to normal after the bout with dengue. "I would never have believed that a little bug bite could lay a person so low, and I have felt half crappy ever since I returned from KPS. I'll feel hearty one minute, then wiped out the next. My biggest struggle is just making it through the long days at the office. I feel like an old fart who needs a nap every afternoon."

Then, Max realized he was being far too expressive to Emily about his condition, and added, "But, I'm feeling stronger each day, bit by bit, and in the morning, I wake up feeling well-rested." The latter was intended to allay fears on Emily's part by ending the letter on a positive note.

CHAPTER FORTY-SEVEN

*M*ax was slightly ill at ease when he was scheduled the next day for pickup at Pochentong at 0830 for transport to yet another Logistics Base south of Takeo, whose main supply route (MSR) had not been interdicted (cut), as yet, by the Khmer Rouge. Max had hoped he would feel better by now, and wasn't certain how he would hold up if things got dicey during this EIUI.

Max was pleased to see that the Air America crew assigned to this EIUI was none other than Corky Finlen and the same crew chief who accompanied them to Neak Leoung. It was like old home week as the three men heartily shook hands and slapped each other on the back. The high-pitched whine of the gas turbine precluded a lot of chatter, but Max reminded himself of a previously apt observation, "Good guys to have around when the chips are down. Now, let's hope and pray that today's visit is routine, with no chips to fall." When everyone was securely back on board, Max put on his headset and clicked the vox button to talk to Corky.

"Have you had any more interesting EIUIs since our trip to Neak Leoung?" inquired Max ploddingly.

Corky responded, "Life has been dull as hell since they snatched our sorry asses outta that hell hole. This mission is my first since then. I've been lying on the beach at Vung Tau, entertaining the ladies in those pretty *Ao Dias* [Vietnamese long dress, worn over black satin pants]. Ya see, all the hullaballoo of that Neak Leoung mission caused the elders of Air America to see fit to award me a bonus of $50K, and I got thirty days bonus leave with full pay, so my ex-wife is happy, as I'm all caught up on alimony. I'm a happy camper, 'cause I still have a small fortune in the stocks and bonds, and the pretty ladies of the night at Vung Tau weren't all that bad either."

"Corky, you're incorrigible," added Max with an almost admiring tone, "but, I think you were underpaid for the things you pulled off during our visit to that sad, unfortunate place. May God rest their souls and aid in the healing of those wounded," the heartfelt words came spontaneously out of Max's mouth. Not normally one to wear his religion or his emotions close to the surface, Max was surprised to hear his tearful invocation.

Corky clicked back, "Roger, amen to that," and the conversation tapered off....

                              *   *   *

On this day, Max's EIUI was headed to an operational area near Route 6 where a reinforced FANK armored column was moving along the highway to clear out pockets of reported KR in the vicinity. Max's mission was to observe tactical supply and transport activities, associated with the FANK Operations Plan (OPLAN). Max noticed that the unit's Admin/Log plan, that portion of the OPLAN that dealt with logistics and support operations, was threadbare. He didn't hold out much hope that the actual support elements would have much organization, or leadership, for that matter.

He had arranged with Corky for a pickup in approximately three hours time, at the same LZ at which they landed. That was more than sufficient time to meet with unit leaders and observe unit's support activities.

As Max arrived at his rendezvous point, he met officers of the 295th FANK support battalion, who showed him around the supply point where the FANK had positioned fuel bladders and tank trucks for servicing tactical vehicles. There was also a small cantonment area for supply vehicles about 50 meters to the west of the supply point. There were several General Purpose Medium (GP Med) tents in the area that were under the canopy of trees about 25 meters off the highway.

The 295th was attached to this operation to provide direct support to the FANK Premier (1st) Brigade Blinde (Armored), which was conducting operations about a kilometer north of the supply point's position. Max could hear an occasional exchange of gunfire in the distance. The rattle of machine gun fire prompted him to inquire to the commander of the 295th, as to security arrangements for the supply point.

The commander was a plump FANK LtCOL named Lon Pham. Pham seemingly always had a wide grin, with clenched, gold-filled front teeth, from which hung a cigarette holder and a lit fag with drooping ashes. The affable commander actually took on the character of an editorial cartoon caricature, in his ill-fitting FANK field uniform. Not only was he one of the only overweight officers Max had encountered, his headgear seemed to Max far too small for his portly noggin.

LtCOL Pham launched into a description of the camp's security provisions, grabbing an old stick, and drawing the perimeter in the chalky dirt, which was routinely churned up by passing vehicles. Max gathered that there were machine gun outposts about every 45 degrees of the circular shaped enclave. Each outpost had a three-man team, one machine gunner, his assistant, who was also an ammo bearer, and one soldier armed with a grenade launcher. These points were connected via landline to the headquarters tent, which was manned around the clock in case of emergency on the perimeter.

Max was walking with LtCOL Pham toward the HQ tent, when one of the perimeter machine guns burst into action. Next came the unmistakable thud of small caliber mortar rounds, probably 60mm, the kind used by almost all KR small units. Then, the spewing sound of outgoing M79 grenade launchers filled the air, while machine gun fire chattered almost incessantly.

Max thought of his M-60 instructor in training bellowing, "Short bursts, fellas, we don't want to melt the barrel of that M-60. That's why they give you two barrels and a set of asbestos-lined gloves to remove the one that's getting overheated. Besides, it saves tons of ammo, and you don't wanna run out of it when Victor Charlie has a mind to pay your sorry ass a visit."

Then, Max's thoughts switched to the fact that he had just arrived, and if things worked out perfectly, Corky Finlen would be back to extract him in about two hours and thirty minutes. "Battles have been won in less time than that," Max recalled from his lessons in history in college, and from his course in American Military History, which was a mandatory subject for all Army ROTC students.

Max's last conscious thought concluded, "I had best follow this portly colonel and see if he has a stash of unused weapons he's willing to loan to a wayward American Captain, who has this penchant for finding action no matter where he alights."

Just then a 60mm mortar exploded near the HQ tent. LtCOL Pham, Max's rotund Khmer comrade in arms, was launched in one direction, while Max was thrown in another. Max awoke groggily several minutes later, and the conscious world seemed less than appealing for his return.

By the time Max shook the cobwebs from his momentary haze, he realized what was happening. The KR had mounted a major attack in the 1st Armored Brigade's rear support area. The fuel tankers were ablaze; the supply tents destroyed; and there were little men in black shorts and plaid, almost gingham scarves (a KR uniform) with AK-47 automatic rifles at the ready pouring through the outer perimeter.

Max checked to see if all his extremities were present and functioning properly. He noticed blood seeping from his ears, and he felt the sting of what he realized were first and second degree burns on his face, chest, and the palms of his hands. But otherwise, he was in one piece.

He had noticed a thirty-caliber machine gun on a table just beyond the HQ tent. Max decided to revisit the area to see if it was still operable.

His luck was true to form. Not only was the gun operable, it was loaded, with two large boxes of ammunition under the table. It had apparently been intended for a final defense of the Supply Point's headquarters.

Max recalled the Cooper Church Amendment's ban on active support or accomplishing any of normal functions that the FANK should perform. A quick survey of the area revealed no FANK soldiers available to man this weapon that Max intended to employ in his own defense.

Max was pleasantly surprised how well the FANK support soldiers held their own against the enemy's infantry probes. The perimeter was littered with KR bodies while the FANK were seemingly acquitting themselves well, in Max's estimation.

Then, out of the corner of his eye, Max saw three KR intruders headed toward the motor park armed with satchel charges. Two short bursts of the old French .30 caliber ended their foray. Then, about 50 meters to

Max's front a small team of KR soldiers had broken through the perimeter, essentially flanking the FANK defenders. MAX opened up with his trusty .30 cal. and mowed down what turned out to be five of the KR intruders. One last assault came from his rear and threatened a complete envelopment of the FANK Supply Point. Max turned, lifted his weapon, which he strained to hold up on the level, and cranked off several bursts that eliminated the KR thrust from that direction.

Max then turned his attention to tending to the wounded FANK soldiers. Many had single rifle shot wounds, but some had suffered the same fate as his friend, LtCOL Pham, who had encountered the lethal effects of mortar shells and grenades. As Max assessed the carnage, he treated the most urgently wounded, stemming the flow of blood, elevating the feet of those in shock, and clearing the airways of those gasping for air.

He made a quick tour of the interior of the Supply Point. He had assembled the soldiers most likely to survive in an area protected somewhat from further assault. He applied what first aid measures he was capable of, and dressed the wounds with what medical supplies that he could police up out of what was left in the HQ tent, the various supply tents, and he even found a small Red Cross kit in the vehicle in which LtCOL Pham had picked him up.

By this time, Max heard the roar of what sounded like APCs, and the high-pitched diesel engines of several main battle tanks, leftover from the early sixties, but still in operable condition. Max breathed a sigh of relief and checked his watch, which miraculously was still ticking away. *"Perhaps I'll make it to the rendezvous LZ on time, after all,"* Max mused optimistically.

He had been at the scene now for a total of just over two hours. He noticed that the assault on the FANK Supply Point had subsided about thirty minutes ago, as he reckoned the FANK armored units were now catching the KR in the open as they pulled back from the scene.

The lead APC crested the perimeter with its fifty-caliber blazing, mowing down the remnants of the KR's assault teams. A second FANK APC swung around about ten meters to the south, reinforcing the perimeter still further. Before another five minutes had passed, Max stood up from behind the overturned table he was using as an assembly and triage area.

By this time, a command track APC pulled into the Supply Point. Out popped a small-statured FANK Colonel, who sauntered up to Max, and, with a saucy Bernard Montgomery style salute, spouted, "*Bon jour, mon capitaine.*"

Realizing Max was challenged in French, the spritely FANK Colonel switched into pidgin English saying, "*Mon* apologies for zeece unfortunate transgression by zee Khmer Rouge, *c'est apres medi*. I am Colonel Sim Vray Ly, *commandant* of zee Premier Brigade *Blinde* [Armored]." As the burns on Max's palms were beginning to fester, the two gingerly exchanged handshakes, and then went about checking for other FANK survivors inside the perimeter.

They came upon the remains of LtCOL Pham, who had apparently taken the full force of the blast from the mortar round. In fact, Max could now recall that LtCol Pham was walking slightly in front of him when the mortar exploded. The evidence: LtCOL Pham's face and torso were badly burned, but, you could not help but distinguish his trademark clenched grin, with the gold-filled front teeth in full view.

Max realized that LtCOL Pham's body had shielded him from the full force of the round, which had exploded no more than three feet from where the ill-fated FANK supply commander was headed. Without his shielding body, Max may not have awakened to assist in the defense of the position. Or, Max thought ruefully, "I may have never awakened."

"May I take you to your point *d'rendezvous*," asked COL Vray Ly, after a quick survey of the scene. FANK losses seemed high in this area, since it had borne the brunt of the KR assault. "It will be hard to replace zeeze specialists *de logistiques*," intoned COL Vray Ly, as he escorted Max to his command track. "*S'il vous plaît*, pass along my thanks to your generous country and ask that they help up replace these brave soldiers quickly, and, *merci*, for zee intrepid assistance by *mon Capitaine* in defending zeece position. We owe you much for helping our wounded and dying."

"I will pass along your message of gratitude to our leader, BG Clausen, *mon* Colonel," Max responded, just before the Air America bird made its landing.

"Again, please accept my thanks for your brave assistance in defending our supply point, *mon Capitaine*," added COL Vray Ly. "I will report your decisive and valorous actions to my superiors at FANK HQ imme-diately."

Corky performed a steep descent, keeping nearly full power pressing as he touched the ground. Max scrambled aboard the UH-1H. Corky wasted no time coaxing the Huey's Lycoming gas turbine back up to take off speed.

"You look like shit," was Corky's first comment.

"Long, hard day at the office," was Max's solitary retort.

Chapter Forty-Eight

*M*ax was told that he'd receive initial treatment at the Embassy dispensary. His wounds were mainly burns, plus two burst eardrums. The attending embassy nurse, a tall, statuesque RN named Lucretia (Lucy) Hanover was more like a Licensed Physician's Assistant (LPA) in today's medical parlance. Not quite a doctor, but far beyond a mere Registered Nurse.

The amply endowed Ms. Hanover was authorized to dispense medications—including administering painkillers and antibiotics. She had taken on Max's case with fervor and intended to prevent any infection to Max's several areas of third-degree burns, and, since she ruled over the Embassy dispensary like the Queen of the May, she took orders from no one, but issued them to the several orderlies and patients like a seasoned sergeant major with exceedingly high standards.

Max had met Lucy several times at Embassy dinner parties and was rather impressed with the ease with which Ms. Hanover, as she preferred to be called, mingled with the blue bloods of the diplomatic corps. It was widely rumored that no career Foreign Service officer made it past Consular Officer without an Ivy League diploma dangling from a prominent place in his outer office. It was clear that Ms. Hanover was highly regarded by the embassy staff and their families, appearing at every embassy social event Max had been invited to.

Lucy looked at ease in this quarter. She seemed to thrive on the singularity of her expertise in a third-world country and was content to enjoy the attentions, although mostly from afar, of the many young diplomats who were cutting their teeth on their first foreign service assignment, while ogling her ample bosom and perfectly formed posterior. Her face was not remarkably pretty, but not homely, either. Her elaborate curvature certainly made up for any shortcomings in the facial beauty category, and, aside from her brusque bedside manner at the dispensary, she was a delightful conversationalist to be stuck with at the many insufferably dull Embassy dinner parties.

"And you, Captain Donatello, will follow my prescribed regimen for keeping these burns clean and well-irrigated. The treatment is going to cause you some grief, at first, but, I can assure you that USAir Force evacuation dispensaries in Thailand are notorious for the prodigious infections that take hold in burn patients taken there. The burn infection rate is off the chart. You may wish to know that an infected burn wound makes for a very long, uncomfortable MEDEVAC flight from Utapao to some Air Force Base or Army garrison hospital on the West Coast. Get my drift?" Max rolled his eyes, as he knew that this particular Florence Nightingale did not mince words.

"We have a hepa-filtered air conditioning system in this facility. That makes this far preferable to the three-paddle-ceiling-fanned facilities in Thailand or Vietnam. I've got you completely dosed up with antibiotics. So, we will simply have to treat these burns topically and hope they heal," added Ms. Hanover with a tinge of doubt, a tone designed to impress on the valorous Captain Donatello the need to follow her orders. "We may be able to allow some visitors next week, if all goes well," Ms. Hanover parenthetically remarked over her shoulder, as she disappeared into her office outside the treatment area.

Chapter Forty-Nine

*M*ax was weary of lying around the sterile confines of the treatment facility after about 36 hours. By then, the burned skin began to pull taut over the most seriously affected areas. His face was a mess, and the palms of his hands were a constant source of throbbing pain. Ms. Hanover had insisted that Max get up and walk around for exercise, use the toilet to the best of his ability, and keep clean hospital gowns loosely shrouding his otherwise naked body.

There was one particularly sensitive area, just above his sternum. Since Max could not remember anything but the initial concussion, he concluded that the burn must have come from flaming debris, caused by the exploding mortar round. Ms. Hanover worried out loud that this nasty burn was third degree. The most serious part of the wound was only the size of a casino chip, but it had a seeping depth that concerned both Max and Ms. Hanover. Besides, it hurt like hell when Max attempted to change his hospital gown.

"Whoever designed this hospital gown piece of dog-doo should be strung up from the rafters," complained Max on a regular basis to the unremitting Ms. Hanover. "Why can't you just have my villa mate, MAJ Bethke, bring me a basic load of my boxer shorts and a few V-necked T-shirts from out of my chest of drawers at the villa," pleaded Max plaintively.

"You know very well why I cannot allow that. How can we be sure that there are no remnants of bacteria on those garments? Right, we can't. And, I will not abide the introduction to my facility of some unknown strain of bacteria that are somehow embedded in your dainties, by virtue of your housemaid's use of unfiltered or suspicious water sources. How do I know that she has not taken them down to the local drainage creek and used that water to work up a soapy lather intended to clean your apparel? I do not. So, kindly refrain from bringing up this subject in further vain attempts at making me pity your poor, miserable state." Nurse Hanover turned and departed Max in a huff.

Max could only think of how miserably heartless this witch of a medical wench was. Max had drummed up charges in his mind that Nurse Hanover enjoyed the spectacle of having a virile young American officer essentially captive for only her to observe. Max imagined her coming to his cot at night to examine his genital portfolio.

"What a lowlife, depraved human monster had been assigned my care," thought Max in a stupor of pain, itching, and mind-bending irony. *"How could this RN, a supposed angel of mercy, pledged to relieve human suffering, possess not so much as a morsel of compassion, pity, or humanity?"* Max went on and on, in a near continuous litany of grievances he had chronicled in his mind about the inhospitable, almost evil nature, of this medically-shrouded emissary from the devil incarnate. Max's other worry was how to couch his condition in the next taping he was due to send to Emily. Since he was unable to write, he would have to muster his knack for downplaying the severity of the situation in this next recording. He had received permission from his formidable medical adversary to have MAJ Hank Benke bring his tape recorder in for Max's use. Not before she sanitized every millimeter of its surface. She even installed the tape, because Max's hands were still bandaged. Max used his oriental Chinese back scratcher to press the buttons on the apparatus.

Max had been apprised that a TELEX had been sent to Emily from BG Clausen notifying her of his injuries and status. Max surmised that Emily would be anxious, if not a bit edgy from the lack of details. COL Jacobson had passed a note that day to Max through Nurse Hanover. It seems that COL Jacobson been directed by BG Clausen to use the Embassy's satellite phone to call the Willis's home in Williamsburg to give Emily and her parents a run down of events leading to Max's current condition, and, since Jacobson was an old friend of COL Willis, the call went a long way toward easing the worry, creating a sense of optimism in the family. So, at least he had an opening to use his 'old soft shoe' approach to describing his condition to Emily and family.

Playing down the severity of his injuries, Max joked about what he called his 'X-rated' hospital gown, always flapping open revealing his exposed, naked tail feathers. "Somebody sold the Army a pig in a poke on that acquisition. Luckily, it's usually just the orderlies and I. However, the senior medical official is female, and she makes no bones about the fact that I must either wear a hospital gown, or I wrap myself up in a sheet like Muhatma Ghandi."

Max figured a bit of humor would demonstrate his positive outlook, and serve to allay any residual fears as to his prognosis. He was just able to get one side of a tape completed, pleading his desire to get it out at the soonest possible opportunity so they could hear directly from him as to his status.

*   *   *

It was almost a full week after being brought to his new 'sanctuary,' when Max heard a familiar set of voices just outside the treatment area. It turned out to be Ambassador Hightower, BG Clausen, and COL Jacobson, along with a diminutive FANK officer, who Max finally recognized as COL Sim Vray Ly, commander of the 1st Armored Brigade.

Max said dryly to the FANK Colonel, "I hope you have come to prevail on these officials to release me from this state-sponsored prison, Colonel Vray Ly."

The Ambassador broke in and inserted, "We have all come to welcome you back to the normal, living world, Captain Donatello. We owe your well-being to Ms. Hanover, who has only left this facility once a day in the past week to seek a shower and a change of clothing. She has personally watched your progress for as much as 18 hours each day, insuring that no infection could possibly be admitted. Orderlies were under strict directions to awaken her from the cot she had installed in her office just outside here, so she was immediately available in case of your need."

Max paled in the light of this disruptive, even heretical, testimony as to Ms. Hanover's virtue. Max had convinced himself, in his stupor, that he would somehow personally preside over Ms. Hanover's demise for her inestimably evil ways.

The Ambassador seemed oblivious to Max's intent on vengeance. "But, my dear young Captain, we have also come to recognize your continuing heroics in the EIUI visit to the Armored Brigade supply trains area along Route 6 last week. Colonel Vray Ly has made it his personal mission to insure that you are recognized for the actions you took after being knocked cold, badly burned, and dazed in the fog of a major KR assault of a FANK position."

"It is my understanding that you personally eliminated several sappers intent upon destroying the support unit's tanker trucks. That was a significant feat in itself. But, I am also informed that your discovery of an aged French machine gun essentially tipped the battle's balance in FANK's favor, when the KR forces attacked the FANK support battalion headquarters in force. COL Vray Ly tells me that you were credited for at least a dozen more kills of KR intruders trying to overrun the FANK perimeter, all accomplished with your hands badly burned and your face obfuscated by a bleeding scalp wound which impeded your clarity of sight."

"Furthermore, I simply cannot fathom your attempts," the Ambassador went on, "at setting up a triage for the wounded. How could you have dragged wounded soldiers to safety, given them treatment, and then have gone out to look for more survivors with those badly burned hands?"

The Ambassador reached out to shake Max's hand, only to pull back quickly in the realization that Max was still trying to heal those two badly burned palms.

"Sorry Max, how terribly thoughtless of me," said the American Ambassador to the Khmer Republic. "Please accept my sincerest apologies. In my exuberance," Mr. Hightower's normally distinct baritone trailed off.

BG Clausen inserted himself at this awkward juncture, saying, "Max, I have another military decoration to present today." He leaned over and pinned the Purple Heart on Max's pillow. "I know that no one ever earns a Purple Heart. I personally know that if you survive any combat ordeal, this little ribbon serves as a starkly minimalist reminder of the suffering you endured. I, myself, know about the feeling you take away from here. You will undoubtedly reflect, probably much later, on the small rewards the Army has to offer for major sacrifices."

By this time the Ambassador had regained his composure. "Max, it gives me great pleasure to present the Army's Legion of Merit Medal to you for your selfless, personal contribution to the opening of the deep draft port of Kompong Som. It was a historical accomplishment, done under the most hostile of conditions. Our country and the FANK government have taken note of this herculean achievement. Please be assured of our continuing esteem, and congratulations on such a significant endeavor in the American support of our FANK allies."

COL Vray Ly accompanied COL Jacobson up next to Max's bunk. Max's boss was first to speak. "My new dear friend, COL Sim Vray Ly has given me an account of the adversity you faced when the KR decided to counter-attack their forces in FANK's rear area. You, of course, have a tendency to find the bleeding edge of every activity into which you are inserted. Your EIUI visit coincided with the KR plan to wipe out the 1st Armored Brigade's supply trains. Your propensity to be at the wrong place at the right time would normally merit my unalterable assessment that you are nothing but a perennial pain in the ass. However, your timing has again earned you a modicum of esteem in the ranks of our FANK brothers."

"To be brief, my dear Cap'n Max, I am here to report to you that the General Sosathene Fernandez, the chief of staff of FANK forces, is recommending to President Nixon that you be awarded the Distinguished Service Cross, the second highest valorous award in the US Army's order of merit, second only to the Medal of Honor (MOH). How they chose this particular award is still a mystery. However, the fact that the recommendation has been made by a decorated combat arms colonel of a foreign army, who was present during a good bit of this ordeal, and that it will be personally endorsed by Marshal Lon Nol, gives it a remarkably high probability of approval."

COL Jacobson related that COL Sim Vray Ly had been a foreign exchange student officer at the US Army's Armor Center as a Captain some years ago. He is well versed in American armored unit strategy and tactics. He has studied the achievements of allied armored formations and their commanding generals in both WWII and Korea. "COL Vray Ly asked me to send him the latest Combined Arms Manuals and the de-classified versions of the US Technical Observations and Analysis of the Arab-Israeli conflict of 1967, for his perusal and enlightenment."

COL Vray Ly then approached Max and said in his own brand of Franco-Khmer English, "You are the model of what a logistics officer should be. You are technically proficient, yet acutely aware of how to conduct operations against hostile attacking forces. Could I persuade you to come back and train the officers of my support units? For I believe that your actions at the Supply Point on Rte 6 would make a significant difference to them in our rebuilding efforts."

COL Jacobson reminded COL Vray Ly of the limits of American officer involvement in the formation of FANK forces.

BG Clausen realizing the strain of this situation on Max, finally interjected, "Let's take this up at the next joint tactical review, gentlemen. Surely the esteemed, but infirmed, Captain needs a well-deserved rest."

BG Clausen looked askance at Ms. Hanover, and nodded her way, and said quite plainly, "Thank you for all your considerable efforts on Captain Donatello's behalf. Ms. Hanover, we are all in your debt."
Lucy Hanover fairly glowed as the Ambassador came by and gave her an air-kiss on the cheek and a perfunctory neck hug, adding, "I was not convinced you could achieve your goal of preventing the evacuation of Captain Donatello. I am happy to admit the error of my assessment of your manifest healing powers, Ms. Hanover. I am duly impressed. Thank you for your dedicated efforts," added Ambassador Hightower as he took his leave.

Chapter Fifty

*M*ax was released to his quarters after yet another 48 hours of round- the-clock oversight by Ms. Hanover, insuring there were no signs of infection. His dismissal instructions were crystal clear. He would make a late morning visit to the dispensary on a schedule, coordinated so that about the time his treatment and bandage change was accomplished, the other members of his villa would simply drop by the dispensary to snag 'Cap'n Max,' as he was now almost universally referred to, as they departed the embassy for their normal trip back to their villa for their mid-day meal.

All was working well for about a week after his 'incarceration' mandate had been lifted, when the burn wound on his chest began to fester. Max thought, "If any portion of my body would be a likely locale for those nefarious gremlins that cause infection, my hands would certainly be prime candidates. Secondarily, the face, then, the damned burn wound on my chest."

The scalp wound had made an almost miraculous recovery, although Max would forever be missing a fine strip of hair just above his hairline. It was as if the KR had made it through the perimeter to incise a tiny piece of this scalp, in a manner that the Lakota Sioux might have accomplished on a fallen member of the 7th Cavalry at the Little Big Horn. But, it would only be so, if the Indian warrior had lots of time on his hands, for such a small, precise scalping.

Only Max's barber would ever know, as Max was blessed with one of those extraordinarily thick manes of extremely fine hair that grew unabated of its own accord.

Once informed of Max's latest relapse, Ms. Hanover declared that his release to quarters was terminated until the infection abated. Her justification: any one of his housemates could be carriers of one infection or another. The drivers who transported the officers to their villa were also suspect.

"Back to the dungeons," Max intoned to himself with a resigned manner. Something had bothered him since he had returned from the Rte. 6 encounter, as he commonly referred to it.

What was Perry Carpenter's condition? He could not believe that a week had passed without word of the Master Chief's condition. Max also wondered what the disposition was of his recommendation for Perry's awards. Max had spent hours, late at night, working on award recommendations, award citations, and feeling guilty about the abundance of attention he, himself, had received since the KPS adventure.

Max, to his chagrin, turned himself over to the whims and ways of Ms. Hanover at the dispensary. Hoping to try to break the ice that had grown Titanic-like since his release about a week ago, Max chose to start with an interrogatory.

"Have you heard anything about my good friend Perry Carpenter? I know you were in charge of and saw to his evacuation." asked Max with genuine interest.

Ms. Hanover said, "Max, we did everything in the book to help Perry. He was doing fine here until he was evacuated to the Naval Hospital in Subic Bay in the Philippines. I was assured that he was making good progress there until an extremely septic infection took hold of him. He did not make it, Max. I am so sorry."

Max felt the genuine caring in her voice. Without doubt, he had misjudged this woman. She cared as much as he did for Perry's welfare and recovery.

"Lucy, please," Max began to speak. "You can be accused and convicted of being too invested in your patients. I loved Perry, too. But, don't forget that he was injured doing his 'thing.' He was a rare character who could get people he could not even talk to lined up to do his bidding. And, they would love doing it."

"We need to reflect on our good fortune to have known a man so deserving of the love of his troops. The FANK soldiers in KPS were the last batch of his near-children," Max trailed off, hiccupping a sob as he lapsed into thought.

Lucy came forward and gave Max a genuinely loving embrace. Then she said, with obvious affection that was hard to refute, "We all should have such discerning friends as you, Max."

Max' still raw, tender, bandaged hands, reached out for Lucy's hand, as the two new friends headed to the treatment room for Max's next period of seclusion.

CHAPTER FIFTY-ONE

*I*t was only 72 more hours in 'solitary,' as Max proclaimed it, until he was again released on his own recognizance with similar orders in effect as after his last medical furlough. Max added to the regimen that he would not shake anyone's hand or use anything but a new cake of soap when he washed his hands or hit the showers.

Max actually relished the down time, even though he listened intently to the radio chatter on the radio's villa base station stashed in their front room. Catching up on overdue correspondence was the order of the first two days home from the dispensary. Having the villa to himself during the day allowed him to be much more expressive and intimate in his recordings to Emily.

Max had received a tape from Emily in the APO mail the day he was released. He was anxious for the lunch/rest period to be over so he could have the living room to himself to listen to Emily's tape. When the group headed back to the Embassy, Max asked Tran for some ice. He made himself a strong drink from the bar and settled down with his tape player to enjoy listening to Emily's loving voice.

Emily began, "I'm recording this at 10:30 PM as we just got the kids to bed. COL Jacobson called earlier this evening, just as we were finishing dinner. I had a hard time getting the phone away from Daddy, as I guess he and your COL Jacobson go way back, and you know how these old colonels go on and on. When I finally got to speak to him, I was impressed with his Southern charm and his obvious high regard for you. Talking to him was like a throw back to Charlottesville, with all the southern touches and affected drawls among my friends at UVA. Your colonel can certainly coat a story with sugar. I couldn't help getting a sense of genuine concern, even worry about you from him, in spite of all that syrup."

Max took a deep swig of his scotch and sighed deeply at how perceptive his lovely spouse was. She could read between the lines of the very best of BS artists, knowing that the truth was the most likely victim of such obvious yarn spinners.

"It was sweet of BG Clausen to have him call. I am thankful that he made the effort to play down the seriousness of your injuries. Very gallant! Under other circumstances, I'm certain I would have fallen under your Southern colonel's spell," added Emily in a kidding tone. "He told us about the distinguished awards Mr. Agnew presented to you and Hank. Congratulations! I am so proud of you. When were you planning on sharing this rare event with me?"

Emily continued, "I can't decide whether to scream out of frustration or to applaud your heroic actions. I'll just have to wait to get you home and fully healed before I smack the living shit out of you for being so reticent in telling me about your distinctions. 'Nuff said. I still love you, even though I think you're a sorry schmuck for downplaying all this dramatic, important stuff!"

"*Whew*," Max exhaled in a moment of relief, now that the cat was out of the bag on a lot of fronts. "*I was trying to fly below the radar about the significance of all these episodes*," thought Max sheepishly. "*I was hoping to make it through this damned tour in one piece with nothing to report home about but the numbing boredom of the experience. I guess my adventurous encounters and illnesses made that plan a bust. Then, getting my ass nearly blown to bits didn't exactly advance the plan*," rued Max as he chomped down on an ice shaving. Max decided to pour two more inches on top of the remnant of his first drink, thinking it would certainly enhance his chances of getting a late afternoon snooze in an hour or so.

As Max crawled painfully out of his chair and ambled toward the villa's well-stocked bar, his mind wandered. As he allowed himself a pause to digest Emily's spirited missive, he surveyed their ample bar.

For some reason, Max remembered how awestruck he was when he first arrived. This was the stuff of movies. But, here he was with a war raging all around him, and he was sitting in what many would consider the lap of luxury.

Max's supply-oriented mind went inexorably onward: the normal monthly Embassy ration for every household was: one bottle each of Grand Marnier, Courvoisier, Drambuie, Benedictine, Amaretto, and every other liqueur available at the moment in the Embassy store. The facility opened with ample notice every month so that each villa's house warden (villa-marm) could requisition its allocation.

In addition, each villa was authorized to buy monthly: two each 1.75 liter bottles of Johnnie Walker Black Scotch, two each large bottles of Tanqueray Gin, three large vodkas, of whatever brand the store had received, and two each large bottles of bourbon or sour mash. One liter bottle of Bacardi Rum was also authorized. Periodically, the store received its wine ration. On these quarterly occasions, each villa was allowed to claim three cases of each type of wine received. One can imagine that after a few months, a villa could amass quite a stash of adult liquid refreshments.

Max settled into his easy chair and continued his logistics-oriented musings. Emily's tape was in the background of his mind being processed.

The Embassy admin office would charge each villa's account for these purchases. Then, members of each house paid an equal share of the sum, just as they did for their share of the groceries brought in to resupply their needs.

The Embassy account was paid at the first of every month, as was the members' contribution to the commissary store's account. The latter bill arrived whenever it came in from Saigon.

Thus, the conservative senior officers, serving as de-facto villa-marms, developed a means to accrue a portion of the monthly contributions for just this purpose. So, whenever the commissary bill arrived, the villa was prepared to deal with it, without assessment, or awaiting the next payday.

This approach suited the finances of most MEDTC officers, who budgeted a fixed amount each month to defray in-country costs such as these. The remainder of their compensation went home to support wives and family.

Max figured that his total household contribution amounted to just over $225 per month. *"Not bad, when you think of it in terms of three squares a day, board, maid and laundry, plus delectable menu choices provided by their incredibly gifted chef, Sakun,"* thought Max wrily.

Max also rued that $225 was also an amount that his family did not receive to sustain itself while he was away. To Max, it seemed like an unnecessary burden had been placed on officers' families by virtue of their having to essentially support two domiciles.

No compensation was ever made to the families of officers for this unfair burden. There were countless officers who served in the war-zone two and three tours. Max felt that there was no doubt that the country rode heavily on the shoulders of untold thousands of officers, who repeatedly answered the call to duty in SE Asia to do their duty to God and country.

Somewhere, in the history of our armed services, it was decided that officers should pay for their meals in mess facilities. In Vietnam, officers forfeited their Basic Allowance for Subsistence (BAS), when they were in the field on tactical operations. Accordingly, in bases where there were mess halls, officers paid each time they used the mess for a meal, supposedly out of their meager BAS.

In Cambodia, there were no mess facilities. So officers had to pool their resources to defray the cost of their subsistence, which was flown in by either Air Force C-130, or Air America on their routine courier runs from Saigon or Sattahip, Thailand.

The process had become refined by the time Max had arrived in February 1972. Now, each officer who was scheduled to spend his tour in Phnom Penh was briefed ahead of time, so that on arrival he had the funds necessary to "buy into" the villa's inventory. The amount varied from villa to villa, but in Max's case, he needed close to $500 up front to pay for his share of the villa's resources.

Again, it seemed to Max that this requirement was an unfair burden on married junior officers. In the early 1970s, $500 represented a significant amount for a young Captain like himself to come up with. While he never complained about it, there was an abiding part of him that resented the fact that his country had asked him serve in Cambodia under these draconian strictures.

"Why wasn't his country willing to adequately compensate him for housing and subsistence?" pondered Captain Donatello resignedly.

With this thought, Max fell soundly asleep in his chair.

Chapter Fifty-Two

$\mathcal{F}$or the next several months, Max's life took on a routine tempo. Aside from infrequent EIUIs, Max got in step with the flow of life and work at the Embassy. Late in October, just before the 1972 presidential elections, the KR picked up the pressure on Phnom Penh with both rocket and mortar fire.

On one night alone, the KR fired over 150 rockets into the city center. In addition, countless mortar shells dropped in neighborhoods on the outskirts of the capital. The house radios crackled to life at about 8:30 PM as the Marine guard on duty was trying to reach one of the villas located not far from where Max and his villa-mates resided. When that villa responded, the Marine alerted the members of that household to prepare for imminent ground attack. KR units had been reported near the Cité Sportif, a large private sports complex with the city's only clay tennis courts. It was located less than a mile from Max's villa, and the villa's sedans had to pass by it daily to access one of the several routes taken to the Embassy.

'We'd better take similar measures," suggested MAJ Hank Bethke.

"Yes, it appears we need to implement our villa defense plan immediately," echoed LTC Ed Czenko with a concerned tone. "Let's get upstairs and get those flak jackets on. I'll alert Sakun and his family, and I'll get the drivers and FANK security detail to batten down the hatches."

On the roof, each of the officers had been assigned a sector that covered about forty-five degrees of the villa's defensible perimeter. Almost 180 degrees of the villa's perimeter backed up to a thick stand of tall trees, which were bounded on their other side by a fast moving tributary of the Tonle Sap River. Since this was an unlikely avenue of approach, the officers concentrated their attention on the street side of the villa. This approach was also protected by two FANK guard towers on either side of the 10' high steel gate that normally provided access to the villa compound. The remaining perimeter of the villa was encircled by a 1' thick, 10' high stone and concrete fence.

Max and Captain Larry Hemphill took the far left and right defensive sectors, while MAJ Bethke and LTC Czenko manned the two central-most zones. Each of the officers was equipped with a pedestal mounted M-60 machine gun with two wooden ammo boxes stashed close by, endowed with a thousand rounds each. Each position had an M-16 assault rifle and an M-79 grenade launcher with enough ammunition to hold off the Chinese Army, much less the lowly KR. Finally, each officer had an automatic-loading 12-gauge shotgun. This weapon normally stored eight shells inside the weapon, but it had been specially modified for the US Special Forces with a mechanism that allowed it to mount a magazine that held 25 rounds in a circular drum, which snapped on like the circular magazine on a '30s-era Thompson submachine gun.

Two boxes of twenty-five M-79 grenade rounds were stationed at each position. One box of 25 fragmentation grenades rounded out the defense of each position. Certainly, this arrangement represented the worst-case scenario that the KR would storm the villa, and it would be a shooting match to the death, with decisive firepower on the American officers' side of the equation.

The men could hear the now almost continuous small arms fire that seemed to be emanating from a couple of blocks away from their position. The mortar fire had stopped, but the different sounds emitted by the different caliber weapons gave off a cacophony that emphasized the sheer and abject chaos that takes place in a close quarters fire fight.

The roar of high-powered motors drowned out the pop-pip-bang exchange of small-arms fire. FANK APCs were arriving with the rapid boom-boom-boom of their .50 caliber machine guns tearing into walls, defensive positions, and KR bodies. A couple of really loud explosions pocked the night, as the explosive rounds of the FANK armored vehicles erupted, adding their 105mm main guns to the deafening din.

Max estimated the battle to have taken about two hours. Looking at his watch, it was only nine thirty-five when the shooting stopped. They had been in their rooftop defense positions for merely an hour.

Just then the Embassy Marine guard announced over their closed-channel radio net that, while monitoring the FANK tactical network, they had heard a report, in the clear, that the FANK forces had routed the KR assault at the Cité Sportif, killing more than sixty-five lightly armed KR infantry soldiers. They had captured another forty-five and were in hot pursuit of the retreating remnants, who were reported to be retreating in in the direction of Pochentong Air Base aboard several stolen FANK cargo trucks.

"Hoorah for the FANK," yelled MAJ Bethke. "They gave those slimy little KR bastards a real knockout blow."

LTC Czenko added, "We may need a nightcap downstairs after we get the tarps over these M-60 positions. Last one down at the bar is a rotten egg." With genuine soldier-like precision, the four hastened to secure the four machine guns under heavy Army tarpaulins, secured by the ammo boxes against the frequent rains that struck Phnom Penh at any hour.

Max finished his duties second among the four, leaving LTC Czenko and CPT Hemphill to compete for the distinction of being the 'goat,' or last in a competitive endeavor. Max and MAJ Bethke were seated with drinks poured when the two late contenders came trekking down the back stairs, with LTC Czenko in trail. As they burst into the villa, the advantage was too great in Captain Hemphill's favor to for the 45-ish Czenko to overcome. The only comment Hemphill had was, "Age before beauty, mon colonel. You look like you could use a drink. I can wait," added the not-so-deferential Captain to his superior in rank and age.

If LTC Ed Czenko had any one, redemptive quality, it was his quick humor. He howled at the prospect of being last but was still chuckling when he came to join Max and Hank. "RHIP [Rank Has Its Privileges], I always say," LTC Czenko intoned in a sardonic tone meant for Captain Hemphill's ears, as the young Ordnance Corps Captain poured himself a double dose of Johnnie Walker Black over a tumbler of ice.

"Do I smell rotten eggs, or is it sour grapes I'm catching in my nostrils," queried the decidedly unrelenting Captain.

"I do recall a challenge of that sort up on the rooftop, about 30 minutes ago, wasn't it Max? I vaguely recall that our esteemed Villamarm said something about the last one down from securing their weapons position may not be deemed a rotten egg, but would certainly smell like one," MAJ Bethke jibed even further.

"But, then again, it could be the latent smell of cordite from that position a few blocks away, or the beginnings of the smell of those rotting little KR bastards, who will undoubtedly be stacked like cordwood by morning, by our favorite force, the FANK," added Hank Bethke mordantly, with obvious disgust.

"Easy now, Hank," coaxed LTC Czenko. "Remember, it's their war. We're just here to deliver the goods."

"That's a crock and you know it, Colonel. We're here as a political expedient to give Nixon his "Decent Interval," while the US makes nice with the Vietnamese. We're overseeing the final guppy breaths of a country that's about to be overrun by one of the most savage revolutionary movements to emerge since Marx invented communism," retorted Hank Bethke, in a tone that neither Max nor Larry had ever heard between two American officers of differing rank.

"Easy now," chided Ed Czenko. "Let's not get on different sides of the same argument, the principles of which we both agree. It would be a lose-lose proposition for all concerned," added the calm-but-collected Army 0-5, suggesting that pushing this envelope any further would be considered a breach of officer conduct and loyalty at a very rudimentary level.

"Apologies, Colonel Ed. You don't deserve my stored up hostility. I feel continually disgusted, to my core, for this Oz-like scenario we find ourselves prominently a part of. However, I should not have popped off like that. I think you know that I have nothing but the highest respect and admiration for you, your thoughts, opinions, and even how you run this household. Please forgive me," said Hank Bethke in a very sincere tone.

"No offense taken. Now what about a refill before we hit the rack?" offered the diplomatic 'villa-marm.'

*   *   *

175

The conversation from that point took on an un-shrouded personal dimension on this starkest of evenings. No one present felt that he could simply cast aside all the rockets, mortars, the onslaught of the KR a mere two blocks from their villa, and expect to get to sleep this soon after all the excitement.

Most evenings, the conversations were simply a review of the day's latest news, a comment or two on any *Stars and Stripes* syndicated op-ed piece, or the group took up whatever appeared in one of the three daily newspapers Max's family inundated him with, which he, in turn, passed onto his villa-mates. Max was often cursed by the overworked mailroom orderly. Tonight, however, was totally different. It was like all the ice between these guys had melted. There were no boundaries on the discussion.

Topics included the enormous frustration and futility that was universally felt about the progress, or lack thereof, of the FANK forces. Tonight's decisive exposition of force impressed none of these officers. It was a clear example of a superior armored FANK Force overwhelming a poorly conceived, badly led, KR infantry raid. Most of the officers thought that the morning media would undoubtedly conclude that the KR was making steady, incremental progress in re-taking the outermost districts of the capital, in spite of the fearsome casualties the FANK forces had sustained over the past several months.

After midnight, the chat turned to families and the incessant worry that must accrue when weeks would go by before the folks at home received updates that assured them that things were still going along swimmingly.

Max, on his third stout drink, brought up the issue of officer compensation, especially regarding the operation of two domiciles. "Do you ever suppose that the government of the United States will wake up and smell the fetid issue of officer remuneration, especially regarding the expenses we sustain in a war zone, while our families are home trying to scrape by on allotments of our remaining monthly resources?" asked Max rhetorically to the assembled group.

"That's a very raw topic, one, which we have long gone round and round with Congressional staffers. We've had lots of assistance from all of our patriotic and veteran support lobbyists, but the congressional staffers seem to think that the Basic Allowance for Subsistence (BAS) is an adequate tax-exempt payment, intended to make up for an officer's subsistence expenses while deployed. A specious argument, for sure, because everyone knows that it's impossible to live on a little more than five dollars a day, even if an officer's mess were available," offered LTC Ed Czenko.

"It is almost an inverse way of thinking. Since officers make more per month than enlisted, the staffers feel they should not be entitled to a penny more than it costs to feed a lowly private in a mess hall. Thus, goes the argument, and thus we have a moot issue," added the senior officer ruefully.

"If you were to ask me to give you the truth of the matter, I would say that this and other compelling issues affecting career officer retention have been put on the back burner, because of the country's weariness about the war in SE Asia, our presence here in Cambodia, and the fact that the American military has not delivered our country victoriously out of this vale of tears."

"So, when it comes to personnel issues like the one you have brought up, the Congress has essentially relegated them to the bottom of the priority list, as a sort of negative tax on the officers who have been prosecuting the war. So, if you follow that train of thought, the order goes like this: "You officers go off and fight our wars, and if we are not pleased with the results, we will undermine programs that underwrite your careers and support to your families," LTC Czenko's voice trailed off.

"Sorry, we are supposed to keep a positive attitude, right? Please do not take my comments out of this room, or out of context in your own minds. I, too, have my gripes about the conduct of this war, and the manner in which the Pentagon, the Congress, and the Administration have performed their duties. I have nagging doubts about the efficacy of our efforts here. I wonder how it all could have come to this," LTC Czenko ruminated out loud.

Max said finally, "I am exhausted beyond belief. If the KR decides to make another attack on the city tonight, my part of our defensive post would be toast." As the others groaned at Max's failed attempt at a pun, as he hastened up the stairs to his quarters. He yelled back over his shoulder, "Wake me when it's over."

*   *   *

Max would never forget the next morning. The awful stench permeated every breath of air as the team sedans made their routine morning passage near the Cité Sportif. Several FANK APCs were still present, as if on sentry duty overseeing the piles of dead KR stacked up, on display for the newspaper cameras. Stark images were routinely and prominently placed on the front pages of the Khmer newspapers. Certainly, this blatantly nasty scene would make it just below the banner of the local newspaper's afternoon edition.

An American-provided M113 Armored Personnel Carrier (APC) had been hit, and it had burned to about half of its normal height. Max recalled that at the time, he was not aware that aluminum would actually burn when exposed to sufficient heat. MAJ Bethke mentioned that the APC must have been loaded with explosives when it was hit, most likely with a Rocket Propelled Grenade (RPG). "The secondary explosions would have generated enough heat to consume the aluminum plate," was Hank Bethke's conclusion

CHAPTER FIFTY-FOUR

THE PRESENT

*M*ax could still recall that gruesome spectacle, as if it were yesterday. The FANK showed no respect for their dead adversaries. The KR dead soldiers were, in fact, piled up like so much cordwood, with limbs jutting every which way. It reminded Max of the old WWII films and newsreels that showed how the Nazi's piled up the Jews, Gypsies, and other unwanted groups that had been gassed in one of their heinous extermination camps. At the time, Max was struck with how very little humanity the Khmer soldiers showed for their adversary.

In retrospect, Max contemplated the irony of that situation. A couple of years later, in April 1975, the Khmer Rouge would make the FANK treatment of KR dead pale by comparison to the wholesale slaughter that KR leader Pol Pot and his fundamentalist Marxist regime perpetrated on the Cambodian people. From the time the KR marched triumphantly into Phnom Penh in that April, until the Vietnamese invaded in 1979, an estimated two million Cambodians lost their lives.

On that fateful day in April of 1975, members of MEDTC and all Americans at the embassy were evacuated by helicopter in an operation dubbed *"Eagle Pull."* Max had made a major contribution to drafting this plan prior to his departure in February 1973. *"Eagle Pull"* was then a contingency plan. It was the Cambodian equivalent of operation *"Frequent Wind,"* which was the larger scale, but comparable, operation that took place when Saigon was evacuated in a widely-publicized and televised operation, involving helicopters landing by the dozens on the deck of the American aircraft carrier, *USS Midway.*

Max recalled that day. He had watched the Saigon evacuation unfold on network television. Who could forget the images of sailors rolling helicopters over the side to clear the decks for others to land?

Stimulated by these reflections, Max climbed up to his attic and dug out a trunk which stored remnants of what had been his military career. He recalled stashing a two-inch stack of calling cards in the trunk. These were the calling cards given to him by each of the FANK officers he'd come in contact with during his tour in Cambodia. Max still had his CGSC Modern Military History thesis sitting on the kitchen table. In it, he had written at the time, the following passage:

The Killing Fields *is a catch phrase used to depict the wholesale slaughter of more than 1.7 million Cambodian people during the Khmer Rouge regime from 1975 till 1979. It is also the title of a biography and subsequently, a British film, written about Dith Pran, a Khmer citizen, who through his own guile and tenacity, succeeded in escaping the 'year one' slaughter at the hands of the Pol Pot's frenzied annihilation campaign. During this period, Cambodian cities were actually emptied of citizens. They were then force-marched to the countryside to work camps under the philosophical guise of taking up a much simpler, agrarian life as dictated by their fundamentalist communist ideology. Another of the mandates of Pol Pot's political philosophy was that the intelligentsia had to be eliminated outright. This included all educators, administrators, managers, entrepreneurs, and people of any stature who had supported the American military efforts in Cambodia.*

As part of his renewed interest in Cambodia, Max reread the book, *The Killing Fields*, by Christofer Hudson. He had first read it back when it was first published in the early '80s. Max had naturally assumed that all the officers whose names were scrolled on his stack of calling cards must have perished at the hands of the KR.

Max had often, over the years, thought of his many Cambodian friends, most of them Khmer Army officers, who must have died at the hands of the blood thirsty KR. What a shameful loss! Max could still visualize the peace-loving, docile nature of the Cambodian people, which was always very much in evidence in his dealings with the Khmer officers. It was hard to believe, and a source of a great deal of depression for Max over the years. But, Max was sure that from what he'd read, and what he'd witnessed, that the KR's bloody, wholesale revenge and enslavement of the population almost certainly spelled doom for his FANK friends.

Adding credence, Max recalled the British film director Roland Jaffe's movie of the same name, which came out about a year after *The Killing Fields* was published. Even with this compelling story of survival, Max considered it very doubtful that many, if any, of his friends had survived.

No doubt, Dr. Hang Ngor's portrayal of the Cambodian journalist Dith Pran was chilling. It moved Max to further research, which revealed to him that Dith Pran had written several other books about the holocaust in Cambodia. Max also found several articles by Sidney Schamberg, the New York Times' Phnom Penh war correspondent, whose character was portrayed in the movie by Sam Waterson. Mr. Schamberg had worked closely with and had been close friends with Dith Pran during the year before the fall of Phnom Penh. His subsequent articles about their last days together held Pran in highest regard. When Schamberg found out that Pran had miraculously made his way to a refugee camp in Thailand, he quickly arranged for Pran's evacuation to the US. Max took the time to write each of the officers' names from his deck of calling cards to take with him on the trip, in the unlikely event that during his forthcoming visit to Cambodia, someone might recognize one of the names.

CHAPTER FIFTY-FIVE

*M*ax had informed his two adult children of his plan to retire and go back to Vietnam and Cambodia as soon as he could make arrangements. Stumbling blocks seemed to pop up at every turn. The Xerox CEO personally asked him to remain on board until they could perform a search for Max's replacement. That would be at least ninety days after the upcoming holidays. Then, it would be at the height of Cambodia's rainy season. So, it looked like it might be a late as June of the next year before he would be free of obligations and inclement weather.

Max discussed these issues with Chris and Melissa. For his part, Chris was gratified that his dad would make this trip in his mom's memory. If anyone knew about his dad's demons, besides his mom, it was Chris. Chris had lived with his dad for the first two years after Max and Emily separated. He and his dad had gone on many skiing, fishing, or bird hunting trips during those years. He had witnessed the demons in action while his dad slept. The dreams were still vivid, where Max would strike out into the night with fists flailing and loud yelps. They were just not as frequent nowadays.

*   *   *

To Max's inevitable gratification, during those years Chris decided to get serious about school, and with some serious fatherly political help, he got into Stanford. At the time, Chris worried about being so far away from his dad. He had always felt helpless, because there was really nothing he could do for his dad. Chris felt like he was abandoning his dad for his own welfare nonetheless.

Chris, by now, was a successful cardio-thoracic surgeon, practicing in Denver. He was married and had two of the most adorable little girls. Max was proud of Chris, and Chris was well aware of it. They had developed a great adult relationship. Chris was grateful that his dad had made it financially possible for him to finish his Stanford under-graduate degree. Then, he subsequently made it through Stanford Medical School, without incurring any significant student loans.

Chris's wife Susie had an MBA from Stanford, where they had met while Chris was finishing his residency. She was now running the business end of Chris's booming cardiology/thoracic surgery practice.

On the other side of the family, daughter Melissa regarded Max's sudden openness to returning to Vietnam and Cambodia as something of a miracle. She was beginning to understand the complex admixture of culture, ego, and sacrifice that her dad represented.

She had spent many a night with her mom, in her final state, examining the causes of the dissension in their otherwise normal family. Now old enough to appreciate to some degree the sacrifices of her elders, Melissa was beginning to understand the complicated, quasi-unmentionable issues that tugged on each of her parents as they trudged through their lives trying desperately to understand one another.

*   *   *

Max agreed to postpone his trip to the Far East until after Melissa had graduated, yet again, with not only another B.A. in Romantic Languages, but also from William and Mary's Graduate School of Business, finally receiving her MBA, Summa Cum Laude, the school's highest honors.

Melissa had found that trying to help her mom at the B&B full-time while taking a full graduate school load was overwhelming, so she had transferred over to the executive MBA program, where she took only one or two courses a semester. Thus, it had taken her longer than she planned to finish.

In the back of Max's mind, he wondered what would happen to what had become the number one B&B in the Williamsburg area in the AAA travel guide and every other notable rating authority. Max wondered, "Could Emily be beckoning me to recover my soul with a redemptive trip to Vietnam and Cambodia, just as she had retrieved and nurtured her last dream of owning a first class B&B?"

So went the mental conversation. What could Max do at long last to exculpate his intractable actions, over all those years, to redeem the memory of that long-lost, precious relationship?

It was not hard to recall all their fun times—all their loving times—all those passionate times. Max recalled one night, early in their relationship, they actually held hands together under their dinner table at the O'Club at Ft. Eustis at some formal dress up gathering. This furtive hand-holding became a 'thing' with them.

Even in their short sojourn in Bavaria, they were never very far apart. At the end of the day, they would consult the daily bulletin, which was always available at every Caserne. The big decision after dinner was to decide, often at the last minute, that the movie being shown by the local base theater might be to their liking. Sometimes, as late as 6:30 they would summarily don their coats, hike the two blocks to the theater, get their tickets, be seated, and share a fifteen cent bag of the world's worst popcorn, most of which was devoured before the movie ever started promptly at 7 PM, with a ceremonious film depiction of the "Star Spangled Banner."

Max missed Emily's touch and caring voice. What an awful folly he had made of that precious relationship, of their lives, actually! All these thoughts of redemption and healing were decidedly too late to benefit Emily. It smacked ironic to Max that these long-in-the-making changes of heart were not only untimely, but could have potentially unintended outcomes.

True to this latest resolve, Max set out to find a reliable travel consultant in Denver. He had heard of one such consultant through some recently retired Xerox friends, who had just returned from a two-month visit to China and SE Asia.

This agent specialized in cruises and guided tours in the Far East. The owner, Audra Campbell, was a woman of strong opinions, who readily contradicted her clients when she thought they were making mistakes in their choices of hotels, guides, or modes of transportation. Her way was to find out what a given client wanted to derive from a visit. If someone simply wanted to say that 'I've been there,' she would encourage cruises, with brief ports of call in the cities where the client wanted to visit.

On the other hand, with someone like Max, who wanted to revisit the places where he had been stationed, and places, like Angkor Wat, which were off limits when he was in Cambodia, she would recommend private guided tours and transportation. In some cases, she arranged for specialty guides, who had taken other war veterans on redemptive excursions, like the one Max envisaged, and, since Max was giving Ms. Campbell six months notice, she could surely find the perfect set of excursions and guides for Max.

In their first interview, Max informed Audra that he wanted to visit, at a minimum, South Vietnam and Cambodia, if not Thailand and Hong Kong. He gave her a list of the cities he wanted to visit along the way, like Saigon, Vung Tau, Phnom Penh, Neak Leoung, Kompong Som, and Siem Riep.

Max wanted a couple of days in some of the places, longer in others. Audra determined that the best solution was to arrange an itinerary where Max flew into large international cities like Bangkok, out of which she could arrange flights to other destinations like Saigon and Phnom Penh. He could subsequently take local flights to the other desired cities in Vietnam and Cambodia.

In the next three months, Max had lunch meetings with Audra on several occasions to go over what was blossoming into a very detailed agenda. It appeared that it would take the better part of a month for Max to accomplish his extended voyage.

CHAPTER FIFTY-SIX

*M*ax had promised to attend Melissa's graduation in late May, then to spend a few days with her at the B&B, which she was still managing, with the help of a few struggling graduate students at W&M, who filled in part-time when Melissa was at class or working on a project. Since Chris and Susie were also attending, Max regarded this get together as a great opportunity for the family to get together before he headed to SE Asia.

Chris informed Max that they had arranged for their girls to stay with Susie's parents while they were back east for the graduation festivities. Chris and Susie had always wanted to visit Washington D.C., so they asked Max to join them, after the graduation activities, to show them the highlights of D.C., before heading back to Denver. For his part, Max relished the thought of some concentrated adult time, with dinners at some of the top spots in the D.C. area.

Max heartily accepted. He had always wanted to go back to the D.C. area when he was not merely a near-pauper junior officer. If nothing else, he wanted to partake in some of the venerable hotels and restaurants that were beyond his reach when he was here for language school, back in the early '70s.

Max and Chris decided to fly in and out of Dulles and simply rent a large sedan or minivan to get back and forth from Dulles to Williamsburg. There would be ample transportation at the Williamsburg B&B. Vans and limos had been purchased over the years to accommodate clients arriving from the various airports in the Tidewater, Richmond, and D.C. areas. The limousines were used exclusively for VIPs who could be picked up at Dulles and delivered to Emily's highly coveted destination.

Max and Chris intended to stay at the venerable Mayflower Hotel in downtown D.C. during their visit, so having one car was not a bother.

They could leave the rental car parked in the garage at the hotel and simply take the Metro, or taxis, whenever the need presented itself.

* * *

Meanwhile, Max had Audra calculate when he'd have to be back to Denver, taking his D.C.-area travel considerations into account. Max had told Audra that he wanted a few days to settle affairs before he left his home in Denver for this month-long sojourn in SE Asia. So, Audra had Max scheduled to depart Denver on the twelfth of June. He would be flying first class on Singapore Airlines on his first leg to Bangkok.

Catching a glimpse of Audra's thinking, Max noticed that she had scheduled a two-day layover in Bangkok to allow Max to reorient his biological clock. She had him staying at the JW Marriott in downtown Bangkok. She arranged for an English-speaking driver to meet him at the international arrivals terminal and take him directly to the hotel. After a brief tour of Bangkok on the second day, the same English-speaking driver would take Max back to the airport for his flight to Saigon.

In their final meeting before Max headed to D.C. for Melissa's graduation, Audra gave Max his detailed SE Asian itinerary, showing dates, flights, hotels, and guide arrangements at each of Max's stops. She said that a courier would deliver his actual airline documents and his passport, with appropriate visas, to his home on the day after his return to Denver from D.C.

CHAPTER FIFTY-SEVEN

When Max and his family finally landed at Dulles the day before Melissa's graduation, they were weary from incessant turbulence. Mid-morning flights out of Denver, even on first class, were fraught with bumps and jostles whenever the jet stream took a dive in late spring. Storms abounded all through the Great Plains states, so the Donatellos' flight was routed north to avoid some of the more nasty stuff to their south. So, their plane was coming into its Washington Dulles glide path from the north, flying into weather systems, which were shifting, converging, and dumping loads of moisture in their path.

The pilot chose a long, slow descent that began over Morgantown, West Virginia. The crew gradually eked out a few thousand feet at every interval allowed. At lower altitudes, the bumps, however, became more severe. Their late lunch meal was pressing perilously close against the upchuck button, especially on those privileged to be seated in the first class section. In the rear of the plane, the staff was in near revolt at the sight of all the esophageal reflux.

When the pilot finally brought the Boeing 767 down to earth, you would have thought that a B-25 had made its first carrier landing, with all the ensuing notoriety back in early 1942 when Doolittle's B-25s took off only from carriers. The passengers howled their approval to once again be in the embrace of the earth's gravitational bounds, when the wheels skidded onto the surface at the end of one of Dulles' longest runways.

Passenger optimism was soon dampened when they saw the extent of the downpour outside on the runway. What did this weather portend to Max and his family with the specter of their two-plus hour trek from Dulles to Williamsburg?

The Donatello family had planned to arrive late on the afternoon before the eve of graduation. So, if necessary, an evening in the Dulles area might make good sense to allow any hostile storm system to pass through. A morning arrival in Williamsburg would not be cause of any perturbation to the schedule of graduation festivities, except to delay their long-awaited reunion with Melissa.

By the time the Donatellos had collected their bags and arrived at the car rental desk, the networks were predicting tornadoes all around Dulles and the surrounding counties west of the beltway. The real problem was that they had not made contingency reservations to stay in the Dulles/Herndon area. There were plenty of nice hotels not far from the terminal, but it was not a sure thing that there would be availability, as their flight arrived at 4:30 PM. Since it was now a half-hour later, Max wondered if there would be availability in any of the hotels nearest the airport.

Max said to Chris and Susie, "I'm going to try and pull some strings with Marriott or Hyatt Regency. They both have large hospitality footprints near this area." Max took out his iPhone and hit a speed dial that had him talking immediately to a very solicitous Marriott Platinum Preferred agent.

Max explained his dilemma. It was in mere seconds that the agent was offering Max a two-bedroom suite at the Marriott at Dulles, a short taxi ride from where they stood. Accomplishing his goal, Max then informed a helpful Avis agent that they would pick up their rental before 9 AM the following day. Max had ordered a premium-sized car, which meant that they would have either a Cadillac sedan or a Tahoe SUV, so there would be no issue with ample space for luggage.

Max then picked up the Marriott phone in the rental car area and was told that there was a hotel van pulling up outside, as they spoke. Max intoned, "OK, troops, let's go hide away until all this hostile weather subsides. We're all approved for the Marriott next door, with a comfy little suite I'm sure will be satisfactory for all of us. Our carriage awaits, outside. All we have to do, unfortunately, is to schlep all our bags out that door."

*   *   *

As the Donatellos hurried into the lobby of the Dulles Marriott, they could hear the roar of what sounded like a freight train approaching in the distance. Their check-in was, therefore, exceedingly perfunctory.

They were told to either assemble in one of the meeting rooms, or try to get to their suite. If the latter was possible, the instructions were to get to an interior bath and close the door, with as many arranged in the tub as was possible. While this gathering was later a laughing matter, squeezing three adults into a bathtub did not seem feasible. Remembering that the suite had one bathroom per bedroom, it seemed only right for Chris and Susie to take refuge in their own tub, while Max hunkered down in his. Max declared upon their arrival at the suite, "I'll find the tub to the left; you guys find the bathing refuge to the right."

Just then, the sound intensified as if a high-speed freight train was running just along side of the hotel.

The roof trembled, windows burst, and there was a frightful vacuum just before the windows gave way. Max felt his eardrums coming undone, just like had happened when the KR mortar carried him briefly into la-la land back off Cambodia's Route 6 in 1972.

Finally, the pressure eased, and Max checked his ears to see whether his eardrums had burst. He had lucked out. The freight train sound was trailing off to the east, so Max thought it would be safe to check and see how Chris and Melissa had made it through this rogue tornado's near miss.

As Max approached, he heard the quiet sobs of a woman relieved that the worst was over. Max found Chris and Susie wrapped desperately around one another at the bottom of their tub, none the worse for wear. Chris seemed to be somewhat stunned.

To lighten the moment, Max teased, "First tornado, I'll bet," with appropriate irony dripping playfully from his voice.

"Wow, they don't give you near good enough of a warning of a tornado's power," Chris offered meekly. "You see these things terrorize states like Kansas, Tennessee, Kentucky, or the Southern Midwest. But, who would have suggested it happens this far north into Loudon County, Virginia?"

Max countered, "I was here on business one other time when a storm made mincemeat out of the outskirts of Baltimore. I've read that most areas around Bethesda and Rockville have been whacked at one time or another."

They spent the rest of the evening awaiting room service to reconstitute the kitchen, so they could have a Gastro Intestinal Reflux (GIR)-inducing club sandwich and cold fries at 11 PM. They washed it all down with the remaining beers in the suite's two mini-bars.

CHAPTER FIFTY-EIGHT

*A*ll of their connections thereafter were timely and precise. They were in Williamsburg in time to join Melissa and several friends at lunch in a spectacular new restaurant called *Il Tempo* on the outskirts of the city, a very cosmopolitan Neo-Tuscan entry into the bustling restaurant scene around Williamsburg. When they entered, they were struck by the many authentic scents comprising garlic; roasted Roma tomato; wood–fired, oven-baked pizza, and succulent seafood pastas. Max immediately caught the scent of pesto, with Reggiano Parmesan, garlic, and crushed Pine Nuts.

Their garlic bread made Max think of the one time he and Emily had caught a train to Milano, the farthest they had ventured down the Italian Peninsula, back when Max was a lowly lieutenant on meager pay in the late 1960s.

Max was still intoxicated with the splendid memories of that trip where he took, to his mind, a 'trophy American bride' to show off to all the wishful and coveting young Italian admirers, who would love to have so much as a brief dance with Emily, irrespective of her marital status. Max's thoughts were immersed with the enormous pride he had that Emily was his wife and lover. How proud he was that she was so spectacular, and that she did not notice a single Italian, adventuring male admirer.

Loyalty. Max reveled in the fact that Emily embodied that one commodity as a prime asset. She had committed to Max, and that was the end of the story. Of course, this was only one of the many precious attributes that Emily possessed, as Max would discover to his great delight from their first day forward.

Chapter Fifty-Nine

*T*he graduation festivities wound down, and the B&B had settled down to just the Donatello family left on the comfortable porch rockers, watching the world go by. Melissa asked Max how the preparations were going for his upcoming trip to SE Asia. Max replied, "I'm just about set, with just a few things left to tidy up after I return to Denver."

Melissa said, "I'm so happy that you finally decided to make this journey, and doing it in mom's memory makes it all the more special. I know she would have done flips to think you finally decided to retrace some of those steps into the valley of the shadow of death you took back then." Melissa gave her dad's hand a squeeze. "If you find that place worthy of another visit, let me know well in advance, and I'll go with you. I have always wondered what that area would be like." The obvious intimation was that she would really like to know more about her dad, and to have an opportunity for a closer adult relationship.

Melissa possessed not only a sincere tone, but her facial expression carried signs of real caring, something Max had not witnessed much from Melissa over the years, since the separation. Max couldn't help but sense the irony that the revelation of his finally going back to Cambodia to face his demons had won his daughter's favor.

The folly of the whole matter was that if Max weren't so intractable about redemption and healing when he first came back from the war, he would have most likely saved himself and everyone in his family the tons of grief that emanated from his inability to follow his heart. But, as Max reflected on former intractability, he recalled the old adage, "When the student is ready, a teacher will appear."

He had obviously chosen to follow the more painful, long-term course. It was Max's essential folly in spades. He had decided to try to suppress all those wartime memories. Not only did he pay the price, so did his family. He was lucky that he was realizing his folly, as it were, while he still had time to improve his relationship with Melissa, and, perhaps, in spite of an already good relationship with Chris and his family, he could more freely take a more active role in their day-to-day lives. Surely, he could at least be there more for the grandkids.

Max decided to pry a bit into Melissa's private life, since she had made the initial gambit of warmth in the conversation. "So, Melissa, tell us about the men in your life." Max could not help but notice the surprise on her face, but she smiled broadly and, without any trace of offense, went on to tell her family that she had indeed been seeing a handsome young gentleman, whose family owned and operated a large Honda dealership there in the Tidewater area. Mr. Special, as things turned out, was also graduating that same weekend from Georgetown law school in D.C. Thus, he was not in attendance at Melissa's graduation. The couple had agreed that it was important for their families that they walk up and get their respective sheepskins. They promised to show each other the videos of the two ceremonies when he got back to the Peninsula early the following week.

"So, we are not going to get to meet this prince charming," chided Chris in a sardonic tone. "Why don't you join us on our trip to D.C. tomorrow; then, we'll all have dinner at some swanky place up there," suggested Chris in a dutiful, yet brotherly manner.

Melissa shrugged, "I'd love to, but I don't have anyone lined up to manage the B&B for the weekend. Also, I'm not certain that Rick, that's his name, and his family will have any free time. On reflection, I guess I could call around to some of my regular staff and see if they'd be interested in making some extra cash. And, I'm supposed to chat with Rick tonight at around 10 PM. I guess I could run it by him, and see if they could be available to meet for dinner as you suggested." Max was pleased at this reaction from Melissa. Flexibility had not always been her most prominent trait.

*   *   *

By morning, Melissa had lined up a substitute manager for the weekend, and Rick, for his part, had begged off a planned, but perfunctory, business dinner with his parents, so he would be available Sunday to meet Melissa's family for dinner. They agreed to meet in the lobby lounge of the Mayflower Hotel at 5:30. They wanted to try a nearby lounge that was reputed to be a hang out for Washington's politicos. After a drink and introductions, and with a little help from the

Mayflower's masterful concierge, they would grab a taxi to one of a number of five-star restaurants in the district.

The plan called for Melissa to spend the night at the Mayflower in a suite with her dad. Then, she'd drive back to Williamsburg on Monday morning. Max, Chris, and Susie would make their way to Dulles to catch the early afternoon flight back to Denver. All was set.

CHAPTER SIXTY

Rick Whitely was from a third-generation Tidewater car-dealer family. His personal credentials were as solid as Fort Knox. To his credit, Rick was a natural people-person. There were no apparent airs, no snobbishness, not a trace of arrogance. What you saw was what you got. Rick had worked from the ground up in the family business. Upon graduation from high school he wasn't interested in attending college. It was not until Rick was near thirty that he started attending college classes while still working full-time. It was only the last couple of years that Rick had moved up to the D.C. area to attend Georgetown law school. He and Melissa had met when she was helping her mom buy a car for the B&B four years ago. They had ended up doing the car negotiations over dinner, and had spent many weekends since in either Williamsburg or near Georgetown together.

It was clear that Rick was totally enraptured with Melissa. This captivation put Rick at the top of the heap of suitors Max and Chris might envisage for Melissa. Since his case seemed vindicated almost from the start, the evening went off like a dream. There were no tense moments. There were no condescending judgments, only a decidedly open, free-wheeling discussion of whatever topic anyone thought appropriate.

Chris was impressed with Melissa's beau. Susie withheld her vote, but marveled at how at ease everyone had gotten along. She was not certain that it was Rick's influence, or that everyone was simply relieved that Melissa may have finally picked someone who was worthy of all her manifest potential.

Max took an early liking to Rick, remembering how gracious Emily's father had been when they first met. Rick was clearly a stand-up guy, and Melissa showed a genuine admiration and respect for him. That spoke legions to Max, knowing how fussy Melissa could be.

The evening was a complete success.

Max had noticed that the bartender at the lounge they had visited first, had a Khmer-sounding name: Sisowath Samoeun. Max immediately struck up a conversation, especially when Max found out this person was indeed a refugee who had left Cambodia in early February 1975, when his father determined the family should get out before the fall of Phnom Penh. Max was pleased to hear that this Cambodian American was active in the international support network that was assisting with aid to Cambodian schools. Samoeun related to Max that his father had been a captain in the FANK Army, working at FANK headquarters when he decided to get his family out of Cambodia.

Max was a not a little perplexed, because he had worked with an English-speaking Khmer first lieutenant named Keo Samoeun during his ten months in Phnom Penh. Could it be possible that Keo might be Sisowath's father? Max followed up with a few more questions that indeed identified Keo as the bartender's father. Sisowath pulled out a picture of his mom and dad, and Max immediately recognized a now sixty-something Khmer standing next to his wife, whom Max had never met.

Sisowath explained that his mother and father now lived near Ft. Eustis, VA, not far from Williamsburg. They had made their way to the US via Thailand, where they were detained in a refugee camp on the eastern border of Thailand and Cambodia until October of '75. The Samoeun family was airlifted to the US on a giant Air Force C-141. They were initially housed in 1975 at the SE Asian Refugee Center at Ft. Chaffee, AK, near Ft. Smith, AK.

Max could not believe the sweet irony. At that time, Max served at Ft. Chaffee as a part of the Support Command headquarters, that was itself airlifted from Ft. Lewis, Washington, to Ft. Chaffee to open the sprawling WWII-era training-turned-reserve base to receive and house the tens of thousands of refugees. In fact, Max mentioned to Sisowath that he was there for several months, working day and night to set up a logistics infrastructure for the base.

The conversation became even more involved when Max informed his new friend that he would be returning to Cambodia for the first time since 1973, soon after he returned the next day to Denver. Sisowath insisted on providing Max with a number of contacts in his Khmer support organization, all based in Phnom Penh. Max was now armed with names, addresses, and phone contacts in Cambodia, of what Max was to discover was an elaborate international web of Cambodian patriots, who had nothing but their country's best interests at heart.

CHAPTER SIXTY-ONE

*L*ater, back in the hotel suite, Max was still animated about the discovery that one of his former FANK colleagues had found a way out of Cambodia, avoiding the slaughter that would surely have ensued. Melissa remarked, "This trip really is important for you, Dad. You might find that more of your Khmer officer friends survived than you thought possible."

Max replied, "I have always held an uncharacteristic pessimism about their chances; call it a gut feeling, I suppose. But, all the reports I've read, and the testimonies I've heard, led me to believe that the survivors who escaped were definitely in the minority. But, I agree the trip is bound to do me some good. If nothing else, I will get to retrace my steps and discover what has happened to those places since I left."

Melissa added, "I really hope that it will have a liberating effect for you, Dad. You deserve some peace. I wish I were going with you." She came over to her dad, put her arms around him, and gave him a big hug.

Max said, "Thanks, honey. Your mom always said that." Max kissed Melissa on the forehead. "And, by the way, I think Rick is a great guy. I would be happy to welcome him into our family. I hope you two find a pathway to happiness together in the future. You seem very well-suited for each other."

Melissa put her head on Max's chest and said, "Rick is the nicest guy I've ever met. I'm very fond of him. We are together a lot, and we get along so well. I feel so great when I'm around him. It's almost as if a magical spell had descended on me. Daddy, I think he just might be Mr. Right."

Max gave his daughter a squeeze and said quietly, "You'll know it when you hear it in your heart. Take your time, enjoy the voyage, and just be sure. Rick appears to know his mind, and certainly seems to appreciate the treasure he has his eyes set on. He'll be patient, I'll bet sure money on it."

Melissa gave her dad another hug and said, "Thanks, Dad. That means a lot to me, hearing it from you."

Max said, "Gosh, it's past midnight. I'm going to be worthless tomorrow, and you need your beauty sleep, young lady." They exchanged grins and offered goodnights hugs, and then they were off to their respective bedrooms.

CHAPTER SIXTY-TWO

*A*t breakfast the next morning, served in Max and Melissa's suite, the banter was all about Rick and Melissa. They had experienced a real bonding event as a family over the past few days, capped off with a memorable dinner last evening, when Rick entered the equation.

The lively conversation went on until Max said, "We should probably adjourn this meeting of the Donatello board. I am certain the Mayflower Hotel would appreciate it if we were to make the checkout time of eleven. And, I hear that planes will leave without you if you do not present yourself within a certain number of minutes before the flight is scheduled to take off. In our case, that is 1:45 today. Since it is now 10:15, I recommend we meet in the lobby in half an hour with bag and baggage, ready for departure. I will arrange to have Melissa's car and the SUV brought around, so the bellman can simply take your bags directly to the cars."

While they were packing, Melissa strolled into her daddy's quarters and said, "Dad, I've been approached by some very reputable auditing and accounting firms. I've been asked to take a consulting position with *PriceWaterhouseCoopers* (PWC) in Hampton. The job would entail travel to D.C. and Ft. Leavenworth initially. It seems PWC has a new contract with TRADOC for performance auditing of their officer training programs. If I were to take it, the B&B would have to be left in the hands of a hired manager. That is probably not the best solution for so venerable a business as mom nurtured over the years."

Max countered, "When do you have to let them know?"

"I have one more interview with a senior partner in Washington next week. Then, who knows? Three weeks? A month?" replied Melissa.

"Let me toss the proposition around in my mind while I'm gone. We have several options. One is to sell it outright. Another is to turn it over to a management company. The last is that I come back and run it in your mom's memory," Max proffered.

"Wow, the last one was not an option I had expected to hear. But, I have to say, I'd certainly love to have you back here in the Tidewater area," spurted Melissa with enthusiasm.

They agreed to let Max think it over while on his trip to SE Asia. It would give him a reasonable amount of time to consider the pros and cons of each alternative.

CHAPTER SIXTY-THREE

*M*ax reflected on how enjoyable the weekend in Virginia had been as he got settled into his first-class seat aboard this Bangkok-bound Singapore Air Boeing 777. Time had flown since he got back to Denver, and as Max savored the premium champagne, he recalled that the only two major things he had accomplished in Denver during his brief sojourn was to hire a house sitter, and to buttonhole Chris about the developments in Melissa's career, and the implications of the three options they'd laid out.

Chris had a very busy practice that was growing in the Denver area. He and Susie had been thinking of having a home built not far from Max's place. Chris had no interest in the B&B business, but weighed in heavily against his dad relocating to Virginia. Chris and Susie both insisted that Max stay in Denver where his friends and family were settled. They wanted him to be on hand while their two little girls grew up.

Max continued his ruminations, *"What if I were to deed over my house to Chris and Susie and the kids? Heck, we could live in the space that Chris had occupied above the garage for all those early years after the separation. Or, we could even build a guesthouse, which I could occupy while there. Then, I could swoop into Virginia for a month or two, keep an eye on the B&B, and then come back west. Chris and Susie could redo the main house according to their tastes and needs. It would be less costly than starting a new construction project."* Max took the last sip of champagne and concluded, *"How brilliant, but I'm not certain how long my tail feathers could put up with all those cross country flights every few weeks or months."*

Max concluded that there would be plenty to do to coordinate whatever path he chose. But, he liked the initial flavor and substance of the idea. It would result in his having the best of all worlds. His long-time friends in Denver, Chris and his family, and he'd be able to work on the relationship he saw as budding with his pretty, talented daughter and her beau. Besides, he still felt a certain sense of place around the Tidewater-Williamsburg area. Besides, his beloved Emily had been laid to rest there.

CHAPTER SIXTY-FOUR

*M*ax used his time in Bangkok to adjust his bio-clock. He was not interested in any kind of touring. He used his driver/guide only to venture out of the hotel for meals. Max had concluded back in the '70s that Thai women, of all SE Asia female specimens, were by far the most gorgeous of all. Exotic, was a thought that seemed apropos. Max now confirmed to himself that this characteristic had obviously not changed. The female greeting and wait staff at the J.W. Marriott were no less than stunning, but Max had no interest in an Asian dalliance.

The plane ride to Saigon was brief. On descent, Max switched to an empty window seat on the side where Tan Son Nhut Airbase had once been. He was amazed to see the concrete revetments that were built for American and Vietnamese aircraft still lined both sides of the runway. They stood empty, like hollow shells of buildings existing for some forgotten purpose.

Max was surprised to encounter a new terminal befitting modern times, with all the equipment and services one would expect in any latter day international terminal. Formalities were perfunctory. Max had a lingering worry that since he had held an active Top Secret Security clearance until his recent retirement from Xerox, there might be some interest in him by the Vietnamese intelligence authorities.

Max's concern was all for naught, as the Vietnamese border officials seemed only interested in relieving the congestion in the arrivals terminal. There was less than any concern about some long-retired American Army officer. Max soon realized that Vietnam and the US were allies and trading partners these days. So, whatever concern he may have harbored was quickly dispelled. He quickly came to grips that Vietnam was not really the communist, socialist, paranoid state of his nightmares, but a socialist-sanctioned capitalist state of unbridled enterprise. It seemed that everyone was in business.

Max could not help but recall the last time he landed at Tan Son Nhut aboard a Flying Tiger contract bird stuffed with three hundred soldiers and airmen. He could still remember feeling the blast of humid air wafting strange fragrances along with the typical Indochinese blistering temperatures. This time, he was prepared, wearing lightweight slacks and a loose, tropical-weight, short-sleeve shirt, with a pair of sturdy sandals. Quite a difference from arriving in an Army dress green uniform, fully buttoned, with tie and a garrison hat!

As he walked up the jet way and entered the arrivals terminal, he couldn't help contrasting the up-to-date, air-conditioned terminal with the dour, drab GI welcoming center at the old Air Base, whose only means of cooling were slow-moving tropical ceiling fans.

*   *   *

His contract-provided guide and translator for the following day was a twenty-something, gregarious fellow with an interminably self-absorbed manner. He called himself "Pham, Superman."

It didn't take Max long to conclude that this Viet Cong progeny was the most self-indulgent, arrogant little shit he had ever encountered. With Spartan pride, Pham trumpeted the glories of the Vietnamese ultimate triumph in 1975. He reminded Max how the American imperialists had to be rescued by the ubiquitous helicopter, the metaphor of US involvement in Vietnam. Max was aware, of course, that Pham was referring to the haunting image of helicopters alighting on a rooftop tower, loading passengers again and again until all Americans and their 'lackeys' were evacuated. Then he pointed out a universal mistake: the tower, where the much-photographed helicopters landed in those last hours, was **_not_** the roof of the US Embassy. It was actually a different compound belonging to the Aid for International Development (USAID) organization.

Max was intimately familiar with "*Operation Frequent Wind.*" This designation was the code name of the operation Pham Superman was describing. It was the Vietnam version of the US's SE Asia evacuation plan. It corresponded to the plan used in Cambodia several weeks before called "*Operation Eagle Pull,*" by those familiar with the concept of operations.

"Pisses me off, this brain-washed little gook trying to glorify the events of our unfortunate departure in 1975. I will not get into a discussion with this

know-nothing little bastard about the whys and why-nots of US involvement in SE Asia," concluded Max with a certain venom he had not experienced since his days in Cambodia, when some crazy-ass American B-52 bombardier killed hundreds of innocents in Neak Leoung on a botched air strike, while he watched.

Max was exasperated with the first day's character and content. Why would any tour company accept the proposition that a returning American Army combat veteran would want to visit the Vietnamese War Museum? Hint: the Museum was built after 1975. This place was nothing more than a cavernous propaganda dungeon displaying ghastly images of dastardly deeds done by vicious American military men.

Revolted, Max was not certain he wanted to proceed with visits to Long Binh, Bien Hoa, and Cat Lai. His biggest objection was being stuck with 'Pham, Superman,' in a car for more than four hours. Max finally acceded and was picked up the next morning at around 9 AM.

Recalling his treacherous daily drive from Saigon to Long Binh, Max was encouraged by the manifest development all along the route. The Saigon Port was a beehive of activity. There were even some small cruise ships in evidence. What a change!

As they passed along the route to Long Binh, Max noticed that some things had not changed beyond the grasp of Saigon's tentacles. Numerous roadside vendors, tire-changing facilities, home-wear shops, storefronts of all description dotted the highway on each side, still in competition with one another for whatever trickle of business that happened their way.

What had changed was the density of traffic almost everywhere. There were far fewer cyclo-taxis, having been replaced by converted motorbikes, with a passenger seat up front. Max recalled all the bicycle traffic back in his day. They had been replaced by the ubiquitous motor scooter or motorbike. The fascinating thing for Max was that now these vehicles were mostly new. Every type of Japanese-made cycle was in evidence from Honda to Suzuki. Max marveled that the many homemade versions that he had seen back in the '70s had been replaced with fuel-efficient, non-polluting Japanese vehicles driven by men and women alike.

Long Binh, once the largest US bases in Vietnam, was now a vast commercial industrial park. Companies like Sanyo, Panasonic, and many other prominent Asian and international notables had facilities scattered all throughout the sprawling facility, where the United States Army once had operational combat commands, support commands, depots, logistics units, and an inbound personnel processing center. Max had forgotten the enormity of the place.

He asked the driver to take him to the farthest points along the perimeter. There, he walked and observed the observation towers, the outpost positions, and the delicately preserved communications facilities. The sentry outposts still existed. They had been used to keep the perimeter front, as it were, coordinated. The tall fences were still standing. As Max moved from position to position, he recollected that even as a mere logistician, he saw through the folly of all these perfunctory ruses of a real defense.

Max did his best to ignore Pham, his supposed tour guide. Instead, before returning to the hotel, he asked to be taken to the Chinese district of Saigon, the Cho'lon District. Back in the day, Cho'lon was a beehive of activity for not only the furtive Viet Cong cadre, who infiltrated daily into the bowels of Saigon, but was also the home of USMAAG (Military Assistance Advisory Group) Special Operations Group (SOG), the predecessor organization to Military Assistance Command Vietnam (MACV), going way back when the only US involvement was the Special Forces Group, which trained the South Vietnamese long before the introduction of American combat units into the South.

Max was overwhelmed by the growth and glaring capitalism that now characterized every street of Saigon. He engaged Pham with a tone of irony, "In the end, communist North Vietnam was the victor in the long struggle with the Western powers. My first inclination if I were asked to describe Vietnam would be to call it a capitalistic country."

Pham retorted, "What we have here in Vietnam today is state-sponsored capitalism. We have patterned our society on the success of China, with its obvious successes in Hong Kong and Shanghai. The Vietnamese people are very enterprising, like the Chinese. We don't have to be told to work hard. It is just that now, the average citizen gets to reap the rewards of his or her own endeavors."

Max replied, "I visited China several years ago and found the same phe-nomenon. Everyone was in business in one way or another. Socialist egalitarian ways of the past seem long forgotten."

Pham said, "Do not forget that the US sowed the seeds of capitalism in occupied Japan after WWII. Then, it happened again in Korea. Both those countries have had amazing recoveries after a conflict with the mighty US war machine. Europe can boast the same result. I do not mean to criticize the humanitarian and constructive efforts America has made over the past century. With the exception of the Vietnamese vic-tory in 1975, all the other conflicts resulted in massive infusions of American aid. In our case, we simply adopted the capitalistic approach, and our economy began to grow on its own initiative."

Max took a dim view of this diatribe. *"This upstart whippersnapper was probably not around in 1975. So, what makes him think he can lecture me on the socio-economic outcomes of the last half-century,"* queried a frustrated Max to himself.

Max had experienced this kind of condescension in several other con-versations with Vietnamese people he encountered on this excursion. It was not pretty. It was certainly not noble, and it was certainly distaste-ful and offensive to Max Donatello.

"Have we forgotten altogether all the lost RVN soldiers who fought to fend off communism? It was supremely ironic to have the communist victors adopt the socio-economic model of their former adversary, and then with flagrant hubris, claim vindication. Talking out of both sides of their mouths," was Max's unspoken conclusion, as he ignored the rest of Pham Superman's rant on the way back to Max's hotel.

CHAPTER SIXTY-FIVE

*D*uring America's presence, the little village of Vung Tau had not only been a deep-raft port and a combat evacuation hospital, but also an in-country R&R Center in the war's heyday.

It had by now become not only a town, but also a bustling tourist destination. The largest cruise ships still had to tender their passengers to port for their excursions, while smaller ones could now edge up to the ample piers and marinas that encircled the Florida-shaped peninsula jutting out at the southern-most point of Southern Vietnam.

The town reminded him of every city, town, and village in Vietnam that he had experienced back in the early '70s. Streets were still strewn on both sides with shops, storefronts, small grocers, fruit and vegetable stands, sellers of every conceivable product one could imagine. Many of the storefronts were simply outlets for the elders of the family to tend and trade whatever their suppliers could provide.

Upstairs, the family occupied one, if not two stories of the condo-like spaces that defined the rows of shops and mini-marts. Max discovered that Vietnamese families often cooperatively bought whole blocks of these roadside SE Asia strip malls. One block looked like the next. Max wondered what differentiated one grouping from another, one grocer from another. It was baffling to Max, from a capitalistic perspective, when three different vendors would be selling the very same commodity, but had selected a location less than a block away from his competitor. Or, they were located across the same road, in the same block, ostensibly to catch the traffic heading the opposite direction.

Max recalled being duly impressed with the seafood in Vung Tau back then. He directed his driver to an elaborate restaurant close to the beach for a late lunch just outside Vung Tau, overlooking the bay beyond, where the vistas included a large cruise ship at anchor, as well as local fishing trawlers dotting the horizon.

At this restaurant, guests were asked to select their favorite fish from ponds and tanks surrounding the restaurant. Max sent his driver off to have lunch and informed him that it would be at least 90 minutes before they would head back to Ho Chi Minh City.

Max hoped that a bottle of good French White Burgundy would be a wise selection for a fare of seafood as fresh as he had ever seen, in these tanks.

Since he was just about famished, he decided to try what the menu described as the Sea Farer's delight, which consisted of steamed prawns, oysters on the half shell, and steamed baby clams. The dipping sauces delivered were sublime.

His entrée would be a pan-fried fish, the identity of which he didn't recognize, but it reminded him of snapper. They were offering either a Sichuan or Vietnamese preparation. Max recalled that he absolutely loved Sichuan fish, but he was also addicted to Vietnamese spices and *nuo'c mam*, the venerable fish sauce used in abundance in Vietnamese dishes, so Max chose the Vietnamese traditional preparations.

The meal came with extra fish sauce for dipping, sticky rice, various pickled white radishes and julienned carrots swimming in a spicy sauce that tasted similar to Max's fondest recollection of the taste of traditional *nou'c mam*. "More is better," Max concluded.

While Max awaited the wine and appetizer, he remembered the first time he was introduced to Cha Gia'o. In Max's opinion, it was the most addictive and delicious fried spring roll in all of Asia.

In was at the language school that he and Emily had been invited to his teacher's house for a traditional meal. He remembered watching Emily's face reflect her enjoyment of the wonderful spring rolls. How she would love this place!

Back in the '70s, each of his dining partners received only two of these small gems. The idea was to wrap it in a large lettuce leaf and then dunk it in a bowl of spicy *nou'c mam*. Absolute heaven!

These people had figured out that if you carefully grind shrimp and pork together, add some simple spices, then use it as a filling in thin rice paper which is folded and fried until golden brown, you had achieved near gastronomic perfection!

When his entrée finally arrived, Max's was pleased that his fish selection was sublime. Grilled to perfection on a charcoal grill, it came with several interesting dipping sauces of varying degrees of spiciness and aromatics. In fact, it was so good that, at the end, Max fished around the bones for morsels to dip into two of his new favorite sauces. Max finally realized that he had put away an abundance of food. As there was only a sip of wine left, Max concluded that he had been sitting there in excess of two hours. His traditional excuse for this kind of laid-back behavior was that he was officially on vacation.

CHAPTER SIXTY-SIX

*A*s Max departed Vietnam, he reflected on the contrast from his time there in the early '70s. Vietnam had leapt into the 21st Century in almost every conceivable way. Gone were the many faces of conflict. Streets and boulevards were without a single soldier or Military Policeman. In fact, there was no evidence of military activity at all. About the only evidence of the past were the remnants of old telephone cables bundled together with numerous strands of modern cable. It was as if someone had forgotten what the old lines connected to, so they simply strung up new cables on top of the old. It was the same in each town he visited. It was as if progress took place so fast that it did not make sense to remove the aging, drooping cables. Rather, the expedient choice was that it easier and quicker to follow old routes using old poles than to dig up trenches and bury the lines in modern conduit.

The whole cable-bundling approach was a metaphor for the Vietnamese. They were forever adapting, always adding or tweaking their surroundings and their infrastructure. One constant was the amazing resourcefulness they had manifested through the decades. Max recalled studying about the Vietnamese culture in the Defense Language Institute. These people had literally struggled for centuries. One conflict after another characterized their history. Perhaps this legacy was how their native initiative and creativity became something of a culturally-ingrained phenomenon.

Still, peace seemed to suit them. A modicum of prosperity had descended on the country. There were so many small businesses. Consumerism was thriving, and there was almost no evidence of poverty. Max was impressed by the numerous large Japanese and Korean enterprises that had established factories in Vietnam. Textile and clothing manufacturing firms like IZOD and Ralph Lauren had factories here, and these were not sweatshops. They were modern, well-ventilated, well-lit factories. Signs of prosperity could be seen on the streets, and in the parking lots, with all the new motorbikes lined up outside in the parking lots of these many factories.

Nonetheless, Max had a good feeling about his return to Vietnam. It seemed that the Vietnamese had moved on since the war. With the exception of his latent resentment of Pham Superman's haughty, narrow attitude about the glorious victory in 1975, Max was satisfied that the trip was worthwhile. Moreover, he felt that he could move on to squelch his dark memories of the place.

CHAPTER SIXTY-SEVEN

*A*rriving in Phnom Penh, Max had a momentary quiver of trepidation, not quite sure what he would discover. The airport had been modernized and enlarged. There were still no modern jetways, only roll-up stairways for passenger loading and offloading. The formalities were routine and brisk. It took only minutes to receive your Visa upon entry and process through to the luggage pick up area. In a matter of minutes, Max was standing outside with his luggage, looking for his name among the many drivers holding up signs with hotel names, or surnames of the individuals who were being picked up.

His Cambodian guide and driver, Chansin Keo, was eagerly waving the Donatello sign above his head. Max was pleased to find that Mr. Keo was conversant in both English and French, and was very polite. In spite of his small stature, he vigorously loaded Max's luggage into the trunk of a small, air-conditioned, late-model Toyota sedan. Max recalled the relief he felt when MAJ Hank Behnke retrieved him at Pochentong early in his 1970s Cambodian adventure, with a sturdy air-conditioned sedan.

As they drove out of the airport parking lot, Max asked Mr. Keo, "Where is the Khmer Air Force Airbase from here?" Max was surprised to find out that what had been the Khmer Air Force base, not far from the commercial terminal, was now a large industrial park, run by some large Korean manufacturing company.

Mr. Keo indicated that a large ex-patriot contingent was now providing Cambodia with expertise that had been lost as a result of the Khmer Rouge's elimination of a whole generation of collective Cambodian intelligence during their reign of terror (1975-1980).

This expertise had not been replaced or supplanted during the almost fourteen years of Vietnam's occupation. The Vietnamese simply filled the vacuum left when the Khmer Rouge regime folded in on itself. Vietnam figured that occupation was a better way to control the remaining population and to control the splintered remnants of the

KR. However, rebuilding Cambodia and re-educating its population were not a part of Vietnam's end strategy.

Mr. Keo went on to say that Cambodia was now required to hire large foreign companies to rebuild their business infrastructure and even advise the government. A large presence of Korean-national firms had filled the void, along with a smattering of Indonesian and Japanese companies.

Mr. Keo explained that the current reigning monarch, Prince Sihanouk's son, whose name was also Noradoum Sihanouk, insisted on having foreign advisers. "He often publicly criticizes their suggestions, or rejects them outright. The current Sihanouk was educated in Prague and several Eastern European countries. At this time, his father struggled to find his way back to power in the early '70s, after the coup led by Marshal Lon Nol, who seized power during the Prince's absence on a brief vacation to France," explained Mr. Keo, as if he'd been there.

"The country's current Prime Minister, Mr. Hun Sen, has been quoted as saying he does not trust outsiders or consultants. He considers them the commercial equivalent of foreign mercenaries. Mr. Sen often complains that the cost of having outsiders modernize Cambodia is a shame born by all Cambodians," confessed Mr. Keo.

"The root of this shame," according to Mr. Keo, "was that Cambodians, in spite of outward appearances suggesting passivity and submissiveness, have always been fiercely proud, and had a long history of looking down on its neighbors as inferior and racially impure. Outsiders like China, Japan, and Korea were viewed in the same way. The ex-pat presence providing expertise, in almost all areas of government and commerce, constituted a loss of face for the still-proud Khmer people."

Mr. Keo went on, "Mr. Sen never mentions the latter issues, but he constantly harps on the exorbitant costs being charged by these Asian companies who have been awarded contracts to help rebuild Cambodia. He recently launched into a public tirade about the lack of quality and the inferior workmanship of the foreign workers.

"The real issue," according to Mr. Keo, "was that the government was ashamed that Cambodian workers were no longer qualified to accomplish much beyond basic agrarian tasks."

"We have the Khmer Rouge to blame for all this," said Mr. Keo with genuine resignation, "and now this vexing struggle between the current regime versus the need for outsiders to accomplish the work. It has simply resulted in extremely slow progress toward rebuilding our country. Since Cambodia regained its sovereignty in 1993, with the departure of the North Vietnamese, the country has made very little real progress." Max was astounded at the depth of Mr. Keo's disquisition, reducing the assessment of Cambodia's efforts at modernization to a succinct few paragraphs.

"How is that you have such a keen understanding of the Cambodian condition, so to speak? I thought all the Khmer intellectuals had been rounded up and marched off to the Killing Fields. Weren't you caught up in the Khmer Rouge takeover?" asked Max with his usual directness.

Mr. Keo quickly responded, "I was a professor of history and political science here at the university until 1973. I had relatives at the time in the United States. They encouraged me to get out while I still could. So, I took my family to California, where I lived until 1995. I longed for my homeland, but still bore abiding safety concerns about returning, even after the Vietnamese essentially abandoned the country."

"After, my wife died in the states and my children were grown, I decided to take the chance. I returned, without incident. But, the only job available for me was as a chauffer for a travel company. That's how I came to be here at this moment," remarked Mr. Keo with a toothy grin.

Max was on input overload with all this information, taking in Mr. Keo's remarkable biography, as well as all the sights and sounds of an unexpectedly vibrant city.

While it seemed that there had been several improvements along the route from the airport to downtown, it occurred to Max that of the three SE Asian countries he had visited so far, Cambodia was by far the least modern. Mr. Keo's comments provided ample evidence as to how this situation had come to be.

*   *   *

Mr. Keo delivered Max to the Hotel Amanjaya, which overlooked the enormous Tonle Sap River. Max asked Mr. Keo to pick him up the following day at 9:30 AM for their tour of Phnom Penh. The hotel was relatively new. It certainly did not exist when Max was here in the early '70s. It catered to Western guests and had fine amenities throughout the hotel. Audra Campbell had done a superior job in selecting the hotels so far.

The Hotel Amanjaya provided Max with a suite. It was a long, continuous room, with french doors opening to the terrace, exposing the Tonle Sap, giving Max 180 degrees of visage covering a front of about five miles of river in each direction.

Max was impressed with the bathroom, which was lavishly decorated in dark colors and ultra-modern fixtures. The staff had run a bath and had strewn the surface with red rose petals. It smelled like heaven. Max was certain Emily would have loved it. Max relished the local Cambodian flair of the place, coupled with all the modern luxuries of a large-chain hotel, without all the hubbub of business travelers. Further, it was in an ideal location, with splendid views of life in Cambodia's capital.

 Max decided to take a walk along the sidewalk outside the hotel, which was situated opposite the river's paved walkway. As he left the hotel, he noticed that he was standing about 100 meters from the Khmer National Museum. He recalled visiting this facility while he was here in 1972. A bit sparse back then, but it was still a gorgeous tract of land, with lush, manicured gardens and unique landscape architecture. He made a mental note to allow some time to walk the grounds again some forty years since he'd been here last.

He started walking and noticed numerous pedal-powered cyclo-taxis, as well as a few scooter-powered taxis. There was also a smattering of tuk-tuks, just like the ones in Bangkok. These were the SUVs of scooter-powered taxis. The front was essentially a motorbike with a carriage mounted on a frame of two wheels in the back to allow for a compartment atop with room for two-to-four small seats. It looked like a miniature, open-air SUV, all welded together and decorated in the wildest designs imaginable.

In Bangkok, no two tuk-tuks looked alike. Here in Phnom Penh, they were less ornate, but still pretty ostentatious. The drivers were the same as taxi drivers anywhere. While awaiting a fare, a good snooze was always in order, and on this particular afternoon, there was plenty of snoozing going on outside the National Museum.

Max proceeded along the boulevard for a block or so, until he realized that off on his right was the famed Foreign Correspondent's Club, the FCC, for short. He and his housemates came here periodically back in 1972 during off hours, to harass the war correspondents who often sat up there on the second floor, overlooking the Tonle Sap, creating imaginative war dispatches for their newspapers back home.

It was a safe, civilized solution for these reporters. More compelling, it was a preferred alternative to the specter of traveling out with combat units, where things often got hot and heavy, and, at times, went to hell in the proverbial hand basket. Besides, combat is incredibly confusing. How could a poor, untrained journalist be expected to make sense of a battle that might take two days to resolve?

You could not expect an Ivy-League-trained junior reporter, with Pulitzer-level skills and corresponding ambitions, to understand strategy, much less tactical operations. So, why introduce reality to this poor waif? Creativity needs a supportive environment. What better place than the FCC to create media spin? What better way to impute the fog of war as a matter of record, than to have as many gins and tonic as you could hold, while your story emerged, sprinkled with a peripheral knowledge of the general scenario?

Max walked across the boulevard at what he reckoned was the least perilous point near the FCC. Motorbikes were almost as bad here as they were in Vietnam. Drivers acted like neo-Kamikazes destined for their heavenly rewards.

Max wondered if things had changed. Were there still journalists who hung out here? Entry was on the first level, which was now a casual restaurant/bistro. Going back to the rear of the bistro, Max remembered the staircase that led to the open-air, second-floor lounge, dotted with small tables. There were still terraces with small tables all along the periphery. In fact, the terraces followed the path of windows on the two long sides of the building. There, off to the right, was a long V-shaped bar that seemed to have caught the drift of the architectural shape of the property.

It was late afternoon, and Max caught a whiff of someone's late lunch. When the spritely young waitress came along, he ordered a Tiger Beer, the one that came from the German-operated brewery in Kompong Som. He asked the girl what the folks several tables away were having that smelled so delicious. She told Max that it was the special of the day. They were having flour tortilla shrimp tacos, with fresh avocado, the chef's own salsa-verde, and pico-de-gallo.

"Wow, does that ever sound good!" thought the semi-emaciated Max, whose innards were still getting used to the questionable food handling standards of SE Asia. Max felt sure that the beer would kill any offending biological gremlins that may have slipped through the deft scrutiny of the British staff at the FCC. This was especially true, considering that they could ill-afford an outbreak of intestinal creeping crud to their credit, inflicted on the fledgling tummies of the ever-changing crop of junior journalists.

"Shrimp tacos it is," responded Max with a dash of really bad Spanglish.

Max had commandeered an outside table on the terrace overlooking the Tonle Sap and the boulevard that he had just crossed. Max thought, *"What an exhilarating venue!"* He watched the remarkably odd combination of traditional Khmer fishing boats obliviously plying their trade, while six- and eight-man racing crews gracefully glided through the water in a way that one might see if he were sitting out along the river at The Head of the Charles Regatta in Boston, while the Harvard varsity crew was taking conditioning drills.

The beer was colder than he remembered. Back in the day, if one ordered a beer in a hotel lobby or a restaurant, it would be chilled with an elongated, rectangular hunk of ice that had been sawed off a block in the back room. Back in the '70s, all drinks were chilled in this fashion, even at fashionable embassy parties. This beer hit the spot, and when his waitress came out with Max's tacos, he ordered a second large bottle. Before she headed off, Max asked the girl if any correspondents still came to the place.

"Since the war, not too many journalists frequent our lounge. Not like the old days. We only re-opened in 1995, a couple of years after the Vietnamese left, so now we have to rely on the tourists who have heard about the FCC. Since Cambodia's tourism has blossomed, and its growth has become a big economic factor in Phnom Penh, our business has been prospering. We have a very good cook, and he brought his assistants with him from the Philippines. They were all trained for several years in Texas, San Antonio, I believe, and have good credentials. Besides, they love living in Cambodia," said the Asian-looking waitress who sounded like she'd been raised in London.

Max mentally absorbed these comments as he tried the Cambodian shrimp tacos. The shrimp were grilled to perfection, bursting with fresh, savory flavor. The avocados were lush, and the salsa verde had just a hint of cilantro with just enough jalapeño to give it a subtle boost. The pico de gallo gave the dish a crowning sizzle that both delighted and stood Max's palate to attention. Like a Command Sergeant Major, this spicy additive was decidedly in charge of the formation.

The weather was warm and breezy; the scenery spectacular. Max concentrated on small enclaves of people going about their day-to-day activities. Some were fishermen, some were vendors, and some were simply tending to their families. It was a vibrant, yet serene perspective, characteristic of life in Cambodia since time immemorial.

Max could not help but think of the terror that must have reigned when the Khmer Rouge rode into Phnom Penh that April day in 1975. By the time the celebration and revelry ended, the city's denizens were herded unceremoniously out of the city. Max recalled the haunting photos he'd seen of Phnom Penh, a city of several hundred thousand— abandoned, evacuated, a veritable ghost town. Its population marshaled out to the countryside to work camps.

Unless, of course, they were suspected of being educated. The edict was plain. No intellectuals would survive. Another capital offense was working for the defeated Khmer government. Yet another was anyone who had served in the FANK military. Teachers, businessmen, store owners, entrepreneurs, vendors, property owners were all herded into old school buildings that were converted into collection centers and transient torture centers, where confessions were routinely extracted prior to transport to the Killing Fields.

Max decided to end this train of thought for now. It had been a nice day. He was exhausted and had just enough energy to walk back to the nearby Hotel Amanjaya. Tomorrow would be soon enough to try to deal with torture and murder on a wholesale level.

CHAPTER SIXTY-EIGHT

*M*r. Keo was dutifully on time, showing up just as Max finished his breakfast in the café on the first level of the hotel. Max had prepared a small bag with the essentials of an observant tourist: camera with spare battery, sun block, a floppy hat to ward off the rays of the penetrating Indo-Chinese sun, sun glasses, bottled water, fruit for Max and his driver, and a current 1 over 5,000 scale map of Phnom Penh and its surroundings for reference, and he brought the same scale map of the city produced in the early 1970s for comparison.

Max's initial impression was that in the intervening years, many of the charming French influences had bowed to aggressive change in both directions. Max did not even recognize the sight of what was the former American Embassy compound. Even as they passed through the streets on one of his most familiar routes to their villa, Max was vexed by the lack of familiarity. Mr. Keo remarked, "Not much left of old Phnom Penh from our day."

Max replied immediately, "I was just about to say that the present seems to consume the past, or, at least it seems to cover over old wounds."

Mr. Keo observed, "There is an old Khmer adage: 'the earth covers over the wounds incurred by mankind and returns it ultimately to its natural state.'" Max considered this tidbit of Cambodian wisdom, tossing it around in his mind in the context of all the people killed here. How little difference had all that killing made in the country's eventual outcome?

When they stopped outside the villa where Max had lived, they came upon only the residue of those heady days. The villa was in shambles. The gate had been blown away, and the servant's quarters destroyed. Windows no longer fended off the rain, and it was clear to Max that no one had occupied these forbidden quarters since the American contingent departed back in the spring of 1975.

Max's heart fell when he thought of that stand-up Cambodian family who had, "*dedicated themselves to our collective well-being and comfort.*

Where were they now? What had become of them? Their little boy would be an adult by now, if he survived." So many interrogatives darted through Max's mind that he felt mildly dizzy.

Max could still picture these people, as if it were yesterday. They were a vibrant, healthy, and forward-looking family. Their only hope was that things would somehow work out, and that Cambodia would finally be at peace. Huge hopes!

Max took a moment as he walked around the overgrown landscape and finally said, "I often think of the Cambodian family who looked after the Americans who were billeted here. What a wonderful group of people! I've prayed for their survival many times over the years, never knowing their destiny."

Mr. Keo picked up on this line of thought. "Many city people from Phnom Penh, who were uprooted in 1975, were sent to their traditional ancestral homes in the villages that dot the countryside. The Khmer Rouge tried to reweave the fabric of family and village with local agriculture. It could have been the salvation of your caretaker family."

Max was momentarily encouraged, but could only respond, "Let us hope and pray it was true for them."

As they drove away from his former quarters, Max felt that a sizeable chunk of his life had been torn away from him. How frustrating to think that a whole year of his life had been spent in hopes of facilitating a better end state for these unfortunate, gentle people. It had been a source of constant gloom for Max, and had been for as many years as he contemplated the futility of American efforts to do what they thought at the time to be the 'right thing.'

Max had concluded long ago that Cambodia was a political expedient for the Nixon Administration, a card to play into their secret talks in Paris with North Vietnam's Le Duc Tho. Kissinger's secret shuttle diplomacy at the Paris peace talks, in Max's view, constituted blatant duplicity. This colossal deception served up a second term for Nixon, along with continuing plaudits, Nobel honors, and manifest prosperity for Henry S. Kissinger.

What was, in truth, being served up on a silver platter, was the Cambodian nation. The United States's government never attempted to solicit American public support, much less tried to sway the predominant political leanings of Congress for support of the Khmer Republic beyond late 1974. Thus, the Decent Interval policy emerged which simply stated that the US needed time to get a peace agreement in place with North Vietnam and get out of SE Asia, regardless of collateral damage.

The serial debacles of Watergate, the Pentagon Papers, the workings of the Watergate Senate Select Committee, which led to the ignominious resignation of Richard M. Nixon, condemned Cambodia's figurative head to the chopping block.

Max believed in his heart of hearts that America was abjectly responsible for the failed Cambodian "Side Show" policy. Further, he concluded that this failure laid the psychological ground work for the Khmer Rouge to be all the more savage and retributive in their treatment of loyal Khmer citizens, and especially, those of an intellectual bent.

CHAPTER SIXTY-NINE

---

*T*he plan for the day had a stop scheduled at School 21, in the heart of Phnom Penh. Once a vibrant day school, it had been commandeered by a fundamentalist faction of the Khmer Rouge in April 1975. It was destined to become one of the most infamous torture sites of the KR occupation. History attests that some of the most cruel and vicious treatment of POWs during the entire SE Asian War occurred at his site.

Max was repulsed from the onset of his thirty-minute tour. It was hard to fathom that so much hatred and vengeance had been inculcated into so young a cadre. But the evidence, though ghastly, proved the opposite.

Young boys and girls had honed their skills at exacting confessions through excruciating means of torture. Hanging a prisoner by his or her shackled ankles from the ceiling was a favored technique. Being shackled to a bunk with no mattress was another effective experiment. No water, no food, only discipline was the formula for the day. Others were placed in rooms half the height and 1/8th the width of a normal western closet.

When the KR got aggressive in their fervor for greater numbers of confessed criminals, the detainees were dragged off to the torture cells where the most innovative means of exacting confessions were used. The KR mastered the use of car batteries, whose terminals were clipped with cables and attached to the genitals of the victim in order to maximize pain when the electricity was sent their way. Water boarding grew up as a confession-eliciting technique in the SE Asian War, and was used in profusion in Phnom Penh at processing centers such as Ecole 21, and, of course, prolific beatings were always on tap if the responses that the KR wanted were not quickly extracted.

Sometimes, people at S-21 were awakened at night, herded into trucks, and transported to one of the Killing Fields not far outside the city. The KR did not waste precious bullets on these people. They were summarily bludgeoned to death with shovels the prisoners had used to dig their own shallow graves.

Max and Mr. Keo arrived at the closest of these monuments to human depravity, located just a few miles outside Phnom Penh. This particular one was used on a large scale. Tour guides would accompany visitors down paths into the bush and nearby orchard, where one could readily see the remains of victims' clothing percolating to the surface in the shallow pits along the trails. Vestiges of the colored gingham scarves, worn by average Cambodians to ward off the tropical sun, also peeked up through the soil. The path looped its way around for about a mile leading back to a small, two-story commemorative Buddhist stupa with plexiglass sides, and is filled with more than 5,000 skulls of the victims at the Killing Field of Choeung Ek. The edifice was built as a memorial to the men, women, and children who lost their lives at this site.

Max, while being revolted by this scene, began to fully appreciate the horrific price the Khmer people collectively paid for supporting American policy so late in the war. While the Westerners were being evacuated by helicopters to safe havens that ominous April, the KR had thousands of soldiers awaiting final attack orders to descend upon Phnom Penh and the other major population centers. The citizens were given no options. Their fate was sealed.

CHAPTER SEVENTY

*M*ax knew that this part of the trip was going to be the roughest on him psychologically. Max had seen pictures over the years of these sites in books and articles about Cambodia. Max was convinced that the US bore a major share of the guilt for this holocaust. America essentially set up the Khmer government to fail. In Max's considered opinion, it was all for the sake of America's myopic political purposes.

Max remembered what his father-in-law told him early in their relationship. He said, "success has a thousand fathers; failure has but one." Max thought that this occasion might be an example where the inverse was true, "failure has a thousand fathers, but no one succeeded." In Cambodia, back in the early '70s, the entire American staff of MEDTC was resolutely trying to turn failure into success. Max himself was a member of this small, obscure fraternity. MEDTC was an elite contingent that gallantly tried, in the face of all adversity, to accomplish its ill-fated mission to save the Khmer Republic.

In Max's appraisal, the US could be faulted because it gave the Lon Nol regime impossibly false long-term hopes. The Khmer government was increasingly blinded by its own illusions concerning both the dedication of the US, but also to the steely resolve of the KR. Of course, these delusions were exacerbated by the FANK government's illusory miscalculation of its own fighting strength and the resolve of its citizenry.

After more than forty-five years of study and contemplation, Max was convinced that Lon Nol was not only out of step with the people about his belief in the Khmer population's racial superiority, but he was also gravely mistaken about the common people's spirit of allegiance about accomplishing his goals. Lon Nol was essentially a right-wing dictator, who lived in a dream world of his own creation.

Ironically, like his predecessor Sihanouk, and also his successor, Pol Pot, Lon Nol grew more and more detached from reality and did not truly comprehend the sense of Cambodian society by the time of his impending denouement. This detachment, along with the manifest corruption of the Lon Nol government, made a populist overthrow inevitable. Faced with the specter of America's summarily stark military and financial withdrawal of support, along with the growing strength of the Khmer Rouge, it was only a matter of time before the Lon Nol regime crumbled.

Max, in his long hours of scholarly research back in the '80s, had concluded that the Khmer Rouge were also substantially self-deluded by their idealistic, whole-life communist philosophy. The KR leaders were, like the Bolsheviks of 1917, espousing an untried way of life. The Khmer Rouge philosophy, to add a measure of complexity, also had underpinnings in the fundamentalist teachings of Mao Tse Tung. Sadly, by mid-1975, the essence of these philosophical leanings had long since been tried and discarded. None of the emergent KR leaders understood this context, nor could they envisage the outcome of adopting their own version of this failed philosophy.

The ultra-left founders of the KR received their initial communist philosophical indoctrination from the dream world of France in the postwar 1950s and '60s. They borrowed prolifically from Lenin's Bolshevism and Maoist discourses from mid-1940s China.

The difference, however, was that KR leaders Pol Pot and Khieu Samphan were never truly scholars, nor had they ever demonstrated the sense to pay attention to the countless historical lessons learned by their communist forebears. By the early '70s, they lived in an enclave world, surrounded by jungle canopy, as they developed their own brand of neo-Maoist, propaganda-laden communism.

So, when America departed, Cambodia exchanged its ultra-right leaning government for one on the farthest left extreme of the political spectrum. The blindness of the KR leadership to the implications of their imposingly radical new lifestyle, coupled with the delusion of the corrupt outgoing FANK regime, was a lethal potion to be administered to the Cambodian people after the demise of Lon Nol's pro-western gambit.

Making matters worse, by the spring of 1975, the American public had washed its figurative hands of all things SE Asian. This abandonment left the Cambodian people essentially alone in a most vicious civil war-style wilderness. When the Khmer Rouge massed around the perimeters of Phnom Penh in late April of 1975, the Americans had sounded their final retreat with *"Operation Eagle Pull,"* the plan that ferried MEDTC and American Embassy officials by helicopter safely and permanently out of Cambodia.

Max, as one of MEDTC's few logistics scholarly minions, was a principal author of *"Operation Eagle Pull."* Max remembered wincing at the news in April 1975 when he heard that the team had been forced to evacuate Phnom Penh.

Ironically, in less than a month, helicopters would repeat the process in the Vietnamese version of that evacuation plan. Yet another irony: the Vietnam evacuation plan was unfortunately named, *"Frequent Wind."* It seemed remarkable to Max that all we seemed to have to show for our years in Indochina was consistent and repeated hot air.

In the end, as the American evacuation carrier *Midway* steamed away from Vietnamese waters with a shipload of grateful former ex-pats and pro-American refugees, the American people finally flushed all thoughts of the horror that had occupied their consciousness. It had taken far too long a time, burned away far too much of the nation's treasure, and had expended far too much blood of America's youth.

Max believed that by then, American society rightfully needed to distance SE Asia from its collective memory. The United States had become a country whose fabric was fairly rendered to tatters as a result of distasteful images of war protests, hippies, and the growing prevalence of drugs in our youthful culture. Indeed, America was weary of body counts that were chronicled faithfully every evening by Walter Cronkite at the dinner hour.

Above all, America had recently revolted and was cynical at the demise of a presidency that had promised "Peace with Honor." Max fully understood this aspect of America's collective psyche, but still rued the sheer expediency of American policies toward Cambodia.

Max believed that it could be fairly concluded that Cambodia and its population were nothing but innocent, ignorant pawns whose genuine commitment to the American alliance facilitated our earliest exit from the hell that Vietnam had become to America. Once we left, there was precious little discussion or authoritative American historical analysis of our actions in Cambodia. To make this paucity more relevant, Max had found through his research that historical analysis of America's involvement in Cambodia during 1971-1975 took up a mere speck of an afterthought on the last pages of our sad history in SE Asia.

And, it remains essentially true to this day.

CHAPTER SEVENTY-ONE

*M*ax was scheduled to fly to Sihanoukville (aka Kompong Som) the next day to visit the old port city where his first real challenge occurred after the Neak Leoung errant bombing episode. Kompong Som, (KPS) in Max's lexicon, was the subject of many vivid dreams over the years. Max remembered a rare day off, before his bout with dengue fever, while they were awaiting the arrival of the SeaTrain Maryland. Max had jerry-rigged a prop for his 35mm camera on the beach near the resort where he stayed. There the camera snapped a time-delayed picture of Max in his swim trunks, wading sheepishly in the surf. Much later, he finally saw the image of himself as this pitiful waif, awash on the lavish beach, in an otherwise forgotten SE Asian paradise, all by himself. His expression seemed to be one of loneliness, combined with a forlorn hint that suggested, "Why me Lord?" Max remembered that day clearly because, when there is really nothing to do, and no one to do it with, time weighs heavily on one's hands.

But now no such existential rambling thoughts invaded Max's consciousness. Sihanoukville had taken on a quite different character. It was now a grown-up resort community on the gulf of Siam. Several international resort management companies had commandeered the best of the beach-front property and built five-star hotels. The quaint little resort whose location always caused Max a degree of trepidation when he made his way back there from port in his open jeep at night, no longer occupied the same place it had. In its place was a splendid, modern resort with a heliport out front. It boasted an enormous, outdoor ocean-side pool that housed a peninsular bar that jutted out to the pool's middle so that swimmers could float alongside and order their favorite beverages. It had all manner of the latest luxury spa amenities. Max's cabana was close to the pool, but was also within easy walking distance from the beach where that forlorn photo of him was snapped back in the early '70s.

His driver was scheduled to pick him up for a tour of the environs at ten the next morning. Max was anxious to see how much development had taken place.

*   *   *

That evening, the resort dining room was featuring a lavish seafood grill/buffet, and Max had been told that one of Cambodia's top singing groups would be headlining the evening's entertainment. At around 7 PM, Max ambled down the dimly lit pathway to the main building. As he got closer, he encountered a lively crowd. People from all around the world were selecting small lobsters, prawns, sea scallops, and exotic fish filet for the four grill masters to prepare. While one's selections were queued up for custom grilling, diners had the opportunity to sample an exquisite array of seafood appetizers ranging from peel-and-eat shrimp to fresh live oysters on the half shell, served with the perfect accompanying wine. There were plump seafood salads, seafood étouffés, casseroles fit for Poseidon, and, of course, ahi tuna and smoked eel, served sushi-style with a tempting array of sauces and accompaniments.

Max was further surprised to encounter a contingent of uniformed US Naval officers and senior NCOs, as he made his way to the lounge. As it turned out, an American nuclear carrier group was just offshore, having just completed joint exercises with Thailand, Malaysia, and Singapore. The carrier had ferried some of the lucky furloughed officers and senior non-coms to shore via helicopter to the front entrance of this impressive complex. Their presence accounted for all the bluster and noise earlier in the afternoon out front after Max had checked in and hit the rack for a brief snooze.

As Max approached the group of eight American Naval Officers and senior NCOs, seated on the fringes of the dining room, he wondered if any of them had signed up for the evening's $50 seafood BBQ. Max found that the enthusiastic group was simply awaiting the evening's musical melodies and the hopes of a squeeze from one of the exotic waitresses.

"Who is the senior officer present?" Max inquired. A fine, young looking aviation Naval Commander intoned, "That would be me; I'm Commander Mike Stephano."

Max sized the kid up, and finally said, "Nice to meet you, Mike. I am Max Donatello, US Army Lieutenant Colonel, retired. I'm visiting Cambodia, staying here at the resort, exploring old haunts from my days as a junior officer assigned here in the early '70s."

"Nice to meet you, Max, would you care to join us for a libation?"

Max replied, "That would be great, but I was wondering if you gentle-men have had dinner yet? If not, I would be pleased to have you join me as my guests for this seafood BBQ. The fare is really quite spectac-ular. It would be my pleasure, and my treat, of course. "

Commander Stephano surveyed his always-hungry sidekicks and responded, "We'd be pleased to join you, sir. I know my colleagues would hate to see a fellow American veteran eating alone. Your hospi-tality is certainly appreciated. Most of the guys just snagged a sandwich before takeoff, but we have our growing boys, don't you know."

CDR Stephano's cohorts seemed to rise in unison with wide grins on their faces, to head for the buffet table. "I don't suppose there was any reasonable doubt that we'd accept your generous offer?"

Max replied, "Great. Why don't you please go get started, and we will chat when you get a plate of those scrumptious appetizers. By the way, don't miss that shrimp salad with pesto sauce. I've been told it's out of this world. And, the oysters on the half shell are supposed to be devil-ishly good."

Max gestured to the headwaiter that the Americans would be joining him, and that they would need a table for nine, somewhere close to the appetizer buffet. "And, please bring us three bottles of nice Chardon-nay to get us started."

The eight fell in step about halfway to the buffet. They fairly pounced on the appetizer display, making sizable dents in each bowl that had been intended by the hotel to make it through the evening. Then, they hiked back to the table, where the headwaiter was just opening the first of three bottles of French Chardonnay.

Max took tasting rights since he was the host. He proclaimed that the wine was fit for American consumption, and ordered that each of his naval comrades be served a third of a glass, just in case there were any wine-haters in the group. There was a young chief who sheepishly admitted that he preferred to drink beer, so Max ordered him a large bottle of *Tiger*, the German beer brewed right there in Sihanoukville. The young chief likened as how he had never had a Cambodian beer.

Max proclaimed that it would not disappoint, and, when it arrived, several of the others had a taste and asked to switch to *Tiger*. Max turned to Commander Stephano and said, "all the more Chardonnay for the wine lovers in the crowd," as he raised his glass in a toast the his new comrades-in-arms. A hearty, "hear, hear," was the noisy response from the group.

Max reminded the group that they needed to go to the platters of entrée seafood, arrayed on ice near the BBQ pits, to select their dinner choices. They would then need to hand over their selections to one of the four grill masters working the charcoal-fired grill pits. It did not take much encouragement before the entire table was empty again, as these Spartan young lads eagerly awaited their entrées to come off the grill. It did Max's heart good to see how heartily they were partaking in this seafood feast.

By the time Max's choices were passed over the grill, he thought to himself that he could have yielded to the appetizers only and called it a night. Max's grill choices had been two small lobster tails and four huge prawns. Collecting his sumptuous prizes, Max proceeded to the condiment table, where there was every savory additive from fresh hollandaise to a characteristic American tartar sauce. The horseradish-tomato cocktail sauce had been spiked with a hint of lime and a small dose of Sriracha sauce. Zing! Max's appetite was now fully awakened. There were several dipping sauces that emanated from the region. Some were laced with diced spinach, others included a kind of fish sauce with julienned carrots and several wildly pickled white radishes, also julienned, floating about.

When all were again seated with their plates full of steaming seafood goodness, one of the officers asked Max how he came to be here, and why in the world was he here alone? Max tried to keep things light, deciding not to reveal that it was his deceased wife's wish for him to return and face the ghosts of his Vietnam/Cambodia Era ordeal. Max merely said he had always wanted to return to visit the places he had seen during the war. The banter became less focused as Max changed the subject, asking them about their mission in the area, and about their careers.

The evening passed quickly, and as the music started around 10 PM, Max realized he needed to head back to his cabana because his driver would be beckoning him in the early morning light. Max enjoyed the singing group for a few numbers, but, truthfully, it seemed to Max that everything sounded the same. Not long after this realization, Max turned to Commander Stephano and said, "Mike, I need to be up early tomorrow, so I will excuse myself and say good night at this juncture."

Max added, "Good evening, gentlemen," as he rose to make his departure. "I can't tell you what a pleasure it was to meet you and spend this special evening with you."

Max could have sworn that there was a collective snapping to attention, and a simultaneous hand salute from them as he turned to walk away from the proceedings.

"*Nice American lads, very nice American lads,*" was Max's summary judgment as he quickly made his exit from the assembly.

Max whispered to the headwaiter on his way out to continue to serve the gentlemen at his table whatever they ordered until their departure. Max added that he wanted all the charges to be added to his hotel room account.

*   *   *

As Max sat in his cabin preparing for bed and gathering his thoughts, he reflected on the vitality of the young naval contingent who had joined him for dinner. Max smiled as he conceded, "*They possess so much energy and dedication to the profession of arms; no second thoughts or hesitation among them.*" In fact, they reminded Max of the young Captain Donatello. He was just as dedicated back then, in the same way these officers and NCOs are now. The only difference was that the country was now at peace.

These thoughts were actually comforting to Max in a strange way. All these years, he had carried a modicum of shame for his country's guilt in the loss of so many Cambodians. Here was a new generation of young officers and NCOs, who were just as professional and willing to serve under whatever circumstances the country encountered. They were ready to do their duty regardless of personal sacrifice or potential harm. It was not unlike his dad's service in Operation Overlord in WWII, or his grandfather's in the Meuse Argonne Offensive during the

Great War. Max marveled how generations seem to rise to whatever occasion their country finds itself, with the same vigor and vitality that Max had shown in his perilous tour in Cambodia. Only the circumstances and national policy differed.

Max could not help but conclude that loyalty to one's country and patriotic service occurs irrespective of era, or prevailing political or policy persuasion. And, since policy has not historically been the purview of the American military, it didn't seem very logical for a retired soldier to carry around guilt and anger over the country's manifest policy blunders. The enthusiastic vitality of the naval contingent he observed that evening seemed to reignite Max's own lost faith.

It was very gratifying to have the opportunity to host these dedicated professionals to a first-class seafood feast. In Max's mind, it validated his own success both in his military and his post-military career to be able to give something spontaneously back to random servicemen who would not have been able to afford such a lavish evening. Besides, they were a bunch of stand-up guys whose dedication and devotion to duty were clearly in evidence. Max was proud of them and especially admired their professionalism.

CHAPTER SEVENTY-TWO

S ihanoukville, aka, Kompong Som, had blossomed into quite a resort community. Max hardly recognized the layout of the city. "Forty-five or so years?" Max struggled with the actual length of time between the days of the SeaTrain Maryland and the current times. Whatever had happened to the port?

So, off they drove to the access-controlled port facility. They were not surprised that no visitors were allowed on the actual piers or docks. From the size and dimension of the complex, it was clear that Sihanoukville was now an operational, commercial deep-draft port with several ships alongside that were larger than the SeaTrain Maryland, back in her day. Extensive portside storage facilities had been added. Max noticed that the terminal complex also included a Petroleum Offload and Storage facility that looked to Max like it could handle all types of refined products, including natural gas.

As they drove away, Max noticed several Gantry cranes, used nowadays for offloading containerized cargo. They had even expanded the port to transship containers from a vast container storage yard surrounding the port. Large numbers of stacked containers awaited clearance and pick up by the now numerous commercial port clearance and highway trucking companies that frequented the port.

Max could not help recalling the need to haul truckloads of break bulk cargo up the escarpment to the woefully inadequate facilities on the route to Kompong Som Airport. Max decided to have the driver take him to what was left of the FANK warehouses.

The driver explained that once the Americans left in 1975, the port facilities had languished. The Khmer Rouge philosophy made it plain that the lush fields and ample rice paddies of Cambodia should easily feed their decreasing population. In their jaded economic perspective, there was no need for imports, exports, or facilities to handle them. Moreover, the conquering Khmer Rouge believed it could certainly provide what few implements as would be needed to sustain the neo-agrarian society. Beyond these parameters, there was essentially no planning except to implement the purge of industrial and western cultural influences on the population of Cambodia. The KR scheme was truly intended to be a giant leap backward.

As they closed in on what was the FANK storage facility, the driver mentioned that warehousing facilities, like the one ahead, were routinely converted for use as collection and processing centers to ensure there was an adequate population flow out to appropriate work centers and agrarian plantations. People were also needed to supplement fishing and distribution of raw food products, as well as the numerous farming tasks that were de-mechanized under the Khmer Rouge's retrogressive agrarian formula.

Max suspected that his trip to Kompong Som might have been for naught. Things had so manifestly changed. There was hardly anything he recognized. Progress had made major inroads in this important logistics area for the new regime.

Max realized the truth of this presumption when the driver approached the once teeming warehouse facility. The large, long building had been compartmentalized as a kind of one-way indoor market. All around houses on stilts were lined up, and huts for those less well-off peasants had been hastily erected as well. In sum, what was here was nothing less than a thriving village just off the main highway to the airport. Max mused that one would have to engage the eye of a sharp cultural anthropologist to determine whether there had ever been any vestige of the old FANK supply depot at this site.

Max got out of the car and walked to stretch a bit on the facility's outskirts. He noticed that along the multiple paths, there were olive drab (OD) fence posts laid next to one another in the subsurface, as if to provide the basis of a rudimentary roadbed. On top, there were decades of additional gravel strewn on top. So, what he was looking at was a fencepost-reinforced gravel driveway. The sheer ingenuity of the design gave an ironic, knowing wink to the rebar-enforced concrete highways that coursed through most first and second world countries. But then, Max had always been impressed with the 'chewing gum and bailing wire' approach to solutions used during his 1970s encounter with Khmer innovation.

As they departed, Max focused on the concrete drainage ditch that followed the road on both sides down the escarpment. He wanted to see if he could recognize the place where Master Chief Perry Carpenter had lost control of the Rough Terrain Fork Lift (RTFL), as he tried to pilot the enormous hydraulic-assisted beast back down the long descent to the port. Max had reviewed the photos that had been taken not long after the accident by COL Jacobson. He recalled that the forklift had lost hydraulic power, which negated the steering-assist mechanism, as well as the brakes, making the unwieldy behemoth gain speed as it progressed down the steep highway.

Max asked the driver to drive slowly for about the first half mile after leaving the 'Khmer warehouse.' The only evidence that gave away the fateful spot was an extensive hydraulic fluid stain on the concrete drainage ditch about half a mile away from the gates of the warehouse. Also, on closer inspection, there was a sizable gouge in the concrete where the vehicle impacted the drainage ditch with maximum impact, flush on its side.

Max called to the driver to halt and pull over. He hopped out to walk around the site. *"What a tragic loss of so adept a leader, by virtue of this damned RTFLs untimely encounter with Mother Earth,"* Max repeated to himself. *"What a capital loss. He was doing so much good and loving every second of it. Perry was the quintessential American senior Non-Commissioned Officer, reveling in the progress they were making with these simple FANK soldiers. The good Lord must've had another important assignment for you,"* was all Max could conclude.

Max couldn't help recalling Perry's earthy humanity. Here was a soldier at the top of his career, having made it through a career checkered with tough assignments, long family absences, and periodically hostile environments.

To Max's great surprise and relief, Perry had put up with Max as his boss, never using experience to trump rank. Perry was a quintessentially professional senior NCO, whose mastery of leadership had been developed over a lifetime in the Navy. Max remembered with relish the time that he and Perry had a chat about leadership over a glass of wine one evening at the ocean-side resort.

Max would never forget Perry's offhand assessment of Max. In spite of their normal banter, Perry had clearly expressed his considered opinion that Max had natural leadership traits—emphasizing that most good leaders had to learn them and discover their utility in their own approach to the art of influencing men. That was the greatest compliment and confidence-inspiring statement Max had ever heard in reference to Captain Donatello up to that time.

"Perry, I do miss you so," was Max's last deep thought as he reminded himself that if Master Chief Carpenter had survived, the two would surely have been the closest of friends down through the years.

CHAPTER SEVENTY-THREE

*M*ax's flight to Neak Leoung was routed through Phnom Penh. There was a very short stop, then onward to one of the places that still held the most savage and elaborate memories for Max. The airport was little more than a grass airfield. It was certainly not a bustling hub of activity. A representative from the firm that had been providing Max's private transportation in Cambodia was waiting just outside the questionably dubbed 'In-Country Arrivals Gallery' of this miniscule aerodrome. The driver was an eager young lad, named Haing, who was not only energetic, but a real chatter bug. He did not shut up until they hit the center of town, Max's objective.

Haing gave Max a summary rundown, in pretty good English, on how things had progressed in this backwater since the Cambodia regained its sovereignty. Max was aware that the population had nearly been obliterated in that fateful, errant B-52 strike. What Max did not know was how the population had fared since the KR regime. Max's driver offered a supposition that hardly any of the native families made it back to Neak Leoung after 1980. In fact, there had not been sufficient time between the B-52 bombing and the KR takeover to do much rebuilding. What had been accomplished was minimal and largely cosmetic.

Max was reminded of the horrific carnage as he walked through the center of town. It seemed to Max that farmers and merchants had repopulated Neak Leoung. Tradesman now plied their wares, sustained by the teaming river port near the town's edge. There was also a large farmer's market close to the spot where he and his intrepid comrade, MAJ Bethke, had set up their rudimentary collection center cum triage facility way back then, covered only with a flimsy tarpaulin to ward off the sun's scorching rays. Sadly, the remnants of the bombed out buildings near the city center were still in evidence. Obviously, there had not been sufficient resources to clean up before the KR took over. Clearly, the town had languished, essentially destroyed, since that ominously unlucky day, when bombs from that wayward B-52 rained down on this unsuspecting, peaceful river town.

The former logistics base, which had been located on the town's outskirts, no longer existed. A few huts remained, but the warehouses had been razed, and the motor parks were nothing but open fields.

Max had Haing take him to the site where the Air America helicopter had been parked when the bombing began. Max could still recognize parts of the UH1-H cockpit by the faded Air America colors. The tail boom was about 500 feet away from the principal remains of the fuselage. It was clear that the craft had long since been picked clean for anything of value.

*   *   *

To Max's dismay, a native elder approached Max as he made his inspection rounds near the bones of the long-destroyed UH-1. It appeared that he intended to speak to Max. Max called Haing over to act as interpreter.

Max was told that the elder told him, "Four Americans were here that day. They came in this contraption, but then stayed to help the wounded and dying. We have never had a chance to say thanks to brave Americans who help my people," the elder said earnestly.

Max was stunned by this man's spontaneous testimony. His mind raced, *"How can these people be worried about expressing appreciation for the small gesture of help we rendered when those US Air Force jet-butt bastards blithely flew homeward without even tilting their wings?"* Max asked himself with genuine discomfiture.

Max looked deep into the elder's eyes, then asked Haing to relate, "My friends who were here that day need no thanks. Our Air Force made a horrible error that day in bombing this innocent town. Neak Leoung and its citizens should never have been fired upon."

Max was thinking, *"Before you express appreciation for a few basic humanitarian efforts of several Americans, we Americans should first apologize for our errant technology, our unforgiveable arrogance, and for the corresponding loss of so many innocent Cambodian lives resulting from the bombing here in Neak Leoung."*

The elder broke the slightest smile and said through Haing, "I think you are one of the brave Americans here that day. I remember a tall, dark, strong soldier, and a tall, thin soldier," obviously referring to MAJ Hank Bethke. "And I remember two others, not soldiers. One was short, fat, and older than the others. I believe he was what you call 'pilot' of this remarkable bird. The other was his young assistant."

The elder continued, "You were here. I remember those eyes. You have earned some well-deserved silver hairs, but I know you were here." The elder was almost gleeful, having convinced himself of his long-term memory's clarity.

Max had supposed he would fly in and out of Neak Leoung below the radar as just another curious Westerner trekking through the Cambodian countryside. Never in his vivid dreams would he have envisaged this scene. After a long pause, Max admitted and asked Haing to inform the gentleman, "I was here. And, I want to apologize to you for the tragic error of my Air Force comrades-in-arms, who caused the loss of so many wonderful Cambodian people."

"Could this conversation possibly be happening?" Max wondered in a soulful search of his memories of this place.

The elder shook his head slowly. "I was out on the river in a fishing boat when the explosions began. So, I rowed back to shore, and ran to the center of town. I was twelve years old. My parents were merchants here, trading in farm and river products, fish, eels, and the like. I could see that the storefront of our business had been destroyed in the bombing. I noticed a tall, muscular American soldier carrying my mother to a collection point with a small tarp to ward off the sun. My mother was badly injured in the collapse of the roof of our store. I was very impressed with how carefully you handled my dying mother. You may not remember that I came to the collection point and stayed with my mother until she was here no more. You were so busy. As soon as you had one victim comfortably situated, you were off to search for other victims to assist. I doubt you even noticed I was there for a long time before my mother died."

Max said astoundedly, "My God, I do remember a little fella who remained faithfully at his mother's side until she died. Then, as we were moving her body to another location where nothing more medically could be done, the boy seemed to disappear. That was you?" Max asked Haing to inquire of the elder.

After Haing's translation, the elder nodded. "My father was never found. Every evening for a week, I crept back into the town to look for him. I searched all the places where he would normally go during the day. I sifted through debris at the site of the store. It seemed to me at that time that he simply evaporated from this world."

Max asked incredulously, "What happened to you? How did you survive? When the KR took over, did you stay nearby?" Max's mind was racing, not knowing what to ask first, of all the questions he had conjured up over the years.

Through the interpreter, the elder said, "Let me introduce you to my younger sister. This is Sasowaith. It was you who picked her up and brought her and my baby sister to safety that day. She has never said a word since then."

As the elder spoke, an absolutely stunning Cambodian woman appeared their midst. Years had added character, but Max realized that this was the little girl he first encountered after the bombing started in Neak Leoung. She was the little girl who carried the infant who upchucked all over Max, just as he had dispatched his comrades to make contact with Phnom Penh via the Air America helicopter's onboard radios and avionics assemblies.

Max inquired, "What ever happened to the baby she was carrying? I lost track of her in the confusion while we were sorting through the injured."

The elder slowly shook his head, "Sadly, the baby developed breathing problems caused by so much smoke. She lived only a day or two after the bombs fell."

The woman who had joined them was stone silent. It was as if her essence had been hollowed out. Although she seemed comfortable around Max, walking slowly around him, seemingly examining his eyes from every angle.

The elder continued, "Since we were orphans, the KR treated us mercifully, especially since Sasowaith had been so obviously traumatized. We were sent to a work camp nearby, where we were assigned to live with another family who also had 'retarded' children. As the years passed, I tended to my sister's care, and after the KR and Vietnamese went away, we returned to Neak Leoung. The few remaining citizens made me their leader because my sister and I survived, when so many had perished."

Max was clearly incredulous, stunned by this dialogue. Here were two witnesses of that fateful day, when all hell broke loose from the skies, when fire came unexpectedly from the heavens to change all their lives forever. Max asked, "Has she ever made any social or interpersonal progress since that awful day?"

The elder told Haing, "She has always had a certain sense of purpose throughout her life. She knows that we need clean clothes. She takes action in preparing food for the two of us. She keeps our dwelling clean every day. All these things, she manages well. However, she needs me to provide a supply of rice, vegetables, and the other makings for meals, and she needs simple tools for cleaning the house and doing the laundry, but she refuses to go to the village to obtain these things. It is almost as if she is ashamed to show herself in public. If someone comes to visit, she will hide in her room."

Max had an emergent thought. *"Could this poor soul have been traumatized so badly from the bombing that it left her with symptoms that had gone undiagnosed? Could she be suffering from a form of post traumatic autism?"* Max asked himself. So many compelling possibilities were presented, but no authoritative diagnoses were ever considered or formulated.

As he observed the woman, Max caught subtle glimpses of understanding and curiosity in those hollow eyes. Max thought he could see somewhere in there a fleeting essence, first appearing, then, just as quickly, disappearing. It was almost like a long-slumbering person finally aroused, coming around slowly to the full realization of a conscious world lost because of a terror-induced coma.

Max turned to the elder and asked, "Has she ever been evaluated by a neurologist or a psychiatrist?

The elder again sadly shook his head. "The KR decided she was simply retarded, and Vietnamese never challenged that diagnosis. Besides, her condition was the excuse for our survival. After the Vietnamese left, she was in her mid-thirties and could not leave this area. Where could she go? So, no evaluation was done. We simply accepted her condition and lived with it. Besides, we had no such doctors. If they survived, it was because the made it out of Cambodia. In the new regime, specialized medical care is still scarce. Most people in areas outside Phnom Penh cannot afford such evaluations, or any treatment that would be demanded as a result."

Max understood. His American instinct would be to sweep her up in his arms, and get her to the best analysts available, sparing no expense. His 'Knight in Shining Armor' approach was clearly out of step with the realities of her situation, and although he realized this reality, it only served to intensify his sense of frustration and helplessness.

Finally, Max quietly said, "She's a lovely girl. It is a tragedy we couldn't get her the help she needs. I would like to arrange for her treatment, with your permission. I have contacts with a network of prosperous Cambodian patriots, who live around the world, and who provide assistance in cases like that of your sister. If you would allow me to make some inquiries, we may be able to get her treatment that would enrich her life."

The elder smiled warmly. "Still trying to help us, aren't you? While I doubt that any treatment will improve Sasowaith's condition, you may certainly know of resources of which I am unaware. I would never impede or thwart any effort to improve her physical and mental well-being."

At that moment, Max realized that he was running out of time. The plan was for him to only spend a few hours at this location, catching the return flight to Phnom Penh in mid-afternoon, changing there to a late afternoon flight to Siem Riep.

Max turned to the elder and said, "I must be on my way. But, you will be hearing from my Cambodian friends." The two shook hands, and before Max turned to leave, he obtained the names of his two new friends.

The elder, Chansin Thin, said, "You have a very generous heart. Please accept our thanks for all you have done for us, and, for your continued concern for our welfare."

Max nodded acknowledgement, and started to make his exit when the Sasowaith ran to him and threw her arms around Max's waist, with her head on his chest, and simply rocked slowly back and forth. Holding Max tightly for several minutes, she finally broke away and fled behind her brother to their meager dwelling.

It was all Max to do to keep his eyes dry. He had so many unshed tears from his experiences here, both now and in the past. These were the warm and loving people that Max had known in 1972.

All the Max could muster was, "Wow!" The elder smiled knowingly.

*   *   *

As Haing drove him back to the aerodrome, Max reflected on the remarkable exchange he had just experienced. He had anticipated that Neak Leoung would most likely be a simple, sad encounter with his past. What occurred had left him aglow with encouragement and sincere expectations for Sasowaith's improvement. Finding two survivors of the bombings had made a surprisingly redemptive effect on Max. He had come back to face the horrors that he'd encountered on his first visit. Instead, he found a spark of hope that perhaps some good could be accomplished for this unfortunate woman, even at this late date.

Max was coming to believe that his long-held horrors resided solely in his own repressed memory. Little evidence of the carnage, tragedy, and pathos of that day in the early 1970s remained for a conscious reunion. Max was relieved by this realization. It felt like he had been carrying the pieces and parts of bodies torn asunder around with him ever since that harrowing day. He now knew that what he had really carried around was simply a vividly awful, terrible nightmare, inexorably hung up in his sub-conscious.

Though it was a simple mental image, it always seemed like a burden, weighing tons. Max was beginning to realize that this long-carried form of self-condemnation had been mistakenly self-inflicted. His sense of rage and aggravated powerlessness had emerged over time in the form of an oppressive guilt, along with boundless shame for the actions of his USAF countrymen whose error caused all the carnage he had witnessed.

Thus, he concluded, this guilt was not something he personally owed to the dead and wounded. Max's actions that day were undeniably humanitarian, even heroic. He finally grasped that the damnable guilt and shame, endured for so long, had been unfairly meted out by virtue of his own misunderstanding of who bore the real blame for the tragedy of Neal Leuong. Finding the elder and his sister had a cathartic effect on Max and confirmed this analysis.

"Whew, what a dumb shit I have been," thought Max. *"It has taken all these years for me to realize it was not my fault that all those poor, helpless Khmer citizens were slaughtered. Those who died, or were wounded here, would have died or had been wounded if the raid occurred a week before or after my EIUI."*

The bottom line, Max finally understood, was that it was not his responsibility to bear the burden of guilt for the gross American mistake that had occurred that day.

Something so simply misconstrued in his vivid sub-conscious had been the genus of untold nightmares; had caused him to relegate his wife and family to the background; and had been a starkly real, life-long trauma.

Max departed Neal Leoung with a different, invigorated perspective. And, the possibility of being part of the effort to treat Sasowaith was a refreshingly inspiring prospect to him. His visit to Neak Leoung far exceeded his expectations. Max would later realize, the visit was not only liberating, but also a redemptive form of therapy for him.

CHAPTER SEVENTY-FOUR

*T*raversing Phnom Penh on the journey to Siem Riep, Max started feeling a bit nauseated, and he observed the signals of oncoming hostility in his lower abdomen. Not sure if the condition was simply an over-reaction to the revelations experienced in Neak Leoung, Max insisted on proceeding with his itinerary. He spent most of his short layover in the men's room dealing with his stomach and intestines.

He even considered attributing blame to last evening's dinner escapade in Sihanoukville at the seafood BBQ, with all his newfound Navy comrades. Max's mind bounced from potential causes to the usual suspects. He had been periodically plagued over the years with the residue of the dreaded intestinal symptoms of dengue fever.

Ashen, totally spent, Max finally rose to the occasion and boarded the two-engine, turbo-jet commuter that would ferry him and his unfortunate plane-mates to their final destination on the Cambodian frontier.

Max barely had time to clean himself up. The malodorous result was that the others aboard this flight were destined to be prisoners, in this tubular aviation marvel, to the vestiges of Max's rebellious abdominal track.

CHAPTER SEVENTY-FIVE

*T*he flawless flight alighted on the runway with a merciful screech, rather than a prominent thunk. It was a blessing for the unfortunate, assembled seatmates of this oversized, odor-afflicted American, who seemed to have blithely slept through most of the short flight. Max awoke with a start as the plane kissed the earth.

Max remained in his seat so the others could deplane. Intended as a simple courtesy, Max still exhibited his unfortunate natural tendency to assign blame to himself for the suffering of others. While there was little doubt as to the culprit for the stench on board, Max felt chivalrous that his latest move surely alleviated the suffering of others.

A chauffer from the same touring local company that had escorted Max around Cambodia was eagerly awaiting the last person off the plane. A young man in his late '20s held up a sign reading 'Donatello' that beckoned Max to his side. The young man said, "I am Sith Vann, and I will be your driver and guide while you are here visiting the Siem Riep region."

Max made a pseudo-magnanimous gesture, hoping the energetic guide would spare him the definitive early history of the Khmer people while they made their way to Max's hotel.

With something less than enthusiasm, Max offered, "I have had a couple of bad flights today, and have kind of a sour stomach. Would you mind if we dispense with the normal acquaintance chat while we drive to the hotel? I feel quite ill and indisposed, and would appreciate your delaying any description of Siem Riep until tomorrow, when I will arise with full attention, as we begin our tour of the area."

Mr. Vann grasped the severity of Max's condition as soon as he opened the door to his nice, late model Toyota Camry, which was already running with the A/C on full blast. Max had a putrid–looking, greenish-ashen complexion. Mr. Vann wondered if Max could manage to control his innards for the ten-minute trek to the hotel. If not, Mr. Vann's life savings would be in jeopardy. His Camry and his tour guide business would be in desperate peril if he could not rid his chariot of the stench of a severely troubled esophagus.

It occurred to Max that the ride to his hotel was quick, if not hurried, which was fine with Max. The sooner he got settled into his room, the better. To that end, Mr. Vann convinced the front desk to dispense with the normal formalities and pleasantries of a SE Asian five-star hotel welcome ritual. With the perfunctory red tape cutting, and within in a matter of minutes, Max was soon entering his 12th floor mini-suite. He could not be certain who had the prescience to start the shower, but by the time he had removed his fetid clothing, he found his way quickly into the place where gloriously warm water was streaming earthward in his direction.

CHAPTER SEVENTY-SIX

*M*ax stirred out of his dormant world with persistent ring of the wake-up call that he had forgotten he'd registered soon after his arrival here the previous evening. It became apparent that as he got up and moved around, he was still feeling peaked and, for the most part, under the weather. Reviewing the prodigious schedule he had approved for the upcoming day in Cambodia, it gave Max pause. What he needed was a down day, not a day filled with bumpy dirt roads, steaming heat, and endless ancient temples. And, he surmised, the next 24 hours could provide just such an opportunity.

Max's again looked over his schedule. The itinerary called for three and a half days in Siem Riep to learn all there was to know about the ancient Khmer society, and to tour the acres of magnificent temples in Angkor Wat and Angkor Thom and vicinity. Max thought, surely, one day less doing the tourist bit would not ruin the trip, and perhaps a down day would allow him to gather his strength and make his final days in the kingdom more enjoyable. With the decision taken, Max picked up the hotel phone and rang up the concierge to have him contact Mr. Vann to inform him of the change. This tour ammendment accomplished, Max rolled back onto the comfy, king-sized bed and went promptly back to sleep. It was well past noon when Max again awoke.

Max first plunged into another long, warm shower. Refreshed and feeling somewhat more human, Max decided to wander about the grounds of the hotel. He had not eaten anything the day before, and although his stomach was rumbling, he decided to forego anything until later in the day. The Hotel Angkor was an enormous, modernistic U-shaped building with fifteen floors on each wing. The massive lobby between the wings had several levels for restaurants, lounges, and reception.

A long, saline pool was nestled outside between the wings of the buildings, with separate compartments for children, lap swimmers and sun worshipping floaters. Stepping out of the lobby to look at the pool, Max noticed that each room on poolside had a terrace large enough for two chairs. Max found some shade outside near a quiet area of the pool and sat under an umbrella-shaded chaise lounge. A pretty waitress appeared offering to bring Max a beverage. Max wasn't certain how his system would feel about a gin and tonic, so he simply ordered a chilled bottle of Pellegrino water.

Just as the waitress departed, none other than Sith Vann, Max's driver and guide appeared. "Excuse me, Mr. Donatello, but I came back to see if you needed anything. I can take you to a physician or pharmacist if you are still feeling poorly," said Mr. Vann solicitously.

"Well, that's mighty thoughtful of you, Mr. Vann. Why don't you sit down and visit for a spell, as we say in the American South. I'm feeling a bit better this afternoon, and I don't believe medical intervention will be necessary. I might have taken you up on that offer last evening before I finally settled down and got to sleep. But now, I'm certain that I am on the mend.

Besides, I'm sure that I wasn't exactly the friendliest client you've ever picked up at the airport. Please accept my apologies for my lack of social graces yesterday, and for being such a jerk." Max added.

"No apologies necessary, sir; your ashen complexion made it clear that you were having a bad day, as you Americans are fond of saying," Mr. Vann added with a wan smile, as he bowed in the typical Khmer prayerful way, with hands together like a first grader going to his or her First Communion.

"Are you sure there is nothing you need—some soda, something to calm an upset stomach?" asked Mr. Vann with earnest concern. It was clear to Max that Mr. Vann was committed to making his stay as comfortable hereafter as was possible.

"I've just ordered some bubble water from that pretty waitress. Would you join me for a drink?" Max added with a tone intended to make Mr. Vann feel welcome.

As Mr. Vann settled in, he responded politely, "Thank you, perhaps some tea?"

"We'll get her to work on that as soon as she gets back," Max added. "So, Mr. Vann have you been in this area for long?"

CHAPTER SEVENTY-SEVEN

*T*hus began an almost non-stop two day dialogue between the two men. Max was impressed with the depth of Mr. Vann's knowledge and understanding of Khmer culture and history. When Max queried as to Mr. Vann's education, he learned that in addition to living through the holocaust, he had been secretly homeschooled by his mother and father after they arrived in their ancestral home north of Siem Riep. Then, after the Vietnamese departed, Mr. Vann went on to earn a master's degree in Cambodian history, which made him well-qualified to be a tour guide around the antiquities of Angkor. Max had been informed that professional guides have to have a guide's license, earned by means of course work and examinations. Licensed guides are the only ones who can escort a tourist through the hundreds of temples in the region.

Sith told Max that his father worked as an official assigned to the US Embassy. Ironically, his dad had a graduate degree in agriculture from Iowa State University. He worked for the US Agency for International Development (USAID), assisting Khmer farmers in modern methods of agricultural production.

Over the course of the next two days, Max realized that Mr. Vann's father had been posted to the US embassy in Phnom Penh at the same time that Max was assigned to MEDTC. The two had never officially met, most likely because the elder Mr. Vann was often in the provinces working with farmers.

Sith Vann expressed amazement at this profoundly cosmic coincidence. Here he was driving and guiding this one American, now in his mid-sixties, through arguably the most extensive and majestic network of ancient temples in the world, only to find that Max had undoubtedly crossed paths closely with his father during their common time at the US Embassy in Phnom Penh in 1972-1973. The congruence of their stories had the effect of stirring more fascination the more the two men probed the events that led up to the Vann family's evacuation from the city.

Max wanted to know as much of the story as Mr. Vann was willing to relate. Max shared his concern about the welfare of the many Khmer officers he had known and worked with during his tour in Cambodia. He had mentioned that he had many horrific dreams that stemmed from worrying about Khmer comrades, whose fate he had never learned.

Mr. Vann was very open with his family's story. As it happened, back when Sith Vann was just old enough to remember, the family began to plan to leave Phnom Penh in the spring of 1975. Sith's father required Sith and his older brother to work daily in the extensive family garden, starting in the early fall of 1974. By the time they were about to be forced to evacuate the city the following April, the whole family, his mother included, had heavily callused hands from wielding manual tools to cultivate their garden.

By the time the Khmer Rouge was making its final push on Phnom Penh, the elder Mr. Vann had diligently prepared his wife and children. The children knew they were forbidden to speak to KR officials. They were certainly never allowed to mention having gone to school. Sith's father made it clear that he would answer all questions from KR officials about their family. If, by some happenstance, the parents were separated, the children would always defer to whatever parent they were with to make appropriate responses to questions from their KR inquisitors.

Mr. Vann told Max that his family had begun their trek to family homelands near Siem Riep in the north a full week before Phnom Penh had fallen. Mr. Vann and his family had been able to make their way in a small boat on the Tonle Sap River northward toward Siem Riep. They were stopped several times by KR patrols for questioning.

Sith's father always maintained a very deferential attitude during these episodes, even though their KR interrogators were often teenage boys, only several years older than the eldest of his own two boys. Mr. Vann's father was acutely aware of the many reports of KR savagery. Chances of survival diminished to near zero when a Khmer encountered on the trail or on the river was suspected of being a traitor, or who had supported the pro-American Lon Nol regime. It was far worse if it was discovered that the person in flight served in the Lon Nol administration, or in the despised FANK forces.

One such encounter happened after the family had been forced to give up their small purloined boat to some KR teenagers, who insisted that the new regime's mandate was plain: all former city dwellers making their way to the work camps must walk.

On the trails, the family encountered several bands of young trigger-happy Pol Pot supporters. In one such meeting, several citizens had just been executed, and their bodies were still strewn on the pathway. The KR forced Sith's father to drag the bodies off to the ditches on either side of the path. The KR band then began to interrogate Sith's father.

They thrust a Cambodian newspaper into his hands and demanded he read it to them. Luckily, the KR soldier who thrust the paper in Mr. Vann's direction had handed it to him upside down. Sith's father made no attempt to turn the paper upright. He simply began squinting at the newsprint, with the script upside down. Finally, one of the KR soldiers relented and yelled out to his comrades that this was indeed an ignorant peasant who looked sturdy enough to make a contribution at one of the work camps. The Vann family was allowed to pass.

In another encounter with inquisitive KR on the trail, the family was asked to show the KR their hands. The many months of manual labor had been worthwhile, as the KR leader once again concluded that the Vann family members were certainly not educated urban dwellers, but simply agrarian workers. They were again given their leave.

* * *

As Mr. Vann escorted Max around the main temples and explained the history and meaning of the bas reliefs at Angkor Wat, Max realized that another trip would be in his future. He would love to share these magnificent temples with Melissa, Chris, and Susie.

On the evening of Max's last day in Cambodia, he and Mr. Vann had ventured out to the Banyan Temple at Angkor Thom to take advantage of the setting sun, which was in just the right position for the perfect temple photograph. Max opened the discourse by asking, "Sith, you have never mentioned whether your father ever returned to Phnom Penh."

Sith Vann replied, "My father and mother are still living near the village about thirty miles north of here, where they settled after the end of the Pol Pot regime in 1979. My father expressed to me on more than one occasion that he had made his peace with God and the world, and was happy to live off the land. My mother feels the same way, and she would never leave my father's side."

Max simply shook his head and remarked, "Your father clearly made it through those years out of sheer guts and guile. I admire his tenacious dedication to his family, and the obviously enormous cultural transition he had to experience. Thank you for relating this story to me, Sith Vann."

Max paused then went on, "Your family's story of survival has given me faith that there must have been others who survived that hellacious ordeal, out of personal resourcefulness and raw courage. I have always felt somehow responsible for the lives of the Cambodian officers left behind. I know it sounds silly, but I have held my country accountable all these years for the actions that precipitated the KR takeover and the loss of so many Khmer citizens."

Sith Vann grabbed Max's shoulder and gave him and embrace. "It is not up to you to take responsibility, or to hold your country account-able for what happened here. I have given this matter a great deal of reflection, and have concluded that Cambodian society was suffering from decay from within itself. The Lon Nol regime and the assistance provided by America only made the inevitable come quicker. Cambo-dia was long overdue a revolution. It was unfortunate that so many died in accomplishing it. When you depart tomorrow, you should leave without any burden of guilt or repressed anger."

"Our country is struggling, but we are headed in the right direction for a change. And, we are taking responsibility for our own growth, even though that is happening more slowly than other places in Indochina. The Khmers have their country back once again. It is up to us to make it prosper," Sith Vann finished.

Max again felt like someone relieved him of an oppressive burden. Sith Vann was a survivor of the Cambodian holocaust. He had framed his arguments in a most positive way. Mr. Vann had convinced Max to rid himself of all guilt regarding the inevitable denouement of Cambodia.

It was as if the last two stops on this redemptive journey to SE Asia had been tailored just for his needs. Meeting the village elder and Sasowaith in Neak Leoung, and having spent the past several days with Sith Vann, made an enormous difference in Max's perspective.

Max was leaving in the morning, but he was leaving with an amazing new friend, and a new outlook regarding one man's wartime experience. That night, just as Winston Churchill had said to the British citizens after the Japanese had attacked Pearl Harbor and the United States entered the Second World War, Max, like Churchill, "Slept the sleep of the thankful and the saved."

CHAPTER SEVENTY-EIGHT

*M*ax could not sleep on the long flight to Hong Kong, but it did give him plenty of time to think before the long leg of his trip back to Denver. So much had happened, so many mistaken beliefs had been dashed that Max's head was swimming from all the inputs. His mind began swirling on the flight from Phnom Penh to Bangkok earlier that day.

On reflection, Max believed he owed an enormous debt of gratitude to Emily, who had foreseen Max's redemption, as she loyally pleaded over the years that Max return to Cambodia to face his demons. Max now realized that his intransigence about seeking treatment for his repressed trauma was far too high a price for Emily and the family to pay.

"It's a wonder Emily stuck around and put up with me as long as she did," Max said to himself ruefully. *"She was still my best friend and faithful partner until her last day on earth, in spite of our separation. She deserved better, much better."*

Max tried to think of how Emily would regard his relief at finding redemption, albeit at this late date. Somehow, he felt certain that Emily would be ecstatic to know that Max would finally enjoy some peace. Knowing Emily's unflagging dedication and unconditional love, Max rested easy in the knowledge that if angels are able to look down on the doings of humans, Emily would be dancing on the head of a pin just to know that Max's trip to Cambodia was so liberating.

Another conclusion occurred to Max as he mulled over all the positive aspects of the trip. He must now dedicate himself to the remaining vestiges of his family, for his own welfare, if not to somehow demonstrate to Emily, in his temporal, worldly way, how much her dedication and loyalty meant to him. Doing something positive in the world would be his mission. He would start first with his family.

Max was blessed with two eminently lovable kids who, each in their own right, were capable of significant contributions to society. How gratifying it would be to actively participate in their lives and those of his grandkids. *"Who knows, I might even have a few more little ones to spoil if Melissa hurries up and settles down...."* Max suggested to himself.

Perhaps his most surprising resolution came to him during the long flight to Hong Kong. He had determined that he would engage the network of Cambodian philanthropists to provide long-term treatment for Sasowaith, his taciturn female charge from Neak Leoung. But, taking this seminal thought to its obvious conclusion, Max decided that he would not only be a bit player in helping the care network that Sisowath Samoeun had introduced him to during his stay at the Mayflower in D.C. Max made a solemn pledge that he would actively join this organization with the aim of assisting on whatever level needed attention, be it fund raising, marketing, or enlisting other volunteers.

During his visit to SE Asia, Max realized he needed a project, a personal mission to keep his creative spirit alive now that he had retired from Xerox. His plan to join the international efforts to help Cambodia get back on its feet seemed a perfect fit for the newly invigorated Max. Max assured himself that although he felt a passion for this new role, he must maintain a balance between it and the initial promise to himself that he would make family his first priority.

CHAPTER SEVENTY-NINE

*M*ax couldn't wait to tell Melissa all about his trip. Taking advantage of the 12 hours time difference, Max called her after he arrived at his hotel in Hong Kong just before midnight. The first thing he told her was that they needed to plan a trip as soon as possible so she could join her dad on his return to Cambodia, next time, perhaps as soon as the beginning of next year.

Max was like a little kid telling his mom about the first day at school, spewing out details in volcanic torrents. What a blessing to have made this trip. Max gained a terrific new friend, a new mission to seek treatment for Sasowaith. Max went on and on. The biggest thing Max wanted to relate was how thankful he was for Melissa's mom. Emily was still his source of strength and purpose. According to Max, Emily was still influencing his life in the most positive ways.

Melissa, for her part, was elated to hear the obvious relief in her dad's voice. She said, "Daddy, I am so thrilled that this trip has been so redemptive for you. It was a long time coming, a bit overdue, but richly-deserved. I know mom would be doing flips if she were here."

"And, Daddy, I have some big news for you. Rick has asked me to marry him, and I have said yes. I was offered that position I told you about at in D.C. But, in talking it over with Rick, I became convinced that it involved too much travel. To make things more complicated, Rick is in line to inherit his family's Honda dealership. His dad wants him to come in immediately as a full partner."

"So, I have turned down the job at PWC. And, after a lot of soul searching, I have decided that I am doing exactly what I have grown to love doing, running the B&B. So, after the wedding, Rick and I plan to hunker down and make the Williamsburg area our home. If you'll have me, I will continue to represent the Donatello family as a kind of caretaker manager of the B&B."

Max erupted in joy. "Congratulations! I am so proud of you. I couldn't be happier for you and Rick. You have all my best wishes and blessings on this engagement." Max was wiping tears of joy from the corners of his eyes. He couldn't help thinking how some good things have a way of finding and working themselves out, if you give them a little time. All his concerns about having to either dispose of the B&B, or relocate to run it himself, were just so much scattered energy. He had come up with some excellent secondary ideas by going through his analysis, however. All that was left was to bide his time in executing the best of them.

"I'll hear nothing of this caretaker manager stuff. I was thinking more like general manager or CEO for starters. It will serve as a fitting memorial to your loving mom to have you maintaining the standards and customer base that the two of you established. I know she is looking down on all these developments with a great big grin."

Melissa was speechless, but finally blurted in a sobbing voice, "Oh, thank you, Dad. Your blessing on our engagement, and your faith in me to continue mom's success at the B&B, mean the world to me. I have always had a secret motive driving me from inside. I wanted you to be proud of me, to respect and admire me. I feel I have that now, and I feel the love out there as well."

Max sputtered, "You certainly have an abundance of all those coming from me. I could not respect or admire anyone more, and, although I've made a mess of showing my love for you in the past, I will make every effort to demonstrate to you how very much love I have for you, both now and in the future."

*   *   *

When Max returned to Denver, he invited Chris and Susie out to dinner at one of the mile-high city's newest and swankiest restaurants. After they were seated and the drinks were delivered, the conversation turned to thoughts on Melissa and Rick's upcoming wedding. Chris and Susie were aware that Melissa had turned down the PWC job in deference to remaining in Williamsburg. Max informed them that she had asked to stay on and run the B&B. Chris jumped in here, "well that's a relief to know you won't have to become a road warrior, flying back and forth to Richmond airport ever couple of weeks. We are ecstatic that you will be around Denver with all your friends and family. In fact, we have made an offer on a piece of land in a development adjacent to your property. Our plan is to build a home near you so the kids will be able to see as much of you as possible. And, Melissa is a perfect fit to run the B&B."

"Sounds like you two have been doing some elaborate planning. Well, I have had a bit of time for some planning, too. I've decided that since Melissa will be remaining in Williamsburg, and wants to run the B&B in honor of your mother, I will soon buy a condo out there as a second home. Your mom and her family are interred there, as you well know. I, too, have a sense of place in the Tidewater area, and harbor an abiding wish to cultivate a closer adult relationship with Melissa. That is not to say I am abandoning you here. My primary home will still be here. The Virginia condo will simply allow me some personal space for refuge when your sister starts having a family. Besides, newlyweds need plenty of privacy."

Chris and Susie seemed aghast, but had smiles when Chris said finally, "You certainly have done some detailed planning."

Max broke in again and related his pledge to assist the Cambodian expat network, which had headquarters in D.C., with prominent members up and down the eastern seaboard. "The condo will give me a place to hang out when I'm not busy helping this organization."

After the waiter took their dinner orders, Max continued, "I would like for you to consider another idea I have been nurturing for quite some time. Instead of you building a new home in the adjacent development, why don't you move into my house? I would deed it over to you, and you could remodel it to suit yourselves before you move out of your current place. It would be less expensive than new construction. There is enough room on the property to construct a small cottage for me, or we could even rehab the apartment over the garage where you used to hang your hat, Chris. Either way, it would be a win-win, since I would remain close, but far enough away to have a bit of private time when necessary."

"Wow!" remarked Chris. "You have definitely been up to some serious skulduggery. How could you give up that big house that you have lived in for so many years?"

Max responded with clear purpose, "I actually bounce around in that huge place. I don't use much more than the master suite and the kitchen. I don't entertain at home, and most of the time, the place stands empty and unused. The plot of land it sits on is twice as large as any other in the development. I pay more for upkeep than anyone else in the area. Besides, the girls would have a large safe-haven in the back with all those mature trees and sturdy fences surrounding the back of the house. Heck, I could keep my eye on them as they play from a perch in the cottage or off the back deck."

Not much eating had occurred by either Chris or Susie as Max made his plea. "Don't you care for your entrees? Mine is great! You should dig in before it gets cold!" Max suggested.

"Ahem," Chris muttered as he prepared to speak, "The dinner is delicious. I think I can speak for Susie in saying that your proposal is not only a bit astounding, it's a lot to quickly digest, and it's enormously generous of you to even consider making such a substantial change. Having us in your backyard, so to speak, sounds sensational, but I thought when I finally got serious about school and a career, you would have breathed a sigh of relief to have me out of your hair. Now, you're inviting me to come back and take over your house as my own. I've got to say that you are a very special kind of dad. And, I might say, a real piece of work!"

"Well, thanks," said Max with an aw-shucks wave of his hand, "I've given it considerable thought. When I think of the house, I think of moving into something smaller, then I think of you wanting to build close by, so I ask myself, how can I move?" Max could see he was getting through to Chris and Susie.

"The girls love your house, Dad," Susie began. "They love to run and hide upstairs in all the bedrooms and closets. The designs we've looked at to date, fairly replicate the functional space you have with rooms placed here rather than there. I could grow to love living there. It's just that I would feel better if we were buying it from you rather than having you deed it to us outright. We can afford it these days, I can assure you."

Max responded with a big smile, "It's not about money. I know you're doing well and always will, for that matter. I was thinking of expediency and simplicity. You will one day own my house in Denver when I pass. I already have directed it so in my trust documents. This way, however, you get the immediate use of it while the girls are young, and I would get a suitable place on the same grounds so I can be close to all of you."

Max introduced a related topic as coffee was served. "I want you to know that I have decided to deed the B&B to Melissa as a wedding present. I think your mother would approve. And, it would sort of balance the scales since I'll be giving you the manor in Denver for your family. The B&B deed is being drawn up now in Melissa's maiden name. I want it kept absolutely secret. But, I do want her to go into this marriage to a member of a prominent Virginia family with assets of her own."

On their way back home, Max mentioned, "I believe I'll keep the New Mexico vacation house for the time being. I've always loved kicking around the mountains and lakes nearby, and would like to have it as a family place for getaways. And, I might even have some guests from Cambodia stay there from time to time."

The End

Author's Afterword

*Y*ou may recall that I set out in the introduction to accomplish three broad goals. My first hope was to acquaint another generation of our country's responsibility for its part in the destruction of Cambodia. Namely, mistaken, short-sighted policies had a way of setting off unforeseen consequences, which ultimately cost lives. In this case, it was a sizable part of Cambodia's population. Secondly, it was my goal to explore the warrior ethos and the prevailing attitude that combat induced mental illness is a problem of weakness, even cowardice which, most assuredly, has no place among serving career officers. And, finally, I wanted not only to illustrate the residual effects of combat on one remarkable officer, but how it affected his post-Army life and his family.

So, trying to grasp the threads of truth about the destruction of Cambodia and its population from 1975, until it regained its sovereignty in 1993, proved a formidable endeavor. When I started writing this book in the spring of 2012, I discovered that US library shelves were not exactly bulging with critical, authoritative, historical works on the subject. Our main character, Max, was on the right track when he lamented the fact that the whole matter seems to have been relegated to the trash heap of history. Clearly, it remains mere footnote in the history of the war in Southeast Asia over the last half of the 20th Century.

That is not to say there are no compelling descriptions of how Cambodia poised itself on the cliffs of perdition over the thirty or so years before Pol Pot's regime encircled Phnom Penh. I have shared some of these in the selected bibliography, unless they were specifically referenced or quoted from in the text. The foregoing is my own analysis of how all this came to be.

I would ask what were some of the causal factors leading to Cambodia's destruction? Who should bear the blame? Could it have been avoided? There are hints spread over Cambodia's recent political history, looking back only two decades before the arrival in Phnom Penh of Pol Pot's revolutionaries in the spring of 1975.

A rudimentary survey of Cambodian politics demonstrates several common traits in each of the regimes. These threads can be observed more clearly starting with Prince Sihanouk's paternalistic monarchy, only getting worse as one looks progressively as Lon Nol's dictatorship swings Cambodia off its neutral path to the far right, and finally the deadly 180 degree reversal to the far left in Pol Pot's ultra-communist regime. A high level summary would show the following:

1. The first similarity is that each regime assigned blame to factors and influences outside Cambodia.

2. Critical self-evaluation was essentially rejected by each of these leaders in deference to a common trait of excessive pride coupled with a delusional attitude held by each administration with respect to Cambodia's strength and long-term economic independence. In fact, Cambodia people were living in a dream world created and propagated by each succeeding leader.

3. Each leader shared a belief that Cambodians were not only better than their neighbors, they emphasized, even exaggerated, Cambodia's racial superiority.

4. Each had illusory visions of Cambodia, its people, its capabilities, and its economic and political stability.

5. Clearly, as time went on, the people's perspective of Cambodian society could not have been further afield from that of the leaders and their regimes. And, unfortunately, as time went on, both Cambodia and its leaders became further detached from reality.

Taking a deeper look, Sihanouk ultimately blamed France and its colonial mentality for not preparing Cambodia to govern itself once its independence was realized. France had done little to establish and educate a thriving middle class, from whom the country could draw able administrators and managers to oversee the government and the economic well being of the nation. Sihanouk also placed blame on the Soviet Union and the U.S. for their failed efforts in the 60's at providing adequate support to allow the Cambodian forces to ward off border threats from Laos, Thailand, but especially, Vietnam.

As for Marshal Lon Nol, he blamed the eastern neighboring Vietnamese and their war of unification for Cambodia's problems. Not only did he condemn Vietnam for its use Khmer territory as sanctuaries, but for its wholesale use of large swaths of eastern Cambodia for indispensible parts of the Ho Chi Minh Trail. Moreover, Lon Nol hated and ordered the wholesale slaughter of Eastern Province Vietnamese for tainting Cambodia racially, where proximity and tribal inter-marriage had diluted the precious dream of Khmer racial purity and superiority.

Pol Pot and his regime would blame the U.S. for indiscriminate bombing and its support of the openly corrupt Lon Nol administration. It, too, had a faulty illusion of the character and tolerance of the Cambodian people. With its sweeping, extreme left reforms, the population had to be catatonic with shock, reeling after the Khmer Rouge swept to power.

Other outside influences could be blamed. China, for example, could have reigned in the Khmer Rouge but did nothing beyond providing weapons and munitions for their communist stepchildren. The U.S. could have forced Lon Nol to reduce or curtail corruption. It could have stopped the bombing. But, we know that neither thing happened. The myopic, limited program supporting the Khmer government in the early seventies was strap hung from the onset by strictures of Congress, war weariness, which had a strangle hold on American public attitudes, and the U.S. administration's dismissive arm waving attitude about Cambodia and its destiny.

So, just as no conflict has one simple cause, Cambodia's inexorable path to perdition was attributable to a combination of factors. The traits mentioned above, which permeated the three consecutive regimes, along with the illusory visions of each leader created conditions that made revolutionary destruction inevitable.

Finally, a case can also be made that a Cambodian revolution, with its wanton destruction of institutions and way of life, was overdue. Cambodian society had endured economic and educational repression, drastic swings in governing philosophies, and ultimately, the heartless slaughter of its citizens at the hands of the godless Khmer Rouge. Given the country's relentless stampede toward the cliffs of disaster, a strong case could be made that Cambodia's regrettable fate was inevitable.

*   *   *

Another important theme that permeates throughout this book is the debilitating, even disabling, residual effects that war has on individual combat soldiers. The American 'warrior ethos' imbues a culture of silence, or a 'conspiracy of silence', as I term it in the book. It is a very real, repressing influence on the psychological outlook of soldiers, especially for officers of the Vietnam era and later. The 'warrior ethos,' holds the view that mental illness is absolute anathema to the career potential of any officer or senior NCO who succumbs to treatment through the military. It has been long viewed as an unmanly weakness, which portends unreliability, and the abiding concern that the officer in question lacks resilience and sufficient mental toughness to perform leadership duties. Thus, seeking treatment for mental illness not only makes one a kind of sissy, but it constitutes career suicide.

I refer to it as a 'conspiracy of silence' because it hasn't been until very recently, say the last five years or so, that U.S. Army authorities at the highest levels have seriously addressed the issues of mental illness or Post Traumatic Stress Disorder (PTSD). PTSD, depression, Traumatic Brain Injury (TBI), and other hard-to-detect mental conditions and illnesses are now getting public attention because of the increasingly high suicide rate among soldiers returning from Iraq and Afghanistan.

In August of 2012, New York Times Op-Ed columnist Nickolas Kristof wrote a revealing in-depth piece about how serious the issue has become, and what the service components are doing about it. Kristof reported that for every soldier killed in the war, about 25 take their own lives. Suicide statistics and occasional violence, domestic and public, shroud the underlying bow wave of undiagnosed mental health issues plaguing returning veterans.

Ironically, soldiers with visible combat-related injuries are honored and decorated publically with Purple Hearts. Tragically, the mentally or brain-injured comrades, with no outwardly obvious manifestation of their trauma, are mustered out of the service, with a pat on the butt and an honorable discharge. Kristof's article cites, "An astonishing 45 percent of those who served in Iraq and Afghanistan are now seeking compensation for injuries, in many cases psychological ones."

As outgoing Secretary of Defense, Leon Panetta, made the stongest statement to date, when in December 2012, he referred to mental illness detection, treatment and suicide prevention issues as the Defense Department's top priority. President Obama ordered the Service Component Chiefs to an "All Hands on Deck" alert, mandating immediate attention to issues of mental health in the services.

To the Army's credit, the principal duty of recently departed Deputy Chief of staff, General Pete Chiarelli, was working this issue. New priorities include: better diagnostic techniques, better training for doctors in treatment facilities to make treatment of mental health issues a critical part of the recovery process. General Chiarelli also made progress in sensitizing senior Army leaders and commanders at all levels to their responsibilities in the identification, diagnosis and treatment of combat-induced mental illness and PTSD.

But this brings us to the place where the buck stops. The Veterans Administration is still grossly overburdened. Despite advances in facilities and staff growth, the pace at which multiple neurological trauma cases are appearing effectively swamps any gains made at the VA over the past decade. On the one hand, quick medevac, high quality medical intervention and stabilization close to the battlefield, combined with speedy removal to sophisticated convalescent facilities in Europe and the U.S., have reduced the incidence of deaths caused by wounds. Even multiple traumatic brain injuries or other neurological and spinal issues can be dealt with quickly, resulting in fewer combat deaths.

The consequence is that injuries like these inundate stateside VA treatment and rehabilitation facilites, once the soldier is medically discharged or retired from active duty. The hidden downside is that undiagnosed head-trauma, multiple concussions, PTSD and mental illness often take a back seat in terms of priority. The result is that, irrespective of high-level Pentagon proclamations, indoctrination of commanders and high-level visibility of the issues, there is still a silent legion of veterans and families experiencing the effects of war-induced mental illness.

The VA is now headed by retired Army four star general, Eric Shinseki, himself a combat disabled veteran, who also served as Army Chief of Staff in the first George W. Bush administration. Shinseki has claimed progress, streamlining claims processes, hiring procedures, and improving treatment facilities. One promising note is that since 2005, the number of mental health professionals across the VA has increased from 13,000 to 20,000.

The VA's 2012 annual report indicates that even more assets of this type were added last year. On the other hand, veteran suicide increased by 16% in 2012 over the year before. Some veteran's support groups are asserting as recently as early February 2013 that one suicide occurs every 24 hours, up from one every 26 hours, as reported the previous year. And, remarkably, more than 60% of these suicides are Vietnam era veterans.

Suicide is only one indication of service-induced mental illness. VA director Shinseki has asked each state governor to do a better job of reporting veteran suicides. Accurate reporting to get valid statistics should help assess the real dimension of what the VA is dealing with. But, the mere fact that Shinseki has to plead with governors for information indicates that neither the VA nor the Pentagon have a real grasp on the problem's causes or necessary steps to make progress in prevention and treatment.

Another obstacle: the VA claims process is still daunting. This author personally knows Vietnam veterans with undiagnosed combat-incurred disabilities, who refuse to set foot into the vast, still hostile bureaucracy, that is the VA. When I retired with a thirty percent service-connected disability in 1989, I silently prayed to myself that I would never again have to enter another VA facility for assessment or treatment.

As I got older, my service-connected issues worsened and required re-evaluation. I swear it took all the persistence and tenacity I could muster to deal with the often simplistic, uncaring attitude of the VA staff assigned to perform my evaluations. After about a year, my disability rating was raised to 60% through a formula that defies understanding. In my summary ratings for the specific issues, like knee or back injuries, etc., the total percentage added up to 80%. However, through some arcane regulatory conversion algorithm, my overall disability was reduced to 60%. That determination took nearly a year.

So, it is understandable that veterans have an aversion for stepping up and making claims. General Shinseki has observed that the rate of approval for claims has greatly improved in past years. The trouble is that there are simply more claims being submitted by this generation of veterans than the VA can process. On average, it currently takes eight months to finalize a veteran's disability claim. It takes more than 365 days to process claims for service members who retire with disabilities incurred during their service tenure.

The bottom line is that mental health issues still languish in the enormous pile of unresolved veterans' issues. I am happy to report that diagnostic methods have improved both in the service components, the VA, and across the spectrum of private health care delivery. What is still unaddressed is how to convince returning veterans to seek treatment to preclude lifelong personal and family issues such as the ones Max experienced in this book's story.

Max's story had a positive, redemptive spin. My experience is that examples like his are rare. Far greater are the number of cases that slip through the cosmic-sized crack in the VA and the military's diagnostic and treatment infrastructure. These cases are relegated to lives of pain, manifest unhappiness, and finally despair, as illustrated by the shocking number of suicides each day among veterans of Vietnam, Iraq and Afghanistan.

Public recognition of this growing issue is not widespread. In spite of seminal articles like Kristof's 2012 New York Times Op-Ed piece, public awareness is still lacking. This is not a savory media topic. Veteran's welfare, in the minds of most Americans, has already been addressed sufficiently through the costly military medical apparatus and the VA. In many ways, this myopic public perspective is ironically similar to the callous treatment received by servicemen coming home from Vietnam.

It is as if to say, "We Americans thank you, but you now need to get on with your lives, and don't come back looking for help that might cost the taxpayer more than we are now contributing." A sad counterpoint to this hypocritical aspect of America's consciousness is that it prides itself in its soldiers, sailors and airmen. But, it is also glaringly true that America has an extremely short attention span. Its collective memory is even shorter as to how proud they were of those fine soldiers when they initially sent them off to prosecute the nation's wars and police actions.

The United States lacks the spirit of what Winston Churchill said after the Battle of Britain, "Never in recorded history, have so many owed so much to so few."

In America, the glaring lack of this kind of patriotic attitude regarding public responsibility for not only its military but its veterans, is no better illustrated than by looking at the abysmal state of mental health among returning soldiers. Simply setting foot into a VA facility anywhere in the country is ample evidence of our collective neglect.

The current administration is clearly on the right track making veteran's mental health and suicide prevention a top priority.

Now, we must convince the American public that we need to step up and finally do something about it.

EDM

November 2013

Selected Bibliography

Bowra, Kenneth R., *Cambodia: Analysis of US Military Assistance to Cambodia, 1970-1975*. Ft. Leavenworth, KS: US Army Command and General Staff College Master of Military Art and Science Thesis Collection, 1983.

Caldwell, Malcolm, and Lek Tan, *Cambodia in the Southeast Asia War*. New York and London: Monthly Review Press, 1973.

Chandler, David P., *The Tragedy of Cambodian History: Politics, War, and Revolution since 1945*. New Haven and London: Yale University Press, 1991.
_____, *Voices from S-21*. Chiang Mai: Silkworm Books. 1999.

_____, *Facing the Cambodian Past: Selected Essays, Chiang Mai: Silkworm Books. 1971-1994*.

Haldeman, H.R., and DiMona, Joseph, *The Ends of Power*. New York: Times Books, 1978. London: Sidgewick and Jackson, 1978.

Him, Chanrithy, *When Broken Glass Floats: Growing Up Under the Khmer Rouge, A Memoir*. New York and London: W.W. Norton & Company, 2000.

Kalb, Marvin, and Kalb, Bernard, *Kissinger*, Boston, Little, Brown, 1974.

Kissinger, Henry A., *The Troubled Partnership*. New York, McGraw-Hill, 1975.

Kristof, Nicholas D., *War Wounds*, New York: NY Times Publishing, Op-ed Aug 10, 2012.

Ngor, Haing, and Warner, Roger, *Surviving the Killing Fields*. New York: Carroll and Graf Publishers (paperback edition), 2003. First published in 1987 as *A Cambodian Odyssey* in the US by Macmillan Publishing Company.

Pran, Dith, and Kiernan, Ben, and DePaul, Kim, *Children of Cambodia's Killing Fields: Memoires of Survivors.* New Haven and London: Yale University Press. 1997.

Shawcross, William, *Sideshow: Kissinger, Nixon and the Destruction of Cambodia.* New York: Simon and Schuster, 1979.

_____, *Cambodia's New Deal: A Report.* Washington D.C.: Carnegie Endowment for International Peace, 1994.

Snepp, Frank, *Decent Interval.* New York: Random House, 1977.

Westmoreland William C., *A Soldier Reports.* New York: Doubleday, 1976.

Ed Mooney is a southwestern Montana native. As part of his Army career, he served a year in Cambodia with MEDTC. He retired in 1989.

In his second career, Mr. Mooney held executive positions at both IBM and Lockheed Martin Federal Systems Companies. Retiring from Lockheed Martin in 2001, Mr. Mooney served as Chief Operating Officer of a mid-sized IT firm supporting the Defense Department. Since 2005, Mr. Mooney has owed an executive consulting firm.

Mr. Mooney and his devoted wife of 45 years, Peggy Lee, recently began an extended tour of South America. They are using Cuenca, Ecuador, as their base.

CPSIA information can be obtained at www.ICGtesting.com
Printed in the USA
BVOW07s1702250614

357376BV00001B/42/P